more praise for *A Good House*

"In *A Good House*, Bonnie Burnard imbues the apparently ordinary lives of her characters with a dignity that renders them unforgettable. She has a sense of the moment that gives value and meaning to a life."

—Nico Ricci, Alberto Manguel and Judy Mappin,
1999 Giller Prize jury panel

"...as compelling to the outsider...as one's own family history would be...Burnard manages, with what seems almost magical skill, to bring 11 major characters, as well as the characters of their homes and their shared and disparate worlds, fully to life...Anyone who loves history, legends, architecture, comedies, psychological studies and rambling, delicious novels will love *A Good House* and will never again look at any family in quite the same way."

—*The Globe and Mail*

"It's the small details, bits of ordinary life, that make this story real. These are the kinds of characters we can't help growing attached to; we wish them well and worry for them—even after we've set Burnard's book aside...Burnard is such an accomplished storyteller that she manages to blur the line between fact and fiction."

—*The Gazette* (Montreal)

"It is strange and wonderful to finish *A Good House* and look back at the arc it has followed—the children who began the novel are now old, or gone, their children have grown up, and the reader has been there as they lived their lives, witness to all the turns and tragedies they have encountered together and severally...Bonnie Burnard made her mark on the landscape of Canadian fiction with her first two books. Now, with the publication of *A Good House*, that mark is irrefutably indelible."

—*The Edmonton Journal*

BONNIE BURNARD

A Good House

HARPER**PERENNIAL** ● MODERN**CLASSICS**

NEW YORK ● LONDON ● TORONTO ● SYDNEY ● NEW DELHI ● AUCKLAND

For Anne Szumigalski (1922–1999)

The author would like to thank the Canada Council for the Arts, the Writer's Development Trust and the University of Western Ontario. An earlier version of the 1995 section appeared in *Grain* magazine.

HARPER**PERENNIAL** ●○ MODERN**CLASSICS**

A Phyllis Bruce Book, published by Harper Perennial, an imprint of
HarperCollins Publishers Ltd.

First published in hardcover by Harper*Flamingo*Canada
and Phyllis Bruce Books: 1999
First Harper Perennial paperback edition: 2000
This Harper Perennial Modern Classics trade paperback edition: 2009

HarperCollins books may be purchased for educational, business, or sales
promotional use through our Special Markets Department.

HarperCollins Publishers Ltd
2 Bloor Street East, 20th Floor
Toronto, Ontario, Canada
M4W 1A8

www.harpercollins.ca

ISBN 978-1-55468-526-4

Library and Archives Canada Cataloguing in Publication information is available

Printed and bound in the United States

HC 9 8 7 6 5 4 3 2 1

1949

FED by the rolling fields and the running miles of shallow country ditches to the east of town, Stonebrook Creek approached the town aslant, cutting down through Livingston's gully, then flowing past the burning mounds of garbage at the dump, a ripe, evolving depth of trash that came alive at night with the industrious plunder of raccoons, an afternoon home-away-from-home for the town's mostly good-natured dogs. Beyond the dump, the creek narrowed and angled sharply west to hug the bottom of Bald Hill.

Then it twisted its way through the recently rehabilitated nine-hole golf course. The course had been closed during the war years but when the men returned, crews of volunteers had worked long hours to bring it back to its pre-war self, the greens shaved close and graded to fool the eye and framed by sand traps, the creek a recurrent water hazard crossed by pretty wooden bridges.

Nettles and cattails and goldenrod and Scotch thistle grew on the banks down close to the water and in high summer there were orange lilies and buttercups and thick, hovering clouds of dragon-flies, and butterflies. And you didn't have to follow the current far to see suckers or catfish or carp. There were snakes, of course, and muskrats, and the slight fear of drowning. But at the very worst the water was deemed only a mild hazard, just something natural, something that could safely be ignored. Most of Stonebrook's residents got from cradle to grave with no thought for the creek at all. There was certainly no changing it.

As it left the golf course the creek passed under the narrow, handsomely arched highway bridge that marked the town's southern outskirts and finally it entered the town proper, flowing behind the canning factory down near the double row of tracks and then past the Vinegar Works and the foundry and the last remaining barns.

Dominion Canners was still in business in the forties and a canning factory was a significant thing for a town to have because it meant jobs for men and women both, dirty, respectable, seasonal jobs processing fruit and vegetables. The work was well paid, but because it was entirely dependent on markets and the yields of particular crops, production ebbed and flowed. Jobs had been steady only during the war years, when tons of fruit and vegetables were trucked in to be dehydrated and shipped to the men fighting overseas.

In the winter months, at Turnball's barn, kids who had bundled themselves in bulky, wet-smelling wool rested their lit flashlights in the crotches of the willows that lined the frozen creek to shovel the snow up onto the sloping banks, diligently chipping at the hardest ridges of ice to make the surface smooth enough for skating under the winter sky, which was never black but always the darkest possible navy blue. Brothers and sisters fought for their turns with the family skates and bright red mitts got dropped in a December thaw and then forgotten until they could be seen again through the cloudy ice, trapped, waiting for spring under the barren, overhanging branches of the trees. Some nights, when the illumination sent by the faraway moon and stars bounced off their high-banked snow like thrown bolts of wedding dress satin, the kids switched their flashlights off, proud to be out in the night alone, made safe by the natural light.

But soon there would be no need to shovel Stonebrook Creek clean because people were starting to talk about a Memorial Arena, to honour the war dead.

Sixteen of the town's sons had been killed overseas this last time and another thirty had been wounded, many of them seriously. Amputees were a common sight now, as were torn, badly healed, once-handsome faces and eyes gone hesitant or vacant and, in the heat of summer, out at the lake, backs and chests and limbs defiled by pulpy ridges of flesh which had been pulled shut over wounds by military doctors working without the luxury of time, without the care that time allowed. Many families were slowly and quietly learning how to make their way around small, unanticipated explosions fired by edgy nerves and some of the wounded had been sent home carrying in their toughened bodies the extra weight of shrapnel, which doctors at the big vets' hospital in London were still busy excavating four years after the fighting was done, often, by necessity, one shard at a time.

Stonebrook Creek did not have in it the force of industry. Stonebrook had never been a mill town. The creek did offer good dependable drainage, which mattered a great deal now that so many new houses were going up, and it did provide a bit of work for the town's men, whose many responsibilities included occasional attention to the creek's banks, to hip-high weeds in the summer, and sometimes to discarded, rusted chunks of sharp-edged machinery parts and, once in a while, deep in the current but stopped by stones, a tightly tied burlap sack filled with carcasses, the lazy disposal of an unwanted litter, lazy because the lake was such a short drive away and rowboats so easily rented.

The creek did touch a few properties. Before it finally left town to make its way over to Lake Huron to empty itself, it did turn sharply north to run behind one long street of houses, to move across the bottom of their sprawling backyards. But the houses built on that street were as good as any.

Stonebrook held perhaps five hundred houses in 1949, brick or painted frame and mixed together, big with small, new with old, good with bad. Normally they sat well back on very big lots, sheltered from the weather by five or six fully matured trees, planted maples, sometimes elms or walnuts, the occasional hickory or chestnut. Forty or fifty of the houses were new since the war, and although these had been built on more modest, modern lots, most of them had fancy up-to-date kitchens and laundry chutes and high, dry basements and wall-to-wall broadloom carpet for the living rooms. Almost all the residential streets had been resurfaced and graced with brand new poured-cement sidewalks, and the tall poles that carried the heavy telephone and hydro wires, slung between them and from them to the corner of each roof, were interspersed now with streetlights.

Down near the Vinegar Works, five or six places had been let go too long to be brought back and these could be picked up for next to nothing by a man who had to settle, who had to have some kind of shelter for his family, even if the linoleum floors did slope in many puzzling directions, even if the rooms did hold the stench of all their previous inhabitants.

The magnificent houses, the three old-money brick houses, each with a small turret and a wraparound porch, had been built uptown near the churches when the town was younger and smaller, before the Great War. The wraparound porches were there to hold rainy-day children and morning tea carts and quiet late-evening conversation, cosy, discreet conversation which could not easily take place in front rooms or kitchens or bedrooms, certainly not on the street.

Sitting on one of these porches, hidden in covered darkness, you could feel the weight of the wet summer air on your skin, you could smell it, the soft scent of toilet water and mown grass and lilacs and honeysuckle in that air. You could listen to the endless ringing of a million crickets, hear birdsong flying from nest to nest in the highest branches of the trees, and sometimes you could hear the low mumble of a car or a door slamming or people shouting, streets away. If you sat there long enough, if you were a patient person, you could see through the dark. You just had to start with the most prominent, most easily recognized shapes, the shapes anyone would know, and then concentrate, hard.

THE Chambers house, a storey-and-a-half white frame with a grey shingled roof, was halfway down the street that backed on Stonebrook Creek. Like almost everyone else in town, the Chambers had two big maples out close to the new sidewalk and a few decorative evergreen shrubs planted under the big front window to soften the line of the foundation. In the backyard, which stretched in a gentle slope down to the creek, there were two more maples, one horse chestnut, one pussy willow, three very old hickories, and, on the shallow creek bank, two majestic willows overhanging the water.

A narrow gravel driveway led along the side of the lot back to a too-small garage, which was really just an oversized shed. But this was common. Not many garages had caught up to the bulk of the new postwar sedans. If there were extra people around, and there often were extra people around, they just pulled their cars over onto the grass. The grass had to be tough enough to survive this, to thrive without pampering, because no one paid any attention to it. It was there primarily to keep the weeds down and to reduce the likelihood of mud.

Across the front of the house there was a large living room with three small, leaded windows on the side yard and a big, recently installed picture window facing the street. Since the war, lots of perfectly adequate living-room windows had been replaced with these picture windows, which were said to both nicely frame the view to the street and open the rooms to sunlight.

In the long living room there was a marble fireplace that didn't draw very well, with delicate tulip sconces on either side, and a wide archway leading to the front hall and to the vestibule, which had a mullioned, bevelled-glass door and then a heavy front door that was permanently locked and never answered, except maybe at Christmas, or to a stranger.

The staircase, which turned halfway up at another pretty leaded window, this one translucent with patterned glass stained green and deep rose, and the glowing hardwood steps fanned to make the turn, led from the vestibule up to a small central hall and off the hall to a bathroom and three bedrooms with extra large closets cut into the sloping roof. This was the quiet part of the house, where voices were muted, where privacy was sometimes sought and found.

At the back of the house, behind the living room, there was a dining room with a slippery hardwood floor, a swinging door into the kitchen, and a wide window which overlooked the sprawling backyard. In the winter when the trees were bare, if you lifted the new, silky sheers, you could see Stonebrook Creek from this window, at least you could see where the smooth blanket of snow became the frozen surface of the current.

Sylvia Chambers' kitchen had most of the modern conveniences: an adequate stove, a brand new porcelain sink, an almost new, half-price Frigidaire which Bill had brought home from the hardware store, half price because of the small, harmless dent in the side. The kitchen was big enough to hold the oversized pine table where the family ate most of their everyday meals and anyone who came over was expected to use the never-locked kitchen door.

All the walls were painted plaster, smooth as silk. The staircase and the trim were oak, the baseboards eight inches high. You could run in a circle on the main floor, from room to room to room, around and around. Small children liked to do this, and visiting dogs.

It was a good house. Bill and Sylvia Chambers had bought it in 1941 when Patrick was four, Daphne one, and Paul just born. The bank loan had looked manageable, and although the war in Europe was well under way and not threatening to wind up any time soon, Bill and Sylvia had both felt a guarded optimism about their lives when they signed the papers that fall.

Neither of them had ever lived anywhere else. Their distant ancestry, an unexamined mix of quiet, hard-working Irish and sanctimonious Scot with the occasional black sheep thrown in, either boisterous, bothersome, speech-making Irish or Scots turned soft, was seldom actively present in anyone's thoughts. Bill's paternal grandparents had farmed eight miles north of town but because there wasn't land enough for all the sons, his father had slowly bought into the hardware store, where Bill now worked. That was before the misery of the thirties.

After the thirties, with the hardware let go for a song, Bill's father had started to sell cars and trucks up at the Chev Olds and he'd loved it, the wheeling and dealing, the good cigars, the flask of celebratory rye in the top drawer of his otherwise empty desk. He was now, in late middle age, a minor partner, with no serious thought of retirement.

Sylvia's Ferguson grandparents had moved up from the Chatham area when they were just young to take over the grocery store, which her father had recently sold to the Clarkes, although he'd reluctantly agreed to continue on for a couple of years as their butcher.

Bill and Sylvia had married in 1936, the year King George died, because Sylvia was pregnant with Patrick, a situation which was not especially desired but certainly not unusual. Sylvia's father adjusted himself to the circumstances quickly, he didn't see any reason to go too deeply into these matters, but her mother thought Sylvia, because she was so very pretty, could have done better and like a fool she said so.

Sylvia had to pull her mother down on the front porch steps to try to convince her once and for all that Bill Chambers was a very decent man, a kind man, that while he was obviously neither traditionally handsome nor brilliant he was everything else a woman could want, and then some. Saying these last words she had smiled and raised her eyebrows in an impudent gesture which was both rare and immediately understood for what it was, and which settled the question for good.

Bill Chambers signed up to go overseas in 1942, very soon after they'd bought the house, just when Sylvia was starting to find ways to believe in the life they were making. He wasn't any kid, he was almost thirty. To explain himself, he told Sylvia he simply couldn't stand not going. He left by train, was sent first out to Halifax to be too hurriedly educated by his country, too quickly taught about ships and depth charges and German U-boats, and then he was shipped over with all the others like him to try to apply what he had too quickly learned.

When it was finished, finished for him, he came back to Sylvia and the kids left-handed. In the organized chaos of an attack from the air, in the bitterly cold, loud, black, bloody mess that was a battle in the North Atlantic, the caution Bill had taught himself, the deliberate, sober, rational maturity he'd thought he would need was wasted. He watched the three most useful fingers of his right hand leave his hand, watched two of them land on the deck at his feet, and just before the guy beside him kicked them overboard he had snapped a mental picture that would make itself available to him for the rest of his life: the bloody fingers rolling slightly with the heave of the ship, the pulpy, mangled flesh that was no longer his own split open like burst sausage, the nails, blue-white and still almost real, holding firm.

But none of this made Bill Chambers extraordinary. He had come home alive, to his family, to his job, to his comfortable house on

Stonebrook Creek. And in 1949, with the war mercifully over and won, the only cost to Bill those three fingers and the time it took to train his left hand, with the country ready to enter an unprecedented boom and Sylvia confident that she could get her children safely through their childhood, comfortable was what the Chambers were hoping against hope to be.

1952

THE new siren was installed in Stonebrook's Town Hall tower on the first good Tuesday in April, after the rains had soaked and softened the fields and then abruptly ended, leaving the spring sun behind to warm the soil for planting.

The old cast-iron bell, the original, was not to be replaced but augmented by this new technology. The bell would continue to announce twelve noon but the siren would signal the fires and emergencies. The siren would call the volunteers from their work or their supper tables or their ball games or their beds.

The councillors agreed they could justify the expense, which was substantial, because a tornado had cut through the county the previous July and people complained for months afterward that they had not heard any warning at all from the Town Hall, not a blessed sound above that wind. The councillors and everyone else who had given it any thought believed that the wail of a siren would be more likely to carry, would probably ride the wind undiminished.

Because there were regulations to meet, because it had to be done right the first time, the installation contract had gone to a company from Sarnia, and when the men from Sarnia pulled up to the Town Hall curb at seven-thirty on Tuesday morning with the thing crated up in the back of a truck, there was a small semi-official party waiting on the Town Hall steps to meet them, to unlock the doors and turn on the lights and lead them up the three flights of stairs to the top of the bell tower. The mayor was there and the two councillors who had pushed hardest for the siren. Norma Fawcett, who had worked forever up at the town office taking receipt of the taxes and keeping the town books and scribbling the minutes at the council meetings, had been asked to come along in case they needed someone to fetch coffee and maybe something from the bakeshop.

[9]

Charles Taylor, the town's quiet, well-mannered simpleton, had been dressed in his slacks and shirt and tie and sent up to watch the installation by his mother, who strongly believed that Charles had as much right as anyone to take part in things. And Archie Stutt made sure he was in attendance because as the town's de facto maintenance superintendent, you could bet he would be left in charge of the thing after the experts from Sarnia pulled out.

Bill Chambers joined the delegation on the steps just as the siren was being taken off the truck. He had made his own breakfast and left the house for the hardware store an hour early, walking a slightly different route uptown in order to arrive at about the right time. He was there with the other men not in any official capacity but because two years earlier he had climbed the two flights with Archie Stutt to measure and make an estimate on the lumber needed for a new tower staircase and that day he had seen the old bell up close for the first time and he had admired it.

It wasn't brass like a show bell but the more lowly cast iron. The dull pewter sheen had been fouled here and there with the crusty smear of bird droppings, but it was nevertheless a beautiful thing. Its weight was self-evident, it was three feet across at the base. The clapper was the size of a softball. Bill wasn't convinced anyone would want to harm the bell, the town council had vowed to keep it and they'd said the siren would not in any way interfere with its workings, but sometimes people got wacky, spur-of-the-moment ideas, sometimes people had to be tamed down a little. He thought he'd just stand around quietly for an hour or so and watch out for the bell.

Stonebrook had been built on the rail line, at the meeting of three townships. As was the case with many of its sister towns, its earliest energy came from the tracks. The railway engineers might have imagined a path closer to the shoreline of Lake Huron all the way north to Goderich but the twisting, shallow valley cut by Stonebrook Creek had presented a costly deterrent.

The firmly squared grid laid down by the town fathers had taken its directions from the two main intersecting streets, the original streets, with the only exception to this grid a necessary accommodation for Bald Hill and for the creek. Front Street, which was supposed to be called King, had been cleared of trees a hundred years earlier when the first stores were built but the narrower Town Hall street was still lined with healthy old maples whose massive branches had long before intermingled overhead to form a nearly perfect summer arch of leaves. The high summer heat got through the leaves easily enough but the bright sunlight was filtered and refined by the arch, falling dappled to the hot pavement and the well-kept grass and the slightly heaving sidewalks below.

Although the Town Hall had been given pride of place, its bell tower was not the tallest structure in town. With the exception of the Gospel Hall, all of the church spires surpassed it, and the water tower, which sat behind the Town Hall on thick steel legs which were splayed for strength, sunk deep into the earth and surrounded by concrete feet to hold them steady in a big wind, surpassed everything. The water tower was painted dark green and often, at least once every two or three years, because it stood as the first and most obvious reflection of the town's fortunes, its self-regard. If you were driving into town from the north you could see the word STONE clearly spelled out in large white letters against the green of the tower, but if you were coming from the south, if you were following the short easy curve past the golf course down to the creek and over the handsome old bridge and then climbing the last long hill into town, the word BROOK appeared only as parts of itself, the letters disconnected by the floating reaches of the United and the Roman Catholic churches.

Like the library and the churches, the Town Hall had been built to be taken seriously. The windows and doors and roof line were not elaborate but purposeful, symmetrical, calming. There was a substantial cornerstone and intricate although not ostentatious brickwork around the double front doors and at all the corners and up under the eaves. There were generous concrete steps with sturdy balustrades and, on each side of these, chained-off space and good, regularly renewed soil for tidy beds of geraniums and snaps and pansies.

These broad Town Hall steps were often used for formal photographs, pictures of Girl Guides and women's auxiliaries, of councillors before one of their weekly meetings, of some important or famous visitor placed proudly front and centre in a group of interested townspeople. There was quite a bit of repetition in these pictures, faces recognizable from one grouping to the next, one year to the next. In the summer heat men posed in dress pants and white shirts with broad ties, sometimes in lightweight suits, and the women among them wore conservative print dresses, sometimes perky hats with a bit of light veil. In winter pictures the men sported felt homburgs with small teal feathers tucked into the silk bands, and heavy-looking wool overcoats, and some of the women wore fur, a floppy-pawed fox draped formally around the shoulders or a Persian lamb jacket with a smart little pillbox hat to match.

Inside the Town Hall there was an office on the main floor where people paid their taxes and complained about storm sewers, and another office where the town constable kept a desk and a couple of overstuffed filing cabinets and where he might be reached by telephone if he wasn't in the barbershop or walking up and down Front Street, gossiping. There were four jails cells which were cleaned occasionally but rarely used. There was a two-stall washroom which for many years was made available to kids who'd got caught too far from home.

The auditorium up on the second floor held thirty rows of shiny, hard, dark brown chairs with squeaky flip-up seats. The rows of chairs were attached to runners and these runners were designed to be bolted to the floor, but they were not bolted because sometimes they had to be removed in an afternoon and stacked at the sides of the hall for a demonstration of some kind or a crowd too large to be seated or a big dance, although now the dances were usually held in the Memorial Arena, which had been built down near the fairgrounds. The new dance floor in the arena was top-of-the-line hardwood and it had been constructed right at ground level, which meant a lot less disconcerting spring when there was a big crowd. There was a raised platform for a five-piece band and on the platform an upright piano which had been purchased the year before with the proceeds from a raffle on a humble Christmas turkey.

The arena was the newest public structure in town. Since the war, all across the province dozens of memorial arenas had gone up because hockey was big and would, no question, get bigger. Through the months of fund-raising and construction both of Stonebrook's newspapers gave a running account of activities, and when the doors were finally thrown open the editors proudly put the total value at fifty thousand dollars, careful to include in their valuation loads of gravel and electrical supplies delivered without an invoice, all the cash donations, large and small, some of these sent by expatriates from as far away as California or Calgary, and freely offered manual labour tagged at seventy-five cents an hour. Bill Chambers had taken Patrick and Paul over with him several times to mix cement or haul lumber, and Sylvia and Daphne had spent a few evenings pounding nails. Fifty thousand dollars was still substantial money in 1952. You could build a perfectly adequate house for under six thousand; you could get yourself a loaded Cadillac like Doc Cooper's for somewhere around four thousand.

With the arena up and operating, Patrick Chambers soon began to play clean but earnest and reliable defence for the Stonebrook Bantams and he already had one short ridge of thick, healed stitches just above his right eyebrow. Eleven-year-old Paul, who played offence for the Pee Wees, a little ahead of his time and usually at centre, had such long legs, such an amazing stride, that he had so far escaped any serious bloodletting. Although they were often after him because he often had the puck.

In the arena proper, an oval bank of painted plank seats surrounded the ice surface like a Roman forum. Between periods, enemy teams gathered in enemy dressing rooms to be praised and harangued by their coaches, the dressing rooms firmly separated by a food booth where you could buy pop from a cooler filled with ice water or hot chocolate and french fries and very good hot dogs piled with generous mounds of pungent onions fried in butter.

Above the dressing rooms and the food booth there was a balcony where tiers of plank seats climbed to meet the bulky rafters, which stretched high out over the ice surface, high and massive, as in a barn or a church. Older people or people who didn't particularly want kids crawling all over them could sit up in the balcony to watch the hockey games in peace.

[13]

THE installation people from Sarnia had turned out to be pros. And not one of the men who assembled that morning had mentioned the old cast-iron bell one way or the other, the talk was all about the siren. But nevertheless Bill was glad he'd gone. It had been something to see.

In just under two hours, including a half-hour break for coffee and banter and bran muffins hot from the oven of the bakeshop across the street, the men had the siren securely mounted and wired in and set to go. Bill didn't stay around for coffee. He couldn't spend the entire morning guarding the tower bell. By the time the guy in charge was ready to give the siren its first test run, shortly before ten, Bill was at his job at the hardware store, patiently trying to get two confusing lumber invoices sorted out with the steadfast bookkeeper, Margaret Kemp.

Sylvia Chambers heard the siren's first wail, pausing with her hands on her hips over the long bed of tulips that lined the far side of the driveway, wondering about the possibility of peonies.

Patrick Chambers was at his desk at the back of the room over at the high school, sitting behind Murray McFarlane, conjugating aloud the Latin verb "to win" with the rest of the university-bound grade tens.

Daphne in grade seven and Paul in grade six were standing out in the dusty fenced playground with all the other kids from all the other grades, listening. After their principal had got the courtesy call from Norma Fawcett up at the town office he had walked from classroom to classroom to forewarn his teachers, and as they stood in the playground listening many of these teachers were preparing a brief, impromptu civics lesson: the purpose and function of a Town Hall, how people must work together in communities, for progress, for safety, for the good of the group as a whole. Most of the kids were quiet, their arms at their sides and their faces upturned as if such a sound was something that came from the sky.

Two hours later, when the tower bell chimed twelve just as it had the day before and every other previous day, Bill was already out on Front Street. If he could manage it, he usually left the hardware store a few minutes before noon because he liked to hear the sound of the bell clearly, in the outside air.

With a dinner of pork chops and last year's apple jelly and mashed potatoes and creamed corn set to go the minute they all came in the door, Sylvia stood on the back step taking the last of the clothes off the line, snapping and folding shirts and pants and aprons and pyjamas and nighties and underwear, dropping them into the wicker basket at her feet. She had guessed right, it had been a good breezy morning for wash. She could smell the morning in the clothes.

Patrick had split off from his friends to walk the last few blocks from the high school alone. As he walked, conscientiously planting exactly two steps in each new square of cement, he was trying once more to successfully tell himself a story in Latin. The story had to be about war because almost all the verbs and nouns he had learned that year from the dour Mr. Stewart lent themselves best to war.

Paul and Daphne, each of them having just received a quickly conceived civics lesson, were walking the few blocks side by side, not a word shared, their coming home together unusual because long-legged Paul walked so fast. He liked to be where he was going *now*, liked to eat dinner quickly so he could get himself back to the playground to join his rowdy friends. Daphne had to take two or three steps for each one of his but that was all right, she could do that.

Spotting the kids, Bill had stood on the sidewalk at the front of the house to wait as they approached from their different directions and when they all came around the corner of the house Sylvia stopped folding clothes to watch them. She liked to watch her kids come and go, she did it regularly. Occasionally, in the hope that this might allow her to see them differently, maybe as other people saw them, just as they were, she tried to pretend that they didn't belong to her at all.

Paul came up the steps first, taking them double, six steps in three. On an April whim he stopped on the porch to open the door so his mother could go into the kitchen first and then Patrick slammed into him and he was stuck holding the door open for Daphne and Bill. As soon as his father was clear, Paul threw Patrick off to beat him into the kitchen. There was a time when he always lost to Patrick, to his confidence rather than his strength, but those days were over.

They all took their places at the table and waited until Sylvia left the stove and removed her apron to sit down with them. This waiting was a rule, one of very few. Bill lifted the bowl of potatoes toward Daphne to start things off and after all the food had been around the table he passed his plate down to Sylvia so she could cut up his chop and asked, of everyone, "And where were you when the siren went off?"

Each of them told their stories in turn and then Paul, reaching for the bottle to pour himself a most-days-discouraged third glass of milk but thinking about the playground, about who might be back there already, said, "What's it matter?"

"It's just a habit you could get into," Bill said. "Remembering where you are."

NEITHER the Chambers kids nor any of their friends gave much thought to remembering, or to the development of habits. They were content to keep pushing forward through undisciplined time, and anyway, habits were what you caught hell for, biting your nails to the quick, picking at scabs to keep the sore going, sneaking down to Stonebrook Creek in your pyjamas to watch the moonlight shiver on the dark water. The kids used their time to do the things they needed to do. They occupied the town on their own terms.

Most of the adults believed that as long as no one got any big ideas, and if everyone kept a general eye out, the worst that could happen would be a dog bite or a bee sting or a superficial slash from some broken glass left lying around in an alley somewhere. They did not want to load the kids up with the burden of possible but highly unlikely danger because most of them disapproved of exaggeration generally. Nothing good came from blowing things out of proportion. Right after the war a partially deaf drifter who had not been able to find steady work had hanged himself under the grandstand down at the racetrack, and no one had forgotten the day he was found and cut down, but most people had decided that, as bad as it was, his decision was pretty much the kind of thing that had nothing to do with anyone, least of all the kids.

As well as the Town Hall and the arena, the kids were familiar with miles and miles of train track and with the smoky, always burning fires over at the dump, with the canning factory and the Vinegar Works and the foundry, the stores on Front Street, the racetrack, the churches, the Rotary Park, the library. They chased after pea wagons on their way to the canning factory, pulled at the tangled vines to feed on pods of sweet new peas. Their pockets empty but their heads crammed with schemes, they drifted into stores, left if they were told to, returned the next week entirely uninsulted.

And they knew the intricacies of Bald Hill and Stonebrook Creek. In the winter, the hill was called Toboggan Hill because what could be more enticing than the threat of a good soaking at the end of a fast ride? The wide toboggan run, pristine under the bright haze of a winter sun, was flanked on either side by tall, descending, close-set spruce and fir and pine and the new snow fell from the hovering clouds to a smooth, blinding whiteness. The kids did not go to the hill so regularly in the spring after the snow disappeared, but when they did wander across it, taking a shortcut, if they saw that the evergreens that lined the sides of their toboggan run had tried to reproduce themselves, if seedlings had taken root, they just ripped them out. Wandering their territory, they believed as children do that both the hill and the creek were quite large. But they were wrong. They could pull their sleighs and toboggans back up to the top of Bald Hill in just a few laughing, shouting minutes and they could easily jump the creek where it narrowed, where the flow of the water was partially blocked, slowed by good-sized rocks and by smaller rocks worn stone-smooth over time by the current. They could get across the creek almost anywhere if they got their hands on two or three old planks.

They followed Stonebrook Creek through unfenced backyards and out into the countryside hunting for mysteries, for bloodsuckers or two-headed toads or unfamiliar skeletons or, please just once more, a boxed-up, thrown-out stash of dirty magazines.

It was Daphne who discovered the dirty magazines. Wandering alone one morning along Stonebrook Creek a mile out of town she had spotted something new, a box that hadn't been there the last time, and she'd crawled down and stretched out over the bank to pull the box open. Patrick and his friends soon took the magazines away from her but this find did provide Daphne with a brief reputation, a bit of status. She'd got the boys something they wanted.

They had all run back to the creek together, Daphne in the lead, and when they shoved her aside and knelt down to grab at the soggy women in black panties, their frantic enthusiasm made her stomach quiver, although she knew better than to let on. She just left them to it, walked away whistling.

It was not unusual for the kids to learn something important from the carelessness of adults. Most of them eavesdropped with considerable skill, easily recognizing the cadence, the tone of voice that indicated a desire for privacy. Given the opportunity of a morning alone at home or a neighbour's house left empty, many of them could snoop through a closet or a chest of drawers without a trace of remorse. Sometimes they took things, just some small thing needed as hard evidence of something they now believed to be true, although they almost always meant the theft to be temporary.

In spite of the efforts of their teachers, most of what they learned about the outside world they learned Friday or Saturday night at the movie theatre, a sloped, narrow space wedged between Taylor's Fine China and the Legion, with tight rows of hard seats and dusty red velvet drapes framing the big screen. War movies were big in 1952, and jungle movies and Westerns. You could usually count on a tough but beautiful, big-breasted, dark-haired woman the hero couldn't bring himself to love and, in the Westerns, close to the end, a gunfight or a fistfight on the top of a fast-moving train. Good guys didn't like to talk much and bad guys died slowly, often in quicksand, their repentance loud but useless because they could never be saved. Even the bad guys themselves knew no one would save them.

The kids were haphazard in their play and quietly disorganized. Their eager enthusiasms died as quickly as they had been born. They got to know each other on their own.

There were tough kids and kids not nearly tough enough, but most of them were assumed to be somewhere in the middle of these two extremes. If there were quarrels or fights, and occasionally there were, these were not reported back to parents because parents never did anything anyway. Parents couldn't save you. When kids came home muddy and soaking wet or bleeding from an unusual wound or cranky or worried or defeated, there was no great fuss. A dish of ice cream, a bowl of cereal, a joke, a bath, a bandage, a good night's sleep, these were the solutions.

PATRICK and Daphne and Paul Chambers came together in play just the one summer, the summer of the circus. Along with a couple of dozen other kids they had been seduced by Murray McFarlane, who had previously been more or less invisible to them, negligible. For no reason anyone could have named, Murray was the summer's sudden leader.

After his grade-ten exams, as a reward, Murray's parents had taken him to Detroit where they had shopped for clothes and eaten in restaurants and gone to see a Hollywood film called *The Greatest Show on Earth*. Home from Detroit with the dialogue almost entirely forgotten but the big-top scenes still throbbing in full Technicolor through his brain, Murray remembered and imagined and dreamed and then carefully described to the others, at first just a few of them sitting on the Town Hall steps, a circus, the possibility of a circus. In spite of the fact that he didn't play hockey or ball, or perhaps because he didn't, Murray was prepared to claim his time in the sun.

Patrick was soon to be fifteen, Daphne was twelve and Paul was eleven. Their separate clusters of friends, normally grouped according to small but significant age gaps and assumed to be distinct for good reason, were joined by Murray into one mass of kids, eager and serious, performers and workers alike cooperating for the larger cause.

Murray was quite a bit taller than the other kids, with a long torso and gangly arms and skinny, long-boned legs. And like his notorious Uncle Brady, who had come home from Italy with just one eye and then died at a railway crossing too drunk to get his car door open, he was very badly coordinated. He was Patrick's age but not in Patrick's cluster. He usually roamed Stonebrook alone, attaching himself to other kids only when he felt the urge and then abruptly leaving them, as if he'd thought of something more important to do.

They would see him wandering down along the creek or sitting on the Town Hall steps or sometimes up in the balcony at the arena, watching the game or, more usually, watching the crowd watch the game. Occasionally on a summer night, just as the sky got as dark as it was going to get, just before everyone had to start home, he would sit with them on the swings at the Rotary Park for a while and listen to the taunting innuendo and the dirty jokes. He could laugh easily when he was supposed to, when it was time. But he was quiet. He contributed nothing worth repeating or remembering.

Murray's comings and goings were of no concern to Mrs. McFarlane, who was much older than the other mothers and who suffered from debilitating migraine headaches. He was just out somewhere, that's what he told her and what she believed.

After a few nights of talking on the Town Hall steps, certain now of his authority, Murray advised the other kids that if the circus was going to be any good, everyone would have to agree to do what they did best. He called the first meeting after supper one dreamy evening in late June under the water tower.

The town's work yard, an open expanse of hard-packed dirt maybe twenty yards square, was more or less hidden from view behind the Town Hall, accessible only by a short side street, an alley really, lined with broad, smooth maple stumps. You had to know where it was to get there. The water tower stood in the middle of the work yard and on the north side there was a large cement-block garage with oversized doors for the fire truck. No one but the firemen and a few necessary officials were supposed to set foot in this garage and the boys who propped the Town Hall washroom window open to share a stolen pack of du Maurier cigarettes or climbed the bell tower with burlap sacks, for pigeons, accepted this as a fair-enough rule, disciplined themselves to accept it because they knew without having it explained for them that fire could be a very big deal, that fire could take anything it wanted, any time.

A larger garage on the other side of the yard housed the garbage truck and the town's two smaller workaday trucks, which were used for ongoing street repair and the scooping up of dead squirrels or groundhogs, for small emergencies like attendance at a drain after a big storm or the occasional capture of a mangy, shifty-looking dog no one knew from Adam. In the deepest recess of this larger garage there was a long workbench and an assortment of very serious tools which were kept clean and sharp by Archie Stutt, who had been the town's man for years, both before the war and after, his temporary absence overseas covered by a drifter who had since drifted on. There were coiled heaps of greasy rope on the floor and five wheel-barrows hung high up on the wall, out of his way. Archie wore overalls and a heavy, beat-up jacket all winter because the garage was cold but it was cool in the summer and it suited him fine then.

As in the Town Hall itself, the lights in the garage, eight of them, were dropped from the ceiling on thick cables, and sometimes, if the double doors had to be thrown open in a storm, the lights would swing and squeal and hum in the wind and Archie, looking up, would shout to the kids huddled around him, "By Jesus, one of these times ..." Archie was famous for anticipating the worst.

Patrick Chambers' friends, five boys at the mercy of growth spurts who represented the widest possible range of height, weight, intelligence, and confidence, were held together mostly by their skill with mockery. But they had been mesmerized by Murray, by his surprising ability to talk, to tell everyone exactly what could happen, what they could make happen. They'd heard about the meeting at the water tower and they turned up, took their positions just outside the circle of kids gathered tight around Murray, and before any of their repertoire of snide remarks had a chance to kick in they all had circus jobs, responsibilities assigned by Murray with a seriousness which was new to them and compelling in its novelty. They were caught up in the crucial early stages of planning and thus lost their momentum. A few of them had once or twice played at maturity, usually in response to some contrived expectation from a parent or some other adult, but this was different. They knew it and were ready for it.

Daphne and her friends sat at Murray's feet, their faces summer-time brown, their sleeveless blouses lifted and tied up at their midriffs and their bright cotton shorts dusty, soiled since mid-morning. Some of the younger girls, the ones who still wore braids or pigtails, were particularly untidy because girls this age were done up just once a day, by their mothers, right after breakfast. All of the girls huddled and squirmed on the packed dirt, begging for some important part to play. They understood that this could be their chance to shine, to wear flashy, glamorous outfits, to show people what they were really like, inside.

One of the oldest girls, the one most sure, who could suddenly and boldly talk the way Murray talked, folded her arms and suggested that if it was going to be for real, there should be a high-wire act, and immediately all the others jumped in, insisting on acrobatics and yes, Murray, yes, a trapeze.

Paul and his friends filled the space between the girls and the older, more worldly, mocking boys. They were quiet and patient, waiting as they always waited to see which way it would go.

Murray's plan was to set up the circus right there, on the hard-packed open space where the trucks backed out of the town's cement-block garages. His plan was to have auditions to see who was best at what.

He tried to be fair-minded. He had hoped to audition in groups of two or three to avoid humiliation but nearly everyone always showed up. There was only one attempt at mockery. One of Patrick's friends, an unstoppable heavyset boy with one leg slightly shorter than the other, who was a stranger to restraint, directed a quick bit of ridicule at the least graceful cartwheeler, but his attempt was killed ten times over with "Shut your stupid face" and "Just shut the hell up" and "So leave, jerk-off." Everyone did what they believed they could do best and Murray watched patiently, judged what he saw, and made notes in a little black notepad. After a few days of consideration, he divided them according to their abilities.

They practised all through July, four times a week, Monday, Wednesday, and Friday evenings, and Sunday afternoon. Murray was firm with schedules, merciless with absences. The mothers who were inclined to get involved got involved. Sylvia Chambers sewed, swapped material with other mothers, took her shears to dresses she was sick of, to ratty towels, and grey dress pants shiny at the knees and rear end. The McGregor kids unearthed a navy blue cape with bright-red satin lining that smelled of mothballs. Clown costumes were adapted from Christmas pyjamas that fathers would never wear anyway and bathing suits were tarted up with sequins and organza frills and bits of velvet ribbon tied in bows.

Jugglers trained hard in the privacy of their own backyards. There was a ventriloquist with a stuffed old-man dummy whose head he had severed from his sister's happily no-longer-favourite baby doll and an animal act, not just dogs leaping high through hoops but two miraculous cats, mother and daughter, who could walk around on their hind legs for a long time and another equally miraculous tabby who could almost talk, who could almost say *mine* and *never*.

One of Paul's friends practised short riffs on a bugle which belonged to his older sister who marched in the high school bugle band and another boy learned to do a half-decent roll on an ancient snare drum loaned to him by his neighbour, an old, old man no one had ever imagined beating a drum.

Murray selected the acrobats, the girls who cartwheeled every spring day across front lawns on the way home from school. He deferred to their wishes when it came time to pick the handlers, the boys who would lift and throw them up to each other's shoulders and try to catch them, to protect them from injury when they fell.

Charles Taylor, Charles the First, they called him, came every night, dressed up in his shirt and tie and, hanging from his neck on a braided cord, his silver safety whistle, his signal. Everyone was familiar with the sound of the whistle because Charles blew it when he thought he was lost and when he didn't like the look of the dog that was following him and once, very loudly, when he tripped running across the train tracks and hurt his back. Charles stood off to the side and watched with devout attention as the girls practised their routines and the kids made him help sometimes, but not with saving the girls.

A trapeze was suspended from one of the girders under the water tower. Murray bought the rope new at the hardware, to be safe, to be sure, and then he had to ask to borrow the town's extension ladder, and when he did Archie said he'd better climb up there himself. Archie had volunteered a three-foot length of pipe for a bar, but after he'd drilled the two holes and threaded the rope, he refused to climb as high as some of the kids, the boys in particular, wanted, telling them as they steadied his ladder that they'd be smart to get themselves into the habit of thinking twice.

Archie got into the habit of leaving the garage door open when he was pottering around on one of the town trucks or cleaning his tools and the kids talked to him, worked themselves deeper and deeper into the garage until they found a length of braided steel for the high wire, and by this time Archie, a widower with no kids left at home or anywhere near it, was shrugging his shoulders and nodding to almost every jumping-up-and-down request. He hauled his ladder out again and tied one end of the wire to another girder and the other end to a foothold on a telephone pole on the street. It was eight feet off the ground and it sloped, slightly, but Archie said that was all right, high wires could slope.

Below these main aerial attractions Murray called for mattresses which were volunteered by their owners and pulled from beds and carried back and forth daily through the streets. Patrick had stepped forward to take charge of the mattresses and he made sure they were returned every night after practice to the right beds and then set them up again the next time, organizing his friends who were the oldest, sturdiest boys because it took at least two of them to keep each mattress from dragging itself to shreds on the sidewalks.

During practices, while the girls perfected their acts, each time pushing themselves and each other further, harder, Patrick and the other boys stood at a slight distance with their arms folded, trying to keep their eyes on the mattresses in case some moron shoved one of them out of position by mistake.

Daphne was the youngest of the girls chosen for the trapeze and the high-wire act. She was chosen because she was slight and fearless and because her natural expression was an open smile. Showmanship, Murray called it. He said it was more important than anything else and he told the older girls to watch Daphne smile, to do it that way. Daphne had known she would be picked even before Murray gave her the nod because at twelve she already knew quite a bit about showmanship and its rewards. Like many happy girls, she had long since learned that a laugh or a smile paid off.

Paul was a clown, he asked to be, and he volunteered to stand on the stump beside the telephone pole on the street to take the money when everyone lined up to get in to see the show.

One of the scout tents was hauled from the scoutmaster's garage and set up as a change room and Archie gave them a long length of his own greasy rope which they strung to cordon off the performance area. Strings of Christmas lights, enough to cover a dozen trees, were draped from girder to girder to telephone pole to make a canopy.

The girls who couldn't cartwheel created elaborate signs with circus scenes and information, the date, the time, and the price of admission, or they organized a stand for Freshie, the ice-cold coloured water that people would buy at five cents a glass, distribution of profit to be decided later. Murray's father, who owned the feed mill, was a very busy man and only vaguely aware that the kids were up to something behind the Town Hall but at his wife's insistence he threw in the money for hot dogs and buns and onions. The hot dogs were to be cooked on the Rotary grills by two other fathers and sold at a substantial mark-up to pay for the things Murray had needed to buy with his own money: a roll of yellow admittance tickets, a box of bandages, extension cords for the Christmas lights, some twine, a few cans of cheap tuna for the cats, and soup bones for the dogs.

THEY began their performance at seven-thirty sharp the Thursday night before the weekend of the Town Frolic, which was always held down at the fairgrounds. Everyone but the performers and the babies and the two fathers who were cooking onions and hot dogs was supposed to pay Paul twenty-five cents to walk past the telephone pole. The bread man, whose daughter was one of the sign painters, had loaned him a money belt with chrome cylinders, which he'd loaded up with the quarters and dimes and nickels Murray had solemnly counted out to start him off, a float, Murray called it. Just before people began to arrive, after he was into his clown suit with his face painted on, Paul took a few minutes behind the tent to practise sliding the coins into the cylinders and pushing the thumb-sized levers to release them down into his palm. Murray had admonished him that it had to be right, it had to balance. He said they should know how many people came, to plan for next year.

Nearly everyone showed up: parents, grandparents, aunts, uncles, bachelors and old maids, babies in buggies, teachers, the ministers, the priest, the old priest. A few summer cadets from the army camp out at the lake turned up, which sent the older girls into spasms of dreamy hope, for a walk home in the dark after the circus was over, for an arm over a shoulder, or the very serious promise of letters after the boy had left the army camp to go back to his real life in Peterborough or Toronto or Galt.

Several kids from the reserve had got themselves into town and they stood around quietly, mixed in with the crowd separately or in pairs. People slipped them quarters to get in or to treat themselves to Freshie and hot dogs.

Standing on the stump waiting for Murray's signal, Paul took the expected abuse from the people waiting in the line-up. Several of the women said loudly how much they liked his clown suit and when Margaret Kemp, who had worked at the hardware store with Bill Chambers for years, said, "That's Sylvia," another woman said, not exactly kindly, "Yes, isn't it just." The bank manager, who knew full well who Paul was, asked him, "How do we know you're not some stranger? How do we know you won't pocket our money and vamoose?" Charles Taylor stood close beside Paul on the stump like a guard.

When he got the signal from Murray, Paul didn't hesitate to make everyone wait so he could add and subtract properly. One guy, some rich farmer he didn't even know, gave him a five-dollar bill, told him to keep the change.

They had what was called a full house. Murray wore the satin-lined wool cape and an old black homburg which had belonged to his grandfather, a man he had never met. He draped his father's white, monogrammed, silk scarf around his neck and to finish it off, to bring attention to his hands, he wore a pair of his mother's white cotton wrist gloves, which he had found beside the Bible in the drawer in the front-hall table and tried on without her permission, a trick that was both out of character and effective because once he'd tried them on the gloves were forever useless to Mrs. McFarlane.

He welcomed the crowd using elaborate circus language. "Ladies and gentlemen," he said. "Feast your eyes...." he said. "Ask yourselves if you have ever seen...." He praised each act as he introduced it, indicated with a broad sweep of the cape where the crowd's attention should direct itself. He gestured dramatically with the baton that had been loaned to him by a retired drum majorette who was new in town and who worked in the Bank of Commerce. She had pushed it through her teller's window after she'd changed his bills to coins, asking him only to promise her he would be careful with it.

They were good. Nearly all of them were very good. People applauded generously, laughed in appreciation for the obvious effort behind the performances. Archie's ropes and cables held fast and the girls' tarted-up costumes looked almost professional under the Christmas lights. The dogs and the cats seemed oblivious to the crowd, did what they knew they had to do to earn their treats out behind the tent. The smell of onions frying in butter prompted people who were not even slightly hungry to fork out an exorbitant fifty cents for a hot dog and someone put a baby in Paul's arms for a picture. The baby stared up into his white clown face and oversized red lips calmly, as if these were just one more thing to learn.

When Daphne fell near the end of her thoroughly practised trapeze routine, the mattresses, although laid down just as Patrick had ordered them laid down, were not enough. People who'd had experience in such things immediately agreed that the loud cracking break in Daphne's right forearm would mend, kids broke their arms regularly, but the break in her jaw looked like it might turn out to be a dog's breakfast.

Sylvia Chambers had just finished telling Margaret Kemp about her new sewing machine. Watching her daughter drop and then seeing her hand go to her face soon after she'd landed, she said aloud, "Oh, Daphne. Oh, honey." And looking quickly up at the trapeze, which was still swinging in the twisted air, still moving with the last of Daphne's tricks, she thought, Why does it have to be us?

[27]

Bill Chambers was standing over near the Rotary grills, talking to some of the other men. He had watched the first part of Daphne's performance but then someone said his name and he'd looked away. He didn't see her fall. After the guy beside him pulled roughly on his arm to turn him around again he thought only to move forward, to push his way forward, and kneel to hold his daughter gently under the shoulders. Holding her he told her to go ahead and yell if she had to. "Let it out," he whispered. "There's no need to be brave." The skin at her wrist had been pierced by a small nub of bloody bone and he recognized the break for what it was, knew that it could be set and that it would in time heal. But her mouth and inside her mouth. The skin covering her jaw was firm, unbroken, but the bones under it had been knocked out of alignment. The bones were completely askew. He had to steel himself, counsel himself not to look away.

He was leaning over, watching her face, waiting, as if the next move was up to her, and Daphne did make a sound but when it came into the air it was not the sound she had sent from her throat. She could see as soon as she heard it that she had terrified her father. He hadn't been ready at all.

Sylvia was on her now too, cradling her bare legs which were shaking and blanched white, as if the fall through the air had bleached the deep summer tan. Sylvia told her, "Hold on, sweetheart, that's a girl." She told her that Doctor Cooper had left for his office already, that they were going to carry her right on the mattress and take her over to Cooper's in the back of somebody's truck, which was parked just in front of the Town Hall and coming around for her now.

Daphne looked away from her parents to the other worried faces hanging over her and then she looked up past the faces at the Christmas stars. She swallowed a mouthful of blood, and recognizing the warm, sour taste and knowing that you weren't supposed to swallow your own blood she pushed herself up with her good arm and tried to spit, leaning over as far as she could to keep the mattress clean. Then the silence she hadn't heard was broken by loud crying, girls crying, her friends, and turning again to spit, she said, "I've hurt myself."

Patrick pushed his parents aside and took one corner of the mattress firmly in both hands, watching the men on the other corners, lifting when he was told to lift. He told Daphne it was all right, meaning we're all here. When she looked up directly at him, he said the worst of all the words he knew to comfort her. "Bugger it," he said, just loud enough for her to understand before she blacked out.

He was glad she'd blacked out. He knew it was better from playing hockey. What he didn't know was why he'd ever let himself believe that one layer of mattresses would do any good. He was supposed to be learning stuff, he was supposed to be understanding things like the cross section of the earth in his geography textbook that showed miles and miles of strata down there, most of it rock. He tried to remember if Murray had told him one layer of mattresses or if he had decided one layer himself.

Paul, whose feelings were usually written on his face in plain English for anyone to read, stood in his clown costume at terrified attention directly under the water tower. He was on his own and in a state but because Sylvia had meticulously reshaped his tight little mouth into a fat red smile his crying made no difference, no one came to him. He had been close enough to hear the bones break when his sister landed and he had seen her body go limp in their father's arms, but he didn't know how bad it was, what it meant, and no one thought to walk over to reassure him, to tell him that his sister had blacked out because of the pain, that it was a natural reaction and likely a blessing. He gulped at the air with his smile, working hard to get the extra air he needed.

After the mattress was lifted, people stepped back so Bill and Sylvia could see Daphne safely out to the truck. Bill pulled Sylvia tight to his side, which made their progress more awkward than it would have been normally, if they'd walked separately. "She'll be all right," he told her. "There isn't much that can't be fixed now." He tried to kiss the top of her head. "We'll get this dealt with."

The men lifted Daphne up into the truck bed, and when the last of them jumped down to close and bolt the tailgate, Sylvia pulled her skirt up to her hips and crawled in after her. "She's not going alone," she said, turning to offer Bill a hand. She knelt and Bill crouched and finally the truck began to move. Daphne was still unconscious. "Did you hear what she said?" Sylvia asked. "She said, 'I've hurt myself.'" Now that they were moving she was allowing herself the release of tears. "Something this bad happens and it's still, I've hurt myself, it's still, This must be my fault."

"It's just an expression," Bill said, although he knew it was more than an expression. Even in the midst of a loud, bloody battle, when they should have screamed, Jesus, some bastard tore my leg off, some bastard has just blinded me, some grey-haired captain of industry sent me all this way only to bleed to death, he had heard grown, dying men say only, I'm hurt, I am hurt here.

"She was doing really well," Sylvia said. "She worked so hard."

"We'll get her through this," Bill said.

Murray had followed the mattress out to the truck too, running along beside the carriers. A few people in the crowd, the old priest foremost among them, were taking the opportunity to mutter quietly that such a thing was bound to happen. As if they'd known there would be an accident, as if they'd been waiting for it. But most people took a different tack. Murray was told repeatedly by men and by some of the women too, "It wasn't your fault, Murray. Accidents will happen." And, "Don't berate yourself, son."

He didn't hear any of it. He was talking faster than he'd ever talked, eager to articulate and receive all of the blame, ready for someone to yank him around by the shoulders and yell, It's your fault, Murray, you and your big-time ideas. Sometimes ideas are better left alone. You are old enough, you should know that.

All he wanted from this night and from this whole summer was blame and another chance, to choose an older, stronger girl or to lower the trapeze down closer to the ground or to stand directly under Daphne with his arms braced as she slid and turned and dropped and caught herself and then didn't.

DAPHNE went back to school that September almost immediately after she came home from the hospital in London. Sylvia had decided that even with the pain, which was sometimes severe, sometimes just plain pain, even though the doctors seemed to like the word *discomfort*, Daphne would be much better off involved again in some kind of normal life with her friends. In Sylvia's experience, distraction was more often than not a good thing.

Daphne's friends called for her in the morning, sometimes lifting her books off the table to carry them in their own arms, and one of them usually came home with her after school to hang around the house until supper. Sylvia wondered occasionally if all this solicitude could be real. Once or twice she caught herself thinking that these girls were just playing, just impersonating grown-ups, with one of them, Daphne, the pretend-hurt girl, and all of the others the pretend-loving friends. Bill was more than a little unnerved by the unrelenting high-pitched babble that filled his house now, the wild giggling, the running up and down the stairs for no good reason. But he didn't let anyone hear him complain. He told Sylvia he only hoped it wouldn't just suddenly evaporate one day, like some fad.

Sylvia made hearty soups to get the necessary nourishment past the wiring in Daphne's jaw and she helped her with her teeth, most of which had been left, miraculously, intact. She held Daphne's pretty lips open to get the toothbrush inside her mouth and after her teeth were clean they moved from the bathroom to Sylvia's bedroom vanity. She sat Daphne on the upholstered vanity stool and played with her hair, twisted it up in a high bun and then pulled it back into a french roll, which she said was much too old for her now but might be something to think about later on. They experimented and laughed into the three-way mirror as the blood-red bruising down Daphne's throat turned to brown and mauve and then to a sickly yellow and then was finally gone.

As bad as Daphne's jaw looked, and was obviously going to look, both Patrick and Paul were secretly relieved that it wasn't worse, glad it wasn't her spine that had been shattered. Although, of course, they didn't say that out loud.

THE first time Murray McFarlane came over it was an October Sunday afternoon and they were all outside raking the leaves back to the creek to burn them. Bill found Murray an old, semi-retired rake up in the rafters of the garage, and while everyone else gathered the leaves into bigger and bigger mounds, Sylvia used a shovel to contain the fire, to over and over again scoop the red-hot ash back toward the centre of the fire. The still-burning leaves that drifted slowly in the updraught like charred butterflies or papery crows sometimes floated up out of sight and sometimes they dropped back down, either into the fire or into the creek, sizzling when they hit the water. Paul threw chestnuts into the burning piles, pitched them as hard as he could to sink them deep, and each time a hot chestnut exploded, Daphne jumped and someone else laughed, making light of her fear, which was new to her, and to them all.

Hearing Patrick complain about a wasted Sunday, Sylvia had to stop herself from taking a strip off him. She thought it had been a good day. "Your reward is that smell in the air," she said, nodding her head to the rusty, bittersweet smell of the fire.

When it was almost done Bill and Sylvia left the kids to finish and went inside for one of their quick Sunday naps. Pulling the bedroom curtains shut, Sylvia thought about the coming winter, the snow that would drift across the backyard, the dirty ice that would crust the creek, and she began to describe for Bill the work they had ahead of them that year.

"First we have to get her properly healed," she said, closing the door. "Everyone's spoiling her now but that's all right. We'll spoil her for a time and then we can toughen her up again." She curled into him, her smoky clothes already discarded over the side of the bed. "And there will be some guilt to get rid of. It's guilt I'm seeing in the boys." She played with the drawstring of his boxer shorts, pulling it again and again but never quite hard enough to release the small looped bow. "What matters most is that we get her back to herself somehow," she said. "I don't want her changed by this. I want her to be exactly what she would have been without the fall."

"Sign me up," Bill said, pulling the drawstring open himself.

"It's her nerve," Sylvia said. "We'll have to help her get her nerve back."

A little later when Sylvia came downstairs to start the meal Murray was still there, sitting with Patrick on the back steps, so she

invited him to stay and eat with them. He phoned home immediately to let his mother know, and after this day of raking and burning and a supper of pancakes and the premium bacon Sylvia always
got from her butcher father, Murray started to turn up regularly to
sit around the kitchen and talk to whoever wanted to take the time
to listen to him.

1955

SYLVIA Chambers got sick the year her kids were all in high school. She was forty. Miracle drugs, said to be on the horizon, were not readily available and, although she spent several weeks in hospital, surgery was thought to lack promise in her particular case, was thought finally to be too high a price for her to pay. Rescue was not anticipated. She just began to feel a little strange in January, got quickly worse through the spring, and died in late July.

Bill didn't put a name to his wife's illness. He sat Patrick and Daphne and Paul down at the kitchen table and told them only that it was very serious. They heard their father's word, *serious*, and they knew the word was meant to warn them, but they didn't want warning. In these earliest months they put their faith in Doctor Cooper, who was old and lame and sure of himself, and in the strength of the prescriptions they picked up at the drugstore, and most of all in their mother's resolute nature. They expected her to get better.

At the end of February they took their parents' cherry bed apart as they were asked and brought it downstairs piece by piece and they helped their father move some of the living-room furniture into the front hall so the bed could be set up facing the picture window. Bill had told Sylvia that he was moving down with her. He could have borrowed a bed for the living room, could have kept the cherry bed upstairs for himself, but he'd decided he would not turn away from her at night, he would not leave her to go up the stairs alone. Barbaric, he thought, imagining himself on those stairs.

He knew what people around town believed, that Sylvia had married him because he was so obviously a reliable man, that she had simply made a sensible, level-headed choice. What people couldn't know was how good they had it here. How calm she could be, how capable, in spite of the fact that she was always open to nonsense. How with her sweat still sharp in his nostrils she could come down to breakfast looking so serene, so unaffected, right away able to become whatever the kids or the rest of the world required her to be. She moved so fast from the one kind of woman to the other. She'd told him once that it was kind of fun and, besides, didn't he realize, it was what a woman had to do. How else? she'd asked him. Against the odds, expecting almost nothing, he'd got it all. And now was going to lose it, was going to have to sit still and watch the step-by-step approach of his own loss.

The kids soon got used to having their mother in the living room and they got used to manoeuvring through the crowded hall to get up the stairs but each time they squeezed past the sofa or banged a shin on the sharp corner of the coffee table they were thinking, This won't last. This is just for now.

Patrick Chambers was older than Paul by four years and, finished with his growth spurts, had settled in at Bill's slightly less-than-average height. He would never reach his brother. He shared most of Daphne's facial features, although where her mouth was pretty his was simply firm and sharply defined. His eyes too were that bright, beautiful, Wedgwood blue, like Sylvia's, like Sylvia's father's. In addition to his size, he'd got broad, heavily muscled shoulders from Bill and dark, thick hair that he wore slicked back in a carefully groomed duck's ass, a D.A. When he compared himself to the other guys he decided it was safe enough to believe he was good-looking, the evidence seemed to be there in his school pictures, in the way some girls tensed up when he looked at them.

Daphne was Sylvia's height exactly and it was obvious that if her jaw not been broken in such a peculiar way in that childhood fall, if the malformation of the healed jaw had not caused the alignment of her face to be noticeably and permanently askew, she would have been a ringer for her mother. She had the blue eyes and Sylvia's sturdy smile, the extremely pretty lips, the widow's peak under her bangs, the healthy swing to her long hair, the sophisticated, arched eyebrows that already required attention from Sylvia's tweezers.

Only Paul would not have been placed with the rest of the family in a crowd, his difference so obvious it was an occasional suppertime joke. Although the youngest, he had just recently and finally become taller than any of them and much taller than everyone else in grade nine, with most of his length in his hockey-strengthened legs. He wore his regularly clipped sandy-coloured hair in a no-nonsense brush cut, and down the sides of his nose and across his chin there was a ridge of acne which he did his best to ignore. He had just started to take Bill's straight razor down from the medicine cabinet and he would often come to the breakfast table temporarily patched with ripped-off bits of toilet paper, his blood seeping through and then quickly crusting up as he ate his cornflakes. His large eyes were an unusual grey-green, a colour previously unseen in any generation on either side, and the lashes that protected his large eyes were as long and thick and dark as a movie star's. Two of the girls in his grade-nine homeroom had already told him they would kill for those lashes.

If there was one trait the family shared, one thing that might have been locked in their genes and thus anticipated down the line, it was their extraordinarily beautiful, fine-boned hands. Bill's hands too, or maybe especially, even taking into account the fingers that had been blasted off in the North Atlantic.

Murray McFarlane, who was only an inch shorter than Paul but lanky and not so sure, not so deliberately physical in his move-ments, was in grade thirteen with Patrick and over the years since the summer of the circus he had gradually worked himself into the Chambers family. He had not disappeared after Daphne's fall, as another boy might have. He ate with them if he was around when a meal was put on the table, volunteered to help Patrick and Paul with seasonal chores like digging out after a big snowfall, taking the storms down, raking and burning the leaves at the edge of the creek in the fall. He exchanged with all of them modest and unusual Christmas presents: an abacus, a bubble-gum dispenser, a brass nameplate for the unused front door, which Bill promptly nailed to the back door.

In a nod to social convention, Patrick was sometimes invited to have dinner with Murray's family but these invitations were always date-specific and issued well in advance. Murray's parents were extremely devout Anglicans and quite a bit older, in their early sixties. Murray had been a last-chance baby. Both of his parents had been the only surviving offspring of very prosperous families and this misfortune allowed them many of the formalities and much of the ease of wealth. Mr. McFarlane's younger, bachelor brother Brady, whose boisterous good nature had been admired by some, had lived a short life ruled and eventually ended by the bottle and Mrs. McFarlane had lost a very young brother before the first war, to meningitis, and after the war a sister, her twin, to what the doctors thought must have been a cancer of the breast. Along with a double portion of prime, leased-out farmland, the McFarlanes owned a good third of the buildings on Front Street and the biggest feed mill in the county, which Murray's father continued to run, to keep himself occupied. They lived in Mrs. McFarlane's family home. It was one of the houses with a modest turret and a wide wraparound porch and Mrs. McFarlane sometimes entertained a few friends on her porch, with card tables set up for an afternoon of bridge or a summer luncheon.

Murray carried the loneliness common to his circumstances with no complaint. On a summer night he might take Daphne and maybe a couple of her girlfriends out to the lake to drive up and down the wide beach road in his father's dark blue hardtop Buick, cranking all the windows down to make the car feel like the convertible his father wouldn't buy. With no gears to shift and one hand light on the steering wheel, he would run his fingers back through his own severely trained D.A. and undo his shirt to his belt, exposing a narrow but nicely shaped chest. He always gave Daphne the front seat so she could control the radio and she'd find Bill Haley or Brenda Lee or Buddy Holly, turn them up full blast and sing her lungs out, sometimes hang out the window to sing her lungs out.

Tired of cruising, he'd stop the car on the beach to talk driver to driver to some other guy from school, the girls quiet when this happened, watching, listening, and then he'd pull away and swerve into the shallow waves, leaving long brief arcs of tire tracks behind them in the wet sand.

He studied with Daphne at the dining-room table, taught her how to write a convincing essay, challenged and praised her because

A GOOD HOUSE

he could see, anyone could see, that she was way above average. And he sat tight beside her at hockey games watching either Patrick's or Paul's team take on some other town. He didn't touch her or try to, didn't watch for a chance to shove her off balance or ruffle her hair or take one of her small expressive hands into his own. He had not yet outgrown his awkwardness, but he had a kind of skinny, lanky strength. One evening in the spring after Sylvia's illness had got a hold on her, after everyone understood her need to conserve what was left of her stamina, she called to Murray to say it was likely his turn to carry her out to the kitchen for supper. At her call, he hurried into the living room and scooped her from the bed easily, taking a firm grip on her back and her thin thighs so she would feel his confidence through her housecoat. He held her tight to his chest as he turned to get her through the door.

IN the time before Sylvia died the family often sat around after supper talking, their empty plates pushed toward the middle of the table to make room for their elbows or their folded arms. All her life Sylvia had been a better-than-average mimic. From the time she was a very young girl she had been able to cancel her own voice and bring someone else into the room, someone with an easily recognized cadence, an easily scoffed opinion. Although her face was thin now and her Wedgwood-blue eyes unnaturally large, she could still do a few people dead on, among them Katharine Hepburn and the town's shy young mayor and, with relish, her hopelessly cheerful sister-in-law, who had firmly established herself as the kids' least favourite aunt. All of the impersonations brought applause.

If Paul's height was mentioned, and it often was mentioned as one way to lighten the talk, Sylvia would say he must have been a foundling, a switch, brought to her hospital bed by mistake. She would describe some very tall mother somewhere puzzling over her short kid. But no one believed that this had actually happened because it was Paul and Paul alone who could do his mother's trick. Like a monster from a horror movie he could claw his hands, he could bend the top knuckles of his long fingers and keep the other

[38]

knuckles locked straight. Paul and Sylvia often performed their trick together, smiling across the table at each other, pleased to be giving the others the creeps.

Two or three times in these months Sylvia called up some energy and tried to say what was actually on her mind. One night, with a deliberation only partially camouflaged by her casual approach, she said she was going to describe each one of them, their skills and their particular talents. She was going to explain why they'd been put on this earth.

After she said, "Patrick is quiet but steady. He can steady other people when they most need it. This has always been true and always will be," Patrick stood up from the table and bowed.

After she said, "Daphne has a mystery about her, something to remind people if they are capable of being reminded that things are not necessarily what they seem," Daphne got out of her chair to stand in the middle of the room and curtsy in all four directions, as if an attentive crowd surrounded them.

After she said, "Paul moves fast and thinks fast. And he is funny, and that is a wonderful and useful thing, never to be underestimated," Paul assumed the exaggerated modesty of a truly humble man, lowering his head solemnly, which made them snort with laughter because what Bill sometimes called his newfound cockiness had once or twice prompted a necessary reminder to Paul that his glorified status as the centre on the Bantam hockey team didn't automatically carry over.

Not finished, because under no circumstances would she have left him out of this, Sylvia turned to Murray. "Murray," she said, "is just good. Good as in, born that way." Believing he knew the truth about himself, Murray stayed right where he was, turned his face away, and shrugged his narrow shoulders.

Bill had been nodding yes while Sylvia spoke, as if they'd talked it over and decided together what was true. The kids knew full well that this kind of testimony was rare. Other kids whose mothers had not been moved down to the living room didn't get to hear themselves described so kindly. But in spite of their clowning they soaked it up, believed what their mother told them, took the words and stacked them away for future use against other words, a few of which they'd already heard.

Sometimes when supper was finished everyone would drift into the living room to surround Sylvia on the bed and talk. They would begin with shamelessly enhanced reports of recent events: somebody's drunk, raging brother-in-law evicted from a dance at the arena, a wedding already planned for July with the bridesmaids to be decked out in dark red velveteen, the highest stained-glass library window unaccountably broken on Thursday night, likely in the middle of the night by a book-hating cult, Daphne said.

From there they would move on to casual, recreational gossip, to conjecture and guesswork. When the momentum picked up they would home in on the oddest people, the misfits, or the ones they knew the least about, or the ones they didn't like. In full swing they encouraged and contradicted and interrupted and accused one another and lied as much as they had to, to keep it going. Sylvia still knew everyone they talked about, she hadn't been in bed long enough to forget how the world worked, and she egged them on and sometimes topped them with mildly nasty but apparently precise accounts from a distant past.

When she couldn't continue she would fade back into her stack of pillows and pronounce, "We are really, really despicable, every one of us," and Bill would respond with his own line, "We're not so bad we can't get worse." If Sylvia was very tired, the kids just squeezed her feet through the blankets as they made their way out of the living room.

Bill left Sylvia's daytime care to her mother because he still had to show up for work at the hardware store. And he still sat in the front booths of the Blue Moon with the other men who worked uptown, the wits, as they were called. The wits knew the situation with Sylvia Chambers and they tried to accommodate it, tried to group their working bodies around it. Normally they passed the time talking politics, casually confusing the facts and enlarging the issues to the point of hopelessness, repeating like slogans the words damnpoliticians and highertaxes. Some days, for a change of pace, they attacked rumoured advances in science or technology, their suspicions banked up by the always reliable tag team of half-baked information and rampant skepticism. But with Bill's situation as it was, they stalled, hesitated a half beat before they spoke, tempered their jumpy, mocking, scatter-gun talk with oblique half-phrased sentiments and couched clichés carefully aimed to miss the mark. They endured the occasional silence, asked short, gentle questions, not for any answer but for the gentleness itself.

This couldn't last. Worn down and fed up with gentleness and care, they conceived a plan.

The men knew that Sylvia had been moved down to the living room and that there was only the one bathroom in that house, so they decided that a group of dilettante carpenters would build her a downstairs bathroom. Archie Stutt was signed on and both grandfathers and the Anglican minister. Trevor Hanley, who had the Chev Olds dealership, said he'd come, said he was all warmed up because he'd just put the finishing touches to a shed out at the cottage last fall. And Archie said that he'd talk to the new guy at the Esso to see if he could be had.

Bill didn't put up any resistance. Although he'd pulled the old picket fence down on his own when he got home from overseas, he couldn't help with something like this because even now, more than ten years after he'd had to start relying exclusively on his left hand, it wasn't entirely trustworthy, not with precision work, not with heavy tools. And he wasn't in any position to leave his job at the hardware.

But he used his discount to pay for most of the materials and he borrowed a thirty-cup coffeemaker from the Presbyterian church. He made new coffee every morning and put it on a makeshift table in the kitchen near the back door because it was March and the ground was hard, the work was cold.

THE construction started from the outside. In the beginning the neighbourhood dogs congregated to bark their interest and this caused the yard squirrels to run straight up the hickories to hide in the winter branches. The squirrels returned when they saw there was nothing much to be feared and the men gave them names, engaged them in conversation. The new guy's language was rougher

A GOOD HOUSE

than what the older men were used to but they toned him down by declining to respond in kind, by taking the trouble to choose their own words. They were in the habit of controlling talk this way and they didn't think badly of him, they just assumed he'd been raised differently. Perhaps by wolves, the minister suggested early on.

Most of the men brought their own shovels and hammers and saws, their own tape measures. They dug through the thin snow into the earth, broke through the shallow frost with the mildest profanity and a bit of extra push from their steel-toed boots on the blades of their shovels. They hauled the lumber from the snowed-on pile in the driveway, built a frame for the foundation, and mixed cement in one of Archie's wheelbarrows. After it was poured, Archie fired up a propane heater under a makeshift tent, which was only an old stained tarp thrown over the lawn chairs, to help the cement set.

They framed three walls out square on the cold ground and pounded them together and after the walls were up Trevor Hanley made a sketch of a low-pitched roof that he said they would have to build with particular attention, making sure that the join to the house proper had integrity because if there was ever going to be a leak, that was where it would want to be.

The plumber came over to install the drain. He drilled holes through the old foundation wall and soldered extensions to the existing waterlines in the basement and when he said he had all the lines he'd need they built the subfloor, leaving him only a trap door, which he said was likely good enough. They covered the wall studs with plywood and tar paper and with siding that someone would paint white in the spring to match the rest of the house. The Anglican minister threw a half-dozen bundles of shingles onto the roof and climbed up after them.

Archie and a couple of the men on the town payroll dug a long trench from the new bathroom drain to the sewer line out on the street and laid a five-inch pipe to make the connection. Soon after the pipe was buried the wide snake of mounded dirt that would settle and sink by summer was covered by the last of the drifting snow.

The men moved inside, brought their tools and their noise and their blunt male talk into the kitchen. They used mallets to gouge a door-sized hole in the kitchen wall, trimmed the opening carefully with handsaws. The kids cleaned up, shovelled sawdust and chunks of plaster into boxes to be carried out to the garage and hauled away to the dump when someone had the time. Insulation was stuffed between the studs and covered with top-grade plywood and then a cupboard arrived and a mirror and a sink and a toilet. The plumber came back, and the electrician, bringing with him a small electric space-heater. A thick grey carpet was glued to the floor so it would be warm on Sylvia's bare feet in the middle of the night.

The grandfathers took off in one of Trevor's brand new '55 Chev pick-ups, a demonstrator, he called it, which meant it was the truck Trevor wanted to drive that year, and after cruising up and down the streets discussing just who might have a loose door lying around they pulled into Bert Wynne's driveway and, sure enough, Bert had an oak door that he'd saved for just such a purpose up in the rafters of his shed. They offered him twenty dollars but he settled for ten, and after the door was home and hung on its frame with new, stronger hinges, Archie patched and smoothed the ragged plaster that surrounded it.

When the work was finished a dozen men pulled chairs around the kitchen table or leaned on the counter to share a forty-ounce bottle of Canadian Club, courtesy of Archie Stutt. They drank quietly, satisfied with themselves. There were no jokes and the few starts at gossip faded off from lack of worthwhile embellishment.

Sylvia's mother stripped the old kitchen wallpaper and burned it in the barrel down by the creek. She stayed with the paper as it burned, used the crowbar to push it down and down again into the fire. Waiting for the fire to do its work, she pulled her thick old cardigan tight and turned to watch the rush of the cold April creek on its way to the lake.

She repapered both the kitchen and the bathroom with a pattern very close in colour and design to what she'd stripped. It took her three days. She was helped by Margaret Kemp, who let herself off early from the hardware store.

The bathroom fixtures were pale sandy pink. Because she asked him to, Patrick drove Daphne down to Sarnia and over the Bluewater Bridge to Port Huron to buy two expensive sets of thick pink American towels and on the way home they stopped uptown at Clarke's for pink Kleenex and toilet paper, which was new on the market and very popular.

When the bathroom was absolutely finished, the men were invited back one evening for coffee and a slice of Sylvia's mother's specialty, double dark chocolate cake. Paul was the one picked to throw open the door on their work. Sylvia sat in a kitchen chair pretending she hadn't been watching and listening all along, hadn't already begun to use the toilet. She told them they'd done a tremendous job, said it would be so convenient for her, and, "Tell me, how can I ever thank you?"

Two months after its completion Sylvia was standing in the bathroom in the middle of the night, washing her sweaty face and neck, when she fell. She watched herself go down in the mirror. In the few seconds it took their father to get to her, the kids had time to make it only as far as the stairs where they could hear her loudly going after God a dozen different ways and then after their father, telling him in a cold middle-of-the-night voice that he would be doing them both a favour if he would just give up on pretending to understand.

"Give it the hell up," she said to him. "It doesn't help me."

And then they heard him helping her up to her feet, trying to soothe her with choked words and his own disciplined sobs.

Doctor Cooper dropped in twice a day every day after the night of the fall to give Sylvia shots in her hip, telling Bill privately that he should be warned that this drug might alter her nature a bit, there was no telling really, but it was the very best available for now.

Reverend Walker from the United Church came once a week, usually in the morning. On his first visit, after he had been served his coffee and muffin, he asked Sylvia's mother if she would leave them for a time and she did so reluctantly, closing the door behind her with perhaps a bit too much force. Bill told Sylvia he'd back Walker off if that was her wish but she said no, it was all right, he was only doing his job. She told no one what they talked about those once-a-week mornings.

Margaret Kemp began to come directly from work at the hardware to cook supper. She was an exceptionally tall, plain-faced, buxom woman in last year's low-heeled shoes who took care to camouflage the fullness of her figure with a slouch and close attention to dress patterns and pretty print blouses that she did not tuck into her narrow skirts. She wore just a touch of lipstick and it had never occurred to her to pluck her eyebrows. She would sometimes lick a finger to shape her brows but she would have been surprised to hear this.

Margaret dug right in. She scoured pots, scrubbed the kitchen floor on her hands and knees, stood Paul up on a kitchen chair to unscrew the ceiling light fixture so she could rinse the long-dead flies down the drain.

She could cook all right, but with no past experience judging appetites, she had a difficult time getting the quantities right. After a week of it she decided there was no such thing as too much, that whatever might be left over could be used up some other way, in a soup or a casserole or a stew. She decided better too much than too little and often she didn't have to decide anything at all because Bill's mother had sent a pot roast or someone from down the street had dropped off another ground-beef casserole.

She didn't sit down with them at the table. While Bill and the kids ate she went into the living room and found some nice music on the radio beside Sylvia's bed and then she brought basins of hot water and a washcloth and the softest of the towels, closing the door to the others and pulling the paisley drapes, turning back the sheet. When the bathing was finished she returned with a fresh basin and they washed Sylvia's hair, which had been cut short for the first time in her life and was now completely without sheen. There was always a jar of Noxema on the table beside the bed and Margaret rubbed it on Sylvia's back and arms and legs and feet, vigorously working the skin to try to keep the circulation going.

After Sylvia was clean, *refreshed* was the word she used, she chose one of the dozen nighties she'd been given since she'd been known to be sick and the two of them got it on her. Margaret changed the bedding religiously and quickly, helping Sylvia up and over to a chair, stripping the bed and making it new in no more than a minute. Without asking anyone's permission, she brought out the best quilts, after she'd found them carefully wrapped in the linen cupboard on one of her few trips upstairs.

She cooked separately for Sylvia, holding back a little on the salt and spices as Cooper had advised. She made good cream soup, mushroom or chicken or potato, served it in one of Sylvia's china soup plates. Sometimes she made salmon croquettes or Waldorf salad, enough for the two of them and no one else.

Sylvia appreciated all of this, particularly the bathing. She said that was almost the worst of it, not being able to keep herself fresh, and she refused to let her mother or Bill or Daphne bathe her. One late afternoon, while Margaret held a large hand mirror so she could comb her wet hair into place, Sylvia said to her, "Isn't life strange?"

Margaret held the mirror steady, tried to keep her own face hidden behind it. She had no way to guess what Sylvia was going to say. She had heard that some people spoke honestly when they believed they were dying, and sometimes to near strangers. She attempted to prepare herself, wondering how she could possibly be of any help to Sylvia when she herself had no faith, no magic, no way to believe in anything except the life that was right there in front of her. All she believed, all she'd ever been able to tell herself, was, You can't know what is going to happen to you and there usually isn't much choice when it does. Of course she could be strict with herself about this, that there was nothing whatsoever to be gained by crying or complaining or quitting, but how could she say such things to this pale woman in this bed? If there were other things you could say, they were not presenting themselves today.

But it wasn't about that, not at all. When Sylvia continued she said only, "We have known each other all this time and never really been friends until now."

Margaret put the mirror down on her lap and bravely reached to tuck a strand of hair behind Sylvia's ear. "Oh, well," she said. "Separate lives."

"But not now," Sylvia said. "Not any more."

Margaret nodded.

"I need you to help me with something," Sylvia said. "If you could."

"Yes," Margaret said, anticipating something practical now.

"Some time soon this is all going to get quickly worse," Sylvia said. "Like everyone else, I've been thinking about the kids." She stopped for a minute to measure her words. "I'd guess Patrick will go to anger, and Paul to tears. Daphne, I just don't know. Is there any way you could ...?"

"Yes," Margaret said, not because she understood what was expected of her but only because Sylvia believed it had to be a woman, otherwise she would not have asked. And here she was, a woman. "Yes," she said. "I will."

Margaret sometimes showed up with a few groceries and one time books from the library, some light history, a couple of dog-eared mysteries, but none of the books got read. Sylvia did ask for a good atlas, which Margaret drove into London to buy, and she spent some of her hours studying the changes in the world.

After a few weeks Margaret brought Daphne into her mother's bed and gave her the tray with the china soup plate and the silver spoon. She stood at the dusty picture window until the soup was half gone, asking Daphne questions about her schoolwork and her friends. She knew who Daphne's girlfriends were because she often saw them walking on the street together uptown, nudging shoulders as they talked, still a bit playful but serious too, newly careful with Daphne and with each other. You could see it in their posture, in their stern faces, the eyes that brazenly searched another's eyes with the promise of understanding. None of the girls came inside the house now, the farthest they could be coaxed was just inside the kitchen door, but this was easily recognized as one more clumsy, misplaced, well-meant gesture of respect.

As Daphne finished spooning the soup to her mother, Margaret asked herself how the boys would feel if she sent them out to the dusty windows with some newspapers and a bucket of vinegar water and then after the dishes were cleaned up she got her Harris tweed coat and her purse, said her goodnights, and let herself out the back door.

THE grandparents usually dropped in after supper, after Margaret had left. They were sometimes accompanied by one of Sylvia's brothers and his wife or by her sister from out of town or by Bill's brother from Windsor with his cheerful wife and their young children. Kitchen chairs were carried in and placed haphazardly around the room, facing Sylvia. The nieces and nephews were allowed to sit briefly on the bed to embrace their aunt and then they sprawled out on the carpet to play secret little whispering games or snap or jumping jacks.

The adults tried to talk about things Sylvia might find interesting, Sandy Koufax and the Brooklyn Dodgers, Lassie, James Dean being killed like that, but everyone listened too politely, too attentively to the speaker, almost all of them were too unnaturally quick to laugh or offer agreement. Sylvia heard their words not as sentences deliberately formed to tell a person something but as dull, one-at-a-time thuds against the dull silence that had begun to wall her in. She heard the words as small, well-meant blows against a concrete bunker. Although she did not ever ask, Could they please just shut up and go home.

Occasionally they would forget themselves and talk just to each other, for which she was occasionally grateful. The most astute among them watched her closely as they talked, recognized for what they were the small, jerking movements of her hands, the slight ducking of her head as if to avoid something flying too low above her.

Daphne decided it would be nice to use the silver tray from the buffet to serve the cookies or squares the women always brought, and Bill's father, a heavy, large-boned man who spoke slowly and loudly, made a huge fuss over her as she circled the room with the tray, said she was coming along so nicely. Sylvia's father, thin and wiry and wheezing with emphysema, paid no heed to the conventions expected of him. He cried openly and said awful heartfelt things like "You were always the strongest," and "Half a life," and "Why can't I be taken instead," and always when he started the others took a deep, collective breath and prepared themselves to put an end to it.

The third or fourth time this happened Paul had to turn his suddenly streaming face to the living-room wall and, recognizing himself in his grandson, Sylvia's father left his armchair to go to Paul, making it worse. Patrick, who in just these few short months had learned to carry love as an unspeakable pressure inside himself, got up from his chair so fast he knocked it over. He took the stairs in five great leaps and slammed the bedroom door and after that night he wouldn't sit with them, would not even say hello when his grandfather came in the kitchen door.

Sylvia's mother remained stoic. A born coordinator, she discussed practical matters with Margaret to reassure herself that everything was well in hand. She took the laundry home with her because she had a new clothes dryer in her basement and she wrote the letters that had to be written to tell the news that had to be told, attempted to supervise the homework at the dining-room table. And privately but firmly she scolded Paul. "I can't abide this crying, Paul," she said. "Not now. And trust me, there will be plenty of time for it after."

One evening in the middle of a week when Sylvia appeared to have a resurgence of strength, she called Daphne to come into the living room alone. When the door was shut and Daphne was comfortable on the bed, Sylvia said she wanted to tell her how much she regretted that she wouldn't be around to help later, with her marriage and her babies. She lifted her hand when Daphne tried to speak, tried to say, Don't say that, Mom. Don't say that. Sylvia wanted badly to be frank, to be truthful. She wanted to say, Take your time when you think you're ready for a husband, don't just go by looks, make him talk, find out how he thinks. Or, Don't let your heart outshout your head. Or, Whatever happens to you, don't just settle. But she said what she had rehearsed.

"It seems to me that smart women look for comfort and loyalty when they're deciding on a husband and I think men want more or less the same thing. And it never hurts to have a bit of laughter thrown in." She didn't mention the long-ago break in Daphne's jaw, or her apprehension about men whose interest might be queered by the malformed face, who might, instinctively, turn away.

"Childbirth," she said, "isn't nearly as bad as some women will

happily lead you to believe. A young body can be trusted." She put
her hands on her own distended stomach. "There are specialized
muscles in there with a job to do and one job only." She didn't say
anything specific or descriptive about sex, except that Daphne
shouldn't be afraid of it. "Sex is mostly just for comfort and fun,"
she said. "And meant to be."

Listening now with her eyes wide open and her hands covering
her mouth, Daphne nodded and tried to lift her hands away. "I want
three babies," she said. "I'm going to have three."

"Three is a very good number," Sylvia said. "Tell me what you'll
call them."

"Girls will be Maggie or Jill or Paula," Daphne said. "Boys will
be David or Daniel or Michael."

"Those are very fine names," Sylvia said. "I like those names a
lot."

The next evening she called Patrick and Paul and Murray in and sat
them down to tell them that they would soon have wives and children, which made them look down through their knees at their feet
and shake their heads. Thinking about this talk all afternoon, she had
known she would have to thread her way carefully between one son's
rage and the other's anxious tears, and looking at them now she could
see her boundaries announcing themselves in Patrick's clenched fists,
in Paul's wet cheeks. What she wanted to say to them was, Take it
slow, as slow as you can. And, Before you decide, have a good long
look at the mother because a daughter usually turns out just the same
or just the opposite. She wanted to say, Loud, silly girls often grow
up to be loud, silly women, and sullen girls tend to stay sullen.

Instead, she told them, "Women expect strength from men, and
gentleness and absolute loyalty. And a good ear." She said, "You
will have to work hard if you expect to raise a family." Looking just
at Patrick and Paul, meaning it as a joke, she said, "You might even
have to think about giving up hockey." Then she took the deepest
breath she could take. "Of course sex is fun," she said. "Likely, you
have already discovered that. But you should try to get it into your
heads that with just a little extra thought, a little extra time taken, it
can be something altogether different, altogether more." She didn't

make them sit there wondering if they had to say anything back to her about any of this. She shooed them out of the room like small boys told to stay away from the creek in the spring, hoping only that she hadn't lied to them.

Bill had offered to set up a small bed for himself in an empty corner of the living room in case his rolling around in his sleep disturbed Sylvia or gave her discomfort. As proof of his consideration, he borrowed a foldaway cot from the McKellars down the street and wheeled it into the dining room where it stood ready, sheets and all, but Sylvia told him no, she didn't want that, not yet. All these months they had continued to do what they could, when they could. Cooper had told them early on and pointedly to go ahead and take whatever pleasure was available to them.

Cooper told Bill now that Sylvia was on a very high dosage, which he was more than ready to up if he became convinced she needed it. He said that death comes in different ways to different people, more ways than an average layman could imagine, and that an easy death was still possible. He said there was no reason to anticipate extraordinary pain, not with the dosage he had her on.

Bill never did set up the cot. In the last week of July, Sylvia didn't want to eat anything and then she began to fall into an extremely deep sleep that could last the night and through the next day and overnight and halfway through the day again. Cooper said this was the blessing of her brain's own morphine, better than man-made.

When she came out of these sleeps she could speak only a few necessary words, could hardly take a drink, could only breathe and listen and watch. Bill stayed home and the kids got some time off from their summer jobs and someone stayed with her in the living room every minute, often two at a time. On the last of these sleeping days and nights Bill was with her and, exhausted beyond discipline, beyond even his time overseas, he crawled in and slept beside her. He woke from a dream of rolling fingers and knew without looking.

He took a few minutes for himself, stayed mute on his side of the bed, resisting full consciousness, making it wait. As was his sleepy habit, he reached to smooth her eyebrows, to try to smooth the lines from her forehead. Then he sat up, stood up in his pyjamas. He tidied her hair the best he could and straightened the pillow and then he made himself search beneath the quilts to find her hands, to bring them out over the quilts because she looked so strange lying there without her hands.

He manoeuvred through the hall and up the stairs to wake the kids, sitting for a few minutes on the top step to listen to the memory of Sylvia's voice telling him what to say to them when this day came, but by the time he reached the first warm bed he had nothing in him but silence. He couldn't help them when they opened their eyes.

When their first wretched grief, loud and clumsy beyond remembering, was almost spent, when the July sun, which was nothing more to him now than the blunt instrument, the mindless impulse of an emptied day, was fully risen, Bill went into the kitchen to phone Cooper and they all stayed in the living room until they heard the Cadillac pull into the driveway. Cooper brought fresh morning air in with him and turn by turn he put one warm arm around their shoulders, which quieted them and brought them back to their separate, independent selves, to the floating, airless absence that each of them had already begun to define as differently as they might have defined Sylvia's full life, given the chance. Then he asked that they go out to the kitchen.

Bill poured himself a glass of orange juice and sat down at the table, and because he couldn't bear the quiet now, because it was making him sick to his stomach and dizzy, he began to walk his kids step by step through their mother's funeral. He'd done nothing about it before, had been repulsed by the thought of anticipating it.

Paul and Daphne sat down with their father but Patrick opened the fridge door wide and slammed it shut, twice and hard. When he asked, "What the hell difference does it make what happens now?" Bill nodded yes and yes again, told him, "This is what we do."

After Bill finished outlining his plans for the funeral, Paul went outside to stand in the gravel driveway and Daphne went after him. The sun was over the garage now. It was promising to be a very hot day. They stood together for a few minutes and then she pulled on his arm to bring him back to the cool of the kitchen.

Cooper had called the undertaker and he must have called Margaret too because she was soon there, standing at the counter with her long back to them, opening a can of salmon, buttering a double row of bread. Bill went upstairs to get dressed and when he came back down he made the call to the grandparents.

Murray came in the kitchen door just after the undertaker. He sat down at the table and cried on his arms like a child, which caused Daphne to move across the room to stand close behind him.

Then Bill told the kids they might as well go and get dressed, so they went upstairs. After they had their clothes on, Daphne sat with Paul on his bed, her own tears mysteriously stopped by the racked renewal of his tears. Murray was slumped on the floor, leaning against the other bed with his back to Patrick, who was silent. They stayed that way until they heard Margaret come up the stairs to look through Sylvia's closet. Soon after she went back down they heard the unmistakable sound of the hearse on the gravel, backing carefully out of the driveway.

A WEEK after Sylvia's funeral Margaret came through the kitchen door on a Sunday afternoon with a mostly roasted chicken. They had been given so many meals that week, scalloped potatoes and baked ham, meat loaves, baked beans, angel food cakes and butter tarts and fruit pies. A dozen empty casserole dishes, good sturdy ovenproof bowls taped with names to identify the owners, sat piled biggest to smallest on the counter. These were the dishes that moved around from one house to the next, following the need.

Margaret told Daphne as she opened the oven door that the chicken wanted only another quick half hour at three-fifty. She said she'd do up a few potatoes to go along with it and did Daphne think peas or corn or what? As they moved around the kitchen together, Margaret was careful to keep a respectful distance between them, careful not to touch Daphne even by accident. At the funeral and at the lunch in the church basement after the funeral she had noticed that Daphne pulled back slightly when anyone threatened to lay a hand on her. And people did try. People did assume you wanted it. She could sympathize with that, she knew what that felt like.

[53]

After they'd peeled the potatoes and got them started, she took off her apron, mixed a rye and water for herself and a rye and coke for Bill, and went into the living room to sit with him. They talked about nothing in particular for a few minutes and then she asked if maybe Patrick and Paul and Murray should take the bed back upstairs. Bill called the boys into the living room and asked them to do it, please, and he and Margaret watched them take the bed apart and carry it back up to their parents' bedroom, where they would reassemble it.

Margaret didn't mention Sylvia's side of the closet because Bill's mother had said that she and her friend Phyllis would attend to that. She'd said Phyllis had a sister in Toronto who was close to Sylvia's size.

Margaret had intended to stay just long enough to clean every inch of the emptied living room but when she was half finished Daphne led her to the table where a place had been set for her. After supper the boys returned the foldaway cot to the McKellars, and when Margaret was finished in the living room, they emptied the hall and put the furniture back where they thought it had always been.

IN September, Patrick and Murray left for university. The previous spring, just before Patrick truly believed that his mother was going to die, when Murray and everyone else were sending in their applications, he had sent in his own, on the sly, consulting no one. His grade-thirteen year hadn't been his best, he knew that, but he didn't expect to fail anything either. They had written their exams, nine subjects for everyone, in the sweating heat of the June gym, and then they'd had to wait out the summer because the marking was not done by their own teachers but by anonymous markers in Toronto. In August when he got his results, and they were just high enough, he told Murray what he'd done. They had driven out to the lake. They were sitting in Murray's new hardtop Chev on the Casino hill with their transcripts open in their laps. Patrick said he must have been something less than human to be making plans for his future when his mother was dying.

Murray had got straight A's and this meant a substantial government scholarship to start him off. The next evening at his parents' dining-room table he directed the conversation in such a way that his mother was prompted to ask how Patrick Chambers had done and where was he planning to go?

A few days later Alex McFarlane came to Bill at the hardware store to say that he and Mrs. McFarlane would like to help Patrick out with some of the money they had put aside years ago for Murray. His little remaining hair was snow white and he had put on a suit to make his proposal. He said they had always regarded their university fund as money to be invested in the next generation, and now that Murray would be needing less of it, they didn't really want to waste it on anything else. He said they'd been south once for a winter holiday and hadn't found it all that appealing, the traffic, the humidity, the exorbitant cost of a hotel room. He said, "You've had a hard time here and I wish you would accept this as a gesture of our respect for Patrick and for you, and particularly, of course, for Sylvia."

Bill accepted the money on Patrick's behalf. Since Sylvia's death, one of the hardest questions he had been asking himself was how could he make sure the kids established themselves the way she would have wanted. That night when he sat Patrick down to tell him about Alex McFarlane's visit, he explained to him that such money didn't come freely. He said the onus would be on him some time later in his life to give over an equivalent amount to some other young person, someone whose potential was not matched by his circumstances. He said that was the way these things worked and that it was a private matter, not to be bandied about. He said Patrick might want to think about a small gift, a token of appreciation, likely something for Mrs. McFarlane. He said maybe Margaret could help with that.

After Patrick got his next paycheque from the feed mill, he went up to Margaret's apartment to tell her what his father had advised him to do and to hand her a twenty-dollar bill. The next day on her lunch hour she went over to Taylor's Fine China and found a lovely crystal rose bowl. She told Patrick she thought it would be appropriate because Mrs. McFarlane had a large garden and people said she was especially proud of her roses. She wrapped the bowl for him at the kitchen table in muted, all-occasion paper and when he asked her if he should get dressed up to take it over she told him, "No, you're fine as you are."

Even after getting the answer he wanted and borrowing Margaret's Pontiac to drive over to McFarlane's, Patrick wished he hadn't asked her for help. He had no idea how this consulting Margaret business had got started. Before their mother died they hardly even knew her and now she was supposed to be the one to ask. It wasn't that she was around too much, she only did what they wanted her to do and they appreciated it, it was that she was always ready to be around. Just sitting somewhere, ready.

Mrs. McFarlane came to the front door. She told Patrick that Mr. McFarlane had decided that morning to make a trip into Toronto, so he wasn't home. But because she knew what this was about, she invited him in and sat him down on the brocade sofa in her living room and brought him a bottle of Coke. She asked if maybe she should unwrap the present on her own. Patrick told her sure, why not.

She was very careful with the paper and the ribbon, and when she had the bowl unwrapped she held it in both hands up to the light coming in from the wide hall. She was very pleased. He had never seen a woman so pleased. "I saw this up there," she said, "and you know I almost bought it. Imagine." She set it carefully on the table in front of her. "I bet this is Margaret's doing," she said. "Your father has such a friend in Margaret."

The first week of September Patrick and Murray loaded up the hardtop Chev to make the move into London. Bill and Daphne and Paul followed in Bill's car, which was equally loaded. The university campus, thought to be one of the country's most beautiful, was spread with casual grace across fifty rolling acres at the edge of the city and set off from the city by high stone gates. The large sandstone college buildings with their bell towers, costly replications of British institutional architecture, had been distributed with precision, set carefully on the green hills like medieval jewels.

The boys soon found their separate residences and Bill and Daphne and Paul helped them carry their belongings up the stairs to their rooms. Both buildings were crawling with parents and boys hauling suitcases and boxes, the boys eager to be left on their own, the parents not very anxious to go. Some of the most reluctant parents had to be patiently shoved out of rooms and guided down the stairs to their cars.

Just before he started down, Bill turned to face Patrick. "This is an opportunity I myself didn't have," he said. "You be sure to make the best of it."

AT home, Daphne and Paul learned to cook. They could each do a good omelette and sausages and chops, although they never risked a roast and there were always potatoes, mashed or warmed-up mashed or fried, and pale green peas from a can or string beans or creamed corn. Paul, unaccountably, taught himself how to make pastry, went up to Clarke's for cans of cherry pie filling. They discovered him more than once rolling out pastry on Sylvia's marble board, his damp face smeared with flour.

The pages of Sylvia's cookbook, a large standard volume stuffed with all kinds of loose recipes in all manner of strange handwriting, were interspersed with a dozen black-and-white pictures of trim, energetic housewives. All of the housewives smiled big smiles and had short, tidy hair with crisp, crimped waves and narrow, belted waists and open-toed shoes and, flowing from their mouths, dialogue bubbles filled with handy household tips, their tried-and-true solutions for the persistent problem of small, unwanted visitors in the flour and the oatmeal, for mildew in basements, and for those noisy cupboard doors that can disturb a peaceful household.

Some of the book's pages were stained and many of the margins were filled with Sylvia's own handwriting, cryptic notes she'd made to herself. Often she had devised variations or substitutions. On some pages there was a check mark or a question mark, sometimes a warning to herself: Careful when doubling, or, Sounds better than it is, or, Everyone hated this, except Bill, who maybe just didn't want to say. On some pages a name had been written in the margin and firmly underlined.

Standing over the stove after school started that September, absent-mindedly stirring a soup that had been dropped off by her grandmother, Daphne leafed through the pages, looking for her own name. She eventually found it beside the recipe for Sea Foam Icing: Daphne, it said. Birthdays and other.

Margaret did not impose herself. She left them more or less alone to sort things out, calling only occasionally to ask if there was anything extra that needed to be done or to say that she was going over the border and did anyone need socks, underwear, khakis? The first time she was invited for a meal she hadn't prepared, she restrained herself, behaved as a guest would, graciously accepting Daphne's no when she asked if she could help with the dishes.

She didn't work with Bill at the hardware now. She had accepted an offer to cross the street to the pharmacy, where she was paid a substantially higher wage to keep a set of books that were not much more complicated than the hardware books. Bill told her he hated to see her go but he wasn't the guy in charge so he couldn't do anything about raising her pay.

As a going-away gift he gave her a pearl cluster brooch that he'd found nestled in cotton batting in a small blue box in Sylvia's dresser. When Margaret asked, he had to say he had no idea how Sylvia had come to have it.

Six weeks after the supper when she didn't wash the dishes, Bill and Margaret began to meet at the Blue Moon for their coffee breaks, sitting always in one of the smaller booths at the back. Sometimes they met for lunch, BLTs or soup of the day.

When it became clear to the wits that Bill had abandoned them, one of them told him in what passes in men for a whisper, "Just don't be too long about it. We can't guarantee your spot forever." It was the first joke anyone had directed at Bill in a long time. They all recognized a possibility when they saw one and they could see no purpose in his trying to continue on alone with those kids. None of them could have done it.

IN January, after one of Margaret's roast beef dinners, Bill asked everyone to stay around because he wanted to talk to them. Patrick and Murray were home for the weekend. Patrick had been coming home regularly, picking up every hour he could get at the feed mill.

Supper had been conversational, lively. The boys were full of talk. Classes were indeed huge, professors were indeed weird, jocks thought they ruled the campus and were pretty much correct. No one bothered much with small-town boys.

Bill had not bought Margaret a diamond because she told him she would be happier with just the one ring, but the kids all knew what was coming and Bill knew they knew. He said the words he had decided to say, careful not to show any undue affection to Margaret, who sat across from him. He mentioned the word "mother" several times and, near the end of his very short speech, the words "make a life."

He understood that what he was about to do would be seen by some as too big a change too soon, or worse, just plain selfish, as if he was thinking mainly about himself. He had tried to prepare Margaret for a bit of resistance because he believed the kids were entitled to it, although he couldn't guess how their resistance might show itself. When they only nodded and tried to smile, each nod around the table an indication to him that they were ready to offer up the hardest gift they had ever been asked to give, before he'd even felt it coming he had made a private, lifelong promise to each of them, separately.

He had made his decision about Margaret in the late fall, the night he took her to the horse races in London, to thank her for all her time and trouble. It was the first time in twelve years that they had been absolutely alone together, with no expectation of interruption. On the way home, after she told him he was more than welcome, he reminded her of all the years they had worked side by side and then without flinching he asked what she would think about getting married.

Margaret smoothed her silky skirt over her long legs and then reached to touch his arm. She told him yes, she thought that would be the best idea.

If anyone had wanted to know, Margaret would have said that she felt honoured to be asked into Bill's life. There was that kind of formality around him now, maybe around any man in his position. But she would have said too that a man's love for a woman should get its start when the woman is young. She would have said that a man's love for a woman past thirty, say, was in fact love for the younger, remembered woman, the feeling strengthened maybe with time and familiarity, but really and always, if you could strip away the time and familiarity, you would see it was the younger, remembered woman who was loved, the basic woman. She would have said that she believed this was one of the main differences between men and women, because you could begin to love a man any time.

After they'd got back to town, Bill had parked his car on the street and gone up the stairs with Margaret to her apartment above the Hydro office. She stood very still while he lifted her sweater over her head and unzipped the long silky skirt. She was wondering as she stood very still how she could possibly begin all this with him, the actual touching, the actual movements of intimacy. She was forty-one years old. A good part of her experience with men had been gained when she was quite young and, more recently, before the possibility of Bill Chambers, while the lovemaking in her narrow bed had been by necessity discreet, perhaps because it had been discreet and limited in possibility and self-contained in its secrecy, it had been, compared to this, now, dreamlike. *Like a dream.* This *now* was meant to be the pleasurable evidence not of a true, prohibited, longed-for love but of Bill's plain desire that she should be with him in his life, through his life. She waited for her body to accept this difference. She relied on her instinct. Bill moved slowly, took them through it slowly. Her instinct told her to let him do this.

Once begun, it was not so difficult. The missing fingers were not missed and his skin under her tentative hands, under the surprisingly symmetrical islands of his dark body hair, was like warm crushed velvet, like something you might touch in the real, daylight world, a very fine, once-in-a-lifetime gift.

When their first moving together was done, curled into herself, holding herself, she told him that she could feel it in her fingertips. It had travelled like an undertow all the way through her. Gone everywhere.

Bill stretched out beside her in her narrow bed, sated and confused and quiet. He could not tell her, he would never be able to tell her how strange it was, the way Sylvia, a smaller woman, had seemed to fly apart when it happened for her, how he sometimes had to hold her tight to keep her in one piece and how other times he just pulled away to laugh and watch her fill the bed, watch her fly, and here she was, Margaret, a much larger, beautifully long-boned woman, making herself so small in his arms and in her own.

He had not tried to convince himself that he loved Margaret, not yet, but he did believe that a certain kind of marriage could be made from need and gratitude and amazement. He believed that Margaret's long-boned presence among them would keep the house safe, and familiar, and that in time, after some months or years, he would discover that he did love her. You could find love waiting for you. He believed that. And besides, he was not young. He did not wish to be young again.

Comforting her, stroking her arching neck and resting the back of his hand against the vein pulsing there, he began to construct a small sealed room to preserve and protect his life with Sylvia, to hold and protect all the past. There would be no end to what the room could contain and he would step inside at will, he would for the rest of his life remember everything, anything, any time he pleased. But he would never allow himself to speak to the things housed in that room because there could be no answer and he believed that such a silence would be the hardest thing his life could ever give him.

1956

BILL and Margaret were married at the Anglican manse on a Friday night in early February. They had talked about going in to the courthouse in London but then Bill suggested the minister who had shingled the bathroom roof and Margaret voiced no objection.

The ceremony was small and quick and private. Bill's parents had not been invited, although they'd told him to go ahead and do what he thought was right, because Margaret's mother and father had both died quite young, in the war years, and Bill didn't want her to feel entirely outnumbered. She had only one much older brother who had long ago moved to Nova Scotia and he could not have been expected to make the trip just for a wedding. The kids were there, of course, and Murray tagged along, arriving at the house in his suit ten minutes before they left for the manse. Bill's brother Gerry and his beefy wife Eileen came up from Windsor to witness the nuptials, the sister-in-law a determined, spirited woman who was always interrupting people with apropos quotes from Doctor Norman Vincent Peale. After an hour of listening to Eileen's relentless cheer, Margaret was glad to remind herself that Windsor was still thought to be a very long drive. There was no formal reception after they left the church. Celebration wasn't really wanted.

Angela Johnston, who was Margaret's bridge partner and oldest friend, had made an angel food cake with pineapple filling and dropped it off that afternoon, had opened the fridge and rearranged things herself to make room for it. Good wishes and a few small gifts came to the house over the following weeks, but informally. The wits and their wives bought them the blue punch bowl set that had been sitting in the window up at Taylor's, calling it when they brought it over one big gift instead of a lot of smaller, useless things.

Margaret sold most of the furniture she'd had in her apartment over the Hydro office to an auctioneer. What she didn't sell she stored in the basement at Bill's, expecting that it would be carried up some day down the road and used by someone just starting out. Otherwise she brought with her only her car, a 1954 Pontiac which she said she was ready to make available to Patrick for dates and to the others when they started to drive, a low, round, mahogany table with scalloped edges that was one of the very few beautiful things her mother had possessed, a nearly complete set of good bone china, her hardly used silverware, and her small, recently purchased television set. Although the house did not yet have an antenna up on the roof, Paul carried the television in and placed it on a table in the living room, rearranging all the chairs to face it.

Margaret tried to be careful not to disturb things. She did partially empty Sylvia's kitchen cupboards and organize the dishes and the canned goods to suit herself, explaining to everyone as they watched her do it that a tall woman wanted a slightly different set-up.

Bill had convinced himself after that first night when they got back to town from the horse races that it was going to be all right for them, but sometimes with no warning he would have long, hard days of remembering Sylvia, bits of her from different times, and he would want her back, badly, he would want their time back. He told Margaret it was like a rancid ache just under his skin, between his bones and his skin. He said this was the only way he could think to describe what was wrong with him.

A month before she died Sylvia had told Bill that anything might happen. Lying in their damp bed he'd listened to her worries about the kids and then he'd heard her describe a probable life for him in the arms of some other, unimagined woman, heard her say clearly that he wouldn't have any choice, he would just have to trust his needs and take it as it came. She said she believed that if she were in his shoes, that's what she'd do. She would just have to.

Although Margaret was carefully casual with Bill in the company of others, in their own bed she stroked him and tried to soothe him. She praised Sylvia. She talked about Sylvia with all the affection she could muster, about her courage, her spunk, how she had loved her children, the way she could mimic people, the way she could get everyone laughing. She prodded Bill to remember Sylvia's take on his sister-in-law, made him laugh with her, remembering. Margaret believed she could do this, allow Sylvia to continue on in him. They weren't kids.

Gradually her kindness began to work its magic and eventually she found the courage to say that, like it or not, life simply has to be for the living. She told him it was a good thing to keep living. When Bill confessed like a sinner that what he really felt was lucky, lucky having had Sylvia and now having her, Margaret nodded yes in the dark and pulled him down, hoping only that because her own body was so different from Sylvia's he would be able to believe that this was a very separate thing he was doing now.

In the early spring, after some blunt but encouraging counsel from Doc Cooper, she allowed herself to become pregnant, guessing correctly that babies sometimes alleviate suffering. Walking uptown to work on a bright, clear morning, watching the branches on the trees along the streets sway with the new weight of buds, she willed the sperm she had just received an hour before to give it their very best effort. There will be prizes, she told them.

The kids didn't bother themselves with thoughts of Margaret in bed with their father. They, too, were not without instinct. The harder adjustment was watching her large hands on their mother's belongings: her aprons, her mixmaster, her clothespins, her sewing machine, the junk in her junk drawer. The irritations were petty and jolting, the way she blew her nose in short, quick bursts, and her bags, her growing cache of bags, the way she flattened and folded every bag that entered her domain and tucked it in a drawer, just in case.

Living on her own in the long, narrow apartment above the Hydro office, working at her oversized desk at the back of the hardware store, all those years entering her ledger numbers precisely for an easy balance at month end, her only deviance an occasional ticket for speeding on her way into the city, Margaret had once in a while taken some time to imagine a life something like this one. Among the many choices she'd imagined she would have, things like clean windows and lots of them, good meals carefully prepared and nicely served, a mirror in a bathroom opening on a private, ordinary mix of male and female toiletries, she had always thought she would call a daughter Kathleen and a son Tom.

But late in the summer, when her condition became so evident it had to be taken into account, Daphne, meaning only to make a show of maturity, to be seen to be accepting of this baby and all its implications, brought the naming to the supper table as if she were absolutely entitled to do this, asking Bill as she added another possibility to her list, "So who named me?"

Margaret sat back and let them do it. Stephen it was. Stephen Thomas. Or Sarah Kathleen. Sally.

HOME for the summer in early May, Patrick had got a promotion at McFarlane's mill. He was now driving a one-ton truck around the countryside making deliveries, heaving sacks of feed on and off the truck, getting brown and bulking up. Late in the afternoon Margaret would lay out fresh underwear and pants and a shirt in the downstairs bathroom and watch for him at the kitchen window, listen for his footsteps on the gravel driveway. He'd come home coated in a cloud of feed dust and stand in the middle of the back-yard to slap his pants and shirt hard and bend over to shake the dust from his hair and then he'd quickly strip to his underwear on the back porch, ducking into the bathroom to shove his head under the tap and wash for half an hour before anyone heard from him.

Although he had assumed he would, Patrick had not liked living in residence much at all. The room was a lot smaller than the bedroom he shared with Paul at home, and John, the roommate assigned by alphabetic proximity, was a loud-mouthed, back-slapping jock from Ottawa who called girls wimen and acted like he'd just discovered booze and couldn't seem to get enough of either.

John introduced Patrick to his many, many friends and prodded him to come with them to the Brass Rail to find some friendly small-town wimen who might have their own apartments, their own apartments being the first and only consideration. Thinking there was a chance he had the guy all wrong, Patrick did go along for one of John's "crime and corruption" nights but at the end of it he found himself in the arms of a not very pretty girl who had no idea what was going on, who said almost nothing but welcomed him into her bed as if it meant something. Her own roommate was in the other bed with some other guy, not four feet away, moaning and whispering, and when everyone else fell asleep, he got dressed quickly and left. He didn't even want to remember the not very pretty girl's name.

He said nothing, certainly didn't tell Murray, and he turned down all further invitations. He watched John's marks nosedive and hoped he'd flunk out, thinking, If there's a God, this guy's gone. Some small hesitation had kept him from telling John that his mother had just died and by October he was glad he'd hesitated.

All his classes were huge. He hated that, the amphitheatres, the fact that not even the professors knew him by name. He and Murray ate lunch together between classes and they worked in the library, went to the odd Mustangs game, drank quietly at the Ceeps where they met but did not take up with several pretty, lively young women who were away from home for the first time too and game for almost anything anyone might propose.

But now it was summer and he wanted someone, needed someone. After several weeks delivering feed, twice to the Elliot farm, he had phoned Sandra Elliot to ask her to go out to the Casino dance on Saturday night. Sandra was going into grade twelve with Daphne and he remembered her from high school, vaguely. He'd heard from Daphne that she had just broken up with some guy from Parkhill and he assumed correctly that they had worked all this out ahead of him, that his call was expected. Both times when he'd pulled into the yard with feed Sandra was just coming out of the house, as if by chance, and when he'd finished unloading she leaned against the truck to talk to him, turned and lifted her head quickly to make her dark red hair swing. She focused on him with big easy smiles, used her posture to make sure he was aware of her breasts, and bending to pet one of the dogs, offered little glimpses of very white cheek not quite hidden by short shorts.

When he picked her up on the Saturday night, getting out of Margaret's Pontiac to go inside and meet the mother, Sandra came down the stairs in a sundress her mother said she'd got an A for in Home Economics. It was dark red with a full skirt and thin straps which Sandra identified, when they were in the car on their way out to the lake, as spaghetti straps. Spaghetti straps required a strapless bra, she told him.

Less than a year later, when they were finally finished with each other, Patrick guessed it was the irresistible weight of her breasts against those straps, that and nothing much else that had got him through the summer.

The Casino sat high in the dunes above Lake Huron. It was large and square, cream stucco with a dark red roof. Downstairs there were slot machines on a gritty cement floor, not very clean wash-rooms, and long benches against the cement-block walls. There was a concession where swimmers and sunbathers could buy potato chips or Coppertone for their tans, and, beside it, a big pop cooler. You had to lift the lid and reach down through ice water for a bottle of Coke or Canada Dry or Orange Crush and more than once a kid who had just come in after hours and hours of playing in the after-noon sun stuck an arm down and promptly slumped to the gritty cement floor, out cold.

Upstairs, the hardwood dance floor was surrounded by a wrap-around balcony with shutters that could be dropped quickly if a storm came up off the lake. You could stand out there between dances and listen to the waves lapping on the sand and stare out over the shining water toward Michigan. Or you could look up at the stars and the moon in the dark sky above the water, at the clouds that threatened to obliterate the light as they drifted across it. Patrick had been coming out to the Casino dances since he was fifteen and he had never once been with a girl who didn't like to do this, who didn't soften looking out at the water or up at the sky.

The band was always the same. They played mostly country and western with a few polkas and square dances thrown in, sometimes a jive. On a good night they could be talked into trying "Sixteen Tons" or "Moments to Remember" or "Blue Suede Shoes" or "Heartbreak Hotel." There was no booze, not inside anyway, not that you could see.

Patrick and Sandra recognized nearly everyone around them but they danced only together, oblivious to the people they would ordinarily dance with at least once or twice. And no one bothered them because a first date gave you that right, to ignore people you knew, to pretend you couldn't see their faces, couldn't hear them speaking even though they surrounded you, same as always.

On the way home after the dance they didn't talk as much as Patrick had thought they would. Standing on her porch under a naked two-hundred-watt bulb that lit the entire yard and half the barn, with one of the black Labs thumping its tail eagerly against his legs, he leaned in to kiss her and when she kissed him back, he took his chance to cup her heavy breast in his hand. But she pulled the hand away and wrapped it around her back. He assumed she had a set of rules in mind. Although it was the biggest breast he'd touched, it wasn't the first. And a guy could be forgiven. The rules varied from girl to girl, more than you'd think.

The Wednesday night after the Casino dance he took her into Sarnia to a show, a war movie, which they watched low in their seats, holding hands as soon as the plot was well established, Patrick's arm quickly closing in around her shoulders. On the way home after the show there was finally quite a bit of talk. Sandra started it by saying how sorry she was about his mother's death and when he tensed up she quickly said she understood how awful it must be for his family. She told him she was sure it would make him feel better to talk about it, that she really believed talking helped. When he reached to turn up the radio, meaning to say that the song shouldn't be missed, she was obviously annoyed that he wasn't even going to try to put it into words for her but she went on bravely to more ordinary things: what he was studying, what he wanted out of university, where she herself thought she might want to go when she graduated. The goodnight kisses took place in the dark of the car, although they were still too few for Patrick and his hand was still very firmly guided. He knew what he'd be doing, wasn't very happy about what he'd be doing when he got home into his own warm bed.

The show had been a slacks-and-sweater-set date but on the Friday night, when their only plan was to do something and Sandra appeared at her door in a pale pink angora sweater and a wrap-around skirt, he drove straight out to Lake Huron. He made two slow trips up and down the beach, nodding and waving at the other guys, mostly high school types who were driving the beach with their girlfriends, and then he turned off to follow the road that twisted back to the inland lakes. He parked the car beside one of the smallest lakes and they leaned forward together to look up through the windshield at the stars. After what he believed was long enough, he said he'd check to see if there was a blanket in the trunk and she helped him spread it out on the soft grassy sand.

Sandra was easy enough to get along with. She laughed a lot and sometimes threw her head back when she did as if she'd never in her life had such a good time. He started to miss her through the week, got so he couldn't remember how he had filled his time before he'd asked her out.

He did miss Murray, who had stayed on alone in London, to work. They'd both decided that residence was not for them so before Patrick moved home they had hunted around one morning and found an apartment near the campus and Murray was living there until September, working at the Ancaster Inn on the other side of the city. When Patrick told Bill about their decision, explaining that residence was more than half full of assholes, it seemed to Bill that Patrick might be getting unnecessarily surly.

Their apartment had once been just the upstairs of a normal house. It had a narrow living room across the front with big windows overlooking Richmond Street, two bedrooms, a small kitchen, and off the kitchen a back porch with a staircase leading down to a derelict backyard. There was an old fridge, a stove that was on its last legs, and a grey arborite table with two red chairs. They had borrowed a truck to pick up a couch and a couple of armchairs at the Sally Ann, bought two twin beds at Eaton's, and raided Margaret's stash in the basement at home for lamps and curtains and pots and pans and dishes and cutlery.

Patrick and Murray tried to describe their apartment one night when everyone was in the living room watching "I Love Lucy." Bill's face looked attentive but he laughed nearly every time Lucy opened her mouth, pounding the arms of his chair in appreciation. Margaret wouldn't let Bill watch his other favourite show, "The Honeymooners," not if she was around anyway, because growing up she'd had enough of sloppy, angry men screaming to last her two lifetimes and how could this possibly, possibly be funny?

She had understood for a long time that the invective at her own girlhood kitchen table, the blind faith in strict rules and the outrage that followed their breaking, had been prompted mostly by a sick longing for order, for a kind of peace, and she knew this longing was not unusual, probably not even despicable. But now, from the vantage point of middle age, standing at the kitchen sink, at her kitchen sink, she recognized that all of it together had been nothing more than ordinary selfishness and stupidity and perhaps even laziness, all of it together had only been her father's way to make things easier for himself.

She guessed Bill likely turned on "The Honeymooners" when she wasn't home. He'd told her that Art Carney was the one to watch, not Gleason, said the way Carney survived Gleason was what made it so enjoyable.

In a commercial for Everlasting pots and pans, when the boys saw the chance to bring everyone's attention back to themselves, they announced that neither Margaret nor Daphne would be allowed to come in to clean their apartment. This claim to independence caused a look to pass quickly from Margaret to Daphne, one look among the many they would come to perfect between them, "the repertoire" it would eventually be called, after enough time had passed.

Sometimes Patrick and Sandra drove into London to see Murray. They would pick him up for an early show or just sit around talking before he had to go to work at midnight. Sometimes they arrived with groceries and Sandra made her Home Economics recipe for chili or stuffed green peppers or apple crisp. A few times a month they stayed overnight, telling everyone Murray was going to be there when he wasn't.

Because Murray never had anyone at the apartment and because he drove home every time he had a couple of days off, Patrick

assumed he had nothing special going for him in the city and it
seemed reasonable to ask Sandra to set him up with someone. She
soon had several possibles for consideration but Murray wasn't
biting. He worked, he slept, he drove home to see his parents, he
went over to the house as usual to spend some time talking to
Daphne or Paul or to Bill and Margaret.

Patrick didn't say so directly, but he thought Murray's reluctance
was peculiar. He couldn't comprehend why Murray was dragging
his feet, especially since Sandra was willing to help with the hard
part and the rewards were substantial. But he gave it up, carried on
alone, left Murray out of it.

He had started to go out to Sandra's and sit around on the porch
with her father and the dogs if she was washing her hair or something, and soon he didn't have to ask her out any more, she'd just
tell him if she had to do something else. They would go to a show
or lie around one house or the other watching television until they
couldn't stand it any longer and then they would drive out to the
lake to find a private depression in a grassy dune.

Like Daphne, Sandra had two more years of high school, and one
night out at the inland lakes after they'd spread the blanket on the
sand, at her insistence they began to discuss a time other than the
present. Sandra didn't see the future as he did, as something entirely
unknown but wide open, she saw the future as something you could
put together, something you could cut out and assemble, like a red
sundress. "What we need to have," she told him, "are concrete plans."

Patrick knew something was required, that he had to offer something up in return for the weight of her breasts in his hands, the
strength of her legs locked behind his back, so he said he'd likely
still be in school, he wanted to keep going as long as he could, so
why didn't she just plan on Western? Thinking this and saying it too
soon after thinking it, he was for the first time annoyed with her,
and then, almost immediately, with himself.

On the way back into town from the lake his annoyance solidified
and shifted and landed square in his lap. Yes, they were having a
good time, and yes, he hadn't had any satisfactory action at Western,
and yes, it was all normal and usual and probably expected, but there

was no damn way it was going to be so thoroughly nailed down, not with him in it.

He replayed the blanket conversation in his head and then pushed back to a couple of other conversations he hadn't paid enough attention to. Now he was mad, and sitting tight beside him in the front seat of Margaret's Pontiac, Sandra picked up on his anger. She pulled away to get a good look at his face.

Almost from the beginning she had said the word love when there was no good reason to say it. He didn't need to hear it, he had never given her any reason to believe he needed to hear it. He thought now, turning onto her concession, that he should have told her right from the beginning that he didn't particularly like all the romantic talk, the love stuff, that he thought in fact it was a bit simple-minded.

And even at the start of this first dissolution of what he would much later in his life describe with a hard-won edge in his voice as a first affair, he knew that ending it was not going to be a cold-blooded exercise. This urge to stop her, to stop himself, was as hot as the urge to begin had been, easily as hot.

How to get it done, that was what he thought about as the summer cooled down. Fast or slow? And was there anyone to ask? Murray wouldn't know. Paul wouldn't know. But not Bill and certainly not Margaret.

MURRAY had finished the year on the dean's honour roll and he was more than happy to stay on in London at the apartment for the summer. After exams he quickly got himself a job as the night desk clerk at the Ancaster Inn out near the highway, undercutting any assumptions people might have had that he was counting on a free ride. He had never before found a job on his own, although he'd done his time in the office at the mill learning how to keep a ledger and he always helped out at Bill and Margaret's and cut the grass at home, washed the cars, sometimes washed the dishes if his mother had one of her migraine headaches.

His parents had called him every two months or so that first year to say they were coming into the city and would he like to meet them downtown at the Iroquois for dinner, and one time they'd invited Patrick and Daphne to come along too, but they never went near the residence and they didn't have many questions. They were content to let him manage the details of his life on his own. When he told them about the desk clerk job, they both said that sounded fine. His mother said he would get to meet people he perhaps wouldn't get to meet otherwise and his father said working with the public was valuable experience for anyone.

He'd got lucky with his residence roommate, a studious Jewish guy from Toronto named Geoff whose marks hadn't been high enough for U of T, but who wanted to transfer there after first year if he could pull it off. Geoff studied all the time, was devoted to his books, asked for and got Murray's help with some of his essays. His father was a big-name journalist who had covered the war in France and Italy and then in the Philippines, and although his expectations never left the room, Geoff didn't see him because he still had to be out of the country a lot, even in peacetime. He just couldn't take the time to visit, understandably. Geoff said his father had a million stories, fantastic stories, and he tracked him through the world not by the pieces he wrote for newspapers but by the postcards taped above his bed, a small but growing gallery of exotic locales with the private, scribbled messages turned to the wall. He went home with Murray and Patrick a few times for the weekend and occasionally they hauled him down to the Ceeps for a wasted evening, buying him beer and telling him his skin was turning a putrid green from too much time at the books, that he'd never get laid if he didn't put out at least a bit of effort. They won't come to you, they told him, all the pretty horses.

Pretty horses notwithstanding, Geoff's marks had been high enough for the desired transfer to U of T and after they were packed up he'd offered Murray his hand and thanked him for the help with the essays and told him if he was ever in Toronto, if he ever needed anything at all, to look him up, for sure.

In June, almost comfortable with his desk clerk job, Murray agreed at the last minute to book a night off sick so he could go home to take Daphne to her high school formal. She hadn't really explained herself when she called to ask him so he assumed her on-again, off-again nonsense with Roger Cooper had left her stranded with a new dress and no date. At the dance, feeling a bit out of it, he spent perhaps too much time standing under the streamers talking to the teachers, but they had a nice time, Daphne told him she'd had a really nice time. And she got to show off the dress, which he understood to be the purpose of the exercise.

He drove home whenever he had a few days free to see everyone. When Margaret began to really show, it seemed all right to say something so he told her she looked great. She continued to make him feel welcome, setting a place for him at the table without making a big deal about it. Once she took his hand and brought it to her stomach so he could feel the soft punch of what she said was probably an elbow or a foot or a baseball bat.

At the Ancaster Inn he hardly saw anyone after midnight. He learned to put the registrations and the receipts in order for the bookkeeper and to clean up any mistakes made during the day shifts, which were the busy shifts. He always had a novel under way. Over the summer he went through all of Faulkner and then Steinbeck, ignoring Hemingway because even though Hemingway was supposed to have been a journalist and Murray was interested in journalism, from what he'd heard he was pretty sure he wouldn't like the fiction. He wasn't all that drawn to the tough stuff, the bulls and balls.

He didn't see many of the motel's usual clientele, the families. By the time he came on they were all tucked in for the night and when he left at dawn they were still sleeping or just up, just getting organized to go back on the road. He did see the evidence of a few obviously illicit affairs, men who registered late and alone and good-looking women who walked out through the lobby quickly in the middle of the night.

And he met Crystal, his first high-class hooker, a long-legged bottle redhead in very expensive clothes who arrived at the inn every three weeks through the summer on the arm of a man who called himself Mr. Crystal, who was her manager, her pimp. Mr. Crystal was a slight, boisterous man in a high-gloss white summer suit. When they registered he always left his mauve Lincoln

Continental under the awning out front with the keys in it, running, and he always took two connecting rooms.

Crystal was a busy lady. All of her calls came in through Murray, through the switchboard which looked just like he had imagined a switchboard would look and which he'd almost mastered by the end of the summer. Sometimes, wide awake and brisk in the middle of the night, she would call down to the desk for tea and a muffin or something. There were no busboys on after midnight and, except for the calls prompted by the presence of Crystal herself, the switchboard was pretty quiet, so Murray would go into the kitchen and make her a pot of tea and grab a muffin or a Danish and take them down the inside corridor to her room. Eddie, the second-in-command maintenance man, would sometimes be in the kitchen with a couple of his crew, eating yesterday's Danish, drinking coffee, and they would razz him, tell him he should demand a real good tip from a woman that well off.

Twice Crystal called down for two pots of tea and Murray found her sitting in a negligée talking to Mr. Crystal, who was always, at least any time Murray saw him, dressed in his classy white suit.

One night she opened the door wrapped in a peach see-through nightie thing with a thick ridge of fluffy feathers at the cuffs, the kind of thing Doris Day might wear to seduce Gordon MacRae. She sat down on the bed to watch Murray put the tray down and when he turned to look at her, not expecting a tip or anything, just looking, she patted the bed with her stubby fingers. He could see her jewellery on the bedside table, a watch surrounded with a heavy circle of diamonds and several large rings that looked cheap but likely weren't. When she asked, clearly making it a question, "Take a load off?" he could feel quarts of blood rushing up through his neck to fill his face. Then she said, "I guess not," and smiled a coy, almost kind smile. He saw when she smiled that she might be older than she looked.

They checked out a few days after her offer, moving on to Windsor or Toronto or some other city on their circuit. Mr. Crystal paid the bill with cash and handed Murray a crisp ten for all his trouble.

When they returned for another week at the end of the summer, and Crystal patted the bed again, Murray set the tray down on the small table by the window, locked all the doors, and climbed in beside her fully dressed, leaving the front desk unprotected and soon entirely forgotten. Unbuttoning his shirt, Crystal told him this one was on the house, because he had been such a sweetheart, such a darling. When he was naked, and shivering, she laughed a little and called him very fine, a fine specimen indeed. If she guessed it was his first real time, she didn't let that spoil things. Halfway through, he decided that she most certainly was older than she looked and that this was not a bad thing but a good thing. She didn't always wait for him to think of things to do and when she was finished with him he was almost laughing too, because now he knew, oh yeah, now he had the inside information.

IN July, Daphne got a job cooking at the drive-in restaurant out near the golf course and soon she couldn't eat much of anything, couldn't stand the smell of meat especially. At home Margaret fixed her cold plates, devilled eggs and cottage cheese and jellied fruit salads and marshmallows rolled in toasted coconut. Already feeling puffed up and clumsy with her pregnancy, she made the same plate for herself and by the end of the summer she said she felt much better.

Daphne had been briefly embarrassed about Margaret's condition, mainly because at forty-two her eggs would probably be stale or at least no longer in their prime, which was exactly the reason not many women that old had babies. Not many women that old even got married. But she didn't say anything because it wasn't really her business and anyway what could she say? Have a nice baby?

After a month of Margaret's cold plates, she dropped down to just over a hundred pounds and stayed there so the next time she drove over the Bluewater Bridge to Port Huron on a shopping trip with her friend Catharine she bought a black two-piece bathing suit, black to show off her tan, two-piece to show off her small midriff.

Climbing up after her onto the raft that was always anchored in front of Doc Cooper's cottage, Roger Cooper told Daphne that he really liked the bathing suit but missed her old breasts. When she stretched out to sunbathe and didn't laugh or even smile he said of course it didn't matter, he understood, he understood completely.

Daphne had started to go out with Roger, who was a grandson to Doctor Cooper, in October of grade eleven. Roger was someone to want, someone to be pleased about getting. She had no idea why he'd asked her out, but if she'd had to guess she would have guessed that Doc Cooper, who had been at their house so often that spring, must have mentioned her name somehow.

Roger wasn't tall but he was on the hockey team and the basket-ball team anyway because he was muscular and fast and accurate under pressure. He was handsome in a Montgomery Clift kind of way, dark, slick, very blue eyes. And he had nice square shoulders. If anyone had been asked to name just five guys in grade thirteen, Roger would have got named.

Daphne was not one of the grade-eleven girls who would have got named. But now she knew about some of the things she thought her mother likely couldn't make herself say that night in the living room. She assumed that Patrick and Paul and Murray would be the same as Roger, anxious with their hands, eager with their tongues, quiet when they wanted something. Why wouldn't they be?

She had not needed Murray's help with grade eleven. He'd started her off with some useful habits when she was in grade nine, how to set logical priorities, when to bluff it through, when to dig deeper, when to quit. Occasionally, if he was home for the weekend, he still sat down with her at the dining-room table after Sunday lunch, leafing through her notebooks the way a teacher would. She told him twice that she didn't appreciate this and when she finally told him please don't do it any more, that she was getting first-class honours on her own, thank you, he quickly lifted his hands up and away from her work and pushed back his chair. He said he knew she didn't need him, he was just curious.

In March, she did go into London with Murray's parents for dinner at the Iroquois. The McFarlanes picked her up at home in their Buick, Mr. McFarlane knocking gently on the kitchen door, Mrs. McFarlane sitting patiently in the driveway. She had agreed to go partly because she had always thought they must be lonely, just the three of them, and partly because Margaret said what reason did she have to refuse? She wore the deep green wool dress that Margaret had given her for Christmas and she had to wear her duffel jacket over it because she had no good coat but Margaret said it wouldn't matter, there would be a coat check any place the McFarlanes ate and she would leave her jacket there, before she went into the restaurant.

Murray's parents seemed really pleased to have her along. Mrs. McFarlane talked a bit formally but quite easily, pausing to include her husband, explaining things to him as necessary, calling him dear. Daphne got the impression that they always talked like that, Mrs. McFarlane leading, directing the conversation toward some topics, away from others.

They met Murray in the lobby at the Iroquois Hotel and Patrick was there too, both of them in a shirt and tie and sports coat. After they checked their coats, walking into the restaurant beside Daphne, Mrs. McFarlane looked her up and down and then quietly told her that the dress suited her perfectly, because of her skin, which was like alabaster, and because she was so tiny. When Daphne told her it had been Margaret's Christmas gift, Mrs. McFarlane nodded deeply as if she wasn't the least surprised. She said that Margaret's taste had always been pretty trustworthy.

Then, almost at their table, she turned to look directly at Daphne's face and said how pleased they must be that her jaw had healed so remarkably well after that awful fall when she was a child. Daphne had to concentrate to keep walking. She knew what her jaw looked like. No one ever said anything to her about her jaw. It was a rule, a way to give her a chance to forget about it. But Mrs. McFarlane apparently made her own rules about what could get mentioned. Only when she turned to her husband to say how very unappetizing the lobsters looked in their tank did Daphne realize that she wasn't expected to say anything back, that no answer was required. Mrs. McFarlane had just wanted to say it.

They were not offered drinks but Murray's father consulted each of them and ordered some of the most expensive things on the menu: smoked salmon from the coast to start, T-bone steak and fries for the boys, Chicken Kiev for Daphne, Chateaubriand for himself and Mrs. McFarlane. The conversation started out a bit stilted but Mrs. McFarlane ploughed on through, including everyone on every topic at least briefly.

After dinner Mr. and Mrs. McFarlane went into the bar on their own for a drink, and when Patrick left to go to the washroom, Murray said to Daphne out of the blue that he'd decided he liked university so much because it was substance, it was something you could get your hands on. He nodded toward the bar and said it had always been this way with his parents, all surface, no substance. Daphne was fiddling with the pecan pie that Mr. McFarlane had recommended and insisted on ordering for her, telling the waiter it might put some meat on her bones. Looking up from the pie she told Murray that maybe substance was overrated anyway. Who could say?

In June she had a huge fight with Roger about his pushing her, even pleading with her sometimes, which made her cringe, so she'd had to ask Murray to come home to be her date for the spring formal. Margaret had already taken her over to Port Huron where they'd found a pale green organza dress with tiny, almost invisible sprigs of flowers, which Margaret said was the finest dress she had ever seen, and they'd bought a stiff, pale green fifty-yard crinoline to go with it and a pair of elegant satin spike heels, dyed to match. She couldn't see any reason to miss the formal and she certainly wasn't going to turn up with a brother.

Murray was a gallant escort. He made a game of being a gallant escort. He brought her a wrist corsage of white sweetheart roses and stood tall while Margaret pinned a carnation to his lapel. After the dance he kissed Daphne's hand at the door as if he was going to turn and leave and then he came in with her to have a grilled cheese sandwich and to help her tell Margaret about the dance, although he had taken no notice of what girl was with what guy, and of course he had nothing of interest to say about any of the dresses.

Roger was back on the doorstep a week after the formal, his assumption being that if his replacement had to be good old Murray, he and Daphne were not really what you'd call history.

Roger was getting ready to go to Guelph to study veterinary medicine. His grandfather had carefully explained the difference in income between veterinary and ordinary practice, he had even estimated the difference in the two lifetime incomes to show him what his decision was really costing, but Roger ignored the numbers. He told Daphne they had all watched his grandfather go through years of deaths and sickness, always getting up in the middle of the night to drive over to see someone he couldn't save anyway. He said he didn't think he had what it took to live a normal life doing what doctors had to do, that his mother had told him when he was a kid that it was a lot worse than people imagined, that his grandparents knew things, miserable, ugly things, and of course they had to pretend they didn't know anything at all when they met people on the street. He said he couldn't see caring much if a cow died, although he understood full well the economic importance of keeping cows alive and kicking.

Saying all this, using the words *couldn't* and *save* and *normal* and *miserable* and *ugly* and *pretend*, Roger had not stopped to think that he might be fouling Daphne's memory of his lame, soft-spoken grandfather leaning over her mother's bedside, and listening to him, she decided that his instincts were correct. He was wise to decide to stay away from people.

Daphne had realized by the end of June just how badly Roger wanted to leave, to get out of town, and through the summer she began to understand exactly how far away he was going, that it wasn't just to Guelph. He had never once said a word about her jaw, about the off-centre look of her face, so she didn't really believe that would be it but she could see her own absence in his future clear as day.

He had been telling her that he loved her and she believed he did in the sense that she was fine for now but she knew he said it only because he thought it was required. It was the thing guys said all the time. He could have put it lots of other ways but he would have been saying the same thing. Some nights out at the lake, lying on a blanket on the soft sand under the stars, listening to the lapping water, she would watch him fall alone into what he described as normal human passion. He insisted that she really loved him and then begged her, ordered her, to prove it. Sometimes he squeezed her arms so hard they were bruised when she woke up the next morning.

None of it was doing him much good. She had been holding the line and she was going to keep holding it. She wouldn't let him take himself out of his khaki pants, would only touch him on the outside, her hand kissed and then directed by his own.

All through the summer they drove out to the lake to the Casino dance every Saturday night, sometimes double-dating with Paul and Andrea or some other couple, sometimes alone. Everybody went to the Casino. To amuse themselves, Daphne and Andrea pretended to have a crush on the lead singer, a young guy with a dreamy voice and a nondescript wife, and they wasted a lot of time trying to catch his eye, which annoyed Roger. Daphne danced with Murray and once in a while with Patrick and occasionally with some of the older guys from town who worked at the mill or the factory or the foundry, who she just sort of knew from working at the drive-in restaurant, who ribbed her and told her she was getting to be too hot to handle. She danced with her father if he and Margaret were there because Margaret usually spent most of the night standing out on the balcony talking to some of the other women and cooling off, pulling at her maternity top until the breeze caught it and sent it billowing out around her.

Roger told Daphne he didn't care who she danced with. He wandered around talking to people or went out to the parking lot or down to the shore for a beer with some of the guys, and on one of the many nights he came back to her at the end of the dance a little drunk, he called her the thing he believed to be the worst possible thing a girl could be. Lying on the soft beach sand, staring up at the stars and thinking about the words *cock* and *tease* and about the men she had just danced with, Daphne told him she thought his brand of passion was just another word for lack of control.

"Yeah," he said. "Exactly." And then, trying as he always did for another way in, he finally hung himself with, "What if this is our only chance?"

Daphne was content to make Roger pay in advance. She didn't want, had no desire to create a heartsick parting at the end of the summer. She hated weak, blubbering movie-star tears and the idea of allowing him to see her shameful loneliness was as nauseating as the smell of the pukey meat she sometimes had to pitch into the garbage out behind the drive-in.

When it was time, maybe after a few fall dates when he was home from Guelph for the weekend, if that's what he thought he wanted, she would let him leave without any fuss at all. He wasn't going to be hurting her. Hurting her, and then after he was gone, thinking about her that way, hurt.

PAUL was the first one to be told outright that Margaret was pregnant. He listened to her throw up one Thursday morning in early June and, tensed up but afraid to even think about her being sick, he asked if maybe she shouldn't go see Doc Cooper. She was sitting in a kitchen chair, clutching a cup of tea, holding a cold cloth to her forehead, groaning. She looked at him and tried to smile to ease his mind and then she laughed and said, "Not for about seven more months."

He caught on fast, although it was the last thing he was expecting. "Holy shit," he said.

She gave this right back to him, "Holy shit," and laughed again.

When he said he wouldn't let on, she told him, "Go ahead. Let on. Your father isn't sure just how to do it and it's likely time. It will be time soon."

Paul had been taken on at McFarlane's mill too, a few hours a week, not driving but loading sacks of feed on the trucks for delivery and hanging around the office wasting the bookkeeper's time with jokes. One day the woman stopped Margaret on the street to tell her that she thought Paul was just wonderful, he was so funny, that he was becoming more and more like Sylvia in that way. But Paul told Margaret the bookkeeper thought everything was wonderful, she was one of those.

He had struggled in grade ten. Margaret had not been able to help him with his French or his Latin but under her eye his geometry marks had improved significantly and after Andrea Sparling materialized it looked like he might pass.

In January, only five months after his mother's death, he had taken Andrea home from the New Year's Eve dance at the arena. He had always thought he wanted a tall girl, that he would look stupid with anything else, but Andrea Sparling wasn't even five feet high. At first when they were dancing they tried to talk but she soon got tired of leaning back to look up at him and finally she just rested her face on his chest. Holding her, he thought, She has such a small back, how could anyone have such a small back.

The New Year's dance was the big one. You could hardly move around the floor. People had house parties first, then they came over to the arena in laughing carloads. At eleven-thirty the band stopped and everyone got their coats and poured out into the cold night to walk uptown to the main intersection, where Front Street met George, to dance in circles around the lit-up Christmas tree, a twenty-five-foot spruce that had been set in a big tub of sand and secured by guy wires to the highest corners of the two banks. At midnight, the Town Hall siren went off to wail in the new year, 1956. Everyone was supposed to kiss everyone else but Paul lifted Andrea off her feet and held her buried in his arms so no one else could touch her.

Andrea lived out in the country, in the middle of eight hundred acres of corn, and her father kept one of his several old half-tons tuned up so she could come and go without bothering him. Like other farm fathers, he expected his kids to grow up a little quicker than town kids might, mostly because he didn't have the time or the patience to wait around for it. Paul knew Andrea's sister's boyfriend Don, who was in grade twelve. They played on the same hockey team, Paul still a star forward because of his long legs, his long reach, Don a squat brute with a scarred face who played defence, who would take anyone on, who lived to throw his gloves off and get serious. Andrea came to all their games although she didn't humiliate Paul, didn't yell at the referee like some of the other girls, or squeal at his accomplishments, or cry into her angora mitts if he got slammed hard into the boards or sliced by some thug's high stick.

And she became a cheerful fixture at the house when she wasn't babysitting the Weston tribe after school. Bill started to call her

[83]

Andy and she befriended Margaret, pitched in whenever there was work to be done. She jumped up after supper to dry the dishes, put the ironing board away for Margaret, grabbed an extra dust cloth on Saturday mornings. She did her homework with Paul in the dining room, eating the taffied popcorn Margaret made for them.

They appeared to be suited to each other. Andy treated Paul the way a young bride would, enjoying him and pleasing him and teaching him how to please her. They made love more often than any of the others and with the happiest enthusiasm. They parked the half-ton in the drive shed out at the farm and climbed into the back with blankets or they crawled into their own beds when they found themselves alone in an empty house. They were firm in their happiness, oblivious, never gave getting caught a second thought. Andy had no questions to ask Paul about his mother's death, although she held him when he cried and listened quietly the few times he spoke about it, remembered from one time to the next exactly what he had said, the specific words he'd used.

Margaret knew what they were up to and one night after the dishes were done she quietly reached into her apron pocket and slipped Andy the folded list of contraceptive possibilities that she and Christine Lucas, who was Cooper's nurse, had come up with between them. She had phoned Christine at home and given her every opportunity to decline the conversation because kids especially were not supposed to be given any official guidance but Christine said she was fine with it. "Go ahead," she'd told Margaret. "Shoot."

"I just wanted to check that there wasn't something I'm unaware of," Margaret had told her. "Perhaps something new."

"Nothing new under the sun," Christine said. "Not that I've heard about. And I'd hear."

They had agreed to list sheaths first, which Christine being Christine called galoshes, then a cap, which she said she could likely get her hands on because there were sometimes one or two lying around the office, then the killer foam, then the Pope's old standby, rhythm, which Christine said certainly worked for him, and finally they threw in pulling out and abstinence. They'd debated a bit about the pulling out and the abstinence, Margaret's position being

[84]

that there was no sense recommending something that wasn't likely to happen and Christine's position being you never knew.

"I heard once that women used to make caps out of lemons cut in half," Christine said. "Which makes you think about lemonade a little differently."

"Really?" Margaret said. "I expect my mother might have used a sponge with vinegar." Until that moment, she had not once wondered how her mother had solved her own problem.

"Then likely mine did too," Christine said. "No such thing now though." And then she couldn't stop herself. "Do you mind me asking who this information is for?"

Margaret did mind and she had prepared herself for the question. But still, she was thoroughly disappointed in Christine. "All and sundry," she'd said. "All and sundry."

Andy just smiled as she read the list of possibilities at the kitchen sink. "It's fine," she whispered. "I know what I'm supposed to know. I asked Cooper and he filled me in. But thanks."

"Oh," was all Margaret could think to say. Cooper was taking his chances. But then again, maybe not. Before Andy could return the list, she thought to ask and was pleased she did, "Maybe you could mention some of this to Daphne?"

"Sure," Andy told her, still whispering, still smiling. "If you like, I can do that."

When Paul wasn't at the mill working, he took it upon himself to stay close to home. Andy had taught him what it meant to be thoughtful and he tried to anticipate Margaret's needs, to prevent her from doing any of the heavy work. He cut the grass and set up a fan in the kitchen. He and Andy helped her empty and paint the cupboards, chucking the odd things that had been sitting unused at the back of some of the shelves: a cracked teapot, a rusted strainer, two tins filled with years of unrecognized buttons. They made room for Margaret's good china which had been waiting all this time in boxes in the basement. Knowing because she was told every time she turned around that she would soon have her hands full, Margaret said what she would really like would be to get the living room and dining room and hall painted. Paul and Andy took right over. They did it all, without any help from Patrick or Murray or Daphne or Bill.

And the three of them drove into Sarnia to buy a white crib with a good mattress, set it up in the big bedroom where it would stay for a while at the foot of Bill and Margaret's bed. After that, Daphne would be gone or almost ready to go and the plan was that one end of her room would become the baby's.

Bill had told Paul when he got his grade-ten results in June that if his marks didn't improve considerably by October he would have to hang up his skates for grade eleven. So Paul was planning to work fairly hard when they went back to school. Now that you no longer needed two languages besides English to do anything, he decided he could afford to drop Latin. He thought things should get easier without the Latin and Andy said she thought so too.

A T the beginning of September, Patrick and Murray started their second year at Western. They liked their apartment and they appreciated the casseroles Margaret sent in, the shepherd's pie and the meat loaf, the baked beans. On their own they ate a lot of bologna and bread, sometimes not even making the effort to slap these together into a sandwich, and spaghetti and meatballs was a time-consuming big deal, a near feast.

They studied hard, compared marks. They brought home armloads of books and went for days without talking unless something actually had to be said. Their papers were twice as good as they needed to be and they both began to rank near the top in all the courses that mattered.

Some weekends Sandra came in on the bus to be with Patrick, telling her parents that she slept on the couch in the living room. She was in grade twelve with Daphne and worked in her aunt's dress shop after school now, so she had lots of clothes. Murray was happy enough to see Sandra, at least in the beginning. He told her she should bring Daphne with her some weekend, suggested they could go some place, the four of them. But she didn't bring Daphne and she didn't say why either, or even if she'd asked her.

After a couple of months of her visits, Murray got tired of

Sandra's presumption, as if her place in Patrick's bed gave her the right to make herself entirely at home. He got fed up finding the cereal box empty, or the cheese gone, used as a middle-of-the-night snack, and he got particularly tired of the sounds she made in bed. He practised asking them what the hell they thought the walls were made of and did they think it was enjoyable to listen to, all that groaning and her stupid cat sounds?

He came in drunk one night and said he wanted some ground rules. He said she could come some weekends but not every weekend. And she could damn well bring some groceries with her. And she could try to use a little vocal restraint when she was on her back.

In a quiet, mincing voice that was worse than screaming would have been, Sandra asked him why he didn't just pretend he couldn't hear anything. She said that's what friends did. And then she wanted to know why someone with all the money in the whole God damned world would take the time away from his busy schedule to worry about who ate what. Murray didn't answer her. He was very unsteady on his feet. He went to bed.

Sandra left in the morning and stayed away for a month. This was what Patrick had been saying he wanted, so it should have made him happy but he soon began to feel marooned without the sex, without sex being there for him, regularly. He sulked around and banged dishes and left the bathroom a roaring mess in the mornings. Murray held back, didn't say, Tough shit, partner.

Murray did start to bring the occasional girl back after a session at the library or after a party he'd tripped into, usually someone who looked to have a bit of spirit. When he got one of these girls in bed he would always encourage her to let herself go, as if he wanted to free her from some sad old restraint. One night after several loud, boisterous sessions in a row, when Patrick and Murray were both in the tiny kitchen, each of them heading for the fridge, Patrick shoved Murray out of the way and then Murray shoved harder, surprisingly hard, and then they pulled themselves back against opposite walls.

"At least Sandra loves me," Patrick said. "At least she knows what she wants. She's not just some little piece, some one-time only...."

"What crap," Murray said, stepping forward to open the fridge door, taking out a beer and handing it off, taking out another. "You don't love her and she's the only one on the planet who doesn't know it because you haven't got the stones to make her comprehend. What pure crap."

Sandra stayed mad. This was her plan gone wrong. Patrick knew that she assumed he was pissed off for the same reason she was angry, that she expected him to do something, to stand up for her, to make it right. But he didn't. Murray had given him his chance and, unfortunate as it was, he pretty much had to take it. Sandra was going to have to stay mad.

He had promised in September to take her to the Christmas ball with another couple, some cousin of hers who was in fourth-year law and his girlfriend from McGill. He believed he should stick to that promise, so Sandra came into the city and dragged him downtown to rent a tux to go with the heavy peau-de-soie dress she had just finished. The dress was a soft sea green to set off her dark red hair and it had a scooped neckline that exposed her freckles and her cleavage, which she darkened just before they left the apartment with brown eye shadow, a little trick she said she'd recently learned.

Before the dance, the four of them went out to a new, classy restaurant for dinner where the guys talked about law and drank too many Rusty Nails, a two-hour start that more or less ruined the rest of the evening. Patrick was hanging over the toilet in his rented tux when Sandra went out the apartment door for the last time, her hair still sprayed to perfection and her sea green dress still beautiful, far too beautiful for rejection.

A week later Murray's father arrived out of the blue to have a talk with Patrick. He climbed up the steep derelict stairs to the back door to ask Patrick if he had a few minutes and then told him to get his coat so they could sit in the Buick to have their talk. Sitting in the car he explained to Patrick that he understood he was doing very well, and he asked if he thought a further degree would be useful to him. Patrick confessed that he had been encouraged by one of his professors to keep going, that law looked interesting. Mr. McFarlane told Patrick that he expected nothing in return for what had been provided so far but perhaps they should look at future support as a business deal. He said he would be pleased to see Patrick continue if he would agree to make reasonable repayments when he was properly established, as he most surely would be, in almost no time. He said, "Business goes in cycles and we're in a slight slump at the mill now, maybe you know that."

Patrick said he understood, and thank you, and when he opened the car door, Mr. McFarlane told him that the next weekend he was home they would go up to the bank together to sign a note. He said he would tell the banker Patrick's word was adequate collateral and a first instalment would be deposited in his account for him to manage as necessary. Patrick recognized Mr. McFarlane's words as only the courtesy of flattery, the wilful thinking of an old man determined to back a younger, unproven man, but he accepted the flattery because by now he believed what Mr. McFarlane said, he did believe he would be able to hold up his end of the deal.

Daphne was working hard in grade twelve, carrying two of the grade-thirteen sciences because she had decided on nursing and to make the following year, which was understood to be rough, a little easier. Now that Roger was gone she had more time on her hands, so in November she started to go down to the arena to help teach the smallest skaters their figures and their little routines, to prepare them for the winter carnival when they would all be mice or rabbits on ice.

She cooked three nights a week at the drive-in and waited for someone to ask her out. No one did. No one else knew that Roger was finished with her and she could hardly make an announcement. She didn't help Margaret as much as she might have but when her father brought this up at the supper table, as casually as he could, Margaret said, "That's all right, Bill. She's already working quite hard enough."

Paul settled successfully into grade eleven, and into Andy.

THE grandparents still stopped in, Bill's mother and father, Sylvia's mother and father. None of them talked outright about the pregnancy although they didn't indicate anything remotely close to shock that Margaret would want and feel entitled to her own child.

In early December Sylvia's mother pulled into the shovelled driveway with her trunk open. She came into the kitchen to put a coat over Margaret's shoulders and then led her out to the car to show her a wicker bassinet, their gift to the baby. She had made a long white eyelet skirt for it and there was a box of satin bows to be attached after the baby was born, when they'd know whether it should be pink or blue. Left on her own, Margaret would not have had bows of any colour, but she was not on her own. She would never again be on her own.

The two of them lifted the bassinet from the trunk and brought it into the living room. That week and the week that followed, as if everyone had been waiting for a sign, other baby apparatus arrived, a big proud buggy for the spring from Bill's parents, a playpen, a high chair, rattles and rag dolls and a small zoo of stuffed animals. People just kept arriving at the door with presents. Margaret was astonished that so many would take the trouble.

On December 19, she went into hard labour straight from sleep. Bill recognized the sounds she made but he wasn't adequately prepared because he had not expected her to hit the ground running. He'd just assumed the older the woman, the slower, the more difficult the labour. He got her into the car and drove out of town through the dark, through the light sleet. The big highway was almost empty. There were only a few hulking semis either on their way to the Bluewater Bridge at the border or just off it, heading for Toronto. He was acutely aware of the black ice that coated the sheltered sections of the road, black the worst of all ice because it was invisible in the dark, it was not even there until your headlights made it shine and by that time you were on it, committed.

As he drove, he talked slowly and deliberately, telling Margaret that from his experience everything seemed exactly normal and that she had to try hard to relax between the contractions, had to keep some of her strength in reserve because she'd be needing it.

At the hospital, he pulled onto the emergency ramp and ran in to get someone, returning with a nurse who pushed a wheelchair. He followed as she wheeled Margaret inside to a desk to do the paperwork and then up the elevator. When they came to the case room doors the nurse pointed him down the hall to an alcove of brown plastic chairs and then she pushed Margaret through the doors quickly, robbing him of the chance to say one last encouraging word to Margaret's back.

They put Margaret out right after the delivery. An hour later Bill was allowed into her room but she wasn't conscious, didn't know he had kissed her forehead. They told Bill his second daughter appeared to be a bit early but was fine and that Margaret's uterus was in shock, a common enough reaction with such a fast delivery. Outside Margaret's room, a nurse wheeled the baby down the corridor and let him look at her for maybe two minutes and then she left him standing there alone. On her way back to the nursery she turned around and said, "You might as well be on your way. Your wife will need her rest."

He drove the thirty miles home just before dawn. The wet snow was thicker on the windshield and the traffic had picked up so he was forced to take it slow.

When he walked into the kitchen Daphne and Paul were waiting at the table with a pot of coffee ready for him on the stove. "A girl," he told them. "And Margaret's all right. She did fine." He said Margaret was sleeping now, that they'd decided to put her to sleep because it had been extremely fast. "It was very, very fast," he said. In answer to Daphne's questions, he said he had no idea how much their sister weighed, all he could say was that she was tiny, a real little runt, and he couldn't say either if she looked like anyone or when they might come home. After only a few sips of coffee he stood to go upstairs to get ready for work. "I'll come home at noon," he called back from the stairs, "and we'll go back in together."

Daphne called Patrick and Murray in London and got them out of bed. She talked to each of them, said the same things twice. "It's a girl and Margaret came through with flying colours. She's absolutely fine. It's sister Sally."

Margaret's uterus gradually came out of shock and when she woke up, alone, she ran her hands over her sore, softened stomach and then up over her breasts, which in the last few months had become ridiculously large and which were now aching and hard as melons.

They fed Sally sugar water in the nursery and brought her to Margaret several times a day to try to take the breast, one nurse staying with them always, even after Margaret told her that it might be better if they were on their own. By the second day Sally had caught on and the nurse finally left them in peace. Bill had brought Daphne and Paul in that first day to look at their sister through the nursery window and the boys drove down from London, coming awkwardly into the quiet of Margaret's room in their coats and boots. After four days of it, Margaret told Bill she wanted out, as soon as possible, yesterday.

When Margaret brought Sally home everyone was ready to hold her, she was never down. Bill called her the Christmas present. After the boys got the tree up and decorated, Daphne wrapped Sally's squirming naked body in a red ribbon and carefully tucked her in among the other presents for a picture. Margaret leaned against the living-room arch and watched Daphne do this not because she was even slightly worried about Sally in Daphne's beautiful hands but because before Sally joined them she had not once seen Daphne reach to touch anyone, man or beast.

Murray's parents were on their first Caribbean cruise, so the big brick house beside the United Church was dark and empty. Murray unpacked but he didn't stay even long enough for the heat to come up before he got back in his car. He had every reason to go over to Bill and Margaret's. More reason now. He assumed he would be welcome to join them for Christmas dinner but he offered to buy the turkey anyway and Margaret said sure, that would be fine, although she would appreciate it if he let her go up to Sylvia's father at Clarke's and pick it out herself. Last year Bill had gone up on his own and after a Christmas drink or two out back with everyone he had come home with a twenty-eight pounder and, although she hadn't said so and would not have said so, she believed the meat in a younger, smaller bird was just a lot more tender. If quantity was going to be an issue, better two smaller birds than one monster. That was her policy.

Margaret knew that with all this help around she had it much easier than most new mothers. She rested, aware of her good fortune. When Sylvia's mother asked discreetly if her milk was coming down all right, Margaret put her hands to her astonishing breasts and laughed out loud, said there was enough for Sally and likely quite a few others. Sally thrived.

IN early April of the following year, at the end of a beautiful first long week of spring, Margaret stood with her hands buried in soapy water at the kitchen sink watching evening overtake the backyard. Sally was in her basket on the floor at her feet, sleeping as she always did with her small fists curled and her arms uplifted in the position of surrender, her soft scent almost visible. Margaret liked to stand at the kitchen window watching the shadows from the trees make their way across the grass. There were patterns she could anticipate now. She didn't know if it was having Sally or just more time alone since she'd given up her job, but she saw things here, lovely things, all the time.

The rolling April sky was threatening to do something before nightfall and three yard squirrels were quarrelling stupidly over the hickory nuts they'd hidden in the fall, chasing each other across the garage roof and halfway up the trees, around and around the lawn chairs, which were still overturned from the winter. Bill had been talking about having the back hickories cut down, using the space they took for a shed to store the odds and ends that accumulated, of their own volition, he said, in the garage. He said he could disguise the shed with a trellis or an arbour, maybe add a garden bench. He said with some of the shade gone Margaret could plant some vegetables out there if she liked.

Patrick had come home for Easter to work a week at the feed mill because one of the full-time guys had some heart trouble, and as Margaret rinsed the glasses under the hottest possible water she heard him coming quietly down the stairs. Sylvia had been correct about her oldest son. Lately he had been spending a lot of his free time in his room with his stereo, listening to records, and he always moved quietly now, you never quite knew where he was. He was too well mannered, too thoroughly trained for much outright anger, for outbursts, and she would not have thought to use the word *depressed* because that word was saved for people who were in serious difficulty, but she did come up with the word *cranky*. She assumed that a good part of his crankiness was directed at her, although she did not dream that Patrick would tell her what was on his mind. From what she had seen so far, they were not in the habit of levelling with each other in this house, certainly not the way she was used to anyway, with screaming matches and foul, ugly words that had to be mopped up the next day, with mindless accusations that still rang clear miles and years away. And she wasn't about to teach them how.

Patrick walked into the kitchen wearing a new ball glove, his Christmas gift from Murray. He was working it with his fist, pounding it, giving it shape, and when he pushed the screen door open to leave she stopped him with a question. "When you consider the fact that men generally have longer legs," she said, "do you believe the greater distance between the bases really does make baseball a harder game than softball?"

His face showed mild surprise but he thought for a minute and gave her a serious answer. "Well, I think that's the idea," he said.

"I wonder," she said. "Sometimes I wonder if I couldn't have played baseball, given my legs." She turned to look at him. "Your mother and I played softball together," she said. "She was a top-flight first baseman and I myself was a half-decent shortstop. You likely don't remember," she said, "but sometimes your grandparents brought you guys to the park to watch in your pyjamas." And then to give him some context, to give him a way to imagine it, she told him, "This was when the men were overseas."

He was halfway out the door, leaning against the screen, waiting. She picked up the pile of plates from the counter and lowered them carefully down through the water. "Although no one ever put it in so many words," she said, "your mother and I were pretty much the backbone of that team. We were good," she said, nodding once and firmly as someone would after any fair judgement. When she said, "One year we came this close to the provincial championship," she lifted her hand from the suds to show him the smallest possible space between her thumb and forefinger.

Patrick looked at her soapy hand and for just a split second, but surely, his face softened. There it is, Margaret thought, and, Now maybe that's done. Then he gave her his own clumsy nod and turned his face to the sound of Murray's car on the gravel in the driveway.

Margaret raised her head to smile at Murray through the window. She knew he would be watching to see if she did, they all kept an eye on her to see what she might do. And she knew he would be able to see the smile because she had been walking Sally up and down the streets in her high, proud buggy in the evenings and now she understood better than some that what looked from the inside like a square of shadowy darkness was really in the dusk a square of framing light. Murray would see the smile and not as a freakish reflection as she saw it, but clearly, unmistakably. Seeing it, he might put one more tick in his Margaret's All Right column. She realized that Murray, too, had needed time to get used to things. She had watched him grieve, maybe not as obviously as the others, but not less.

"Sally and I might come to some of your games this summer," she offered, and although Patrick had nothing to say to this, he did take the time before he jumped the steps to use his elbow against the closing of the screen door so Sally wouldn't be frightened awake by a bang.

The last part of what Margaret had told Patrick had been a lie, had been what her notoriously blunt, profane, and long-deceased father would have called a bare-assed lie. She had hardly known Sylvia. They had never played on the same ball team and neither of them had ever got close to any championship.

She did have a memory of the Chambers kids on the bleachers those summers when the men were away. They would already be bathed and ready for bed, Paul and Daphne wrapped in blankets in their grandparents' arms, Patrick running loose with the other boys. Banks of park lights had been installed to illuminate the diamond for night games, sometimes there were two a night, and she did remember warming up behind the bleachers, glancing over once in a while to see how the other game was going and seeing Sylvia on first base slamming a fist into her glove, yelling ball talk with the other women, jumping funny little jumps on the bag to keep herself revved up.

And what's a lie, she thought, against everything else? Against Sylvia's bone-thin dying? Or Bill's having to learn to love a second woman a second way? Against her own stale life above the Hydro office, the small rooms holding like swamp gas the uncut smell of her own body, her own habits, her own little difficulties. Against her living-room view of the cenotaph, where a name she had once said softly and often was etched two inches high in the granite column, her view of that column fouled by filthy windows she could neither open nor get anyone to wash. Against the secret, muffled, after-the-war footsteps of a man not her husband mounting the stairs late in those long evenings above the Hydro office, the pleasure of his company, his praise, and then the hush of broken, wondrous promises. What, pray tell, is a lie?

She was ninety per cent certain Patrick would never mention the championship to anyone, he wasn't that type, and even if it did get mentioned one day, she could rear up and say, Sure we did, of course we did. She could talk about those years long enough to make them all believe they misremembered. And they would defer to her, just as surely as they watched her. Truth be told, she thought they should be ready to offer a few lies on her behalf.

Alone now, she turned from the window and looked down at the basket at her feet. And then she snapped her sudsy wrist hard in the air above the basket, releasing a cluster of rainbow bubbles that fell in slow time down to her perfectly formed Sally who, sleeping, could neither reach to touch them nor watch with an innocent's bewilderment their bursting.

1963

THEY rented Dunworkin for the entire month of July. Other years Bill had taken his holidays when they were at the lake, but because it was only a fifteen-minute drive from town and because he couldn't see sitting around on his duff for four whole weeks, he decided not to that summer. The plan was that he would go back and forth to work every day and Margaret and Sally would stay put. The rest could come and go as it suited them.

Dunworkin was one of the oldest and biggest cottages on the beach. It was painted a muted light green, and it sat in the dunes, was tucked into the grassy dunes for protection from the winds off the water. As part of the deal, a fourteen-foot cedar-strip outboard with an easily managed twenty-five-horse motor sat beached on the sand in front of the cottage, and after an evening spin out on Lake Huron, when it was time to make the turn to come in for a drink, Bill sometimes made a game of testing the strength of his middle-aged eyesight against the block letters painted on a board above the screen-porch door. Like most of the other cottages up and down the beach, Dunworkin had always had its name, was probably named soon after it was built in the twenties, or maybe before, when it was still just someone's good idea.

It was a magnificent cottage. Across the front, a deep, screened-in, slightly sloping porch with hinged board shutters that in good weather were left hooked up to the ceiling held a picnic table for card games and Margaret's jigsaw puzzle, several Muskoka chairs painted either a deep cherry red or black, an old canvas hammock at one end and at the other a swinging couch suspended from the ceiling on rusty chains.

Inside the cottage proper there was a large main room with two old maroon sofas and several low-slung upholstered chairs, none of which matched each other or anything else, and beside these a few rickety little tables, each with an ashtray, one with a stack of *Reader's Digests* and *National Geographics* for rainy days. The ceiling was a grid of rough-weathered beams and painted plywood. The walls had been finished with good pine panelling and the floor was covered with broad pine planks. Visible footpaths had been worn into the planks' grain from the front door back into the kitchen and from the kitchen past the big oak dining table to the open staircase.

The fieldstones in the fireplace on the end wall had been darkened with years of smoke curling out before the fire got going properly and above them a heavy, broad mantel held a spread-out collection of necessities and treasures: pink shells from some ocean, four arrowheads, a red flyswatter, a flashlight, a transistor radio, a small, decorative Japanese fan, and a large box of Eddy matches. Beside the fireplace the owner had left a well-stacked supply of dry wood and a beat-up wicker laundry basket filled with newspaper and kindling.

There was cottage art. Hanging above the mantel a large, heavily framed oil depicted a man in a small boat who was making his way through dense, drifting fog toward a looming clipper ship, the man sitting hunched against the elements, the long oars just lifted from the water, the only real light the painter allowed caught in the drops falling from the oars back into the sea. On the wall at the kitchen door a small framed needlepoint sampler firmly admonished all who entered to leave their troubles behind them and taped to the wall beside the stove a 1963 calendar, courtesy Trevor Hanley's Chev Olds, had been turned to July, to Saskatchewan. It was the kind of calendar with each month of the year matched to a picturesque colour photograph of a touristy scene from one of the provinces and July was an aerial shot of two lonely but evidently prosperous prairie farms, each of them surrounded by a rectangular shelterbelt of trees and by worked fields, muted tan or green. A small river twisted across the photograph and the sky above the fields was a western summer blue, bouncing with light. And hanging perpetually crooked on the pine wall beside the front door there was another, quite-a-bit-smaller oil painting, this one of a tiny-waisted turn-of-the-century woman dressed in a voluptuous rose dress and a wide-brimmed pink hat. She carried a parasol against the sun and offered the room an old-fashioned, come-hither smile. Bill named her the Tart of Dunworkin and straightened her every time he went out the door.

Compared to town, the kitchen was primitive but adequate. There was hardly any counter space but there were two large banks of pine cupboards, both hot and cold running water at a deep porcelain sink, and a fridge new enough to have a decent freezer across the bottom. The prize was the stove. It was an old six-burner with both a baking and a warming oven. In May, when they'd come out looking for a cottage to rent, it was the stove that had clinched it for Margaret. This was a stove she would have traded her own for.

Upstairs there were five bedrooms and a screened-in sleeping porch that sloped down toward the beach in agreement with the porch below it. There were beds of every kind, old double beds very high off the floor that had once been good pieces of furniture, likely picked up at auction sales, newer single beds on wheels, a rollaway, three army cots.

When the owner had shown them the cottage, he had followed them from room to room and Margaret hadn't had the nerve to inspect the mattresses with him standing right there, but as soon as they'd brought everything in from the cars, the first thing she did was go upstairs to lift and turn each of them. When Daphne brought up the basket of sheets and blankets, Margaret told her she had been hoping for something fresher on the other side but these warhorses had been turned before, many times. Then she said they would just have to do, wouldn't they?

Everyone came for the first weekend, all eleven of them. Bill and Margaret and Sally, who was six, Patrick and Mary who were to be married in two weeks in the chapel at Springbank Park in London, Murray on his own again because his wife Charlotte was in Hamilton at her parents', Paul and Andy with their arms full of Neil and Krissy and all their attendant gear, Andy pregnant again with what she called their last baby for sure, and Daphne.

None of them mourned Murray's wife's absence. He had brought Charlotte up the previous summer, just before they were married in Toronto, and everyone had been first surprised and then disappointed. Charlotte dove right in, and while they understood that working for a television station might make someone necessarily forthright, she couldn't seem to have a conversation without trying to enlarge herself. She paid an extraordinary amount of attention to her appearance, changed her clothes three times a day, expected other people to change theirs. She sat at the supper table puzzled as if she didn't quite know how to manage just one fork, dropped names like Tolstoy and Chanel and Yves St. Laurent and Bloomingdale's, drank only what she called the best Scotch, assumed ignorance, presumed envy. Looking across the supper table at Sally, who at five was freckled and bony and sometimes clumsy and often left in general but happy disrepair, Charlotte told them that she herself had been an unusually beautiful child. She was without question pretty, with her mink-brown eyes and her snub nose and her white, gleaming teeth and she did have the body of a slightly underfed showgirl. But she wasn't the first good-looking person they'd had a chance to eat supper with. They'd never heard anyone say such a thing.

After Murray decided to marry her, he told them that her father had three car dealerships in Hamilton, that he'd got a pretty good start in the fifties. He said her mother was a great woman, very funny, and a big volunteer. None of this explained anything.

Patrick in particular detested Charlotte and was always ready to call her the Queen if Murray wasn't around to hear it. Bill and Paul simply ducked out when she came into a room, the sight of her reminding them always of some important thing they'd forgotten they had to do. Daphne tried the hardest, taking the trouble to slip Charlotte a few easy clues. After the third meal at Margaret's table in town she handed her a fresh tea towel, meaning to say, Margaret looks tired, she cooked, you ate, now maybe you could help dry the damn dishes. She deliberately and repeatedly said Margaret's name, meaning to say, It would be a really good thing if you stopped calling Margaret Marg. She carefully referred to her niece and nephew as the kids, meaning to say, If you'd pay attention, you would see that we are not the kind of people who want the kids called the children. Charlotte might have saved things if she'd noticed and adapted a bit but it looked as if she couldn't be bothered. And they hadn't wanted much. Margaret told Bill the absence of a patronizing tone of voice would have done it for her.

No one could imagine Charlotte at the lake anyway, so far away from a decent hairdresser, the sun so hot, the flies so thick on a muggy day, the mattresses turned but still clearly suspect under Margaret's crisp sheets.

Margaret was forty-nine and Bill had turned fifty-one that March. Bill's hair was mostly grey and he had what he liked to call bandy old-man legs. This would have astonished him even five years before, his legs going. They had always been strong, for most of his life his strength had been in his legs. He was deeply embarrassed to wear the Bermuda shorts Margaret and Daphne had decked him out in the summer before, two identical pairs of them, plaid, but he wore them then and he was wearing them again this year. What else could you wear at the lake? He drew the line at sandals. He was either in his normal shoes and socks or he was barefoot.

It had been a wretched winter, long at both ends, with weeks of high wind and sleet that had made driving treacherous. Then for one solid month after Christmas there was nothing but new snow, wet and dangerously heavy on the roofs. Lots of people had decided to climb up to shovel their roofs clean that year, Bill and the boys among them. Margaret had got herself through the winter imagining this month at the lake and after they had spoken for the cottage she told Bill that it might be the last summer with all of them together, and for this reason they should do what they could to make it one of the best summers they'd ever had.

She was very much looking forward to Patrick's wedding. She had her dress, which was not the expected mother-of-the-groom beige but teal blue with panels and a very low-cut back, and Bill had bought his first new suit since Sylvia's death, a good navy pinstripe that should do him another seven or eight years. Aside from the groom's dinner, which was to be held the night before the wedding and which they had decided to have at the cottage, they didn't have any particular responsibilities at their end. The wedding was to be quite small because Mary wasn't much for ceremony and her parents, nice people who had always lived in London and who had a cottage down the lake, said when Margaret called to offer her help that they had everything under control.

Patrick and Mary seemed to Margaret perfectly matched. Where Charlotte appeared to be just a run-of-the-mill phoney, Mary was forthright, pleasantly frank and blunt. She was never rude, not even slightly, but if you asked her for an opinion, you might as well be ready because you'd get one. You could tell listening to her that she would have been astonished to be told she was blunt. And meeting her mother you could see it was not likely that she would be mellowing with age. Like her mother, Mary had large, wide-set eyes, a very thick head of dark hair, and good, delicately squared shoulders. But she was gracious about her appearance, laughed about it, said she was more than happy to be told that she looked like Jackie Kennedy, who wouldn't be? Although Margaret neither said nor indicated anything of the sort, she was pleased to see that Mary had almost cured Patrick of his habit of taking refuge behind his sulky little moods. When he did try to escape, Mary went right in after him to haul him out.

And Murray had his own someone. Charlotte was quite unlike any woman Margaret had ever known but she'd had a good talk with herself about Charlotte and she had decided that at the end of the day, if that was what Murray wanted, they were all going to have to learn to like it. There had to be something there, something Murray could see. He wasn't a fool.

There was no question at all in Margaret's mind about Paul and Andy. Three years married, two kids, bang, bang, and another due soon. They'd had a big country wedding out at Andy's church on a hot Saturday in June. There were two hundred people in the pews, friends, relatives, neighbours, and then a wonderful country meal and a dance of course. The only thing that spoiled it was Andy's Dad's coughing, not because it interfered with the vows or the music but because it made a few of the people who loved him think they might be back at the church sooner than they wanted to be. And so they were. A year later, after he was gone, and gone quickly, diagnosed, cared for, and then dead inside of two months, his wife moved into town and Paul and Andy had a farm to run. But they were doing all right. They planted only cash crops and there was no livestock, so it wasn't a twenty-four-hour kind of farm.

That left Daphne. As far as Margaret knew there had been no one at all since Roger Cooper. But Daphne was only twenty-three. And she worked shifts at the hospital which had to make a social life difficult, the odd hours, the fatigue, the constant regime of having to grab some sleep when you got the chance.

Aside from wanting each of them to connect with someone who was good enough, who was comfortable and dependable and, given the choice, easygoing, Margaret didn't care much what the kids did with their lives otherwise. She assumed they would be able to make their living. They were all smart, exceptionally smart in her opinion. As far as she knew they were doing fine.

Most of them spent the best part of the first Sunday at the lake lying on the sand on blankets drinking illegal beer from picnic tumblers and then swimming out to the third sandbar and back to cool off. By noon, Bill had taught Sally how to float. He had been a strong swimmer since the war. Before he left for overseas he'd come out to the lake alone and taught himself, tested himself way out past the last sandbar. He'd started Sally off with the dead man's float, face in the water, arms extended, holding her up with one trustworthy hand under her small ribcage. When she had almost mastered that, he turned her over to face the clouds. With his hand light on her spine, over and over again holding and releasing her, he told her that floating was the first and most important part of swimming, that if you could relax your body, if you could get that feeling, the rest was only technique, just muscle control and breathing.

After lunch Bill and Margaret walked down the beach to the store to buy overpriced butter to go with the lobsters. Murray had brought the lobsters, eight of them, packed in ice in a cooler in the trunk of his Mustang, explaining that he'd got in on a shipment from Nova Scotia arranged by a friend of a friend of a friend at work. When they got back with the butter they went upstairs to bed for the most stifling part of the afternoon.

Murray did the cooking that night. He used an old roasting pan he found on the back porch, boiled the lobsters up two at a time.

Patrick rummaged around until he found the extra leaves for the oak table and then Margaret covered it with newspaper, put out two big loaves of homemade bread and a bowl of her potato salad, the sterilized-under-boiling-water pliers from the trunk of Bill's car, and several pretty little sauce dishes filled with melted butter and wedges of lemon.

When they were finished with the lobster eating, she was going to give them fresh peach pie.

PATRICK'S groom's dinner was held the Friday night before the wedding. They'd had two good weeks of sun. Everyone was brown, even Bill and Patrick and Paul and Daphne, all of whom had been going to work most days, Bill just into town and Patrick and Daphne into London and Paul out to the farm. Even Murray, who had been coming and going from Toronto, taking long weekends. Paul tanned the fastest of course. His face and arms were brown all summer, every summer.

They'd got quite a bit of enjoyment out of the boat. Mary and Sally sometimes took lunch and went up the lake to Port Franks, twice all the way to Grand Bend. And every evening after their walk, Bill and Margaret pulled sweaters over their bathing suits and went out on the water, cutting the motor to drift and watch the sun go down, returning in the dark, quiet and sometimes holding hands like middle-aged European film stars as they walked toward the cottage.

At the end of the first week, Mary and Daphne and Sally had gone into London to the bridal salon for their final fitting. Mary had long ago sketched her dress for Margaret. It was plain winter-white satin with a full, ankle-length skirt, a tight bodice, a high collar, and a row of tiny satin-covered buttons running down to the small of her back. She had found the dress in *Vogue*, had taken the magazine with her in March to see if it could be copied. Daphne and Mary's friend Joan, who was to be maid of honour, were going to wear full crinoline-skirted pale pink lace, had been more or less directed to lace by Mary's mother who, having wisely restrained herself from directing her daughter's choice, felt more than entitled to guide the attendants, explaining with blunt confidence that there should be a bit of show to this occasion. Sally's dress was an exact but smaller copy of Mary's, pink to match the others, but satin. And she was to have wrist gloves secured with tiny satin-covered buttons.

Without being asked, Sally had decided that while they were at the lake she would take on the job of keeping Neil and Krissy entertained. It was obvious to everyone that she had set herself this responsibility. She spent most of the time rolling around on the floor with them or flopped in the hammock or down at the edge of the water digging in the fine, clean sand with old serving spoons, filling brightly painted sand pails to build castles for them, pulling them back out of the water when they crawled or toddled too far away. She got them to help her collect unusual stones and pebbles along the water's edge, tried to make them understand exactly why the stones were nice. Her arms were so small it was hard for her to lift or carry the kids, so the others watched her at a confident distance and intervened once in a while when it was necessary. But they did so quietly and quickly, as if it were hardly necessary at all.

Because Sally was so helpful, Andy spent a lot of time on the porch couch reading first *Crime and Punishment* and then *The Feminine Mystique*. She drank a lot of juice, watched small boats pull skiers back and forth, watched the waves roll in. One afternoon she called Margaret out to see a bunch of kids, they would have been eighteen or nineteen, horsing around in the lake. Margaret said she'd heard their antics from the kitchen. Two of the guys were diving and then blasting up under their squealing, laughing girlfriends, between their legs, lifting them up out of the water and tossing them backwards. The third guy was dunking his girlfriend's head, holding her under with both hands, letting her up and holding her under again. She fought it, she flailed and thrashed, but the more she fought, the harder he pushed. And he was stronger of course, he was a very big guy. When the girl finally got free, got her footing, the boyfriend suddenly dropped his arms and bent down sharply into the water. "I bet she kneed him," Andy said, pleased with the possibility.

The girl ran out of the water and grabbed a towel on her way past the blankets where they'd all been sitting, sunbathing. Then she climbed into one of their cars. The others had stopped to watch her go, and just before her boyfriend got to the car, and he was surprisingly quick to come after her, she had rolled up all the windows and locked the doors. "I'd guess that girl has just made up her mind," Margaret said. "Let's hope she can stick to a decision."

Most afternoons Andy carried the transistor radio around with her from chair to couch to chair, sang a wholehearted "She Loves Me" and a plaintive "Return to Sender," kept time with her hands on her distended stomach. Sometimes she got up to dance around the porch with her arms raised above her head and her hips swaying seductively in her baggy plaid shorts and sometimes she sang and danced her way down to the water to cool off, wading in just to her thighs, bending down to splash her face and her arms and her shoulders. Margaret kept an eye on Andy and watching her she thought more than once that she was behaving as if she were all alone in the world, as if she couldn't be seen. She wondered if she had done that herself, carrying Sally.

The morning of the groom's dinner, Patrick and Paul and Murray took Paul's pick-up into town to go to the liquor store and to get what was needed from the house. Margaret wanted the big dining-room table and the chairs brought out because she thought everyone should be seated and there was no way to make the cottage table hold them all. She told Bill she didn't want a buffet, would not serve a buffet for Patrick's dinner. She gave the boys a list of the things she wanted from the house, most of which she'd wrapped and boxed up before they came out. The two linen cloths, her own china as well as Sylvia's, her own silver and Sylvia's, the lead crystal glasses, the blue punch bowl, the trays. The butter tarts from Mrs. Rinker. The liquor. Lots of film.

When Patrick and Paul and Murray got back from town, Bill said they should set up in the porch so they could watch the sun go down over the lake while they ate. So the picnic table and the Muskoka chairs were carried from the porch out onto the sand beside the barbecue and the dining-room table was unloaded from the truck and brought around to the front and in through the wide screen-porch door. Getting the cottage table out to the porch was not so straightforward, and after ten minutes of trying to manoeuvre it through the narrower main door, they had to give up and take it off its pedestal, which wasn't easy, given nuts and bolts and screws untouched for decades. After nearly an hour and three different wrenches from Paul's truck, the two tables were finally joined end to end, and they were not dissimilar. When they were covered with the linen cloths they looked as Margaret had hoped they would look, like one long banquet table.

Bill had gone into Clarke's before lunch to get the roast he'd ordered, a big rolled rib, and he'd started it over a hot fire in the middle of the afternoon, adding a few coals every half hour or so and then just leaving it covered to finish on its own as the coals turned to hot ash. Several people who had been walking the beach with their dogs had to run up to the barbecue to pull the dogs away, and one guy, holding his German shepherd firmly by the collar, asked about the chances for an invitation to dinner. This was just a friendly, aren't-we-all-so-damned-lucky kind of question, asked only to give Bill the opportunity to talk about the meal they were going to enjoy that night and about Patrick and Mary, about having a second son who was ready to tie the knot.

Margaret and Mary and Daphne had got up at dawn to try to beat the worst heat of the day. They'd made a huge pot of lobster bisque, the leftover lobster squirrelled away in the freezer after Murray's dinner. They'd baked the angel food cakes and three dozen pull-apart rolls. They'd scrubbed the sweet new potatoes and shelled the fresh peas, which were to be creamed, and cut up the asparagus and the carrots, which were to be caramelized. While they worked Andy sat on a stool in the corner of the kitchen with Krissy on her lap, talking to them and taking pictures of them washing and chopping the vegetables, stirring the bisque, beating the eggs, picking one last time through the nuts for bits of shell. By noon they were all sweating buckets and Margaret said they likely didn't even need the damned oven, the kitchen itself could cook the dinner.

Late in the afternoon, after a rest upstairs with Bill and then a quick swim with a bar of soap, Margaret made a Waldorf salad with the apples she'd got at the cold storage. Instead of walnuts, which no one liked, she used the hickory nuts she'd gathered the previous fall from the ground under the last remaining backyard hickory and smashed with her hammer on the cement stairs that led to the cellar.

The younger women went for their swim and then they changed into sundresses and put the vegetables on to cook and started to set the long table. The blue punch bowl was filled with Sylvia's lemonade and for dessert, on silver trays, there was the choice of Mrs. Rinker's butter tarts or angel food cake, with a milk-glass bowl of fresh strawberries and another of stiff whipped cream to follow the cake around the table. Murray came to the kitchen with a small jar of expensive British horseradish for the beef so Margaret kept her own back.

There were nineteen of them for dinner. Mary's parents came over from their cottage, bringing with them her elderly grandfather. Sylvia's mother drove out from town with Bill's father and Joan brought her boyfriend Dennis, who had a guitar and very long dull hair. Charlotte came from Toronto, arrived just as they were dishing everything up. She had stopped at one of the fruit stands on the highway and bought a bag of mushrooms and when she appeared in the kitchen offering them, Margaret almost opened the fridge to put them away for another time but then caught herself. "Oh," she said. "Just the thing we're missing." She quickly scrubbed a pan clean and melted a spoonful of butter over high heat to fry the mushrooms with a quickly chopped handful of sweet onion.

When the table was ready, after Bill had carved the roast and piled it on the platter and the potatoes were tossed with butter and a bit of mint and all the bowls were brought out from the kitchen, Bill put Patrick at one end of the table and Mary at the other, insisting. Everyone else sat wherever they wanted and when they were seated, instead of grace, Murray, who was to be Patrick's best man, stood to offer a toast. Happiness, he said. And health. A long life. Comfort. Joy. Great, mindless, sweaty sex. Progeny. Lifelong friends. Naked ambition. Success. Blue skies. A ton of money or just enough, whichever. A split-level in the suburbs or not, whichever. A red Porsche. Holidays in the sunny south. He wished all these things for them, claimed he spoke for everyone here present.

They ate and drank and talked and lied and laughed on that

sloping porch. Neil and Krissy were passed around and across the table like treasures, fed strawberries and peaks of whipped cream from their great-grandfather Chambers' finger. Mary's mother had brought a camera and Paul got up with Margaret's, took two rolls of film, making sure he got shots of everyone. Sally was so happy she cried. She had been walking around and around the table lightly touching everyone as she passed behind them, and when she squeezed in to stand between Margaret and Charlotte, she could no longer hold it back. The talking gradually stopped and everyone watched as she tried to explain her tears, and when they were finally understood, Charlotte was the one who reached out to comfort her.

An evening breeze flowed around their shoulders and the sun went down for them just as they'd hoped it would, slowly and beautifully, the red and orange and pink and mauve descent filling the sky above the shining water and then spreading, moving in across the water toward the shore. They talked as long as they could over the table but when the darkness brought cold air in off the lake they decided to move inside. Paul lit one of his fires and Dennis started to play his guitar, although not very well. The other men got out the rye and the gin and the crokinole board and the cards for euchre and all the women but Mary, who was after all the bride, and Andy, who was by this time extremely tired, and Sally, who was upstairs getting Neil and Krissy settled down to sleep on their army cots, started to clean up the dishes so the men could bring the tables in.

Charlotte stayed out on the porch long enough to pick up *The Feminine Mystique* from the hammock, asking no one in particular, "Who among you is reading this horrid thing?" Then she tossed it down and walked to the kitchen carrying the silver tray of leftover tarts in one hand and the empty salad bowl in the other.

Seeing Charlotte with her hands full, concluding that she had decided not to sit this one out, before she could put a stop to it, Margaret thought, Now this is an occasion. She took the tray and the salad bowl, handing them off to Mary's mother, and then she turned Charlotte by the shoulders and reached to tie a fresh apron around her waist. It was the first time Margaret had touched her. Feeling the jumpy bones beneath Charlotte's firm flesh, she thought, perhaps as punishment for the earlier thought, Oh, how awful for her.

"We'll let you wash," she said. "If you wash, the rest of us can get things put away and then we'll be able to join the men that much quicker at the fire."

To her everlasting credit, Charlotte put her watch and her rings up on the windowsill beside all the others, poured a pink stream of dish soap into the deep porcelain sink, and threw on both taps, full blast.

ALMOST every evening after a light, early supper, Bill and Margaret went for a long walk along the shore of the lake. They would start out barefoot on the warm sand but they carried their shoes because Margaret liked to go far beyond the main beach, she liked especially to go the two miles south to Stonebrook Creek, and they eventually ran into sharp, coarse stones and, at the Point, shale and a broad outcropping of rock.

When she was a girl Margaret had been invited once by a young friend, who was really just the daughter of an old friend of her mother's, to spend three summer days at a cottage which was not on the main beach with Dunworkin and all the other big cottages but down near Stonebrook Creek. Her mother hadn't had many actual friends because she was an occasional kleptomaniac, bringing home things that her father had to quickly find and immediately return or once in a while pay for if it was something that had been partly used up, like perfume, but this one woman had been a true friend and Margaret could remember her quiet kindness. She had been exactly the kind of woman people guessed to be slow-witted but she was not slow-witted in the least, she was simply shy and clumsy the way some women are, the way very young men are before they come into their own, and, regardless, she was very kind.

Angela's parents' cottage was not as old as some of the others at the creek but it was small and dark and ramshackle, with one main room that was mostly kitchen and two bedrooms added on and then another room, a porch, added on to that. On the first day of Margaret's visit, the girls had played hopscotch on the white-sand shore of Lake Huron and practised their swimming strokes both in the air and in the water and then they were given a picnic lunch to eat on a blanket in the dunes. After they'd helped Angela's mother cut up apples for pies, Spies, the apples were called, they used the afternoon to explore, to crouch down low to watch some of the other cottagers through their windows, and to follow the footpaths worn through the trees and scrub brush and poison oak that filled the empty space between the cottages and the road to town.

By this time, Margaret realized that the lemonade she'd shared with Angela at their picnic had worked its way through to her bladder and, because she refused to pull down her bathing suit and squat in the shelter of the trees, as Angela suggested, they had to find the nearest outhouse. At the end of a short dirt path lined on either side with painted stones, when Margaret reached to open the outhouse door, her hand was stopped by the sounds they heard inside, a wet slapping like the hurried beating of a cake at a kitchen table, and then a very sad moan, and then another. Angela put her finger to her lips, the signal for opportunity, for discovery, and they crouched again, as if this position were as natural to them as walking upright, the perfect stance for girls loose in the world. They took their turns at a small knot low in the weathered outhouse boards, each of them encouraging the other with a sharp elbow in the ribs: You look. No, you look. They watched him in silence, although they could see there was little chance they'd be heard. They could not see any part of his face so they couldn't begin to guess his age or his place in the world. It was Margaret's eye at the knothole when he delivered himself, his delivery a big, bursting achievement, and after Angela pushed her away she had no choice, she did have to run into the trees and squat naked to empty herself. And Angela was soon beside her, laughing quietly and holding her stomach and reaching up to pull clean summer leaves from a small maple. When they heard the outhouse door creak open behind them they were careful to look busy, to look away.

Then Angela turned to check and, positive that he was gone, or almost gone, because she did see someone ducking around the corner of a cottage, she said, "You know what that was?" She was erupting with laughter now, so pleased with what she already knew, with the things she did not have to learn. "It was the dastardly one-eyed worm. And that's what they do with it. All the time. Day and night, my aunt says."

Pulling up her bathing suit, Margaret laughed too, but privately, with only the shaking of her skinny shoulders. Although it had been her first sighting, her first true exposure, she didn't believe there was much point to being surprised. And it wasn't the achievement she would remember but the helpless pulsing and the colour, the deep blush of red in the pale, fisted hand, like something left outside the body by mistake.

Back at the cottage, they found Angela's mother sitting halfway down the hill watching the waves pour in and tickling herself, her weathered face, with a long blade of dune grass. She must have been lost in thought because when Angela crept up and hugged her from behind, she jumped and yelped as if she'd been attacked. Then she said she was very happy to see that they were having some fun together and before they went inside she made them stand still against the cottage door for a picture. After she'd got their fun recorded for posterity, she handed the borrowed box camera to Angela and stepped up to the door herself. She ran her fingers quickly through her short, thin hair and smoothed the skirt of her summer dress and then she squared her shoulders to smile into the afternoon sun.

On the second morning the father walked with the girls to one of the farms that bordered the lakeshore to take them horseback riding. This was the surprise he'd promised the night before at the supper table. The men saddled the horses and then Margaret and Angela climbed up on the rail fence, as they were told, to mount. The farmer rode a blue-black stallion, the father was given a big russet mare, and the girls rode strong fat ponies. Margaret's pony was friendly and calm and obedient, its tan-and-white face almost pretty, its knobby flanks patched like the map of a world that was nothing but desert and snow.

They'd gone for miles along the beach, the horses long since trained to walk out into the shallow lake to skirt the stones on the shore, knowing in their horse heads that soon there would be sand again. The men stayed behind the girls, ignoring them, trusting their good sense and trusting the ponies, but their voices carried through the summer air and the girls heard their talk, which was briefly about their time together at Vimy, where they had both been stablers for the cavalry. Because she knew even as a ten-year-old girl that Vimy Ridge had been a battle and that the war these men had fought was called the Great War and because it was the first time in her life she had heard it used like any other word, Margaret remembered that the farmer said the word *gallantry*, and she remembered too, the way you remember a fright, the dark burst of laughter that fell on that word. The men didn't stay with the war for long. Soon they were talking about a stallion stolen in the dead of night from a neighbouring farm and then about a flaxen-haired woman they didn't name but seemed to have known well, both of them, their laughter falling much more gently on the shared memory of this woman.

The horses had to be turned inland to follow the rutted road only at Kettle Point, the Indian reserve, where the wet black shale that covered the shore was dangerously slick underfoot and the rocks extended deep into the lake. There were still kettles to be counted at the Point then, large grey stones worn perfectly spherical by the action of a million waves, resting in the water like oversized pearls. This was before the time when people started to drive onto the reserve to pull the kettles out and haul them home to use as decoration on their front porches.

Margaret's mother had accepted the invitation on her behalf without asking her if she even wanted to spend three days at a cottage but in the end it didn't matter. They had been the best three days of her childhood.

Any summer evening, standing as an adult woman at the mouth of Stonebrook Creek, Margaret found it hard to believe that the creek entered the lake at all, the offshore waves pushed in so surely, with such a steady force. But the creek did join the lake. On calm days, most days, it crept in slowly, nearly invisibly, the only evidence a murky cloud of silt drifting out into the cleaner blue of the lake. And after a storm, after a pounding, roaring, creek-rising rain, the force of the current was more than strong enough to overtake the shoreline waves. Running down the bank, surging down, the creek emptied its mud-churned, overflowing self full force into the larger body.

It was widest there on the sand, meeting the lake, maybe sixty feet across. Back from the shore where the land began its quick sloping climb up and inland, the creek narrowed and the banks soon became steep enough to require buttressing with fieldstones and large broken slabs of scrap concrete, refuse from highway upgrades.

At the edge of the water, swamp grass grew wherever it could find purchase among the stones, and higher up the bank, where the real soil began, sumach took hold, and then trees, beech and maple and oak, leaning in over the creek to make a leafy tunnel above the current. Even in a canoe, you would have needed to duck your head here.

There were still cottages on both sides of the creek, built up on the high ground that overlooked Lake Huron, situated close together and at odd angles to one another, perhaps to catch the extraordinary sunsets through the desired windows. Margaret thought she recognized the cottage she'd visited as a girl but she couldn't be sure because most of them were old and rambling now.

Not long after the cottagers were established, someone, some group of them, had decided it would be a very good thing to be able to get back and forth between the cottages quickly so they'd built a narrow, swinging footbridge high above the water across the creek. It is likely that the idea behind the bridge was to promote evening visits among summer friends or to allow more interesting morning walks, to free the kids a bit. They'd suspended the footbridge from heavy steel cables that were threaded on each bank through tall, soon-rusted posts and then securely anchored deep in solid ground. When it was first built the bridge gave access not just to the south-side cottages but to a grassy picnic spot, with swings and teeter-totters and a fire pit and an open pavilion, for shelter from the rain. The pavilion did not withstand many years of winter storms off the lake, and it was not replaced, but Margaret had seen in Angela's cottage a framed black and white photograph of summer people in their bathing suits getting ready under the pavilion's low-pitched roof to share a meal, the very best of everything imagined laid out with pride on the picnic tables.

Pulling away from the shore of Lake Huron, Stonebrook Creek flowed past the tennis courts and the rough stone pillars that marked the cottage road and then it passed under the first car bridge, under the highway. On the other side of the highway it veered away respectfully from the old cemetery and soon began to cut a shallow valley through the apple orchards and the fields of corn and wheat and oats and barley and white beans, through bush and pasture.

If you were out for a Sunday drive, you could locate Stonebrook Creek from any of the roads by the haphazard trees that followed its twists and turns. The crows and starlings that fed on the crops nested in the trees, as did swarms of hornets, and sometimes you would see herons. In the fall, farmers who watched for bothersome beaver dams became small-time hunters, walked back to the creek with their guns for ducks or pheasant.

Cattle had long since established paths down to the creek bank, had walked the scrub brush flat so they could get to the edge, to drink, and on the hottest days, where the water was shallow, and it often was shallow on its way to town, the cattle waded right into the water, stepping clumsily around the visible stones. Sometimes they'd stumble and go down heavily and then thrash in the mud to get themselves upright and sometimes, once down, they stayed down to let the murky water cool their dung-matted, fly-bitten flanks.

And there had always been garbage. If you were anything like the child Margaret had been, and if, for something different to do, you had biked out from town to stand on one of the municipal bridges to engage in some private dreaming, or to drop small stones into the middle of the current to test the depth of the water, listening for that deep, satisfying plop, you could see, upstream and down, that any number of people used the creek for garbage. Not much of it, only the occasional rim of a tire or a saw blade, a toolbox, a few cement blocks, a few heaps of broken bricks. And you could see islands of drifting twigs. And deadfall, whole trees or rotted, broken limbs blown down by wind storms, resting on the largest of the stones.

And, until the days of DDT, you could enjoy the brilliant presence of butterflies, the rusty orange of Monarchs, the beautiful, shy Northern Blue, lush grey Cabbages, the long-forgotten red of Admirals.

There were five municipal bridges between the lakeshore and

town, on concession roads or side roads depending on the turn of Stonebrook Creek. Most of the bridges were cement and all of them had been constructed high above the water to accommodate spring flood. But the creek seldom overflowed its banks, not significantly and not for long, because the lake was there, just a few miles away, ready to take whatever came.

Although Margaret and Angela had raced across the suspension bridge those hot summer days at the mouth of the creek, protected only by the chicken-wire guard and a light running grip on the steel cable, and both of them loving the rhythm their running made, the snaky sway, she had to coax Bill onto the planks and he went across just once.

"It has never so much as threatened to give out," she said, pushing him gently from behind, her hands on his narrow hips. "Not once."

"And they say that's exactly when you should play a slot machine," he told her. "Just when it seems it will never give out." He was laughing now and gripping the steel cable with both hands, exaggerating his terror for Margaret's enjoyment.

Standing halfway across, they looked straight down to study the water, to watch for movement in the churning mud. Margaret was quickly able to find the ripple of a lost, spinning school of minnows, anxious to get back to the lake where they belonged, and with the minnows found, she turned from the lake and squatted low to look back up the creek. Bill bent down to join her. Through the dark tunnel of overhanging branches they could hear frogs croaking and the squeal of gulls and they could see deadfall and upturned, tangled root balls and drifting twigs. They could gauge how quickly the creek got deep as it began to move inland.

Leaning there, looking with Margaret at all these things that obviously had some meaning for her, Bill put his hand on her sturdy shoulder. "This has been a good summer for all of us," he said. And then he moved his hand to the crown of her head, turning her face toward a perfectly common but good-sized snake that lay curled on the slope of the bank, resting in the damp shade after a hard day of snake work, its long, curved body the boundary, the asylum, for a dozen slithering offspring.

1963

IN their last week at Dunworkin, late on a Tuesday afternoon, lying on the couch in the porch and breathing deliberately, using all of her discipline to relax, Andy tried to describe her cramps to Paul and Margaret. She said they weren't really much different from what she'd been having for the past week, from what her doctor assured her were just fairly common bouts of false labour, except that she was positive they were lasting longer now.

Margaret sat close to Andy in one of the Muskoka chairs, reading Andy's finished copy of *The Feminine Mystique* which, until now, she had been enjoying thoroughly because, as she'd told Bill, in her opinion there certainly was something to it. Paul stood at the screen door.

"You're the only one who knows how it feels," he said. "You have to say one way or the other." He moved over to the couch, leaned down to put his hand on Andy's stomach. "I'm ready to take you in right now."

"If it comes now, the baby will be nearly a month early," Andy said. "I think I should try to hang on. I'm supposed to be able to hang on." She gave into it then, her soft eyes filling with streaming tears, as if the concern expressed by this loving man was itself the cause of her discomfort.

Margaret closed the book. "I think you've got your answer," she said. "She shouldn't have to go through any more of this. And they're promising a change in the weather so it might be a good idea to get her in now anyway." She was up out of the chair. "I'll pack her a quick bag."

Paul helped Andy into the truck and took her straight to Sarnia without stopping in town at the doctor's office. He said he was afraid they'd be told the same old thing and he was real tired of hearing it.

At the hospital, after the paperwork, they put Andy in a wheelchair and took her up into the stage room right away. Paul stood back as a nurse in a white turban and a scrub dress helped her into a johnny shirt and up onto a stretcher, asking as she eased her back on the pillow, "How are we doing?"

"Not all that well," Andy told her.

[117]

"Which baby is this?" the nurse asked.

"Our third and last," Andy said.

"Are you in labour?" the nurse asked.

"I'm not sure," Andy said. "This time it seems to be going differently. I'm not due until next month but I've been having cramps for weeks. And they've been a lot worse today. They've been bad today."

The nurse ran a hand over Andy's stomach to determine the position of the baby's back and then she used her stethoscope to find the heartbeat, counting the rate with a watch pinned to her scrub dress. She put her hand on Andy's stomach again, gently, to time the frequency of the contractions.

Then she asked Paul to leave them, to wait out in the hall. He did as he was told but he didn't go far, he didn't go out of earshot. The nurse pulled the privacy curtain around the bed and put on her mask. "We'll just see how many centimetres," she said, "if any." She pulled down the sheets, arranged Andy's small, shaking legs into the frog position, snapped on a glove, and lubricated her index finger. Andy took a deep, quivery breath as the nurse inserted the finger into her rectum.

"I must be nearly ready," she said.

The nurse peeled off the glove and tossed it into the wastebasket on the floor beside the bed. "Your cervix is two fingers dilated," she said. "And the baby seems to be on a bit of an angle, seems to be coming not quite square. I'm going to call the doctor at home. He should be able to tell you more." She pulled Andy's johnny shirt down, smoothed and tidied it, and then brought the covers up and folded them across her chest. Just before she left the room she turned and said, "You shouldn't drink anything, just in case."

Paul passed the nurse on his way back in and she didn't stop him. He lifted the curtain, ducked under it. Andy was quiet, not quite so apprehensive now that things seemed to be under way. She pushed the covers off, asked him, "Is it hot in here?"

Paul said no, he didn't think so but then he wasn't doing any work.

The nurse returned in a few minutes to check the baby's heart rate again and soon after she left them the doctor on call came into the room. He let Paul stay, which worried Andy, although she didn't say this out loud. The doctor moved his hands over her belly, his fierce blue-black eyes concentrated on her taut, mounded flesh as if the small dips and lumps could be read, could be comprehended. He told them that he didn't think it was a case of anoxia in utero, he didn't believe the baby was in any difficulty. He said Andy could deliver normally, and because the baby was relatively small and not far off true in its position, he should be able to give it a slight turn. He said he was sure a turn was all that was needed and that they would take her into the delivery room in an hour or so, depending.

They waited together through the contractions, which Andy said were the real McCoy now. She said she'd know them in any dark alley. When it was time to go she leaned up to kiss Paul goodbye. "If the baby is born tonight," she said, "it will be Tuesday's child, like Krissy, full of grace."

Meagan started to come just after midnight, which made her Wednesday's child, full of woe, although in the throes of labour Andy would not be able to remember this next line of the verse. Paul sat down the hall in an orange plastic chair with his head in his hands, waiting as he had waited before, ready to wait out the night, but Meagan didn't take long getting herself born.

While the doctor stitched Andy up, good and snug this time, he said, winking, as if consideration for a husband's lifelong pleasure was one of the hospital's policies and certainly one of his own, certainly worth an extra tug or two on the sutures, a nurse took Meagan to the other side of the room to bathe her. After she'd got her cleaned up and wrapped snugly in a receiving blanket she laid her on Andy's already aching breasts, allowing them a couple of minutes before she took Meagan down to the nursery. Andy couldn't see much of her new daughter, could see only her fuzzy scalp and her odd little face and her tight-fisted hands, but by all appearances she was a healthy baby.

Paul spent a few minutes with Andy in the recovery room, just long enough to assure himself that she was all right, and then he went to the nursery to get a look at Meagan through the glass. After they pulled the nursery curtain shut, he drove out to the lake to wake Bill and Margaret and Daphne and Sally, to tell them. They all got up and sat around the big table in their pyjamas and nighties to listen to him tell it.

Just before dawn Andy was deemed recovered and taken up to another floor where she was put into a room with three other patients, two of whom still had the slightly mounded bellies of recently delivered women, the third not a woman at all but a girl of no more than sixteen. She rested, dreamed, talked a bit to the woman beside her who had just had her first baby at an astonishing and likely dangerous forty-six. The nurses appeared regularly with thermometers and blood-pressure cuffs and Andy drank all the juice she could get her hands on, which meant she was soon up to the bathroom on her own.

Paul ate Margaret's celebratory breakfast of bacon and French toast and after he'd held Neil and Krissy on his lap to tell them about their sister, he drove back into the city. He sat out in the waiting room while Andy slept, went down to the gift shop to buy her a small bouquet of cut flowers, helped her with her sponge bath. The first time they brought Meagan down he waited in his mask and gown until the nurse was gone and then he laid Meagan out on Andy's stomach, unwrapped her blanket, and took off her tiny shirt and diaper to expose and examine her, to run his hands over every inch of her long bones, her bright pink skin.

That night he went back out to the lake to tell them everything all over again and to say that Andy was in a normal room now and that he'd had a good look at Meagan and she was just as she should be. He slept alone upstairs on the sleeping porch, his dreams filled with the fishy smell of a boat after a storm. In the morning, Margaret and Sally took Neil and Krissy for a long walk down the beach, leaving the cottage quiet so Paul could sleep through until his body had had enough.

While Paul slept, Daphne drove in to the hospital. She came into the room just as a nurse was finishing up her examination of Andy's sutures so she stood quietly outside the curtain, waiting until it was yanked open. The nurse hadn't heard her and as she was leaving she backed into her and yelped in startled surprise. She told Daphne she should wait in the hall next time. She wasn't much older than Daphne herself, maybe twenty-five, but she did not lack confidence, she was in fact just the kind of nurse people liked. Finished with Andy, she walked quickly over to the girl by the window, who was lying curled on her side with her back to the room, pulled the privacy curtain around the bed, and asked the girl to please roll over.

When Andy saw Daphne standing there with her skin so tanned and her body so fresh and trim and tight and angular and jumped-up with energy, she said, and immediately wished with all her heart she hadn't said, "Oh, Daphne, you look like a slightly different species of woman. Maybe vaguely related to the species in this room, but not really the same, not the same at all."

"And hello to you too," Daphne said, smiling, meaning to let it go.

"It's just because you look so strong," Andy said. Which was the truth.

"I've been down to the nursery," Daphne said. "They brought her to the window for me. She's lovely. She's small but it looks like she's got Paul's bones so she won't stay small for long." She sat down in the chair beside the bed. "How are you doing?" she asked. "Sore bum? Sitz baths helping the sore bum?"

Andy was thinking, I do love this woman. "Yes," she nodded. "Although sore hardly says it."

The nurse who had been examining the girl by the window yanked the curtain open again. "Today makes it three days," she said firmly and loudly. "If you won't do it yourself, we'll have to haul you out of that bed. And we'll do it, believe you me. You've got to get up and get walking and not just to the bathroom. It isn't a matter of choice."

The girl didn't answer. The nurse left the room, shaking her head, fed up.

"Have they had you up and down the hall yet?" Daphne asked. "It's chock-full of slow-walking women in really awful house-coats." She looked at the two empty beds. "Your roommates must be out there already."

"No, I haven't," Andy said. "But it's my understanding that today is the day." She started to sit up, pulled herself up straighter in the bed. "The doctor is going to give Meagan a once-over this afternoon and he's supposed to come to see me first thing tomorrow morning. Then maybe we can come home."

Daphne was just about to tell Andy how pleased Bill and Margaret and Sally were when the nurse who had just left returned with another, much larger woman in a different uniform. They walked quickly over to the girl by the window, pulled her up by her arms, turned her, lifted her off the bed, stood her upright, and walked her out the door, not a word said.

"Oh," Andy said, covering her mouth with her hand so she wouldn't be heard. "For the love of God."

"I don't see why they think they have to keep her on this floor," Daphne said. "If they gave it two minutes' thought, they might figure it out." She shook it off, stood up from the chair. "Are you ready to give the hall a try?"

Andy brushed through her wet hair with her fingers to tidy it. "I guess," she said. "I've showered and, after much repeated encouragement, pooped. So what else is left?" She turned and dropped her legs over the side of the bed, wincing. She stopped moving for a minute, looked down at her bare feet. "It's a mighty long drop to that stool," she said.

Daphne eased her down. "We'll find someone out there to challenge," she said.

Andy tried to hold her johnny shirt closed while Daphne helped her into her housecoat. "Your day will come," she said. "And I'll be there just as soon as I can to inquire about your bum."

They went out into the hall to join the flow and halfway down to the nurses' station they passed the girl and the woman in the different uniform who held her up. The girl's eyes were shut and she was walking close to the wall, hugging it. The other women who were up working off their various discomforts looked only briefly and then took care to avoid bumping her.

Daphne and Andy continued slowly past the nurses' station and down to the nursery. All the babies were being transferred to a kind of trolley, a long row of little rolling beds, and Meagan had already been moved, she was lying snug in her receiving blanket waiting to be delivered to her mother. "She has your face," Daphne said. "Your forehead. And your chin."

Meagan stirred a bit, stared and blinked at the ceiling lights high above her. "I saw one of the older nurses pinch her arm and watch to see her reaction," Andy said. "Almost like a test. But she didn't react. Neil and Krissy could raise a complete stink by the time they were a day old but she doesn't fuss at all."

"Paul told us," Daphne said. "I say good for her. There's already too much fussing in this sorry world."

They walked down the hall with all the other women who were making their way back to their rooms, and after Daphne got Andy up onto the bed, she asked if she wanted her new nightie from the suitcase. The nightie had been Daphne's gift. It was a beautifully soft cotton print with two discreet nursing slits, two secret little passages. While Andy unbuttoned her housecoat, Daphne found it and handed it over.

A nurse came into the room pushing the two other babies, and after she had them safely in their mothers' arms, she brought Meagan and parked her close to Andy's bed. Without looking at Daphne she told her she would have to leave now. This was no surprise to Daphne. She thought about asking for a mask and a gown but then thought no, she'd leave them their privacy. "I'll be back in a little while," she said. Just before she stepped back to pull the curtain around them, while the nurse was busy admiring Andy's nightie, she reached out to touch her fingers to the top of Meagan's fuzzy head. "This, my little love," she whispered, "is called breakfast."

She had thought she would just go out to sit in the waiting room and leaving she glanced for some reason over to the window. The girl was there again, covered and turned away and curled up.

She didn't ask herself what she was doing, she just walked over, pulled the chair up close to the bed, and sat down. The girl looked up at her as if she had two heads, two very ugly, unwelcome heads.

"I'm on my way down to the gift shop," she said. "Can I bring you a chocolate bar or something? A magazine? Maybe *Seventeen*?" The girl was silent, her face collapsed into a sturdy frown.

Daphne took a deep breath. "I just thought I'd like to tell you," she said quietly, "that I was adopted. My mother was young, like you. But I've had a really good life. I've always wished I could tell my mother that. And I've always wished that she had a good life too. When I think about her, that's how I imagine her, having a good life of her own."

The girl's eyes were wide open now. She was looking at the high green branches of the elm just outside the window. She spoke so quietly Daphne almost missed it. "That's nice of you to tell me," she said.

Daphne stood and tucked the girl's blankets up around her shoulders, a useless gesture because the girl had already pulled them up as far as they would go. But it was all she could think to do. "Sore bottom?" she asked.

"Yes," the girl said, crying a bit now. "They keep bringing me the heat lamp and I hate it. I really hate it."

"I'm a nurse," Daphne said. "Maybe I can try to put a stop to the heat lamp for you." The girl hadn't moved but Daphne hadn't expected her to. She ran her hand lightly over the curled-up, covered body and left.

She found the head nurse doing paperwork at the nurses' station. By the evidence of her cap she had trained in London too, which would mean that she was a very good nurse indeed. Daphne was careful to introduce herself as the woman's junior, to smile a quick deferential smile. On the way down the hall she had thought about asking if the girl could be moved to another floor, but with the head nurse standing there in front of her, attentive and patient but obviously busy, she decided to settle for the lesser but more probable win. Initially the discussion veered close to the abrupt, although it soon settled down to a successful resolution, Daphne's point being that since the nurses themselves decided on heat lamp treatment, what would be the harm in no more of it for a kid who might be distraught but was likely sharp enough to know whether something was helping or hurting her.

The older, larger woman, the one in the different uniform who had been walking the girl up and down the hall, had come up to the desk and was standing there listening. She was, Daphne decided, the homeliest woman she had ever seen. "You think she should be pampered?" she asked Daphne.

The head nurse ignored this. "I'll have a look at her myself," she said. "As soon as I'm finished here. If she'll try to get up and get a move on, we can maybe put an end to the heat lamp."

Daphne thanked her and went to sit in the waiting room for ten minutes and then she walked back down the hall to Andy's room. The girl's curtain was still open and she had shifted to lie on her back, with her hands out on top of her blanket. That looks like courage, Daphne thought, smiling a bit in case the girl looked her way, which she didn't. She ducked in through Andy's curtain.

Meagan was asleep in her mother's arms, apparently sated, and Andy was still sitting up straight on the bed. She had been waiting for Daphne to come back through the curtain. She didn't speak the question but mouthed it, slowly and clearly. "You're adopted now?"

Daphne just shrugged her shoulders and reached out for Meagan. "Give her here," she said. "I'm her perfectly healthy aunt. They can stuff their rules and regulations."

Lifting Meagan into her forbidden arms she thought, She feels so heavy, why would a baby born early feel so surprisingly heavy?

THE promised storm arrived early in the evening two days after Meagan was born, at the end of their last full day at Dunworkin.

Paul and Murray and Margaret and Sally had gone in to the hospital right after lunch, and while they were gone, Patrick and Mary came in the door from Boston, surprised that there were no cars parked out behind the cottage, surprised to find Daphne alone with the kids. They had timed their return to have one last night at the lake and to help clean the cottage properly in the morning, before the owners moved in for August. They hadn't expected to come home to a new niece.

They'd had a quick rest upstairs and were sitting at the table drinking beer and asking Daphne about Andy and Meagan when they heard the car doors slamming shut. Sally was with Murray in his Mustang and Paul was alone in his truck. Margaret had stopped off in town to come back out with Bill and on the way they'd gone

to the drive-in beside the Casino to get fish and chips and milk-
shakes for everyone.

Margaret set the table and while they ate, Patrick and Mary
answered questions about their trip, about the hotels they'd stayed
in, the seafood they'd eaten, the people they'd met, the traffic. When
the table was cleared Bill said they should start to think about packing up because there was a storm in the air and they were likely
going to lose the lights before the night was out. But they didn't
start to think about packing. They took their coffee out to the porch
to wait for the storm to come up over the water.

At about seven, the temperature dropped quickly, heavy clouds
gathered and settled low over the lake, and the breeze began to
stiffen into wind, to skim the sand on the beach and in the grassy
dunes. You could see the sand moving in the dunes, shifting itself
into new patterns. And then the nature of the waves changed. They
came to shore not in frothy little overlapping spills but each wave
on its own, in a loud, dark rush, smacking the sand.

Margaret and Mary went upstairs to close the windows and drop
the shutters in the sleeping porch and bring the bedding and
mattresses inside and Bill ran down with Patrick to pull the boat
farther up on shore. Paul and Murray got the tarp and the ropes
from the shed and after the tarp was wrestled onto the boat, Bill
walked around it and pulled hard on the ropes, double-checking
their knots. He yelled to them above the wind that they had to be
especially sure because this wasn't their boat. They'd never had
their own boat, although one spring the boys had built a rough raft
and launched it in the creek behind the house. They'd taken it only
a few miles, past the golf course and Livingston's gully but not very
far after that, not all the way over to the lake.

Aside from a bit of quick eye contact, the younger men made no
response to Bill's comment. Just in the last few years, but more and
more predictably, Bill could not restrain himself, could not resist the
chance to teach them a little moral lesson, as if grown and educated
and capable, and as sensible as they were ever likely to be, they
might suddenly begin to slide down the slippery slope to childish or
criminal behaviour, to moral decline.

Daphne had joined them on the beach. She was jumping up and down on the hard wet sand, still in her bathing suit from her afternoon with the kids, wrapped in the quilt from the porch couch. She wanted someone to go walking in the storm with her. "Not very far," she told them. "Just down to the Casino and back. Before it really gets going."

Bill shook his head. "Not a good idea," he said. He was looking back at the cottage, at Margaret and Mary. The sleeping porch was closed up tight and they had dropped all but one of the downstairs shutters and now they stood together at the one open screen watching, waiting for the men to come in out of the storm. Soon Sally was there with Krissy squirming in her arms and Neil beside her, standing up wide-eyed on a chair to see the action.

Bill started back up with the wind behind him, pushing him. Patrick and Paul followed and Murray went to Daphne, put his arm out to direct her toward the cottage. But she ducked and pulled away. When she turned around and opened the quilt to him, he moved in beside her. "Not all the way to the Casino," he yelled above the wind, taking some of the quilt over his shoulders.

Margaret was not surprised to see them go. She stood at the screen and watched the wind as it tried to snap the quilt away from them and then she dropped the last shutter.

Inside the cottage, although it was not yet cold, Paul was ripping and bunching newspaper for a fire. Mary suggested that they rearrange the heavy old maroon couches and the chairs into a circle around the fireplace and Patrick helped her, said they should have thought of it sooner, should have done it the first day. When they were finished, Bill sat in the corner of the smaller couch and Sally flopped down beside him, taking Krissy up onto her small lap. Neil ran across the room and started to climb the stairs, saying he wanted to have some more nap. Margaret scooped him up and cuddled him, knowing that he was both frightened of the sounds the storm made and lonely for his mother, although he wasn't the kind of child who would want this said.

Margaret always made a point of giving generous attention to the grandchildren. She wanted these two and all the ones that followed to get to know each other, to like each other, and later have a few memories of liking each other. She had told Bill she'd had nothing like that when she was young.

They settled in to watch Paul's fire. The wood had been seasoned and he'd stacked it carefully, correctly. Within minutes the bottom log appeared to be entirely on fire, the flames jumping out, stretching to lick the logs above it.

The wind was fully up now. The rain was starting to come down hard on the roof over their heads and the sound of the waves was a pounding roar. Sitting watching the fire, Margaret allowed herself to wonder if Daphne and Murray had found shelter, and where. If the others shared one thought, it was that the two of them would likely come bursting through the kitchen door any minute, would likely come back laughing and drenched from their idiotic adventure.

Looking around the room, from face to face, Margaret noticed that Sally was wanting something. "What is it, babe?" she said.

Sally hugged Krissy close. "Shouldn't we go find Daphne and Murray?" she asked.

"They'll be all right," Margaret said. "Don't you worry about them. They're somewhere."

Satisfied with this answer, Sally turned to the fire to study the quick bursts of firelight that brightened the faces of everyone close to it and then she asked, "Shouldn't we watch the storm?"

Margaret looked over at Bill. "All right," he said, getting up. "But if we lift the shutters, the porch will turn into a sandbox and that means in the morning it will be Sally and Dad who wake up really early to sweep it out." He opened the door to the porch and closed it quickly behind him and they watched him through the big front windows. As he released the hooks the force of the wind pushed the shutters against his chest, pushed them halfway up to the ceiling. After he'd got three of them fastened he turned back to look at Sally, who was standing at the window holding Krissy, nodding her head. He went over to the picnic table and gathered what was left of Margaret's jigsaw puzzle into the box, bent to collect a few pieces from the floor. Watching him from her chair by the fire with Neil snuggled close beside her, reaching back to knock on the window but then not knocking, Margaret said, "That doesn't matter, Bill. My puzzle doesn't matter."

The sky was as black as night. Every few minutes long branching forks of lightning pierced down through the clouds to the rolling surface of the slate grey water. Sheet lightning, broad and quick and unanticipated, lit the whole grey lake. The waves had thickened, they were moving in now like liquid muscle, breaking hard and sudsy white on the dark sand, throwing up driftwood and bits of garbage and stunned minnows and coarse sawdust from the mills on the far side of the lake, the Michigan side.

The first of the thunder cracked just as Bill was coming back in from the porch with the puzzle box in his hand. The lights, two in the kitchen, one above the big oak table, and three in a floor lamp beside Patrick's chair, flickered twice as one light and then died. Mary had been sitting holding the flashlight, ready for the darkness, and when it came she pushed the switch and pointed the cone of light at Bill as he walked back to the kitchen to get a towel to dry his head. Paul was fiddling with the transistor radio by the light of the fire, turning the dial back and forth through the static, searching for the voice of a weatherman. "They'll have a generator at the hospital," he said.

"They'll have a generator for sure," Bill called from the kitchen. "Likely several." After he was dried off he came back to sit down again beside Sally and Krissy on the couch, put his feet up on the hassock, and locked his hands behind his head. "Let's talk about Florida," he said.

This is what they did when there was nothing else for them to do. They talked about going south for a winter holiday, driving down in two or three cars but staying together on the road, finding a nice stretch of ocean, renting some kind of cottage for a couple of weeks. Bill always started the talk. And they had discussed it so often and in such detail, the details always presenting some kind of problem and then one way or another getting sorted out to everyone's satisfaction, that it seemed almost possible that one day they might actually get themselves down there. They would buy loud American bathing suits and jump ocean waves under a hot February sun and when they were tired of jumping waves, they would lie back in black-and-white striped beach chairs, the stripes being one of Daphne's contributions to the dream, to drink perfectly chilled glasses of cheap American gin.

AFTER they'd made love in the small unlocked shed behind the Casino, Murray and Daphne waited out the worst of the storm with Mary's parents, drinking Canadian Club.

They had just started back to Dunworkin when it really broke loose. They'd thought it was likely almost over, but running down the Casino hill they could hardly see their feet in front of them and the crosswind coming off the lake soon slowed their running to a hard walk. Their hair was blown wild and plastered wet to their faces and everything that covered them, the quilt, and their clothes and skin under the quilt, was quickly, thoroughly drenched. When a flash of sheet lightning created a brief, queer daylight under the black clouds, they were able to recognize Mary's parents' cottage and they left the beach thinking just to take shelter under the broad eaves around at the back where they would be protected from the full fury of the wind. But Mary's father heard them and opened the kitchen door with a flashlight in his hand. He knew them immediately and ushered them inside, his only comment a surprised but cheerful, "Good grief, Mother."

Mrs. Wilson pointed them to separate bedrooms and brought towels and dry clothes, a sundress for Daphne and a pair of Mr. Wilson's best shorts for Murray, telling them in a pleasant, straightforward way what fools they were. "Here," she said, tossing them their towels, "get yourselves dried off, for God's sake." She gave them a few minutes and then knocked on the doors holding a plastic basket for their wet clothes. Daphne told Mrs. Wilson if she could please just have a garbage bag, that would be great, and then she went to the bathroom to fix her hair in the candlelight, to search her face for giveaway signs of joy. Murray went out to talk to Mr. Wilson, who was standing in the kitchen pouring the rye with his flashlight tucked under his arm.

The four of them carried their drinks to the fire in the living room, which was furnished much more formally than Dunworkin, the sofa and chairs obviously just one generation off new, likely brought out from the house in London when a better suite there displaced them. The floor was carpeted and there was a new open kitchen with a breakfast bar. Several oil lamps had been lit and placed on stable-looking tables.

Earlier that afternoon, before they'd arrived at Dunworkin, Mary and Patrick had come to tell Mary's parents about their honeymoon, about all the historical sights in Boston and the drive back through New York State, and after the Wilsons got Daphne and Murray settled into comfortable chairs with their drinks and a sincere assurance that they had both enjoyed the groom's dinner just so much, travel was what they wanted to talk about now. They wanted to know had Murray had the chance to broaden his experience with travel? Had Daphne? They themselves had travelled a lot and hoped to do more of it now that Mr. Wilson could take some time away from work. They had been to Florida many times of course and twice to Europe, once to California, to Jamaica, to Banff, to Washington.

Murray was relieved beyond measure that there was nothing to do between the cracks of thunder but drink rye and listen, or appear to listen. He had thought about it so many, many times and now here it was. In all his imagining he had never once imagined it unexpected or clumsy or rushed, or on the rough cement floor of some anonymous cement-block shed in a banging storm. The metal roof above them had been so roaring loud he couldn't hear or understand most of what she'd said to him, and because he was afraid to raise his voice in case someone heard and came to rescue them, he'd had to try to speak with his hands, had to let his hands say what he might have said if it had happened some place else, some place safe and quiet. Near the end, near the brilliant end of it, he understood that his hands were not moving kindly, they were not soothing her flesh and her bones and her muscles as he had imagined they would, given their chance. He was bruising her with questions, the questions being, Why does this have to come to me now? and, Why do you decide you want me now?

Daphne drank her rye and smiled her misaligned showmanship smile. She was not thinking about the trips she might make. She was thinking about the sheet lightning that had filled the high shed window. In its intermittent flash she had seen that he was as fine as she'd discovered, just this evening discovered she had imagined him to be. She'd looked down at many men lying naked or nearly naked, bruised and broken and suffering or healing or dead. But this was a man as he was meant to be seen, and a man's moving body, all bones and angles and shadows, was a lovely thing. She could feel his hands on her face and on her body, all over it and all over it again when they were finished, much harder when they were finished. And her body knew her mind. Her body had known enough to brace itself. Her mouth had gone to his skin, to the rain on his shoulders, to his damp belly, instinctively. She could no more have stopped this than she could in other times have stopped her aching arms from reaching for a sweet bundled infant or her mangled jaw from opening wide in unanticipated laughter.

When it had become clear that he should not be asked to wait any longer she had wrapped herself around him and he held her exactly as she wished to be held, and when he broke through into her it wasn't hurt she felt at all. Or it was hurt with a fine new name.

And even so, even with all of this ringing absolutely true through her comforted, thankful body as she sat there watching the Wilsons' fire and drinking their warming rye, when they'd finally got themselves hidden from the storm, safe under the eaves, when Murray asked her, "Did that happen?" she could only try to look at him squarely and say, "I might be the last person to ask."

1970

PATRICK and Mary bought their house in 1964, the first spring after they were married. Mary had roamed north London with a real estate agent for two months before she decided on tree-lined Piccadilly Street and then it was just a matter of waiting and watching for one of the big old square-jawed houses to come on the market.

Most of their friends and certainly all of the men at Patrick's law firm were buying out in the suburbs, big brick splits with two-car garages and bay windows, shake roofs and two fireplaces and lower levels to be finished soon with shag carpet and wet bars, but Mary had grown up in a once-modern fifties ranch over behind the university, every solid inch of which, the walls, the baseboards, the doors, the ceilings, had been painted a creamy off-white, and now for her own life she wanted some character. She wanted natural wood and high baseboards and thick plaster walls you could sink a nail into and deep windowsills and the muted, unobtrusive yellow brick that had been the preferred brick when the old part of the city was built. Although she would never have said so, the first time she saw Bill and Margaret's white frame house, the house Patrick had grown up in, which was so much smaller, so much the lesser house, she decided that she liked it better than her own family's. From the look of things, Margaret had neither the inclination nor the time for the pristine demands a woman could make on a house. She had moved in with Bill and his kids and more or less maintained what Patrick's mother had begun. This was the kind of house Mary wanted for her own kids.

Because Patrick still had the last half of Alex McFarlane's note to take care of, Mary's father had loaned them the five-thousand-dollar down payment, telling them to go ahead and buy big, buy what they'd need down the line, because waiting was not nearly as wise as it was assumed to be. Moving up was an extremely costly undertaking. He further advised that it would be worth their while to forgo holidays and a new car for a while in order to put every loose dollar they had against their mortgage. Somehow he knew what was coming, knew that the housing market was just on the brink of the kind of growth not seen since the years after the war. He was obviously disappointed to see his money sunk into such an old house but Mary told him she was convinced it would outlast the new houses being thrown up so fast on the outskirts of the city, and besides, the trees alone and the park just a few blocks away and the settled, closed-in feel of the street, these were the things she and Patrick valued. And Patrick's office was so close he could walk and that would save them the expense of a second car, forever.

Mary was just pregnant with Stephen, didn't even quite realize she was pregnant, when she got almost exactly the house she wanted and they asked one of Patrick's colleagues to draw up the papers.

Bill and Margaret said nothing one way or the other about the choice of a house but when Bill saw that the kids were serious about the place on Piccadilly he did bring Archie Stutt in to look over the hot-water furnace and the wiring and the plumbing. Archie's diagnosis was that the wiring was a bit suspect and should likely be tackled some time in the next five years, the plumbing, being copper throughout, was that much better than new and the old boiler could probably fire the *Queen Mary* across the Atlantic, if in fact the *Queen Mary* still existed.

After they signed on the dotted line, but before Paul came in with his half-ton to help bring over what little they owned from the apartment on Oxford, most of it cheap, leftover university stuff, Margaret and Mary stripped all the downstairs hardwood with a rented sander. Then they waxed and polished, both of them on their knees for long hours, their stiff joints screaming because Mary wouldn't have urethane, which she said looked phoney. They went down to Kingsmills to pick out material for drapes, decided together on good understated linen that was neither in fashion nor out. Margaret didn't offer to sew these herself, although she did find someone at home who was an experienced seamstress, to run them up.

A year later, after the drapes were hung and the floors buffed to a soft glow by the socks and slippers that moved across them, Margaret drove into the city more than she normally would have to watch Stephen while Mary took herself off to estate auctions to try to find the furniture she imagined filling all her rooms. Stephen was a good, pudgy baby, happiest when put on the kitchen floor with the pots and pans and a couple of big spoons. Sometimes Margaret brought Sally in with her for company, to dispel the hollow sound of the rooms that was caused, she knew, not just by the absence of furniture but by the extremely high ceilings that Mary liked so much. At nine, Sally appeared to have lost every ounce of her earlier maternal inclination, although she would agree to hold Stephen while Margaret spooned him his pablum. Usually Sally just wanted Mary to hurry up and get home and said so.

It took Mary three years to find all the big pieces she wanted and she was careful not to rush it, not to be swayed from her master plan, which she never did articulate to anyone.

Now they were almost a houseful. The boys were in the second biggest bedroom, Stephen up in the top bunk and John, who was born the day after Stephen's third birthday, just recently coaxed into the bottom bunk. The crib had to be freed because at the end of March Mary had discovered she was carrying her last baby. If it was a girl, and Mary and her doctor both claimed to be sure this time that it was, she would be Rebecca. Rebecca Sylvia.

Patrick was working ten-hour days almost all the time and they hadn't had a holiday since the big family trip to Florida two years earlier, just before John was born. If he'd stopped to think about it, Patrick would have had to say that he was exhausted but he was still only thirty-three and hungry for promotion, for the added income and the status and the responsibility, for the meat a man like him was expected to sink his life into. You didn't get a promotion in a firm like his if you allowed yourself to appear tired. The walking to work helped. He believed it did. And often in good weather he donned sweats to jog the route he'd laid out for himself, changing it sometimes in response to traffic patterns, finishing off with the seven blocks to his office, cleaning up in the small men's washroom and changing into the suit and shirt and dress shoes he'd parked behind his office door. This routine was the source of edgy amusement for some of his colleagues, many of whom paid exorbitant fees to belong to a downtown gym that had a weight room and a sauna and a pool. While his jogging precluded his taking part in most of the jock talk and in the much more significant rounds of boasting about paying so damned much money for fitness, his thirty-minute run down the quiet morning streets, through the large, heavily treed central park, past the tank from the Second World War and the cannon from the Siege of Sebastopol and the larger-than-life soldier high on a concrete pedestal ignoring in perpetuity the larger-than-life woman reaching up to him, became an essential, head-clearing part of his day. Perhaps because it gave him his only privacy.

He did enjoy his noisy rituals with the boys, lifting their tough, squirming, slippery little bodies from the bathtub if he got home early enough, escalating their loud, goofy nonsense with his own at the breakfast table on stretched-out Sunday mornings. And he was content with Mary, who was not remotely like Sandra or any of the others he'd been with after Sandra. They did not very often have sex as he'd imagined a man and his wife might, on automatic, when they were tired at the end of a long day or just coming out of sleep in the privacy of early morning. Mary would do anything, go anywhere, but only when they had the assurance of an empty span of time, only after she'd been held for a long quiet time in his arms. And neither of them liked to talk as they waited for it to come to them, the peaceful energy that Mary in the middle of one long night had called their loving freedom, murmuring her satisfied and slightly smug conviction that, for her money, it was a far, far better thing than free love.

Except for the absence of a decent garage that might actually hold a car, he had come to like the house on Piccadilly and to like what Mary had done with it. The oversized armoires and the odd corner cabinets and the heavy little tables and the several reupholstered chairs you could fall asleep in took comfortable hold in the house and in their lives.

At their first cocktail party, which they gave the third year they were in the house, Patrick's fifth year at the law firm, he'd overheard one of the senior partners' wives say to another senior partner's wife, casually, that she could not imagine surrounding herself with someone else's worn-out junk. But Patrick did not look to such women for any kind of guidance. He didn't look to such women for anything. When they came to him at his office with their husbands, usually to have new wills drawn up or sometimes to sign the papers on a bigger house at a more prestigious address, he pulled their chairs out for them despising their little downtown suits, their immaculate puffed-up hair, their expensive assumptions, their second-hand confidence. When he passed those particularly gruesome women in his own narrow hall with its sconces and its dark oak staircase, which he hoped to be climbing until he was a very old man, they pretended they had not been heard and he almost laughed, but knew better of course. Their husbands were standing just inside the kitchen talking about Expo and the possible implications for international trade. Lifting their almost empty glasses in Patrick's direction, they too pretended the women had not been heard. As he poured the Scotch for his superiors he wondered whether this little bit of awkwardness would help him at the office or hinder him. From what he'd seen, he guessed it could go either way.

It had been Patrick's idea to add the screened-in porch at the back of the dining room. They'd replaced the wide window with double garden doors that, except for the hottest, muggiest days of high summer, were almost always wide open, May to September. Bill had found them an old wrought-iron patio set at a cottage auction, four chairs and a chaise that he'd carefully and thoroughly stripped and repainted white, driving up to Goderich with the cushions to have them recovered in the tough yardage used for boat cushions, realizing when he got there that he'd forgotten to ask Mary exactly what colour she wanted, deciding on his own that she would like the hunter green and she quite sincerely did, nearly as much as she liked Bill himself.

The addition of the screened porch required attention to the garden, which was small but nicely proportioned, with good afternoon sun. Patrick and Mary concluded together that the only things worth keeping were the red maple and the crab apple and a few of the lilacs back near the garage. After Patrick and Paul cut down or hauled everything else out of the ground, the seven or eight too many lilac bushes and the walnut tree, which was dirty, and the old cedars, which had thinned and faded, the first order of business was a new wraparound euonymous hedge, for privacy. They left a good expanse of reseeded grass for the kids and built a sandbox close, but not too close, to the back door, drove out to the lake for a load of fine white play sand. They worked up the flower beds with topsoil and some of Paul's Cadillac manure from the farm, put in a dozen peonies along the side and three climbing roses against the garage wall. They left the rest to Mary and she took her time with the perennials just as she had with the furniture. The first thing she did was paint the small garage door a dark cherry red to set off the roses, which would be white, which were by the seventh year of their marriage white and robust and almost glowing in the evening light when they sat with their drinks in the screened-in porch with Stephen and John at their feet, the boys revving their trucks in preparation for a big crash, their little mouths working hard, exploding with the sounds of carnage.

BOTH of Murray's parents died in May of 1970. His mother suffered a quick, entirely unanticipated fatal stroke while she was standing over her stove grating cheese into a sauce for the broccoli and two days after her funeral his father was gone. He had been sitting alone on the brocade sofa watching Archie Bunker berate Meathead on "All in the Family" when he had a mild heart attack and soon thereafter a second attack that was called massive and which killed him.

Patrick had done their wills right after he joined his law firm. Mr. McFarlane told his own long-time lawyer at home that he wanted to give the will business to Patrick, just to help get him started, and this was understood as an ordinary gesture from one generation of men to another, a handing down. The McFarlane wills were not complicated. Everything to each other and then everything to Murray. The only exceptions were a bequest to the Anglican Church for new carpet and choir gowns and another larger bequest to the Cancer Society, because both of the McFarlanes assumed that if they lived long enough, they would become familiar with one kind of cancer or another. Some of their oldest friends had died of it, quite miserably.

The day after his father's funeral, a Saturday, Murray drove into London to Patrick and Mary's house on Piccadilly, which he'd never seen, to be told what he expected to hear. His parents had always ensured that he understood clearly the specifics of their wills. They did this even when he was a child, to give him confidence, they said. Although neither of them would have shared it with anyone but the other, they had been, in their old age, slightly disappointed in Murray. This materialized in three ways: his mother's worried judgement that he was foolishly and dangerously resistant to his God, his father's proud disappointment that he had deliberately sought a career that took him so very far away from home, and their shared amazement at his choice of a wife. But their disappointment did not in any way interfere with what they had always privately called Murray's birthright. Money, his mother said, was money.

After Mary had given Murray a brief tour of the house, and he did seem interested in the staircase and particularly in some of the cabinets, Patrick picked up both wills from the dining-room table and handed them over, explaining unnecessarily that because Mr. McFarlane had outlived her, his will negated his wife's.

Mary was glad to see Murray although she had never known him well. There was only the quick year before she and Patrick were married and Murray had pulled back that year, giving her room, giving her first claim, and then he more or less disappeared into his work, into his travelling around. Sometimes they heard from Margaret where in the world he was and once in a while they found something of his in one of the Toronto papers, but they saw him only irregularly and only at home if they happened to be at Bill and Margaret's when he, too, was in town visiting his parents. Charlotte had stopped going home with him to see the McFarlanes while they were alive, although she was firmly present at both funerals, thoroughly composed in a severe, black, sleeveless dress. She had moved through the crowded church basement, chatting up the elderly church people and touching their age-spotted arms as she spoke to them, her transparently disciplined liveliness so false it clearly astonished them, left them shocked on her behalf and speechless.

Standing in the dining room in her own very early middle age, Mary thought now that Murray was quite good looking, compelling in a way that Patrick was not. His hair had thinned but this made his face unavoidable and she liked unavoidable faces. His cheekbones were his strongest feature, his cheekbones and his light-filled eyes. She attributed the thinking of these lusty thoughts, which were not at all normal for her, to altered hormones. She was always a bit randy when she was pregnant, a bit open. When she was carrying John, she had confessed this to her young doctor, mainly because she was curious to see if he'd say what he usually said, which was, "Oh sure, I hear that all the time, not to worry." Lying on the table, conjuring fond thoughts about the pulsing baby just there under her thick, taut skin and about herself, her temporarily, she hoped, altered self, she did not pause long enough to realize that she was speaking to a man who probably assumed himself to be fairly good looking and who was just at that moment preparing to insert his gloved index finger into her vagina. When he frowned and offered the opinion that while he'd never heard of such a thing, he would guess that her feelings were likely just a slight aberration and certainly nothing to get excited about, she recognized with a thud her own stupidity and laughed so hard he had to stall his index finger and pretend to laugh with her. Later, when she replayed this scene for Patrick in their bed, snuggling into him, expecting raucous laughter, he just pulled back and lifted his eyebrows, waiting as he had waited before to be told just why this was funny. Disappointed for a week, she finally thought of telling Margaret, who was a better audience for almost anything anyway and who, hearing it, hooted most satisfactorily.

When he'd arrived Murray had made a sincere and appreciated fuss over five-year-old Stephen, who was Stephen Murray, and then over John, who at two was still small enough to be lifted and swung up into the air, and now Mary called the boys back into the dining room to say goodbye. After Murray bent down to shake the boys' hands he turned to her. "You were never in my mother's house," he said. "Patrick gave her a rose bowl once and I'd like you to have it. And she had a chest you might like. I think it's walnut." He held his hand at his own chest to indicate the height. "It has about a hundred drawers."

Mary smiled and nodded yes.

"Come maybe Wednesday morning," he said. "The auctioneers are going to be there Wednesday afternoon to look things over. I'll hold back anything that catches your eye."

Moved by this unexpected generosity, Mary told him she would come Wednesday morning for sure, and thank you. And she decided she would definitely choose something. If there was nothing she liked, she could just pick something small, something she could tuck away in a cabinet.

Before Murray arrived she had told Patrick she'd take off with the boys and it still looked like the right thing to do. She reminded him about all the ingredients available for lunch and then went out the door to settle Stephen and John into the car and take them the hour's drive over to see Bill and Margaret and Sally. Bill in particular loved to look up from the cash register at the hardware store and see her standing there with his grandsons, come all this way to visit their grandpa at work. He always kept a stash of multicoloured Laura Secord suckers in the back of the register for his grandchildren and for all the other kids who came in, who were expected to stand stock-still and quiet while their fathers contemplated wrenches and roach poison.

Driving down the highway trying to find some music on the car radio, Mary found instead a report of a shooting at Kent State University. Four American students had been killed by troops from their own National Guard. The troops had shot into a crowd of protesting students. That was the phrase the reporter used, shot into the crowd. Listening to the reporter go on about Nixon and rallies and demonstrations and Cambodia and casualties, the word *casualties* sounding as always like very much the wrong word, she thought, not for the first time, how good it was to be Canadian, to be alive in this country now. A Canadian in 1970 didn't have to fear her own armed government. Patrick and Murray and Paul were not required by law to hand their lives over to fight someone else's war.

She hoped Patrick would take the trouble to get to know Murray again, that Murray would stay around for a while, that they'd drink beer in the sun porch all afternoon, listen to some of Patrick's jazz, to John Coltrane or Thelonious Monk, get themselves loosened up. They had not seen much of each other for years but this could be understood as simply an ordinary interruption caused by jobs and marriages, distance, Murray's constant moving around. She remembered watching them, especially that summer at Dunworkin, thinking that she heard in their casual, sometimes nasty banter an oblique male commitment, a kind of contract. They seemed to have been steady, easy, dependable friends and why not resurrect that? She didn't know how grown-up men survived without it, or why. Her own friend Joan, who was married now, too, and living on the far side of Toronto, had become indispensable, like a sister who didn't slow things down to a crawl with the need for context or background or explanation.

It might have been better if Mary had stayed with Patrick and Murray in the porch. She might have been able to give Murray more of what he'd come for.

With the wills out of the way, Patrick's intention was to ask briefly about Charlotte and then to take the chance to get Murray to talk if he would about journalism. He thought he might be able to feel that he knew him again if he understood more about his working life. And he had a lot of questions, starting from the almost nothing that he knew about the job and from the assumption that anything Murray could tell him would be at least slightly interesting. But the one question about Charlotte, the simple, She looks good, how is she? took them straight down Murray's line of thought, which apparently had been the plan from the start.

"Oh, Charlotte's fine," Murray said, answering the question with a nod and then adding quickly, as if it were part of the answer, "I'm going to leave her." He tilted his head back toward the wills on the dining-room table. "There is substantial money now. She could live well enough on half of it."

Patrick eased himself back from the edge of the reinvigorated friendship. He didn't like divorce. Not at all. There was nothing to like about divorce. "Why now?" he said. "Why not earlier, before you got the money?"

Murray laughed. "Once a lawyer ..."

"No," Patrick said. "It's just that, well, why would you want her to have any of that money?"

"Because it was not her fault that I married her. I married her because she has the best legs and the finest breasts I have ever seen. And I sincerely believed that would be enough to last me."

"She is a very good-looking woman," Patrick said.

"But you've never liked her," Murray said, watching closely for a reaction that was not forthcoming. "Nobody has ever liked her. And now I don't."

"Charlotte must be similar to the rest of us," Patrick said, getting up from his chair to get a couple of Pilsner from the fridge, calling back, "She must be made of all the usual stuff. Strengths. Weaknesses. Needs." Coming out to the porch again with the beer, he said, "I admit I didn't like her much at first, but I decided some time ago this was probably only because I was used to a different kind of woman. We were unfair to Charlotte, I'm sure."

Murray waited until Patrick was comfortably stretched out in his wrought-iron chaise. "I hope you haven't wasted a lot of your time feeling guilty," he said. "She has never liked any of you. Almost right from the beginning, she had vicious nicknames for everyone."

"Which I don't want to hear," Patrick said. "Not today or any other day. Anyway. I think everyone pretty much came around. I just assumed I couldn't see what you saw."

"And indeed you couldn't," Murray said, taking a long drink. "The fact that she'd been with quite a few other men has always been a bit of a turn-on but I never did get to like the idea that someone like you, for instance, might look at her and imagine her naked."

Patrick laughed a low male laugh, the kind women get to hear only by mistake. "You are deluding yourself a bit there," he said. "I have never imagined the good Charlotte naked." He had, of course. He caught Murray's skeptical gaze. "Call it friendship," he said, shrugging his shoulders. "Call it taste. Yours. Mine. Not necessarily the same."

"If you say so," Murray said. He had rested his foot on Stephen's beat-up dump truck and was rolling it back and forth in front of him. "And you're right, she does have needs. What she needs is to feel superior to everyone on the planet. What she needs is to have received a good swift kick in the ass when she first started to strut her mind-boggling vanity, whenever that was. Before my time."

"This sounds a bit like hatred," Patrick said.

"The problem has become more about what it isn't," Murray said, "than what it is."

Patrick started to run his thumbnail down the sweaty label of his beer bottle, shredding it. Murray dug round in his pockets and found his lighter but no cigarettes because he had purposely not bought any. "I've been smoking," he said. "And now I'm quitting. Everybody I know smokes," he said. "My car stinks of it. My clothes stink of it. Can you smell it on me?"

"Yes," Patrick said. He thought about asking if there was someone new, a replacement, someone who was prompting Murray to admire Charlotte less than he had when he was a lonely, lusty twenty-four. He decided to wait it out. If there was a woman, and if Murray wanted him to know there was a woman, he would bring the conversation around.

"I wanted kids," Murray said. "It never occurred to me that this was something you should have to ask a woman beforehand."

"Charlotte doesn't want kids?" Patrick looked at Murray straight on, as if this surprised him.

"She'd had herself sterilized before I even met her."

"And didn't say so?" Patrick asked, incredulous.

"What she says now is that she just assumed that because I was from the beginning so determined to get a posting in London and from there maybe to Southeast Asia or at least some place with some significance, that because we talked all the time about what she now likes to call with a bitchy little twist 'the world out there,' that I wouldn't want to be tied up or tied down with the extra responsibility of a family. And because she was so up front about her own career, her own ambitions, she thought this made us a match. She assumed it didn't have to be discussed."

"You did talk all the time about your job," Patrick said. "You talked endlessly about your possible career moves. And it looks like you've done at least half of what you imagined doing. She has a point, perhaps."

"She has a point? Perhaps?" Murray sent the dump truck rolling into the dining room. He leaned forward in his chair to face the floor, bracing himself on the long bones of his legs the way he had when they were boys, when he was a sometimes anxious boy.

"No, of course," Patrick said. "She should have levelled with you. Given you the opportunity to make a choice, to do without the legs and the breasts."

"So I'm just your average piece of pond scum?" Murray asked. "The one who sees he has to leave is automatically pond scum."

"Usually," Patrick said. "In my experience. Do you want me to get the divorce under way?" he asked. "Maybe a legal separation first and then see what her lawyer comes after?" He gave Murray a chance to think this over. "We could likely go for irreconcilable differences, which is just new on the market and quite generally applicable." He waited again for Murray to take in what he'd said. "I'm assuming you don't want to go after the sterilization, although we might be able to argue some breach there."

"Irreconcilable differences would suit me fine," Murray said. "From where I sit it sounds almost precise. And I won't fight her, not unless she wants more than half. I doubt very much that she would go after more than half."

Patrick laughed. "Oh, my son," he said. "You might know your way around Heathrow but you obviously know dick about domestic life." He stood up and went to the kitchen, came back with two more bottles of Pilsner and a bag of potato chips that he threw into Murray's lap. "Lunch," he said. "Or we can get in your dazzling new Volvo and go grab a hamburger. Or you could buy me a proper prime-rib lunch down at the Iroquois."

"I'll be wanting to get married again fairly quickly," Murray said.

"As I surmised," Patrick said. Waiting for it had made him more curious than he might have been otherwise. He assumed he wouldn't know the woman. She would be a journalist of some kind, or connected to that world. "Who is she?" he asked. When he didn't get an answer he continued. "She's nice and fertile?" He intended this to be black and funny. Like his taste in women, Murray's taste in retort had long since been established and there was no reason to expect any deviation.

Murray looked up to watch if and how Patrick's face would respond when his brain cells registered the word he was about to hear. "Daphne," he said.

Hearing it, Patrick realized he'd felt it coming, he had felt something coming. He was extremely careful to control his facial muscles, to hold them exactly as they'd been before the question was asked and answered. Mary liked to complain that he could do this in his sleep. "The Daphne I'm thinking of?" he asked. When Murray nodded, before he could stop it, he muttered a quick "God," giving himself away. He could not have explained, not even to Mary, precisely why he did not want this to be true.

He thought he would like to ask Murray if he'd had contact with Daphne lately. It didn't seem probable. She'd been at both funerals, as had they all, and she was her usual self as far as he could tell. She'd handled Murray the way she would be expected to handle him under the circumstances. She had talked to Charlotte, led her around the room to introduce her to the kids, the nieces and nephews.

Then he thought what he would really like to know was if they had been together when they were young, right under everyone's nose, when Daphne was just a gullible, disfigured, innocent kid, taking all that shit from Roger Cooper. And what were the circumstances? Where, for instance? When? And where was he? And did anyone else know about this? And then he understood that there was a better-than-average chance he was going to get extremely pissed off if he allowed himself to go much further in that direction.

Murray felt the air thicken with Patrick's anger, the particulars of which were unchanged. He recognized the economy of movement, the concentrated hold on the beer bottle, the way his eyes quickly located a horizon, in this instance the dark red garage door, and locked on it. There would be no outburst. The stillness was the outburst.

He reached over the trucks at his feet, across the space that separated them, to grip Patrick's knee, hoping that this gesture might break the connection to the garage door, that it might say what it was generally understood to mean in the world of men, which was, Come on, guy. Come on, friend. This can't be such a big deal. And it worked, at least to the extent that Patrick looked at him.

"You can relax," Murray said. "I have no reason to believe your sister has any particular feelings for me."

This was not exactly true. It was, exactly, a lie. From the night of the big storm, the night in the shed behind the Casino, although there had been nothing since, not even the casual weight of her hand on his arm or his back or his shoulder, he had been able to imagine something tangible coming to him from Daphne. For the seven years since, whether he was with her at one of Margaret's occasional suppers or much more usually not with her but in a plane crossing the Atlantic or sitting in a gritty hotel bathtub at two in the morning listening to rocket fire from the outskirts of a ravaged city, he had been able to imagine something tangible.

But he decided on the spot that friends could lie. The best of friends could tell the best of lies if they absolutely had to, to get themselves through something, intact.

O n Tuesday morning Daphne drove up to Murray's parents' house because standing beside her over his father's open grave the week before he had asked her to come.

It was hot for late May, and dry. The lilacs that surrounded the wraparound porch were in full, droopy bloom. She knocked on the double oak door, distracted by their sickly scent.

Before she arrived Murray had gone up to the Blue Moon for two cups of coffee, graciously accepting the condolences offered by the young waitress who took his money and then by the owner who had come to the front immediately when he thought he recognized Murray.

He sat Daphne down at the small kitchen table and gave her a coffee, which was black and only lukewarm now. The table was still covered with one of his mother's many embroidered cloths, which had been ironed, perhaps just ten days earlier, into neat creased squares. "How to start," he said.

"Patrick said you'd offered Mary first crack at everything," Daphne said. "That was good of you. She loves old stuff. She will appreciate anything you give her."

"Patrick called you?" Murray asked.

"He's taken to calling me once or twice a week," she said. "He never has much to say so it's usually a bit of a mystery why."

"We had a good talk on Saturday," Murray said.

"So I heard," she said, her face implacable.

He didn't want any part of this to be an ordinary game between a man and a woman. "Did he tell you I'm leaving Charlotte?"

"Oh," she said. "No." She covered her jaw with her hand as she always did when she found herself in a conversation that might make a difference to someone. "I didn't realize there was that much trouble."

"Oh, that much and more," he said.

She lowered her hand and traced her finger along the ironed crease of the tablecloth, then lifted it from the crease to lightly circle a mauve pansy. "Imagine women sitting around all day doing this work. Or, I guess, doing it after the harder work was done. Think what it would be like to make all your own beautiful things. From plain cloth, from bits of coloured thread. From nothing."

"You do know what's coming," he said.

"No," she said, turning her face to the window above the huge old sink, away from what she could see coming.

"But if you had to guess ...?" he said.

"I would have to guess you're thinking about an unusually bad storm," she said.

He nodded.

"You shouldn't likely plan any kind of life around a storm," she said.

"You hadn't been with anyone," he said.

She faced him again. "But I have since," she said. "You gave me a taste for it," she said, opening her eyes wide, trying to laugh, to make him laugh.

"Don't ever tell me about any since," he said. "It would sound obscene to me."

"I wasn't about to," she said. "Believe me. And 'obscene' is a very strange word. Are you and Charlotte obscene?"

"We should leave that alone," he said.

"I'm all grown up, Murray," she said. "All grown up now."

"If I leave her, will you come to Toronto with me?" He ran a hand back through his thinning hair, which was not a nervous but an absent gesture. "We should get married. I would like us to have kids."

"If I say yes, you will leave your marriage, but if I don't, you'll stay?"

"You are the only really good reason to leave her," he said. "This will hurt her. It will certainly upset her parents and maybe even Bill and Margaret."

"You could try it alone," she said. "Many people do. And successfully."

"That wouldn't be much of a change," he said, although he did not want to go down that road. He'd decided standing at his father's grave that he wouldn't use that kind of thing to win her over. "Look," he said. "It was a mistake. It seemed like a good idea at the time, but it was a mistake."

"You were so wild for her," she said. "You were so obvious it was embarrassing." She covered her jaw again. "You touched her all the time, more than you ever touched anyone. For the flimsiest reasons."

"I realize that," he said. "It was true."

"What you're looking at now is not a woman like Charlotte," she said. "Although I guess you would realize that too."

"Standard issue," he said. "That's one of the only things I could hear you saying the night behind the Casino."

She stiffened. She wasn't laughing now. "You don't get to say that. I do, but you don't." She pushed her chair back from the table a little and crossed her better-than-average legs, smoothed her suede skirt. The skirt, like skirts everywhere now, was very short. "I've never had any complaints."

"Don't," he said. "Come on."

"I'll confess that I've thought about this," she said. "Imagined it."

He reached over to touch her, to take her forearm in his hand, and she let him do this, although there was no change in the air to suggest she was being touched. It moved just the one way, as if the nerve endings in her skin had been tripped to block a small, localized invasion. She knew the feeling, recognized the absence. Her skin had done this for her before. Healthy bodies do this all the time, she thought.

"You picked," she said. "You chose. It wasn't me."

"You could have stopped it," he said.

"And I would have done that how, exactly?" she asked. "I was twenty-two when you married her. I had no idea how I felt. I knew nothing, even less than I know now, if that can be believed. Except that you were so hot for her, so smitten, so gaga, so dumb-as-a-fence-post gone. I thought it must be love. Her perfection, your idiocy."

"All that time you treated me like just some kind of dull old reliable friend and then the summer after I married her, you peeled off your bathing suit for me in the Casino shed."

"But I did not feel that coming," she said. "The Casino shed was a true surprise to me." She finished her cold coffee. "Maybe I thought it wouldn't matter then," she said. "Because everything was decided. Nailed down. Locked up. I wanted what I wanted and maybe I was afraid to go to anyone else. Perhaps I thought you would understand that. And anyway," she said, "although I was probably jumped-up and fairly hot with curiosity, and likely with need, with a particular need, I've tried to think of that episode as just a kind of very detailed hug."

"I remember the details," he said.

She took his empty coffee cup from his hand, dropped it down into her own empty cup. "Maybe something else had happened by then," she said. "Which I didn't understand until very recently."

"What something else?" he asked.

"If I'd loved you," she said, "after you'd decided on her, married her, I should have pined away in some kind of heartbroken agony. When I couldn't have you, I should have wanted you more. But I didn't. I wanted you almost not at all and that's what allowed me to peel off my bathing suit." She got up to pitch their empty paper cups into the garbage bag sitting beside the back door. "I don't think it's supposed to work that way. Is it? It's certainly not the way the story gets told. It's not the way the song gets sung."

"Songs and stories," he said, "do not offer reliable guidance for life."

"I can't do it," she said.

"Explain this to me," he said.

"You were the one who should have known. And you didn't. You didn't take me into account. So why would I trust you now?"

Murray leaned back in his chair. Time, he thought, could be a major player here. And it's all I've got. "What if things just stay the same for now and you think about our options," he said. "I won't do anything. I'll wait as long as it takes for you to make up your mind." He did not describe their possible lives, did not tell her that he was ready to hold her skinny little body every night of her life. He had imagined so much of what they could have so thoroughly it would have been easy to do but he didn't.

"I would like kids," she said, leaning against the sink. "And yours would be by far the best."

"So you don't anticipate marrying anyone else?" he asked.

"No," she said. "I do not."

He was ready to start speaking in paragraphs, to force her into a corner with sound argument, with logic, but he shut it down, hard. She had just said part of what he wanted to hear and he believed if he opened his mouth, she might be prompted to take back what she'd said, and that would be far worse than never hearing it. He hated women most when they said a thing and then backtracked to kill it.

"What if we make love right now?" she asked. "What if I have us a baby? We could go that far."

He had not wanted to hear this. He had not once imagined this. "An illegitimate baby?" he asked.

"The baby would be fine," she said. "Later on maybe you could come back and see how you liked the looks of me."

If she was going to start talking about her face, he was prepared to stop her in her tracks. He'd had the words ready for a while, from the time his guilt had finally, and almost without his noticing, transmogrified into the lesser sin of profound regret. And he did not see it as a self-serving act, this ridding himself of guilt. He would never have hurt her deliberately, not in ten thousand years, and having seen in his travels mountains of deliberate, murderous harm, he now believed that guilt could not exist without intention. That guilt was starved without the nourishment of intention. This conviction freed the young man he'd been and it freed Patrick too, although Murray had never made the offer. He wasn't a priest. Of course Daphne had never accused either of them, not then when she was a kid and not since. What she'd said when Bill ran under the water tower to gather and comfort her was what innocent people always said: "I've hurt myself." This was wrong, of course. Worse than wrong.

"Not just small breasts but small slightly sagging breasts," Daphne said. "Does that sound appealing?"

"I don't understand," he said.

"What I want is a child," she said. "I'm lonely at the core and while some people would say this is the worst reason to have a child, a despicable, selfish reason, it must be the very best reason, or so it seems to me. I've seen women hold their babies as if they've been lonely for them all their lives. No one ever speaks up to say that's suspect."

He watched her small body, watched her cross her arms to protect it. The light from the window behind her framed her sandy hair, which she had lifted and pulled back from her forehead to expose the widow's peak, Sylvia's widow's peak. "I'd make it as easy for you as I could," he said. "I would give you money."

"That sounds to me like a good deal," she said. "I like money. It's one of my favourite things."

"So you're saying now would be the right time?" he asked. "We're going to go upstairs now?"

"When I was driving out from London," she said, "I was thinking about this house. I was thinking in particular about the wrap-around porch, about the lilac bushes and the low branches of the spruce trees along the side."

"It's the middle of the day," he said. "There will be people on the street." He waited for her to come around, to be sensible, but she wasn't going to give an inch. "We will have to be quiet," he said.

"This time quiet in the quiet." She moved toward him, reached down to his lap, and urged him to his feet.

They went out the kitchen door and followed the porch where it turned at the corner of the house. When they came to the place where the lowest branches of the spruce trees were almost as dense as a man-made wall, Murray stopped.

Daphne stood very still. She was facing him, staring at the creamy surface of his shirt, at the still-hidden chest and shoulders. She was making for herself a sharp, reliable memory of the time before she saw him exposed to the light of day, before she knew every part of his daylight body.

Almost always, until now, when she was with a man, trying like a child to guess exactly what was wanted and, more exactly, what was not wanted and, more crucially, what the final cost of all of it might turn out to be, she recognized in herself and quickly tried to blunt a nearly irrepressible and surely hurtful impulse to cringe when the hands reached out for her. Standing quietly on the porch protected by the spruce trees, she was thoroughly enjoying the absence of that impulse. And she believed that she understood the reason for its absence. This understanding was a release, a fine, small release. "I'm thinking it might be important, it might be best if we try to keep some space between us," she said. "Quiet should help."

Let her get this said, Murray told himself. It's only what she believes now. He took for his own memory the top of her small, beautiful head which was almost ready to lift itself up. Her face is going to be calm, he thought.

It was not absolutely quiet on the porch. There was a bird of some kind hidden among the boughs of the spruce. The bird was agitated, likely fearful for the safety of a nearby, recently constructed nest. They couldn't see it but they heard its loud defence.

MARY and Andy were out by the garage deadheading end-of-July roses when Daphne came into the backyard to tell them that she, too, was pregnant. The boys were busy with their trucks in the sandbox and "Midnight Cowboy," a song Andy especially liked, a song she was humming along with, was playing on the stereo in the screened porch.

Mary and Andy didn't know each other well. When Mary and Patrick were first married, Andy had had her hands full with her kids and lately Mary had been equally busy with her own two and now she was going to have a third, a last baby. Paul was the one who had encouraged Andy to start coming into London, to make the effort to get to know Mary a bit. What he really meant, what almost everyone meant, was, Get away, take some time for yourself. Get your mind off Meg, at least for a few hours. You're entitled.

Andy's first response to Daphne's news was a loud yelp. Then she reached out to embrace her husband's slightly older sister, moving aside when she was finished to give Mary a chance. When Mary didn't take the chance, Andy quickly began to talk nonsense, starting with the first thing that came into her head. "But all this time I've been hoping for one more bridesmaid's dress," she said. She looked over at Mary, who was about to speak, and carried right on. "Mary and I decked out in matching peau-de-soie, and with pretty little pumps dyed to match. I was thinking baby blue. You're saying there won't be any baby blue peau-de-soie in our future?" She was trying to give Mary some time, to fill up the air between them so Mary could take a minute to think, so she wouldn't speak any of the words that looked to be banging around in her angry head. It didn't do any good.

"Did I hear you right?" Mary asked. She had taken a step back, an actual step back, from Daphne and Andy beside her.

Daphne said it again, just the one word. "Pregnant."

Mary looked at Andy to see if this might have been a set-up, prearranged, to see if Andy had been already told and won over. But Andy's face was blank. She looked back to Daphne. "Is there a man connected with this?" she asked, her voice scraping like fine steel wool across the word *this*. "You don't have anyone ..."

Mary's tone of voice was brand new to Andy, but hearing it, Daphne recognized the stilted cadence and the quick drop to a lower, deadly serious pitch. Knowing without a doubt that she had heard hints of this tone of voice before she wondered at her own foolhardiness, at her own casual assumptions. If it had been even slightly appropriate, if there had been any room back there beside the roses for a quick acknowledgement of absurdity, she would have smacked her own forehead hard with the heel of her hand. If they'd been alone, Andy would have laughed. Margaret certainly would have laughed, hearing it.

"Yes, there is a man," Daphne said. "Likely the difficulty is not going to be with the word 'man' but with the word 'connection.'"

Andy felt exactly as she did when she was trying to drive the loaded half-ton up an incline through greasy spring mud. She geared down, hoping for traction. "Okay now," she said.

"Kids need a father," Mary said, gearing up. "And so will you. You'll need help. It's a hell of a lot harder than it looks. About a thousand times harder. Childbirth is nothing. Childbirth is a bloody piece of cake."

Aware that this could get very bad very fast, Andy decided that she was not going to get sucked in any further. She would do whatever Daphne wanted, whatever she needed, anything at all short of turning on Mary. Because the only future she could actually see had all of them in it. As far as she knew none of them were going anywhere. Mary would just have to stretch her mind to accommodate this little bit of reality. But in her own time. Because how else did people do this kind of thing? She could not credit herself with a tolerance greater than Mary's or a heart that was bigger or more yielding. She just didn't care, she just truly didn't give a damn, not as long as Daphne was all right with it. Whatever it was.

Daphne was turning to go, not in anger, not crying but turning firmly, ready to head for the gate and down the driveway to her car.

Mary reached to put a hand on her shoulder. "I'm sorry," she said. "But you're not some hippie freak, you are a nurse, for God's sake. You're a grown-up."

Daphne had anticipated this from Patrick, maybe. Patrick, probably. Although she would not have claimed to know her well, she had thought Mary was a bit like Margaret, perhaps because they had always got along so well. She had expected Mary to offer some variation on what Margaret had said that morning.

Margaret had taken time for one of the deep breaths she always took in the instant before she reconciled herself to something and then she'd said a mere "I see." Such fine words. And by the time Daphne had finished her tea and muffin and was ready to come back into the city, to Patrick and Mary's, Margaret already had her strategy prepared. "Leave me to get your father through this," she'd said. "There are far worse things and he is one of the people who knows what some of them are. If he thinks he's forgotten, I can remind him."

"I'm thirty," Daphne said to Mary. "I have thought this through. I can work until I start to show and I've got a bit of money and I'll be getting some help."

"From ...?" Mary said.

"From the person who wants to help this baby." Daphne could hear her own tone of voice adapt itself to the circumstances, a ready weapon, automatic. "If you can't take my news in the spirit in which it is offered, then don't take it at all."

"But this isn't just your problem," Mary said.

Andy flinched, not at the tone of voice but at the word. This was not a problem. She was the one who got to define the meaning of the word *problem*, thanks anyway, and these two lucky, lucky women were the last people in the world who should have to be told that. Meg not walking quite when she should have, not talking when she should have, and then talking strangely, slamming her fists, hitting out all the time now when she was frustrated, which was practically every waking minute of the day. Meg changing everything, changing even breakfast into tension. That was what you could call a problem.

In her head she already had Daphne's baby safely born. She couldn't stop herself. The baby was perfect, as her own first two had been. She already had it dressed in some of the things she'd kept, against this time, she realized now. She let it grow up quickly in her mind because that's what kids do, had it visiting them at the farm with Daphne, who would be a good mother, an easygoing mother, had it sitting on Paul's knee on the tractor for a picture with Neil and Krissy perched on the wheel wells and Meg standing behind Paul on the hitch, Meg happy about all of it, jumping and squealing with excitement.

She threw her garden gloves down on the grass and told them she had to go home. She walked along the path and out the gate without a sound, the muscles in her shoulders braced so they would heave only slightly, almost imperceptibly.

Mary was the one who broke down.

Daphne watched her, unmoved. She didn't reach across to touch her and she was not for a New York minute prompted to offer the consolation usual to such circumstances: I know you didn't mean to be hurtful. And Andy knows it too. I'm sure she does.

She looked at this pregnant Jackie Kennedy lookalike, this small, dark, bony-shouldered, thick-haired woman who would remain connected to her as long as Patrick was alive and likely long after, and thought, Mary, you've pulled yourself away. Nobody did it for you. And how do you like being away? Is it better out there?

And then she left, stopping for a minute at the sandbox to tousle John's hair and smile down at Stephen, who was just old enough to have been listening, to have noticed his mother crying into her hands back beside the roses.

WHEN Murray phoned, Patrick had asked him to come up to the office. He'd started a file, made some notes. He didn't have much information yet, only October, 1962, Toronto, which was the date and place of their marriage, and a sketched-out offer of settlement that he had deliberately lowballed. He had no idea how much money Murray made, or how much Charlotte made. He didn't know if they had saved any money themselves because from what he'd gathered they had been living a fairly extravagant life, but he assumed Murray's inheritance would constitute the bulk of the assets. He was sure Charlotte's parents were both alive and well, so her probable future security would not be up for discussion, not in front of any judge that he knew. He wondered what the late Mr. McFarlane would have made of this, Murray allowing his carefully husbanded money to dissipate to this god-awful woman.

Murray had said on the phone that he would rather they meet for dinner downtown some place, so Patrick booked a table at the Iroquois. He deliberately arrived one drink early and after his drink was served he took the file out of his briefcase and placed it squarely in front of him. He wasn't happy, he had even considered passing this thing off to one of his colleagues, but he wanted it done as fast as it could be done. Just to look at her, you wouldn't know Daphne was pregnant, but walking to the restaurant in the muggy August heat he had thought about late February, how fast late February could come. Normally he could not truly remember winter in summer or summer in winter. Normally he found it impossible to bring to mind the opposite season, its pleasures and drawbacks.

When Murray walked into the restaurant he was empty-handed, no briefcase, nothing. Maybe he had an accountant. Maybe he was going to refer Patrick to his Toronto accountant.

As Murray sat down, he glanced at the open file laid out on the table. "Nice suit," he said. "New?"

"Hardy Amies," Patrick said. "Not all that new."

The very attentive waiter had watched Murray settle into his chair and was soon right there with his "What will it be for you, sir?" They ordered their drinks and after the waiter left them Murray said, "What the hell's happened to us that middle-aged men are required to call us sir? If this is achievement, I don't think I like it. We're not nearly smart enough to make people feel servile," he said. "Are we?"

"No, we're not," Patrick said. "How are things?"

"Good," Murray said. "Extremely good. I just found out that I'm going to Saigon in September, which almost, but not quite, makes up for the fact that I didn't get there last year."

The waiter was back with the drinks and two oversized menus. He recommended the veal and they both said veal would be fine, although they'd pass on the salads. When he left again, Patrick asked, "Should we get at this or do you want to wait until after we've eaten?"

Murray reached across the table to close the file.

Patrick set it down beside the legs of his chair. "Fine by me," he said. "I won't start the meter until we actually begin our discussion."

"I'm going to pay you for the work you've done so far," Murray said. "Just send me the bill. But I've decided to hold off on anything legal."

Patrick found his horizon, the restaurant's name painted in heavy black capitals across the plate-glass window. He held his drink steady in his hand, an inch above the pink tablecloth. "You might as well keep talking," he said.

"She won't marry me," Murray said. "There is less than nothing I can do about it, so don't you go weird on me. Don't lay all of this at my door."

"I wouldn't dream of it," Patrick said, meaning that he hadn't yet found the words for his contempt.

"So I'm not going to put anything to Charlotte immediately," Murray said. "Things have not been exactly spectacular for her lately. At work. With her parents."

"This would be the same woman you couldn't stand the thought of carrying on with three short months ago? The one with the legs and the breasts and the extreme, what was your word, vanity?"

"Charlotte and I are nearly but not quite played out," Murray said. "Nearly but not quite dead. And I think it will be better all around if I stay until we are absolutely finished, until it is obvious to both of us. And thus unavoidable. Why should I get to miss the worst of it?"

"Some people might call that commendable," Patrick said. "But the reason you should get to miss the worst of it is, of course, because you are soon to be a father. I had assumed you would not want it to be born a bastard. That is what many people have agreed to call kids who arrive mysteriously without fathers. You've likely heard the word."

"Of course it has a father," Murray said. "I am the father." The waiter was there again, silently placing their plates of veal in front of them. Murray thanked him and he padded away. "Did she tell you I'm the father?" he asked. "Did you ask her?"

"No, she didn't tell me," Patrick said. "And no, I didn't ask her. No one is asking her. Except Mary, who had to take a large load of abuse for her trouble, which she did not in any way deserve. Not from Daphne or anyone else." He was not going to go on much longer with this. He was going to pull the discussion up out of this shitheap. Practising law, he was required to keep clients focused, disciplined, well away from the murky, useless, self-indulgent talk

A GOOD HOUSE

that could waste hours of his time and truckloads of their money. He was required to keep them firmly concentrated on what the law allowed and he was extremely good at it.

"She won't have me," Murray said. "Not now or any time soon."

"And if she's got a kid, nobody's going to be having her. I don't think you two realize what you are playing at. This kind of mindlessness has repercussions all the way down the line."

"And when did you get to be the great moral centre of our lives?" Murray asked. "You must be a busy man...."

"You can't expect non-reactions all around," Patrick said. "Dad isn't exactly jubilant."

"Margaret will be able to help Bill with it," Murray said.

"Jesus," Patrick said. He used his fork to lift the overcooked asparagus and drop it onto his side plate. "Everyone depends on good old Margaret. There's no escape. Almost for as long as I can remember. Almost that long." He scraped the sauce from his veal, turned it over to check the other side. "And she's always right in there, ready and willing to decide what everybody thinks. Christ. As if it's been agreed she's got some kind of wisdom. Which she does not have." He had cut a slice of his veal but it stayed on his fork.

"Margaret's only solution is to smooth things over," he said. "Make the phone calls, smooth things over, clean out a cupboard or two, and build a stack of salmon sandwiches. And then assign her little jobs to keep us busy, in case we might want to articulate what's on our own God damned minds."

"That sounds a bit like hatred," Murray said.

Patrick leaned back from his dinner. "I shouldn't have to explain this to anyone and certainly not to you," he said. "We should have been left alone longer after my mother died," he said, making his summation. "It should have taken a lot longer."

"I have always thought Margaret was a bloody saint," Murray said.

Patrick counselled himself, swallowed the words sitting ready to go at the back of his throat. He offered instead a calmer, "I have always thought her moving into our lives was perhaps not entirely altruistic, not without significant and obvious benefit to Margaret herself. And if my understanding is correct, you don't get to be

[160]

declared a saint unless you're dead. It's my mother who is dead," he said. "Do you remember any small part of how deathly ...?"

"Why should you be the only one who remembers?" Murray asked. He hadn't stopped cutting his veal. He hadn't stopped eating and he wasn't about to. "I was there. You haven't got a lock on it."

"Do you know what she said to me after Daphne fell?" Patrick asked. "After all the surgery and the wires and the clamps, when it became obvious the price Daphne was going to have to pay and still she refused to even cry a little, to even let on that something serious had happened to her?"

"I know what she said to me," Murray said.

"She said it had to stop at Daphne's jaw," Patrick said. "Right there. She said if I went through life blaming myself, it would only make things that much worse. And that I was to take care of her, that Paul couldn't do it because he didn't have the right kind of heart, Paul had her own soft heart. She said I had exactly the kind of heart Daphne would need."

Hearing this, Murray remembered some of the other things that had been said in that kitchen, in that living room. And he felt a bit cheated. He wished he could find someone right then and there to ask precisely what kind of heart he had. Maybe the waiter would know. But of course there was no one to ask, not any more. The goodness Sylvia had dreamed up and assigned to him at the kitchen table, her generosity in assigning it, would have to do him. And it had done him. It was probably the reason the boy he'd been had gone there, as if he'd known if he just hung around long enough, Sylvia would give him his goodness.

"Listening to you," he said to Patrick, "I can hear something close to her actual voice. That's what she understood, you know, when she was dying, that we choose our own words. That we make what we say. We own what we say."

Patrick was spent. Maybe it was just a combination of the August heat and the Scotch, but he'd had enough. He could feel his body tightening up, and as he concentrated on relaxing the muscles in his back, he wondered if this rummaging around in the muck for something that might be called true, this spilling your guts, your unsightly guts, was what women did, what girls and then women did, when they huddled together to listen to each other with their rapt, intimidating exclusivity. He wanted it over and done.

But he was cornered. He believed he had very little choice. If he was Murray's friend, and he was sure of only that, it would not be humane to leave the question unasked. "What did she say to you?" he said.

"She said, 'You'll have to take your lead from Daphne,'" Murray said. "She said, 'You and I are the only two people who know how much you care for her.' She said she believed things would be all right in the end."

"So this is your 'in the end'?" Patrick asked. "Daphne and her illegitimate baby here with us and you off somewhere else living your normal, busy, sophisticated life?"

"I trust her to know what she's doing," Murray said. "Do you remember when she used to call herself 'dee-formed'?"

"Without even trying," Patrick said. "I hated it. Her jaw is wrong but it's not that wrong."

Murray laid his knife and fork across his empty plate. "She needs more time because things like this go slower for her. She knows that. We know that. But she seems to be ready to take the time. And she wants my kid with her while she's doing it." He pulled his cheque-book from the pocket of his leather jacket. "I'll leave you with a good chunk of money," he said. "I can't be writing cheques to her. I don't want you to tell me how much she should have, she can have whatever she wants, but if you would administer the payments ...?"

"Fine," Patrick said.

Murray was leaning forward on the edge of his chair now, writing his cheque. His joy was apparent in his still very serious face, in the shoulders hunched confidently across the table. He folded the cheque and handed it over. "Maybe you could just be happy for us?" he asked.

Patrick looked at Murray's long-fingered hands, which were open, palm-up, in the middle of the table. He was trying to think, Maybe there is nothing to lose here. He was trying to look at Murray fairly, as a man in a great heaving mess, as a troublesome, irksome, loyal man. "Be very careful with Charlotte," he said. "It can be pretty rough on women. Even when it's what they want."

"Could you bring yourself to say something good about this?" Murray asked.

"We will make sure they're all right," Patrick said.

Murray closed his hands, tightened his fists, and then opened them one more time. "Say, happy," he said. "You don't have to make a sentence. Just try the one word."

Patrick drained his glass and put it down carefully on the tablecloth. He took one of Margaret's deep breaths. "Happy," he said. He searched the room and lifted his arm to get the waiter's attention. "Ecstatic."

CHARLOTTE had had enough long before she decided on Mike. She didn't care that Murray was away much of the time because she had always known this would be the reality. She'd believed from the start that he would do well and that doing well would mean travel and moving from assignment to assignment, sometimes on very short notice.

She did care that when he did get the chance to be around for a while he was always and obviously preoccupied, preoccupied being just another word for absent, another way to be gone. There was a song, she couldn't remember what kind of song or who sang it but she did remember the one phrase: "solid gone." Somebody was solid gone.

He didn't even seem to need sex much any more, not from her anyway, although she'd had some occasional evidence that her body could still, as it were, hold his attention. She supposed she instigated this intermittent sleepwalk coupling out of pride, for the opportunity to remind him that he was absenting himself from something that even he thought was exceptionally fine. There was no sadness in it. By this time she wasn't a believer and neither was Murray.

What she had learned from Murray, and after learning it realized she had learned it late, was that a man's physical attention, occasional or otherwise, should not be taken as hard evidence of anything. That wondrous, breakneck need that appeared to speak for something too complex for words, something beyond ordinary articulation and astonishing and touching in even the most mundane of men, spoke for nothing but itself. It was a need gratifying nothing but a need. This was the way it had been quietly and modestly explained to her when she was a disbelieving girl who had wanted with all her pumping heart for it to be otherwise, who had wanted the men she would love to be exceptions to this shitty rule, to be absolutely her own. And it was the truth.

With Mike, she had adopted an entirely new attitude. She had decided it was safer to go in knowing. Knowing didn't necessarily cancel the possibility of happiness because there was still a satisfying and surprising range of affection and fun and respect. Working with men, working seriously and productively with men, she had early on got wise to their deceptively relaxed drive for power, she had learned by watching just how they got what they wanted and came out clean. But all of that was nothing compared to understanding, at long last, how men loved.

Sometimes she wondered if she had stalled around with Murray, putting up with it, because she was terrified of the absolute vacancy she might feel living on her own. Something awful being better than something empty. But it didn't matter now. It would be all right now because Mike was there, ready and willing and wonderfully able. Murray, of course, had never been in danger of feeling empty.

She had long since stopped being intimidated by the cast of characters that accompanied Murray into their marriage, or tried to. She'd started to refuse to go up there ages ago. When? After that failed Hallmark Christmas, in 1962? No, it was a bit later, out at the cottage, Dunworkin, it was the summer before the motorcade in Dallas, before Jackie Kennedy showed the world that sometimes a woman just wants to crawl out of the damned car. Anyway, it was soon after it became crystal clear that they expected her to make a gargantuan effort to get to know them, to warm up to them, to bend to them. That they expected her to stand at the sink and wash the fucking dishes. She was working a fifty-hour week in those days, for God's sake.

Coming back to Toronto in the car with Murray after the last time she'd made one of her efforts, and she would have called her efforts gallant, anyone would, she had finally let her thoughts be known. She'd told Murray that while she could see they were nice people, they were just not particularly interesting to her. None of them. She had asked him to please explain to her why on earth he believed they were exceptional. Could he name anything at all? When they weren't breeding, the women worked, sure, but at only the expected jobs. The jobs you'd guess. And the men. Right, the men. They risked nothing. The biggest risk in all their lives was setting a place at the table for the minefield that was Meg, waiting to see what outrage she'd put them through, or Paul and Andy planting the damned corn, watching the futures market to see if in the fall they'd be simply rich or stinking rich. And the worst of it, the inescapable worst of it, was their perpetual, mind-boggling awareness of each other, their constant gatherings, their relentless, tedious assumption that they could rescue each other. That rescue was possible.

She had truly expected Murray to put up some defence. She assumed she'd hurt him. But he just shrugged his sloping shoulders, which she had loved then, oh, she had loved pretty much every inch of his bony body then, and kept driving.

His parents weren't that bad. Mr. McFarlane was a kind of slow-moving, old-school gentleman and his mother, stuck in little old Stonebrook with no hope of release, had made a valiant effort to create a quiet, civilized life for herself. And Patrick wasn't bad. She had been fond of Patrick. But there was no way to get near him without tripping over the rest of them. They were a mob, a tight little pack of yelping, nondescript, self-satisfied, what? Yokels? That was likely a bit cruel. Anyway. Anyway. All of it was ancient history and having Mike would soon make it dead history.

She had known Mike at work. He was a writer on her news team and they had been working almost side by side, slamming stories together, for nearly twelve years, had looked at each other perhaps a million times before that one-more-night-among-many when they'd all gone down to unwind in the bar. They were discussing Peter Finch's performance in *Network* when they looked at each other differently. Mike was very, very bright and fun, tons of fun. He was a terrific gossip, had delicious, nasty stuff on lots of people and he loved to get down and dirty. But his primary attribute was that he did not automatically assume that beautiful women were dim and from her perspective this was a substantial attribute. He wasn't any better looking than Murray but he was blond with a grey-blond beard and great clothes, great style. And he was absolutely comfortable with himself, which made bed just so much better.

All the best people she had ever known, even or maybe especially the people who were not particularly good looking, had style and none of it was accidental. Contrary to most assumptions, style didn't require a lot of time or even a lot of money. You didn't have to look like Warren Beatty or Diane Keaton. You just had to decide to look like bloody someone, to behave like someone who counted in a world that counted.

When she'd poured Murray his drink and told him that she had been sleeping with Mike for a year, give or take, he'd had nothing to say except, "I've met him. He's the one with the good teeth." He had no accusations to heave. There was no yelling, no hard breathing that might dissolve into gloomy sobs and, thank heaven, no massive melodramatic pain rising up between them on the sofa, which was a very good thing because she really, really hated melodrama. Despised it. She could have got quite worked up if Murray had taken the thing in that direction, tried to make a production out of it. But he just set his drink on the table and stood up and left the townhouse. Like a man, she'd thought. He believes he's walking out like a man. All she could think to say to his back was "Thanks, Murray."

She supposed he would get himself to Patrick right smartly to begin his defence of the great McFarlane fortune. He would soon discover that she'd already been to a lawyer herself. He would soon be learning how to divide by two. Mike had almost nothing left because he'd had to split what she'd guessed was a substantially smaller amount of money when he left his wife, and since then, of course, every year, month after month after month, he was required to hand over child support. For most of the years of his marriage his wife had not worked "outside the home." She had chosen the domestic life, home with the kids, home with the cookies. She had chosen to spend his money as if it were her own and seven years later she was still at it. "The bottomless pit" Mike called them when he was pissed off, when he once again found himself wanting something he couldn't afford.

But that first wife had taken care of Mike's paternal needs, so there wouldn't be any difficulty there, there wouldn't be any unexpected hope there. Anyway, she was almost past it. In two quick months she would be forty years old and people would soon stop asking the dreaded, dreadful question. People would soon stop looking at her like some apparently vigorous houseplant in a pretty pot that refused to flower.

Mike's children, whose nicely framed photographs sat on every flat surface in his apartment, lived year round with their mother and her new husband, really a fine guy, Mike said, usually, out in Victoria. The children would continue to come to visit of course. She had already met them several times. Not bad little people, quiet, polite, perhaps a bit terrified of her. But this was natural given the circumstances. The last time they'd seen them, in March when she and Mike had flown out to Whistler on a quick, impulsive ski trip, both girls were in desperate need of a good haircut but one of the boys seemed quite bright, which could be interesting.

DAPHNE wasn't surprised to get the phone call, although she had never once indicated any interest in the particulars and the few times Murray had seemed eager to talk about Charlotte, about his ridiculous marriage, she had stopped him cold. She expected him to stay married.

This wasn't decency or anything close to it. It was because she was a grown-up, because she guessed, albeit without the benefit of direct experience, that the long-term investment of time and energy and of what she had always assumed to be good sex, although Murray was careful to deny it, would be very hard to cash in. Hard for both parties. Even in a ridiculous marriage.

She had heard lots of married people use the phrase *work it out*, and other, workmanlike phrases too: *wait it out, ride it through*. *It* being the thing that was never quite touched on. She'd been at enough weddings, although now that she was thirty-seven the regularity of these was diminishing, to be familiar with the childlike, skipping rhyme rhythms of the vows: in sickness and in health, for richer for poorer, for better for worse.

At least they had no kids. People used that phrase a lot too.

At least she did. Have a kid.

She was back to work full-time at the hospital now that Maggie had started grade one and she was glad to be weaning herself from Murray's help a bit, finally. Although she had been pleased to cash the cheques when she needed the money. A woman with a child gets it both ways in several respects, more expenses and less income, more demands and less energy, more sorrow and more joy. More heart-wrenching sorrow and more inexplicable joy. Sorrow always when Maggie was hurt, not physically, that was pretty straightforward, a scraped knee, stitches here and there, but hurt in her trusting eyes, in her small trusting heart. And inexplicable, absolutely indescribable joy in her resolute accomplishments: walking, going to the bathroom alone for the first time, saying as she careened down the hall that it was private, setting the breakfast table for two, accumulating secret, treasured, junky things around her in her bedroom, drawing detailed pictures of three-storey houses and horses running wild on cloud farms, telling jokes to Grandpa Bill, saving them up to make him laugh and slap his knee.

Once when Maggie was small, just beginning to talk, to make herself understood, she had climbed up onto Margaret's lap for a restful cuddle, and settling herself in, she'd turned and used her capable little hands to lift and fluff Margaret's breast, like a pillow. Sally was there, she'd been about fifteen, and standing close behind them she had blushed with embarrassment for her mother. But Margaret allowed it, easily. She'd only laughed and said, "This kid's going to do all right for herself."

Still, even with all this, there had been days, many, when Daphne was what her own Grandma Ferguson would have called wearied, when a kind of lonely, godforsaken fatigue left her slumped in a chair, drinking cold tea, stunned. When she had to ask herself what she'd done. And why.

When Maggie first started talking, first started giving people names, without any prompting and maybe because she had been told that "uncle" was the word for the other men who sat for a long time and comfortably at Grandma's table, she'd pointed to Murray

and named him uncle. As soon as she had it out, Daphne spoke to
stop her. "Just Murray," she told her.

"Because I'm not your uncle, honey," Murray said. "Because I'm
way better than an uncle."

Patrick had kicked in immediately, claimed there was nothing in
the universe better than an uncle. This made everyone and then
Maggie laugh, which had been his determined intention. He was
still the only one who knew. He had never told even Mary, who
assumed the father was some married guy who had lied his way into
Daphne's affections or some other nondescript, irresponsible, shift-
less jerk, same difference. Patrick didn't argue with Mary and keeping it to himself eventually became like any other discipline. Once
firmly decided, you just kept on.

He had made up his mind that if Maggie ever started to resemble
Murray, as she some day might, he would go along with whatever
Daphne said she wanted. If she decided then that the others could
be told, fine. If not, equally fine. You didn't invest your time bothering Daphne with rational argument or an appeal to common
sense, not productively.

MURRAY was just back from Jordan. He was very brown and thin
or at least more wiry, more angular than usual. And tired. But forty
wasn't old, how could it be? He had continued to aggressively speak
up for overseas postings, particularly to the countries that were just
beginning to be called Third World and which were crawling with
creatures like himself, men excited and sometimes even amazed by
climate and topography and architecture and the massive stench, the
stupefying force of poverty and disease released by war. Men who
were close to impotence, struck dumb by the relentless confusions
of barbaric sensibilities, impaired by a limited tongue and stranded
in their useless, indulgent assumptions. Once, hungry himself and
filthy dirty and slightly wounded by a grapefruit-sized chunk of
concrete that had glanced off his shoulder when he was running
with a television cameraman from Spain out into the safety of an
empty, bombed-out street, he caught himself believing for one
quick second that war was the least of it. Why would these people

tolerate war, he wondered, these of all people? Of course such a question marked a man to be about as naive as a man could get. The people in these countries didn't vote for what they had any more than they watched their children thrive in comfort or drank good water or sought proper medical attention for their own undeserved wounds. And what they endured in country after country was nothing more complicated than a few ruthless animals at the top who were not the pasty-white desk generals you'd get in a declared war but hard, fit, middle-aged men who were so silky smooth you'd think they'd been to charm school. Men who had found a dependable, foreign source of arms and who worked their charm, their magic, prompting the chaotic, anxious rage of thousands of younger men. And no resource anywhere was as renewable or as ready to be tapped as the rage of young men.

Since Watergate, which at the end of the day had been understood most usefully to be a signal, it seemed to Murray that journalists had split into two distinct camps, those in the muckraking camp who positioned themselves right up against privileged power and dug around there for the dirty truth like private dicks, like archaeologists, and those in the other camp, his own, who roamed the almost beaten world like sometimes bombastic but nearly always terrified, appalled explorers. Although that was the one word you never heard. *Appalled.*

He had taken the train down to London to talk to Daphne because for a long time he and Charlotte had owned only the one car, the old Volvo, which as far as he knew would be sitting unused in the parking stall under the townhouse in Toronto. For years Charlotte had wanted to get rid of it because she always took cabs and she said he could more cheaply rent a car to get himself home, but now she said they'd better wait to see how things shook down, by which he assumed she meant that she wanted the option of saying, You can have the Volvo and I'll take the prints. There were prints he wanted, that he'd found and bought, but he doubted he had the strength to get them. He wasn't going to waste his time and energy going after any of the furniture, the beloved neutrals that Charlotte and the decorator had chosen, the decorator an enthusiastic, courtly young man looking for referrals who had promised that they themselves would give colour to their rooms.

He hadn't been on a Canadian train in years and he wasn't liking it. Flying, you had no control but at least you got there fast, and while driving soaked up time, at least it was your foot on the gas. The train was both slow and tedious, and where in other circumstances he might have chatted up the shy but friendly, hefty, middle-aged woman sitting beside him, who looked exactly like Andy might look in fifteen years if she stopped taking care of herself, while he might have taken the trouble to learn all about her town and her no-doubt-gifted grandchildren, it wasn't going to happen today. He might have killed the time working but he was empty-handed because he had nothing back at the hotel except a new shaving kit and one new change of clothes.

Everything had stayed with Charlotte in the townhouse: the prints, his typewriter, his files, his books, most of his clothes, the overpriced magnetic travel chess set that he'd bought in Madrid but never used, never taking the time to learn, his prayer wheel, which he'd seen masses of men use in earnest, his mother's tarnished silver tray packed away somewhere, the crystal snifters Bill and Margaret had given them as a wedding gift along with a bottle of Courvoisier, which they drank a lot of then, in their confident, pretentious youth.

Charlotte had agreed that he could come to pack up his personal things, which he assumed all of these to be, some time very soon. She had just asked for notice. She said she didn't want him dropping in unannounced. Murray guessed she had enjoyed that, setting up and then offering the image of a relaxed Mike wandering around the townhouse, wrapped in a towel that had not so long ago dried his very own ass, rinsing their dinner plates in the sink, flossing his pretty teeth, getting ready to climb back into their great big king-sized, maple four-poster bed. Back into her bed. The thing had cost Murray more than he ever thought he'd be paying for a bed but he didn't guess he would be listing it when it was time to divide the assets.

He didn't torture himself long with this kind of thinking. And anyway, thoughts of Mike with his hands on Charlotte didn't grate nearly as much as thoughts of him pouring brandy into one of Bill and Margaret's for-all-these-years-unbroken crystal snifters. Or blithely opening his filing cabinet, lifting out his files, one of which held the few letters from Patrick about Maggie's money. He had been a cretin leaving those letters in an unlocked cabinet.

He had already decided that he was not going to tell Charlotte about Maggie or about Daphne. There would have been some pleasure in it, watching her digest the meaning of what he'd said, watching her try to think back, to recognize in hindsight some comment, some averted glance for what it was, but there would be more pleasure in keeping it back. He would probably hurt her, sure. But not with that. Not with them.

When he'd phoned Daphne, he had asked if he could come this time when Maggie would be in school. He was quite used to tempering his conversation when Maggie was around, to offering his affection for Daphne in a way that would not confuse anyone. You could get good at some things after six years. And he was very careful with Maggie's affection. Every time he came in the door she would pull off his jacket, perch him on the edge of a chair, and climb up behind him to play artist, using her small index finger to draw pictures on his back: a horse, a lunch box, a watermelon, the turtle she'd seen crawling along the bank of Grandma's creek. He always made her draw the same picture again and again, struggling to guess what it could be, carefully guessing the wrong thing, prolonging the delicate touch of her hand long after he began to recognize the shape.

He and Daphne had adapted to the inconvenience of their occasional intimacy, always going out to a motel, telling the sitter in Maggie's presence that they would be at dinner and a show, that they hadn't yet decided which show, and that they might stop off somewhere for a drink or two on the way home. But he was about to be divorced and now things had to be talked about straight up. He'd decided he wanted the talk to be direct.

He caught a cab to Daphne's apartment, which was in a modest, orange-brick, four-storey bunker over near the river. She took his jacket from him and sat him down near the window in one of the two chairs that overlooked the Thames, actually the large parking lot and then the Thames, although she said that sitting there herself she always saw the greater distance, the better view. She offered him a coffee, which he wanted. Needed, he said.

Holding her own cup in both hands Daphne took a hard line, as she had on the phone when he'd called. "You two," she said, as if they were merely one more self-indulgent, middle-aged couple. "God," she said. "Why go looking for misery? Really."

She was wearing a dark blue cashmere sweater, Murray knew it was cashmere because Charlotte had four of them, and he was hoping he'd bought it, that she had taken some small part of the money and used it for herself. "I said I'd wait until it died on its own and now it's dead," he said. "I am soon to be a free agent."

Daphne tried something different. "They say there's a grieving period with divorce," she said. "Anger, grief, refusal to believe. Not in that order but in some order. You will have to give yourself time to get used to this."

"I've just had a two-hour train ride," he said. "How about I believe it, I accept it, and I'm happy?"

"If I were you, I wouldn't be too happy," she said. "Not too publicly happy. It might hit you later, people often talk about a delayed reaction and then you'd feel like a fool. You have a lot invested in her."

"Will you move to Toronto now?" he asked.

"I don't think I can," she said.

"Not right now?" he asked.

"Not for a long time," she said. She got up to get the coffee from the stove, to reheat their not even half-empty cups. "You know better than anyone," she said, pouring, "how good it's been for Maggie living here. Not too close to home but close enough. That's the thing with family. When you need them they can be like family."

This was precisely the answer he had expected.

"I've just got back on at the hospital full-time," she said. "Patrick has probably told you. Nights, Mrs. Warren across the hall comes to sleep over. She needs the money and Maggie likes her and I trust her. She raised six kids of her own and I think I've met them all. They look like they've turned out all right."

"I've thought about moving up here," he said. "I might be able to make it work. Staying in Toronto maybe four nights a week, keeping a small apartment."

"When you're around," she said. "When you're not away."

"Of course," he said. "When I'm not away."

"I can see how it might work in the practical sense," she said.

"But not otherwise?" he asked.

"When was the last time we were together?" she asked. "Three months ago?"

"And that too will be a thing of the past," he said. "Now we don't have to go without each other. Not for so long." He looked at her the way all lovers look when they are remembering some of what they've had from each other.

"I think I might like that part," she said. "Although I've been doing quite well with your random hits, with your intermittent affection. I must store it up somewhere. Sort of like a camel."

"You are not saying you want me here," he said. He swivelled his chair. Her face in coffee-sipping profile gave not a hint of damaged, reconfigured bone. "I've been listening closely and I haven't heard it."

"No," she said. She took a minute. Murray had gathered up his nerve coming here and now looked like the time for her to gather hers. "If you're a free agent you could adopt Maggie," she said. "I'd like that very much. And no one would object. They might think it was just an exceptionally decent thing for you to do."

Murray had not considered adoption because it had never been feasible but hearing the word, he thought he would like to adopt Maggie right now. Today. They could call Patrick at his office to get the legal work started. They could tell Maggie when she came in the door from school. Then he thought again. If this was what Daphne wanted, it had to be worth something. "That would be unusual," he said. "Given that her mother won't have me."

"Oh, I'll have you," she said. "But I don't see how we can turn ourselves into some kind of normal married family. It would be a shock to Maggie, and to me. And to you. And at the end of the day," she said, "it might be true that I love best, that I'm best loved, from a slight distance. It might be true for you as well. Have you given any thought to that? Your own affection for distance?"

"If you let me slip away again this time, I don't know...." He drained his coffee, turned the cup upside down on the saucer. "When I was a kid I hated being alone. The feeling doesn't leave you."

"I've always thought you were alone because you preferred it that way," she said. "Because you judged the rest of us and found us wanting. I thought you did it because you were smarter than we were. That's why your circus was so great for the rest of us, because it allowed us to think that maybe we were smart too, like you."

"I was just a clumsy, scared little boy," he said. "Smarter than nobody. Of all those ragged kids, you were the only one who made any effort, the only one who sat down beside me once in a while, on the Town Hall steps or up in the balcony at the arena. You don't likely even remember making the trip."

"No," she said. "Did I?" She tried to remember but couldn't. It was a long time ago, it would have been long before he had established himself in her, what? Heart? "But you're not clumsy now," she said. "You're not that boy now." She had never before heard him go backwards in time and this softness in him, this remembering was not something she wanted to embrace. Because what did it matter, their childhood? "You've got more than what it takes now, my friend. I look at Maggie, how bright she is, and I think, That's her father in her. She's intelligent like her father. Like your dad and your mother. Your mother was an accomplished woman. That's so clear from this vantage point."

"Maybe you should allow Maggie the chance to see who she's smart like." This was as rough as he was prepared to get. There wasn't going to be anything after this. "It must be a bit strange for her. At school, for instance."

"She is a cherished child," she said. "You have seen the evidence. Regardless, who doesn't have some place to go to find grief? If this does turn out to be a grief for her, which I really, really doubt, given the fact that she is so beloved, at every turn." She waited for him to say something, to argue his position. But he wasn't going to argue. "I was secure and safe and extremely legitimate and my mother still died on me," she said. "My mother still moved down to the living room and died."

"Marry me," he said.

"Adopt Maggie," she said.

"I'll adopt her," he said, "the minute after you say you'll marry me."

She covered her jaw. So much talk. Too damned much. But now that it was started, there didn't seem to be any reason to stop before something at least had been achieved. "If you won't adopt her, then give her a brother," she said. "Or a sister."

"Jesus," Murray said. "What I want is not abnormal." He dropped his head to look down through his knees at the floor. "I'm crazy in love with her."

"And she knows that," Daphne said. "She is rock solid sure of you. You can believe what I'm saying here."

"When I finally got away from home," he said, "I promised myself I would never expect to influence a child. I would never try to turn a child into just some renewed version of myself."

"You're talking about your parents," she said. "Religion."

"They just assumed I'd be content to believe what they believed," he said. "That there was no need for me to work through my own life. They thought they'd done the work for me, took it as their right to do that work. As in, this is your name, this is your town, your country, these are the rules you'll live by and, oh, by the way, here is your faith, here is your God. And no questions, please. No asking where did this nonsense come from and why is it called sacred."

"You survived them," she said.

"Just," he said. "And now I'm realizing that what I really want is to have an influence on Maggie. I want to help her shape her life. This is extremely important to me. And of course I am sitting here assuming, I am convinced my influence would not be presumptuous or simple-minded or absolute. As did they, no doubt."

"You can help her shape her life," Daphne said. "You've already helped her. And you can always, always see her. At a moment's notice. When she's old enough, you can take her with you sometimes, wherever, in to Toronto, down to the States, to Europe later when she can handle it. That day will come soon enough and she'll love it. All I'm asking now is that you give her someone to grow up with."

"Why have you never connected with someone else?" he asked. "Made a family for her that way? There must have been guys...."

"What the hell is wrong with you?" she asked. "How could you think that such a thing would be possible for me?" She was looking out her window at the distant muddy Thames. "It's you."

"It's me what?" he said.

"All right," she said. "Okay."

She had never said it. He believed she would never say it.

"We've got an hour before she gets home," she said.

He stood and pulled her up out of her chair. "Maybe I should just figure out a way to make you very lonely," he said. "Maybe I should make you sit and wait for what you think you want. Waiting can unsettle a person, you know. It can make a person ready to agree to anything. In desperation. Pathetic desperation. You should give it a try."

"I don't think either one of us is going to be lonely," she said. "I think we're going to be lucky. Same as always."

"Lucky?" he said. He had not once associated this word with this woman. He reached to lay his fingers on the skin of her exposed throat, which was always warmer than he expected it to be. Then he quickly had her naked and she began to work on him, uncovering his narrow, fuzzy chest, unbuckling his belt to expose the sand dunes of his belly, which she would recognize blind.

"Lucky," she said. "Think about it."

He was watching her hands. "Are you saying this should happen now?"

"Probably," she said. "It's that time, or close. I feel quite fertile and you certainly appear to be."

"What about your job?" he asked. "You just got back."

"I wasn't planning this," she said. "I didn't see how I would get the nerve to put it to you. I wouldn't have asked if you hadn't decided you were finished with Charlotte or, I guess more accurately, if Charlotte had not decided she has had enough of you. But now it seems, well, not unreasonable."

"Only if you can tell me why it has to be me," he said.

She looked out at the muddy Thames. "You can likely manipulate me enough to make me say what you want to hear," she said, lifting her head, lifting her hand to touch his mouth. "I think I can feel the words just on the tip of my tongue."

She turned to lead him to the quiet of her bed. They had from the beginning got into the habit of quiet, perhaps because twice it had been required, perhaps for other, better reasons. On the way to the bed she was deciding that this time she would tell him what he wanted to hear. It was an easy word, she knew that now, having Maggie and wanting another, and it looked to be true.

"You are one crude woman," he said, following her close enough to touch her again, to run a lonely finger down the deep furrow of her back, which made her go weak every time he did it, made her quiver, as if she had never before in her life been touched there, not like that.

THERE were conversations about Daphne's second pregnancy, full-blown conversations whose fitful purpose, whose work, was to find an acceptably humane context for unexpected or unacceptable behaviour. Bill and Margaret talked, Paul and Andy talked. The first time almost everyone had thought, well, anyone can make a mistake. And they had been more than willing, almost immediately eager, to fall in behind Daphne, to help her make it as right as it could be made for Maggie.

Maggie was beloved, there was no other word for it, and she had emerged a confident child. She was not particularly precocious, she did not constantly nag at the outskirts of adult life as beloved children sometimes do. She was just a relaxed little girl, easy inside her own skin.

Patrick knew again of course. He simply deepened his resolve, disciplined himself to speak carefully. Mary, almost ready to accept that she wouldn't ever learn what was going on with Daphne, tried to undergo a change of heart.

Paul and Andy, who were wanting to rebuild some kind of social life now that they no longer needed a sitter, now that Meg had moved into the group home, had come in to London for an evening of drinks in the screened porch. After Patrick and Paul had each asked about the other's work and exhausted their ball talk, recent catches and hits and errors, questionable trades and undeserved salaries, Mary started to tell Andy about the strawberries she'd got her hands on, how small they were, how sweet, and at nine-thirty the women decided out of the blue to make up some freezer jam.

Patrick had been refusing to discuss Daphne's situation, so Mary hadn't had a chance to speak her thoughts out loud, and she needed to. But standing next to Andy at the kitchen counter, hulling berries while Andy mashed, listening to Andy quietly sing, as she always did when she was happy, she was coming up empty. Her thoughts wouldn't get themselves organized and they didn't even seem to be actual thoughts but just clumps of words banging around in her head, bouncing off the side walls, having themselves a bit of fun. She heard her own rational voice start several sentences and leave them hanging, unfinished, and she saw Andy quietly waiting as she sang, knowing better than to push it. Oh, Andy was smart. Finally, tired to the bone of the sound of her own banging, bouncing thoughts, of her own noisy half-finished sentences, she dropped her paring knife down on the edge of the sink and said, "Oh, hell. At the end of the day, what's it matter."

In all the time Andy had known her, this was the first and only thing Mary had ever said that impressed her. "That's pretty much what I think too," she said. Pushing down hard on the berries, adding the cups of sugar, Andy told herself that from this night of jam making she and Mary might finally be able to rely on each other for a bit of womanly comfort, for an occasional bout of womanly fun. Friend, she thought, maybe.

Mary had never been a quiet talker. Sitting in the porch drinking their beer, the men had heard her change of heart. Looking back through the dining room into the kitchen, watching these women make up the jam he would eat all winter, Paul said his problem was that while he wished things with Daphne could be otherwise, they apparently couldn't. So there it was. He said if there was going to be hell to pay, he'd pay his share. He smiled, saying this.

Patrick would have described his brother's smile as one part strength to two parts oblivion. But he said nothing. Sometimes, like now, he caught himself believing that Paul was not much more than a belligerent innocent, that he simply preferred the luxury of being in the dark and would fight very hard to stay there. Once in a while people like Paul paid an extremely high price but more often, more usually, they were spared, excused from the full cost of realizing what was actually going on in the world.

Paul was watching Patrick watch a squirrel balance on the crest of the garage roof. He recognized the concentrated attention, the temporary silence, the threat you couldn't quite hear. He knew his brother's anger as well as he knew his own. "Jesus," he said. "You could lighten up a bit."

Almost immediately after Patrick said, "Could I? Is that your considered opinion?" Mary was beside him with a spoonful of strawberry jam.

"Taste this," she said. "Tell me if it needs more sugar."

And then Andy came to lean against the garden doors that opened to the porch. She, too, had heard the edge in Patrick's voice. "Whatever's going on here," she said, "it has to be fixed. Now." She moved to sit at the foot of Patrick's chaise, facing Paul. "I will not allow another drop of trouble in my life. Not another God damned drop." She turned to look at Patrick. "Can I make myself any clearer?" she asked. "Because I'm ready to try."

Patrick had nothing to say to the severity in Andy's eyes. He nodded once and then he took the spoon of jam into his mouth to declare it sweet enough for him. Paul got up and followed Mary to the buffet to get the cards out for a rubber of bridge.

Sally found it very tough sledding this second time. At twenty-one and having just about completed her first biology degree, she was more than sometimes fiercely judgemental about even the smallest transgressions, so her attitude about Daphne was not a surprise to anyone. But the word she slung around this time was *humiliation*, which did seem a bit strong, even for her. On a Sunday evening over one of Margaret's roast chickens, in Daphne's and Maggie's absence, she tried to share her theories with the others. She said it was clear to her that Daphne's pregnancy was either an act of aggression or an indication of a lack of caring on both sides, theirs and Daphne's too. She said she could not understand why this couldn't be faced head-on. "It's our business," she said. "It's obviously our business." Patrick was the only one who watched her as she lectured them. The others looked at Margaret's new plaid wallpaper, or out the window above the sink.

When she tried to provoke them into joining her discussion, asking, "What kind of family are we?" they did begin to look around the table at each other. But no one could come up with a satisfactory or useful answer.

"Can't tell you," Paul said. "Not on the spot like that." His face was deadly serious with concentration, as if this were a quantum physics problem that might be solved had any of them been anything other than mere idiots. The rest of them laughed but Sally didn't. She judged their refusal to join her, to engage, to be evidence of a shared shame that had left them understandably inarticulate, and forced them to retreat, as usual, to the false comfort of a limp joke.

That night, tucked into Bill in their bed, Margaret said, "I suspect there was quite of bit of ridicule when Daphne was a girl, when she was out of Sylvia's sight, away from her protection. Kids do god-awful things to each other," she said. "It isn't any myth." She pulled away a bit to look at his craggy face, which had too quickly aged there on that pillow, year by year, as had her own beside it. "Ridicule has a way of sticking to the ribs." She reached up to rub his shoulder. "Maybe Daphne just lost her chance to believe in her own worth."

Bill shifted his shoulder slightly, like a tamed animal moving its body under an affectionate, trustworthy hand. "Sylvia and I both watched for that kind of thing," he said. "It seemed to us that she regained her confidence not too long after she fell. She appeared to be more or less her same old self. From what we could tell anyway."

"What I mean is," Margaret said, rubbing him harder, "maybe she lost her chance at truly believing. There is perhaps a significant difference."

"She's made her bed," Bill said.

"I don't suppose it's ever a good idea to make assumptions," she said, lifting her hand from his shoulder. "I'm going to have something to say to Sally about this, and if Patrick doesn't climb down soon, I'm going to have something fairly straightforward to say to him as well." She flipped her pillow, to get the cool side up. "He might be surprised to find out that I can win an argument, but we know I can, don't we?"

"She has made her bed," Bill said, turning away from her, to sleep.

If any of them could have asked her, Daphne might have tried to say that it wasn't the deformity of her jaw. It was hardly her jaw at all. There certainly had been some cruelty, sometimes more than she'd thought she would be able to withstand, but in her experience kids with a physical oddness were not mocked so much if they'd had an accident, as she had. And she'd had herself a famous accident. From what she'd seen, from what she knew, you had to be born with something wrong to get the worst of it.

She might have tried to tell them that she didn't even remember much about what happened in the time after she landed on the mattress: the bleeding, the pain, the painkillers, the trips into Toronto to have her jaw reconstructed, the wires, the clamps, the months she was not allowed to chew, or able to speak clearly, to make herself understood. And it wasn't the actual fall she remembered either.

It was the time between, between the hard-swinging, show-off happiness under the Christmas lights and the dropping straight down through the cold air. It was that everlasting split second when there was nothing she could do to save herself.

1986

PAUL and Andy had been married for twenty-six years. Sometimes Paul found this hard to believe. When they started out together at nineteen they'd had lots of energy, lots of momentum, and then, running the farm and their lives, they'd slowed themselves down. They'd got into the habit of talking things over, planning things out, and they were conservative with money, deliberate. No one had told them that they should live this way, in sync and carefully. It was a kind of gut instinct that came naturally to them, from their careful natures, from their natural affection for each other.

Besides the farm, for almost fifteen years they had been operating the feed mill in town, hiring extra help when it was needed to keep things moving. Now Neil was almost old enough to take over. He appeared to be a mature twenty-five and it looked like he might be able to handle it.

Right after Murray's parents died he had come out to offer them the mill for a lot less than he should have got for it and the steady income from that had paid off both the loan and most of the mortgage on Andy's parents' farm, which was now their farm because Andy's mother had sold it to them and moved into a bungalow in town out near the golf course. Over the last ten years there had been enough extra money to modernize the old farmhouse, to put on a new roof and insulate the draughty walls, to replace the furnace, and then to build a fourteen-by-thirty-foot addition with an efficient, sunny kitchen that Andy had designed herself and a breakfast nook and a downstairs bathroom with a shower. And recently there had been enough money for the seventeen-foot Bowrider that Paul docked at Grand Bend.

With a dedication that was a surprise even to himself, after the crop was off and between Oldtimers' hockey games, Paul had begun to look into his ancestry. It wasn't a deadly serious hobby but he was interested enough to make a couple of trips to the county library, to talk to the people there and let them help him with his searches. He had got his start from Grandma Ferguson, who was not just old now but elderly, frail, although she was still getting along all right in her own place. Near the end of one of what she called Paul's too rare visits, she had opened a closet door on three cardboard boxes of very old pictures, most of them formal in the extreme, all of them black and white. And, while not inheriting any land, wheeler-dealer Grandpa Chambers had been left in recompense a very old, dried-out journal called *Our New Life in Lambton County*, which he handed over to Paul casually, as if he himself had no use for it. The formal faded script described in full the backbreaking demands of daily life without the ease of technology, the awkward, slow-moving courtships, the sicknesses and some of the early deaths, the marriages, the many births, the stillbirths, the visitors, the families that moved on, often to the West, to the promise of sections of very good land. It described the years of stubborn work, the need to clear farmland properly, the threshing crews, the accidents, the food poisoning, the quilting bees, the prized horses and the barns that burned in the night, the roar of the fire and the frenzy of the prized, dying horses that could be heard for miles around. The journal had been written by a woman who would have been Paul's distant, many-times-removed aunt, and the assumptions she made, the attention she paid, could not have been mistaken for anything but a woman's, although she had tried, she had taken some trouble to describe the life completely, as a whole.

Paul didn't talk much about his little project and no one pushed him, not even Grandma Ferguson. He guessed they were waiting for some finished product they could hold in their hands, and dispute.

Even after twenty-six years of marriage, Andy was still very small and this pleased Paul because it made her body so available to him. And she was still outgoing, easily friendly with people. She was tired of course. She had been tired since the summer Meg was born. Neil and Krissy had always been good with Meg and still were, but they had a perfect right to get on with their own lives.

With a bit of help from Paul and Andy, Neil and his wife Carol had bought a house in town down near the arena, which Carol called the big old dilapidated monster but lived in quite happily, talking non-stop to her toddlers as she painted all the rooms, commandeered a crew to jack up the porch and got the yard in shape. Krissy was in Sarnia working as a dental assistant, making pretty good money as far as Paul could tell. Although there were guys around now and then, she hadn't yet found anyone permanent. Paul believed privately that Krissy might be a bit headstrong, independent, perhaps to her own detriment. Most of her friends were the same. Once he had heard a bunch of them, all of them flashy, long-legged, good-looking girls, sitting around on the front step talking about not getting married until they were at least thirty, not giving up their freedom one split second before they absolutely had to. Privately he hoped that Krissy would settle soon, that she would find someone good enough to make her want to break away from these friends and get a young start, a head start, as he and Andy had. Independent or not, he didn't like to think about her alone. It made no sense to him.

Usually he left this kind of thing to Andy. She would come up with a way to describe Krissy's situation, a way to make it sound right, like it was nothing to worry about. Once in a while he wondered if he and Neil and Krissy didn't just dance to Andy's tune but then he would pull back from that line of thought. There were worse things than listening to a smart woman.

Meg, their youngest, was twenty-three. She was living at the group home in London now. Like Neil, like Paul himself, she was extremely tall, but where Paul and Neil were lanky, Meg was bulk. She'd got really big when she hit puberty, and although Andy had trimmed her down with more vegetables and less meat, had stopped baking altogether, since she'd left them she had filled out again. She was heavier and stronger by far than her brother or her father.

Given her circumstances, Meg got along well enough. She could talk with people if she felt like it, if she decided she liked them, and when she was home to visit she could work with Paul in the barn. There was no question of her going out into the fields because today the fields meant massive machinery, the fields were about as close to industrial as you could get.

They had held Meg at home as long as they could, the teachers at the school in town doing their best to keep her occupied with some bit of busywork at the back of the room while the other kids progressed. The parents of her classmates, many of whom Paul and Andy knew or had known one way or the other, were ready to understand Meg's limitations, her frustration, they were ready to understand almost anything theoretically, but when the fights started, when their sons and sometimes their daughters started to come home with broken glasses and torn clothes and bloodied noses, they'd had to complain. And who could blame them? Certainly not Paul and Andy.

They had got the chance to put Meg in a group home in London when she was thirteen. Their names had been submitted by their family doctor, the fourth young guy from somewhere else who had taken over what everyone still called Cooper's practice, which meant they were contacted, sent information. They had decided to try the home, at least for a while, and it had worked out. A group of people from London with problems of their own had got the home under way, got their hands on a good chunk of government money to get it up and running. It was in an older, ordinary residential neighbourhood and from the outside it looked like just a really big brick house. It looked like the kind of ridiculously oversized new-money house that was going up regularly in the suburbs.

Meg had liked it there at first, or said she did. They had a young staff to run the place, to teach the kids things, normalization, it was called, how to go shopping for groceries, how to go to the dentist, how to have your parents come for lunch on Saturdays. Their meds were strictly supervised and they were often taken out on excursions in a van donated by the Kinsmen, which was fine except for the big sign on the van advertising exactly who was inside it.

Every morning through the week all ten residents, six young men and four young women, Paul wasn't supposed to call them kids, were packed into the van and delivered to a sheltered workshop where they sat at long tables with a hundred other similar souls to do contract piecework for 3M or some small local company. They were paid, the point being that their work was worth something, but not much, a token really. Most of the money from the contracts went back into the place itself because there was a large staff. A lot of individual attention had to be available to each worker.

Paul and Andy were allowed to visit while Meg worked and from the start they had wanted to make these visits. People were stupid and cruel, all the time, people who should know better, adults as often as kids. You got to recognize that, to watch for it, if you had a daughter like Meg.

For the first few years a former army man had managed the workshop but now a Mrs. Bradley was very much in charge. She was a British woman in very high heels with orangish hair that she puffed up and sprayed way too thoroughly every morning, who was nevertheless polite and forthright in her comments to Paul and Andy. She said Meg was aggressive, yes, but they often saw that in their clientele and she could be distracted, she could be calmed, and when she was calm she was a very good worker. And the others were learning to keep their distance and never to tease Meg. In fact there was one boy, a Down's syndrome boy, who had taken a shine to her, who followed her around like a puppy, who liked to sit beside her at breaks and when they ate their lunch. Mrs. Bradley told Paul and Andy that Meg was extremely patient with this boy, very understanding. She said Meg had an enormous heart.

Paul and Andy visited the group home too. During their first visit they were led upstairs to see Meg's room, which she shared with the three other girls. It was large enough and bright enough, but after they'd had a cup of tea downstairs in the oversized, beautifully furnished living room, as soon as they were in the truck on the way home, Andy erupted into a small rage, turning on Paul to ask, Lord, didn't he notice? She said the room was just horrible, that it needed a good cleaning, a good airing, that it smelled of old food and sweat and stale underwear. She said she would give anything to be let loose for an afternoon in that bedroom.

On their next Saturday visit, sitting on Meg's bed, trying not to look perturbed, Andy asked Richard, the supervisor who was on duty that day, why didn't he either stand over them and make them do it or get someone in to do it for them? She told him she could see no reason for them to live like that. But Richard just looked around the room and shrugged his shoulders. The girls were expected to do their own wash and to keep their room clean. That was the rule. They were pretty slack, sure, but according to Richard the idea was that they themselves would get sick of the mess and the smell, he believed they were capable of getting sick of it, and then they'd clean it up. And anyway, he didn't think it was particularly bad. "Maybe you should see my bedroom," he said.

They didn't go in quite so often after that visit, maybe once a month, once every six weeks. At home, hoping to help Andy get used to things as they were now, Paul told her that Meg was absolutely safe and cared for and at least slightly happy some of the time and that this was likely as good as it was going to get. "You don't have to think about her so often," he told her. "She can make a life for herself there. And better there than here with us. There is nothing for her here." He didn't know if he believed any of this to be true, but it was important to him that Andy believed it.

Meg came home every Christmas and for a couple a weeks in the summer, and any time Krissy or Neil and Carol and the kids were going to be around for a few days someone drove in to get her. Later on she would fall to them. Everyone knew this.

WHEN Meg hitchhiked home the first time, on a Tuesday afternoon in the late fall of 1985, Paul and Andy had just got back from Bill and Margaret's and were sitting in the breakfast nook having a coffee together, talking about their mutual suspicion that something was up with Patrick and Mary, that they were in trouble, and that as usual Margaret knew more than she was willing to say. Margaret *had* been willing to say that Sarah, who would no longer answer to Sally, had called the night before from Vancouver to tell them that she and Rob had decided to get pregnant.

Sarah and Rob had been out in Vancouver nearly four years. Rob was an English software engineer who had come over from London just before they met to take a big job with one company and then, six months after they were married, unsatisfied, he'd moved to another company and they had been transferred West. After Margaret had told Paul and Andy her bit of news, that it looked as if she was finally going to be a grandmother in her own right, she confessed that she had been almost ready to accept that there wouldn't be any babies because Rob didn't appear to be big on family, his own or anyone else's. And then she said it was likely just the waiting that had thrown her off, the idea that a woman could bide her time and then decide to do it when she felt ready. "A modern convenience," she'd called it.

Paul saw Meg first because he was facing the window and then they watched together as she ran up the long laneway toward the house, a large woman running like a child, her strides clumsy, her arms wild, clouds of cold panting breath bursting from her mouth as she ran. Her new jacket was wide open to the wind, her Blue Jays hat pushed firmly down on her head.

She had been dropped off at the end of the lane by a grey Chrysler, they could see the car waiting out there for her safe welcome. She turned back several times to wave at the driver, a lone male, who returned her wave and honked the horn several times.

Andy went to the door and opened it, letting in the cold air, and when Meg saw them she stopped running and began to walk in long strides across the frozen grass. She stopped once to bend over to catch her breath, lifted her head to look up at them, grinned her widest grin. Paul waved at the driver of the grey Chrysler, signalling that it was all right, he could carry on.

Slumped down on the step, Meg said to Andy, "I came home. I got rides home." She was so proud of herself.

"Who was that man?" Andy asked. "Did he tell you his name?"

"Mr. Brown," Meg said. "That was Mr. Brown from Sarnia."

Andy hesitated but not for long. "He didn't touch you or say anything creepy, did he?"

Meg had been taught that she was vulnerable to strangers, to unkindness and worse, that she had to understand this and work to protect herself from it. "Nobody touches me unless I say so," she said. She made a tight fist in front of her face and shook it hard. She knew what her fist could do because when she was nine and very annoyed with Neil one morning, getting ready for school, she'd knocked him out cold in the back hall.

They took her in and Andy got started calming her while Paul dialled the phone. Meg pulled her cat's cradle out of her jacket pocket and began to work it.

Richard was the head supervisor at the home now and he said he had been calling them and that he'd been just about ready to call again. He said Meg hadn't got in the van after work, that there was a new driver who wasn't used to everyone yet. He said Meg must have been hiding because no one noticed that she wasn't around, and by the time he'd got hold of Mrs. Bradley, who was home herself by then and who had no idea that Meg hadn't got on the bus with the others, they knew they had lost her. He said nothing like this had ever happened before and that he was so sorry. And was Meg all right?

Paul didn't see any point to anger. "I think she had herself a fine time getting home," he said. "I'll bring her back in the morning."

Richard said that would be appreciated. And then he asked could Andy come along too because he had been planning to call them anyway to come in for a talk, and maybe this would be as good a time as any.

Paul said fine and hung up. He assumed it would be something about aggression again, maybe shoving some of the other people around, yelling, maybe throwing another wrench through a window. Likely it was time for a trip to the doctor to ask one more time about upping Meg's downers.

Andy cooked sloppy joes and apple crisp and after supper Meg pushed back her chair and announced that she wanted to go into town to see Grandma and Grandpa. Everything about her, the way she sat forward in her chair, the way she held her chin up and out, told them, If you won't take me, I'll get there on my own, I know how to do it now. They took the truck. Meg sat in the middle between them and played with the radio, played air guitar when she found a station she liked.

Sitting at her kitchen table doing a crossword, Margaret heard the truck and, knowing the sound, walked to the sink to fill the kettle.

Just before she looked out the window she thought, This is odd, they just left here three hours ago, and then she looked. Bill was in the living room watching television and she called loudly to him, "Bill, come out here. Something's wrong. Meg's home."

When she was born, that summer they were out at Dunworkin, none of them had any way to know precisely what Meg's future might hold, but Bill had a sense of it, from the war, he told himself, because he had seen things you couldn't imagine. Because he'd had to accept things no one should have to accept and say nothing.

When Meg was four or five and just beginning to hide under the combine, to run deep into the rows of corn and deliberately try to hurt the barn cats that followed her, to bust nearly everything she touched, to eat so fast she choked herself, Paul and Andy tried to discipline her with a sharp tone of voice or a quick slap on the hand or on her little squirming rear end. But Bill had intervened. It was the first and only time he had ever done such a thing with any of his kids. He told Paul he was likely going to have to find another way. "We'll help you," he said. "Margaret and I will be here to help you. And your brother and sisters will help you." The drugs had started then. The doctor experimented until he found something strong enough to keep Meg steady but not dopey and for quite a while the drugs had done the trick.

Watching Paul and Andy and Meg approach the back door now, Bill asked himself one more time what God could possibly mean with all this bullshit. He knew there was no God to wonder about, had known this since the North Atlantic, since Sylvia, but that didn't change things. He still caught himself asking. And not less often as he got older, but more often. He thought maybe it was a kind of weakness, like his legs going, or the hair all over his body turning white.

Opening the door he opened his arms to his granddaughter, knowing his own hug would be overpowered, braced for the strength of her arms. "Meg o' my heart," he said. "What the hell are you doing home?" He grinned and stood back to look up at her. "Have you quit your job or did you get yourself fired?"

Meg laughed down at her grandfather and stomped her feet on

her grandmother's doormat. "I got rides home. Three of them. All the way."

As they took off their coats, Margaret made the pot of tea and got a Pepsi out of the fridge for Meg, which she poured into one of the indestructible glass mugs they still had from 1972, the year the town celebrated its centennial. She set Meg's drink on the table, an invitation for her to sit down.

Leaning forward over his tea, Paul said to Bill, "She hitchhiked. They didn't know she was gone until she was halfway home."

Margaret lifted Meg's ball hat from her head and took it onto her own lap. "You'll go back in the morning, sweetheart," she said, meaning to say, Listen to Grandma, this is acceptable to us only as a one-time-only whim, a lark. "They need you at that home," she said. "I could see that. You were helping Richard paint the back hall when your grandfather and I dropped in to see you in the summer. You could hardly take the time to visit. Do you remember?"

Meg looked at them, each of them, one at a time, turning not just her eyes but her whole head. "Richard always makes me and Matthew do the hard stuff for him, the shit work. Matthew says he pisses us off." Matthew was Meg's friend at the home.

"And Richard is lucky to have you," Bill said. "He told me that. He told me you did a good job of whatever you put your hand to."

This was a lie but Bill thought, So arrest me. Tonight was going to be one more of those nights they'd just have to get through. Maybe he would go in tomorrow with Paul and they could talk together to this Richard, find out just what jobs needed doing, what kind of jobs they were, find out who was on a salary at that home and who wasn't, who was maybe picking up a bit of extra cash by saying he'd paint the back hall for instance. Although he did believe work was good for Meg. About the only thing that was.

"So everybody wants me to stay there," Meg said.

"Oh, no question in my mind at all," Margaret said, cheerfully. "You can do all kinds of things in the city that you can't do on the farm. And with people your own age."

Meg didn't say yes, she hardly ever said yes, but she didn't say no so they left it there. Margaret poured more tea for herself and Andy.

Bill got out the rye and the Coke and two more of the centennial mugs because Meg liked everyone to use them. Meg put on her hat and her jacket and went out into the backyard to walk down to the creek, which was running slow under the bare branches of the willows, and perfectly safe. Bill had often taken her back to the creek when she was small, to show her the wonders, the surprises, and to teach her how to keep herself safe near water.

Bill poured Paul his drink, asking, "What's she been up to?"

"I have no idea," Paul said. "Likely more of the same. They want us both to come in tomorrow for a talk."

"They want us both?" Andy asked. "You didn't tell me that." She laid her head down on the table. "They'll want her on stronger drugs," she said. "She's going to be so souped up she won't even know her own name."

Margaret stroked Andy's hair, combed through the grey-blonde streaks with her fingers. "Such a time," she said. "Such a time."

Sitting, waiting for Andy to lift her head, Paul was telling himself to smile, to make the effort. Just a quick we-can-get-through-this kind of smile. Waiting, he realized that they likely smiled a lot less for each other now than they did for other people, people they didn't even like much, and why should that be?

Meg rode back in the truck bed on the way home. When she was small she rode there with her old dog Stanley as often as they'd let her, both of them happy, full of themselves, barking for the fun of it.

Before she went up to bed Margaret called Patrick and Murray and Daphne and Sarah, to tell them. She didn't expect them to rush home, she didn't expect them to do anything. Paul and Andy could handle this on their own. But she believed the others should be told.

She had long ago taken it on herself to make sure these kids stayed aware of each other. And she shared the good news as quickly as the bad, never exaggerated, never betrayed a confidence, not even to their father.

In the morning, Paul and Andy took Meg back into London, first to the group home to change her clothes and then across town to the workshop. After they'd delivered her into the safe hands of Mrs. Bradley, who chastised Meg, told her that her work was waiting and that she would have to move fast to get caught up because they had a new contract coming in that afternoon, they drove back over to the home to talk to Richard.

It wasn't aggression this time, it was sex. When Richard said the word they both knew they had been waiting to hear it, prepared to hear it, for a long time. When she'd hit puberty they had tried to anticipate her behaviour, they had talked with each other and with the doctor about the difficulty the most common urges would cause her. Since then they'd hoped her apparent disinterest was either the result of the mix of drugs she'd been on almost all her life, or hormonal, because why shouldn't her unhappy hormones be screwed up too? But it seemed they had just been lucky. And now it seemed they weren't.

The boy in question was one of the other residents at the group home. It was her friend Matthew. Richard said that when he caught them in the basement, just getting started, Meg spoke right up, told him that Matthew loved her and that she loved him. She'd looked to Matthew to back her up but he had gathered his shirt in his hands, was hiding his face in it, crying, embarrassed to be naked in front of Richard. Finally, as if to explain everything, Meg said, "It's my fault, Richard. It's my fault because I like it so much."

Richard told Paul and Andy that he had seen no evidence of birth control. Meg's city doctor hadn't put her on the pill because he would have been the one handing them out to her every morning and of course she hadn't been sterilized or anything and he was certainly not recommending that. He said he had no reason to believe that Matthew could be trusted with condoms. And what did they think?

Of course Matthew's parents had to be told. It was easy enough to agree to that.

In the end, both Meg and Matthew were allowed to stay. They were told they could be friends, that everyone understood how much they needed each other's friendship, which was a good thing, a normal thing, but they shouldn't go down to the basement any more, not alone. The deal was that they would both be given something to quiet their needs and Meg would take the pill, to be doubly sure.

At home, the doctor told Paul and Andy that he was sorry he

hadn't anticipated or recognized Meg's enthusiasm. He said the new drug would work with Meg's other drugs to further blunt her aggression, which could only be a good thing for her, and that it would not necessarily kill her capacity for ordinary affection.

Meg and Matthew both claimed they understood. They were supposed to be friends. Just friends. They began to volunteer to do the supper dishes and a little later they started to do their wash together again in the basement, mixing whites with whites and darks with darks, being sure to talk a lot and really loudly because Richard or someone would be standing up there listening. They volunteered to rake the twigs and the dead grass off the lawn in the spring and as a reward they were allowed to go downtown on their own to see a movie starring Jack Nicholson, who was Meg's favourite actor because he was both handsome and out of his mind. At the workshop they were inseparable, most of the time allowing the Down's syndrome boy who'd taken a shine to Meg to hang around with them, taking him along if they were going to the lunch-room or outside on a break to sit in the sun, to lean against the warm brick wall at the side of the building and neck.

Their public touching was soft and discreet. In Mrs. Bradley's opinion, it was in fact charming. If they engaged in anything more forceful, if they found a way through the haze of pharmaceuticals handed to them in little paper cups each morning, they weren't talking.

For a while after this business, Paul and Andy themselves stopped making love. Andy had always called it that, making love, refusing to use the other words even in the midst of their slippery, lusty acrobatics. When they were just starting out, before they were married, she'd said that was what they did, they crawled into an empty place where no love existed and made it, created it every new time from nothing but themselves.

"What power," she'd say, laughing, grinning up at him from the comfort of a pillow or mounting him, taking his shoulders in her hands for balance.

THE second time Meg hitchhiked home, in early summer, she had Matthew in tow and they went first to Bill and Margaret in town.

This time they were expected, although not by Bill and Margaret.

A young woman wearing cowboy boots had stopped to pick them up from a corner in downtown London. They had got the morning off to do some shopping on their own for clothes when the stores weren't crowded. This was a big deal, a big responsibility that they had earned with mature behaviour and an eager willingness to help Richard with his little jobs. They were supposed to take a city bus out to the workshop at eleven but after Meg told Matthew what they could do and how much fun it would be, they decided they didn't want to get on that bus.

The woman in the cowboy boots dropped them off at the end of Wellington Street where it meets the 401, and when Meg asked with the door hanging open which way they should go now, the woman pointed to the ramp. They walked the long curve down to the highway, staying safely to the side, off the pavement, and before long they were picked up by a trucker who was just coming off the ramp himself.

As soon as they were up and into his cab, the trucker could see what he had on his hands. He asked them if there might be someone looking for them right now, and when Meg politely said no and told him honestly where they lived and where they worked and less honestly that they had the day off and had been invited to visit her grandparents, he didn't necessarily buy in, but he let it be. They seemed smart enough to him. In spite of her size the girl was pretty, she had a perky little face and a great rack. And he thought the kid looked like he could almost take care of himself.

He veered off the 401 onto the 402, telling them about Michigan and Chicago, about his wife and kids in Windsor. He let them play with the radio. After forty-five minutes, when they were coming up to the turn-off for the town they said they were going to, he told them as much as he'd like to he couldn't take the time to make a detour. He dropped them and watched them walk up the ramp to the old two-lane, waited the five minutes it took for someone to stop. The someone was Margaret's long-time friend, Angela Johnston, who was just coming back from Sarnia where she'd had an appointment with a chiropractor. She recognized Meg before she stopped for them because, except for her size, she was just so much like Andrea, her colouring, her mouth especially. She had seen her close up at Margaret's once before an evening of bridge when she'd come in with her dad to pick Bill up for a hockey game down at the arena. In the car, when Meg asked if Angela could take them to the Chambers house, she said she would be pleased to do that. She said she knew Bill and Margaret, they were her grandparents, wasn't that right? She assumed correctly that Meg didn't know her from Eve.

Bill's car wasn't in the driveway so Angela got out and went to the back door with them, which made Meg quite angry, she could tell. But they found Margaret home. She told Margaret what she knew, the 402, the trucker who waited until she picked them up. Then she accepted Margaret's gratitude and left, knowing she would be counted on to keep her mouth shut about this.

Margaret called Andy, who said that they had been expecting the kids there, that they'd got a call from Richard this time, and that they would be right in to get Meg. She said she had better hang up and call Richard back and then she'd better phone Matthew's parents in London, which was another number she didn't have to look up now. Matthew's parents seemed to Andy and Paul to be very fine people. They hadn't overreacted at all the year before when the kids were first discovered and they might have, they would have been forgiven a bit of shouting, a bit of protective rage. Perhaps they, too, were tired. Perhaps they too had long ago given rage its chance and found the returns negligible.

Paul backed the truck out of the drive shed to pick Andy up at the front door of the farmhouse and after she climbed in and was belted up he smiled over at her. "We can do this," he said. "We've done harder things."

Andy didn't say anything. She was remembering when Meg was younger, when she was Meagan, and how easy things had become when they could finally make her obey them just by asking, how she used to grin proudly and say, "I'm going to do what I'm told," accepting it as just another skill she'd learned, an accomplishment.

And she was thinking about the last time Meg had pulled this stunt, the effect it had had on them, the comfort of touch gone, the possibility of its absence unforeseen and astonishing, as if all through these long years the comfort had been not their own creation at all but only a visitor to their bed.

When they were very young, it had been so easy to tell Paul that she loved him, to watch him shine when she used the words. If she'd known then what she knew now, she would have said instead, I trust you, Paul. It's trust. Meaning, these are the naked, sweaty, only times when the world is safe for me. Meaning, it's not love that makes it so fine, so reckless, it's trust that makes our skin shine in a dark bed.

But it was love everyone believed they wanted. Love was supposed to make the world go round. And what a big job that was. How could she ever hope to make trust measure up to love?

They were passing the Fulbright farm, just minutes from the turn-off onto the highway into town, when two things happened. First, although Paul was driving as he always drove, which was just a bit too fast, he saw in his rear-view mirror that they were being tailgated by a red pick-up. Watching in the mirror, he asked, "Whose truck do you suppose that is?"

Andy turned around to look but she didn't recognize the truck either, nor did she know the driver, who was alone in the cab. When the truck came alongside them, taking its time passing, they got a good look at the driver's unknown but uncommonly serious profile, and then they saw something they found even more difficult to believe. An elderly, well-dressed woman with thin white hair was getting a very rough ride back in the truck bed. She seemed to be trying one more time and with great difficulty to sit up straight, but she couldn't get purchase, her arms were not strong enough. Seeing her struggle, Paul laid on the horn. When the driver picked up speed, Paul yelled, "Asshole," and laid on the horn again, pounding it with his fist to make himself understood.

Excited by the blaring of the horn, the Fulbrights' new dog, a black Lab who had been sitting in the shade of the barn watching, waiting for some action, came tearing out onto the road barking up a storm. The dog wasn't exactly a pup but it wasn't old enough or experienced enough to know how to run after a truck and stay clear at the same time, and in an attempt to accommodate the dog's inexperience Paul swerved. Swerving, he braked too hard and lost control of the truck.

Normally, he would not have taken the dog into account at all. He would have kept the truck moving at a steady speed because this was what charging farm dogs expected from you. He'd learned this at fifteen behind the wheel of Bill's 1952 Ford Fairlane and he had never in the thirty years since run over a dog.

The truck jumped the ditch and came to rest on its side, stopped there by a substantial old maple.

A N D Y came to consciousness still belted in. She could hear a woman crying, crying out as if from some distance, and she thought, Oh, that poor woman, and then the sound got louder, closer, and she recognized it as you might recognize a friend approaching down a country lane on a dark night. It was her own voice calling out for Paul.

Opening her eyes she could see, and almost could have touched if she'd thought to move her hands, the solid blunt mass of a tree, ridges of grey bark. She could feel her own weight against the seat belt. And the sharp sting of a hundred small cuts. Shards of glass had pierced her face and her scalp and her arms, she could see the blood trickling across the skin on her bare arms, feel it seeping into her eyes. And she could taste it. A man was climbing up across the hood to get to her, taking his footholds on the bent frame of the windshield, which had shattered and collapsed.

Ed Fulbright got her door pulled open and her seat belt cut but as small as she was he couldn't hold her. She fell down onto Paul's body. She had no way to stop herself. Ed had to ask her to try to turn toward him, to try to give him her hands, and when she was able to do this, to turn and reach out for him, he gave her a smile of encouragement.

As soon as Ed had her laid out on the side of the road, his wife was there carrying a blanket and sheets in one arm and a shotgun in the other hand. Amy Fulbright nodded toward the barn, where the dog was curled up and panting hard, refusing to look at them, and handed Ed the gun. Then she knelt down beside Andy in the gravel and covered her with the blanket. She began to rip some of the sheet into strips, starting the rips with her teeth, and as she pulled the shards of glass from Andy's face, she brought the cloth to the cuts to soak up the streaming blood. Pressing very gently, smoothing Andy's hair, she said, "I've called the ambulance. They'll be here soon. But I think you're all right."

Andy didn't want this woman's care, this soothing, didn't want the hands trailing over her arms and her face and her neck. She wanted an answer to the question, the only question.

Amy Fulbright composed herself and said that Ed didn't think he could or should try to get at Paul. She said that because Ed was afraid to move him she didn't know for sure but likely Paul was just still unconscious, likely he was just more badly hurt. She said, "We'll pray for that," and bowed her head, covered her entire face with her large hand, and began to mumble.

When the gun went off, even though Amy Fulbright was the one who knew it was coming, who had insisted it be done, she jumped nearly out of her skin. Andy didn't flinch. She had gone into shock and she stayed there.

THE police came to the kitchen door, two of them. Meg was there immediately, with Matthew right behind her, but Bill let them in. When the police said what they had to say, Meg dropped to the floor wailing and Matthew backed himself up against the stove, his hands raised in front of his face for protection. Bill turned from them all to sit down at the table, his seventy-four-year-old body collapsing in on itself, becoming instantly and permanently smaller. He sat very still, clasped one shaking hand in the other. His face was calm, his mouth closed. His eyes were wide open and fierce, focused on something that doesn't exist in the real world.

Margaret came into the kitchen knowing nothing, assuming this commotion would be about Meg. When she looked down at Bill sitting at his place at the table, she thought, He's lost his sight, what's the hell's going on, he's gone blind. And then she took in the uniforms in her kitchen and realized the kind of thing it must be. She knew that there was only a certain kind of news that came this way. "You are going to have to tell it to me too," she told them.

The police let themselves out, but even after they were gone, Bill would not let her touch him. He said he was finished with God. He said he understood now that he'd thought he was finished when Sylvia died but all the time since he'd been holding out the possibility, he had left some room in his doubt for doubt itself. He told her it wasn't disbelief he felt this time. Disbelief meant you allowed yourself to hope for something and then found you couldn't believe in it. Climbing the stairs, he called back loudly that God was only a black hopeless hole, God was nothing.

Margaret made all her phone calls. When she was finished she called Angela Johnston to please come back over to stay with Meg and Matthew until Matthew's mother could get there and then to sit with the wailing Meg until Daphne or Patrick arrived from London. She didn't know if Angela could manage this, but there was no one else she wanted to ask. And then she drove alone into the hospital in Sarnia.

Sitting behind the wheel on the four-lane highway, for the first time in all her driving life made uneasy by the semis that one after another gained on her and then thundered slowly, stupidly past, she thought, I don't know how to live the next few days of my life. I do not know how. She sobbed hard around each of these simple words, wrenched finally, now that there was no one to witness the wrenching. It didn't stop after five miles, or ten. It didn't end until she was in the hospital parking lot, where it had to end. She turned off the ignition and took the deepest possible breath. She wiped her face dry with a Kleenex and tidied her hair with her fingers and then she adjusted the rear-view mirror to try a brief smile. The smile was a horror, as false as anything she'd ever seen. But in the horror she was able to anticipate, able to prepare herself, for Andy's larger grief. Her own sorrow would be as nothing. That was the truth of it.

She found Andy in a ward. Her mother was there with her, sitting on a chair close to the bed, stroking the sheet over Andy's shoulders. Margaret found another chair and watched quietly while Andy's mother tended to her, watched her bring the water glass to Andy's mouth. The few nurses hurrying around the hall clearly had little time for anything but the wounds, the dressings and bandages.

They were kind enough and respectfully gentle and they moved quietly but they could only do so much.

When Margaret thought Andy was ready, she told her what she knew, that they had been told that Paul was alive when they got him out of the truck, that he lived for a while in the ambulance. But he hadn't regained consciousness, hadn't spoken. "So we've got that," she said. "The suffering he didn't have to go through."

"The old woman in the truck," Andy said, her words slurred with sedative. "He was so mad. He died angry." They didn't know what she meant and they didn't ask.

Later in the afternoon, when Neil and Carol and Krissy came into the room, Margaret stood up and said she'd best go home.

Patrick and Mary were the first to arrive in town. Right after she'd got the call from Patrick at work, Mary had phoned Stephen at McGill and then gone to the high school to pull the other two, and by the time they got back to the house on Piccadilly, Patrick was there, locked in the upstairs bathroom with the shower running, although when he came out he was still in his suit and bone dry. She'd heard him, his dry screams, when she was walking to the front door with the key in her hand. They were packed in half an hour and on the road. Patrick had not wanted to let her drive. She'd had to take the keys from his fist and lead him around to the passenger door. She'd had to do up his seat belt.

When they got to the house they thanked Angela and sent her home and soon Daphne arrived with Maggie and Jill. Murray and his wife Kate were driving from Toronto, he had told Margaret they should be there around nine or ten that night. Patrick went out to the golf course motel to arrange for rooms.

Margaret had called Sarah in Vancouver and she was trying to get on a flight. Sarah had been planning to come home in a couple of months to show off her baby and Margaret had told her on the phone that maybe she shouldn't come now, not alone, it was such a long flight she should check with her doctor and do what was best, that they would understand if it was better for her to come later, after the baby was safely born. But Sarah had said no, she would be there. She'd get on the first available flight.

After a dazed supper of scrambled eggs and toast, Margaret tucked Meg into Daphne's bed, which was where she liked to be, making her promise to sleep. Someone turned the television on and, one by one, Patrick and Neil drove all the cars uptown to gas them up and run them through the carwash. Just before eleven, Daphne and the girls went out to sleep at Paul and Andy's, to check on things as much as anything because Krissy had decided to stay at the hospital overnight with Andy, sleeping if she had to on one of the plastic couches in the waiting room. The others went out to the golf course motel because there wasn't room for everyone any more and because Rebecca, Patrick and Mary's youngest and only daughter, was afraid of Meg at the best of times.

The next morning Patrick and Neil took Andy's mother into Sarnia to get Andy from the hospital. When Margaret called, the hospital had told her today or tomorrow, depending on what she was going home to, whether there would be any help at home. They hadn't mentioned clothes and Margaret didn't think of clothes until Patrick had backed out of the driveway and was halfway down the street, too late. She had told Patrick and Neil to bring Andy back to her, that her mother should stay too, maybe on the McKellars' rollaway. She was sure of just two things: that Andy's kids would need her help in ways no one could begin to anticipate, and that Andy would be strong enough to give it to them only if she was cared for herself.

Krissy had sat awake all night beside her sedated mother. In the morning, when she sensed the others coming into the room behind her, she stood up and walked straight into Patrick's arms. She told them a nurse had given Andy another shot of something at midnight and that she had finally fallen asleep around two. They had just made her wake up. A breakfast tray sat untouched on the table at the foot of the bed and she was supposed to be getting another sponge bath. Andy was curled on her side, dressed to go home in her bloody clothes, shivering.

Neil half carried his mother from the wheelchair to the car, and making his way through the heavy city traffic, Patrick told them that Margaret wanted Andy there, that Andy's mother was to come too, that he hoped this would be all right.

Murray and Daphne had volunteered to make the airport run. Murray had been able to tell her at the kitchen table how wonderful Maggie and Jill were, because this was something he could say in front of anyone, but as soon as they were in the car and belted up he said it again. "You are doing such a job."

"They are wonderful in themselves," Daphne told him. "It's possible that you and I don't even matter all that much."

They were both in a stupor. Murray took the old highway because he said they had lots of time and this was a chance to get a few minutes away from it. They didn't talk for miles and then Daphne told him that every time she looked down at her hands they were clenched. "My palms are sliced with fingernail marks," she said, examining her opens hands. "These extra little curving moon lines cutting across the normal lines, what are they called?" She did know the names. "The heart line," she said. "The head line. The health line. The life line. The fate line."

Murray reached over to lay his free hand in her lap and she took it, touched her fingers to the warm, soft pad of skin on the back of his hand, lifted them away, waited a hard few seconds and then touched the skin again, over and over again giving herself the pleasure of his existence. Anyone seeing this, she thought, even from a distance, would recognize it as love. Easy love.

But sometimes, most often those times when the bully guilt dislocated her ease, she wondered if the thing she had always been after, and still wanted, even now when she had no earthly use for it, was semen. Only his, but still, only semen. For a long time, from the first time, she had been able to feel her cervix moving in pleasure, the knowledge sent to her every time from just behind, just beyond the sweet delirium, and because she'd wanted an image of this mystery, a miniature image that might be worn in a gold locket, she had imagined a small, hidden, happy muscle yawning open like the mouth of a fish. But recently she'd seen a documentary, a film of a woman in orgasm, the woman on her back in some lab, the minuscule camera and light carefully inserted, this for the sake of science, of knowledge, and she had seen that it was not at all as she'd imagined. The cervix was not like a fish. It dips down into the pool of semen, again and again, like a small, thirsty dove.

They hadn't been together for three years. Two months before he married Kate, Murray had told her, in a rehearsed, controlled phone call, that it had to be over. He'd explained that while he probably could continue on alone, he didn't want to, not any more. He needed someone who was ready to sign on full-time.

A trusting soul, she'd thought, listening. Could this be what you want? What you've found somewhere?

He told her he thought he might have fallen in love. It felt like that.

He had tried something similar once or twice before, when it wasn't true, hoping with his practised lies to shake her loose. But this time it was, true.

As she'd listened to him tell the truth, Daphne had recognized the change immediately. He had given himself away because the other times there had been a trace of bravado, a whiff of threat in his voice, and this time there was only a dull regret, only the quiet retreat of a man who had made up his mind.

"Then I guess we go on," she'd said, saving herself, "slightly altered." She was sitting at her window overlooking the muddy Thames, with Maggie in school and Jill at her knees offering one of her storybooks. "This can't come as a big shock to me. You have been more than generous. All this time you've been generous." She waited for him to speak but he evidently wanted her to say something more. "What about this for a plan," she said. "We go straight to remembering the best of it. Full bolt. No detours." Still he didn't speak. "And of course the girls," she said. "They're yours. No games will be played there."

Murray had not been surprised that her control was absolute, that she didn't even ask who it was he thought he loved. He knew she wouldn't fight for him. She didn't have to fight for him. He didn't push for any kind of guarantee about Maggie and Jill because Daphne did not waver, she did not say things she didn't mean. Her promises were few and far between, but they were kept. And he didn't ask what she would do, who she might find for herself, because if he'd asked, she would have said only that he was not to worry, she would be all right. And so, as easily as that, it was done. Twenty years, done.

When they turned onto the airport road, she was holding his large hand completely in her own two smaller hands. "I like Kate a lot," she said. "Everyone seems to." She was quiet again for a minute, thinking of a way to convince him. "I've been trying to figure out why whenever she sits down at the table, the kids come alive for her, every one of them. I've decided it's because she doesn't make them nervous. She makes them the opposite of nervous."

"I've named the girls in my will," Murray said.

"Your will?" she asked. "Is something wrong?" She was staring at his hand in her lap, as if its strength had deceived her. "You're not sick?"

"No," he said. "I'm fine. It's just a normal update."

She lifted his hand to her mouth, briefly rested her lips on his warm skin. "Does Kate know about this will thing?"

"Yes," he said. "I told her it was because they have no father and I have no children. It's fine with her. She has quite a bit of money of her own. And a very good pension plan with the university. She's been there for almost twenty years."

"Will you tell them?" she asked.

"We should maybe let it wait," he said. He slowed to make the turn into the airport parking lot. "And I want to sell you the house," he said.

"The house in town?" she asked. "I don't live in town."

"It's been rented out. You could continue to rent it out."

"Even so," she said, "I don't really have the money. I haven't been able to save very much. Sweet-shit-all is how you might describe what I have been able to save."

"The price would be negligible," he said. "A dollar, just to make it a legal sale. Patrick is going to send you the documents for your signature, the deed of land."

"And we tell no one?" she asked.

"We tell no one now," he said.

"All right," she said. She reached into her satchel for her wallet, got out a soft one-dollar bill, and tucked it into his pants pocket. "I love that house," she said. "Maybe I'll retire there. I could grow roses in my dotage and give them to people. Buckets of fresh-cut roses from the odd, old woman who lives alone in that big house with the wraparound porch. Who wears earmuffs and high heels and overalls. Whose nails are too long."

"Or you could live an ordinary life there," he said. "Another option."

When they approached the terminal they could see Sarah and Stephen waiting with their bags at the pick-up curb. Stephen already had his suit on, he had apparently worn it on the plane from Montreal. As she was getting into the car Sarah told them she'd been able to make an earlier connection at Pearson because the flight from Vancouver had got in a bit ahead of schedule, so she and Stephen had waited together in the coffee shop. She said she had called the house from Toronto but the line was busy. Except for her eyes, which were without make-up shadowed and puffy, she looked fit and healthy and strong. She was wearing a dark green maternity jogging suit, the material stretched taut over her high, broad belly. Daphne was a bit surprised at the jogging suit because Sarah had always been a disciplined, slightly flashy dresser. She would not normally have been caught dead in this outfit, not in public.

They put her in the front seat with Murray for the ride home. Stephen rode in the back with Daphne, his head turned toward the passing outskirts of the city, the small industries, the packaging plants, the car dealerships. Sarah didn't break down until they were on the highway, after they had answered some of her questions.

Paul had been fifteen when Sarah was born and four years later he was married and gone out to the farm, but of all of them he had been the one closest to her in age. Before Andy married Paul, before her own kids were born, she had pretty much taken over with Sarah, dressing her up in little sunsuits, taking her out to the lake on her days off to play in the sand with bright plastic pails and serving spoons from the kitchen drawer, colouring with her at the kitchen table, cutting out paper dolls from one of Daphne's old books.

Daphne guessed that Sarah was remembering some of this. She stopped talking to let her remember in peace.

Mary and Kate had gone back over to the house to stay with Meg while the others went in to the airport because Margaret had to get some sleep and Bill was still in very bad shape, it was all he could do to stand up from his bed and get to the bathroom. The two of them switched off, took turns, one of them lying down with Meg up in Daphne's bed while the other answered the kitchen door. Mary didn't recognize many of the men and women who arrived carrying gifts of food but she bluffed it through, claimed to remember meeting them somewhere when it was suggested that she had. The people who stood at the door had the advantage of course.

Kate wasn't expected to recognize anyone because she and Murray had not been married very long. She was understood to be the second wife, a wife who wouldn't know much. But she was not unfamiliar with the gestures, the nature of the gestures, the men slowly shaking their heads, saying almost nothing, the casseroles in their hands wrapped thickly in newspaper, still warm from someone's oven, the pies and all the desserts recognizably made from scratch because the women who sent them were careful to send only the very best ingredients, the very best effort.

Although her parents had moved to Oakville after she and her sister left for university, which turned out to be for good, Kate had grown up this way, in Dresden, a town not far away and almost this small. Her great-great-great-grandparents had been brought up north just a few months before the Civil War, when slaves were pouring across the border. Dresden was where they'd ended that trip, where they'd built their lives. As she took the warm dishes into her hands she watched the friends and neighbours stare briefly and discreetly at her pink upturned palms.

Meg could not be consoled. Margaret had said she was to be kept at home, that she was not to be taken back into London before the funeral, that they should be able to calm her down somehow. But Meg could not or would not sleep. She was wide awake crying for days and nights running. She could not cry herself out.

After Andy was settled into the boys' room, quiet and clearly needing quiet, Neil and Carol tried to take Meg home with them but she wouldn't stay, Neil had to get dressed in the middle of the night to bring her back to Andy. Margaret waited up with Meg until dawn and then she called the doctor at the clinic and asked him please to prescribe the biggest belt of whatever he had in his arsenal because it simply could not go on. One of the two new druggists, a young East Indian with a red Mustang and large, calm eyes who had been in town long enough to know that he should come to the back door at a time like this, brought the prescription over himself and Meg took the first capsules standing at the sink, asking as he handed them to her with a glass of water why was she the only one, why was she always the only one?

After the druggist left, Kate, whose field was chemistry, lifted the capsules to read the prescription and then Krissy said that she would do it. When the funeral was behind them she would arrange to take her holiday time and go back into the group home with Meg and stay there with her for as long as it took.

Although most of the flowers had been sent to the funeral home, a few plants, mostly mums, were delivered to the house and there were already over a hundred sympathy cards. Meg, who was calmed by mid-morning and sluggish, decided that she should be the one to open the cards and with her fine-boned, beautiful hands she opened and arranged them in larger and larger circles on the dining-room table. She took great care with this, did not swear or punch herself when one card knocked another over.

THERE had to be two afternoons and two nights of visitation because one way or another Paul had known so many people. The funeral director, who was almost ready to take over the business from his father, was very considerate, very attentive. At Patrick's request he had not tried to darken Paul's high forehead to match his tanned-from-the-fields face.

Andy's mother stood just inside the doors with her sister and brother-in-law, Don, who had come down from Barrie where Don had been for all these years a cop. Their job was to greet people as they entered the main room, to ask that they sign their names in the book. Neil and Carol and Krissy and Meg took their places beside their mother, Meg securely wedged between Carol and Krissy. Andy stood closest to the casket, braced to take the brunt of it. Her face and neck were sliced with small stitched cuts but otherwise, thanks to Carol's steady hand, she was properly made up, her lips and her eyes. She was dazed and sick with sorrow but soon grateful too, for the kind words, for the extravagant praise she was accepting on Paul's behalf. She had gone through lines like this herself, many times. She knew people struggled.

The rest of them flanked the casket on the other side, Bill first. Not many people had ready phrases for Margaret and Bill. Margaret guessed this was because they hadn't had nearly as much experience offering their condolences to the parents of the deceased, and she thought, Wasn't this a good thing. She recognized clearly what she saw passing in front of her. One by one by one, these people made the larger circle and most of them knew to keep a certain distance, to come just so close and no closer. Standing in that one place, Bill sometimes seemed to stagger a bit and when he did he reached back to touch the glossy wood to steady himself. He had not yet cried. His eyes were still firmly focused on the thing that didn't exist.

Except for Daphne, the others were able to fall back on their social graces, to smile and thank people they hadn't seen for years, even ask them brief questions about their own lives. Daphne said nothing to anyone. Standing in this room with the body of her brother, with the masses of flowers and the syrupy music, hearing over and over all the useless words of comfort, she had found God, she finally had God squarely in her sights. Her head was packed solid and the hate seeped through to her unruly face, was recognized for what it was by the people who took her hand and then quickly moved on past her down the line to the others.

Several times throughout the two afternoons and evenings, Patrick moved out of his place in the line to go across to Andy or to Neil or to the girls. Going to them, to encourage and reinforce their strength, their forbearance, he would stand straight with his head high and reach to put a firm hand gently on a shoulder. "You are doing just fine," he'd say, or, "Hang in there. Only another half hour and then we can go home." And once, to Krissy, who was having some very bad moments, especially after her girlfriends had come through, wrapping his arm around her small, quivering back, "Honey, it's only harder for people when you cry." It had to be done. Someone had to do it.

Although he had insisted that, to the extent possible, Paul's skin should be left alone, that the pale high forehead should ride as it always had above a ruddy, bronzed face, and although he escorted several of the older aunts and uncles to the casket and stood waiting with them there as they blotted their eyes, and although he had several times counted the profusion of baskets which had been placed around the casket and on the closed bottom lid, and could have described in some detail the stems and leaves and petals of the robust arrangements of flowers held in those baskets, he did not once look directly at the body. Two afternoons and two evenings and not once did he look. Because Paul was gone. Not dead but gone.

Late on the second afternoon Charlotte arrived with her condolences, alone. She moved down the line to take their hands in her own, embracing only Andy and then Bill, who would not remember her thin arms encircling him. She spoke to no one at any length, certainly not to Murray or to Kate, whom she had never properly met. Watching everyone give Charlotte the courtesy of a disciplined, civil greeting, Margaret thought, You could part water with that woman.

On the third day the young United Church minister conducted the funeral service. He was a very sincere man. He hadn't known Paul but this was not unusual now, ministers buried people they hadn't known all the time. And he had done his research. He tried to capture some part of the kind of man Paul had been. He told the mourners that so many people had mentioned Paul's sense of humour, how much they had come to enjoy it. And what a good father he'd been. And how he had borne his burden, meaning Meg, with courage.

The tone of his delivery was friendly, familiar, his phrasing casual. The words he used were everyday words, even a bit slangy. He talked this way at all his funerals because he was a city man who mistakenly believed that rural people preferred a less formal approach, that they wanted to be talked to this way, appreciated it. For his text, he turned to John, Chapter 11, to the story of Jesus raising Lazarus from the dead, and when he spoke about the sisters, the distraught Mary and Martha, he called them "the girls." He finished his lesson with Verse 23: "Thy brother shall rise again," and for the rest of her long life, whenever she thought about Paul, before she could get the words stopped, Margaret would think, Thy brother.

After the story of Lazarus resurrected, Patrick went to the lectern to read an Updike poem, "A Pear Like a Potato." Although she had never before mentioned it, it was Mary who had stored the poem in her head, who had called the library in London to have it found and read so she could copy it down. Patrick had no words of his own. He held the lines of poetry in his shaking hands and read quickly, aware as he read that it was Krissy who sobbed so loudly. Krissy and Mary beside her.

Four of the pallbearers were friends of Paul's, men he had curled with, played hockey with when they were kids and who still played for the Stonebrook Oldtimers, as had Paul. The other two were nephews, Patrick's Stephen, who was twenty-one, and his John, who was eighteen. When it was time to lift the casket up onto their shoulders the older men put the younger men in the middle, one on each side, giving no specific instruction but watching them and patting their backs when they looked to be all right with it.

On the way out to the cemetery, which was a slightly rolling twenty acres of very well treed, nicely maintained land beyond sturdy stone gates just at the edge of town, across the creek, the mourners' cars followed so slowly behind the steel grey hearse there might have been the beat of a drum in the air. As was the custom, when other drivers saw the headlights they stopped at intersections or pulled over to the side of the road to wait quietly while the procession passed, some of them with their heads bowed, some of them holding kids still in their laps.

The interment was over quickly. Just ten minutes before they'd come out of the service to get into their cars to form the procession,

there had been a brief, early summer sun shower and all the headstones shone with rain. Although it had been chosen, Paul's stone
was not yet placed. They gathered tight together under the green
canopy at a grave that was not yet a grave, not yet a small part of
the world grassed over and marked with a chiselled name, with
chiselled dates to mark a time on the earth.

Driving back to the house with Bill at the wheel because he had
insisted and Stephen and John in the back seat, Margaret told the
boys that she remembered when she was a young girl that men
would carry the coffin all the way from whatever church it was and
down the rutted road to the cemetery, with the mourners following
behind them on foot. "And there was no backhoe," she said. "What
you got in those days was a hand-dug grave."

Stephen gave no indication that he'd heard anything at all. He was
quiet, and watchful, proud enough of the way he'd handled himself
but afraid too that more would be required of him. John leaned
forward slightly at Margaret's words because he was interested in
history, especially the small particulars of history, the way things
worked, the odd things people used to do.

Margaret was thinking about her parents' graves on the far side of
the cemetery, which she did not very often visit. When her mother
died in 1941, her father had bought just the two plots, telling
Margaret there would be another place for her somewhere some day,
meaning there would be a husband so why in hell should he waste
his own hard-earned money. When Sylvia died Bill had bought a
package of eight, apparently and mysteriously imagining that his
kids would marry but have no children, would not reproduce themselves right out of consideration. Now two of the eight plots would
be marked with headstones. Andy had agreed to let Paul go beside
his mother, it was almost the only thing Bill had said in four days, the
only sentence he could put together, but she had insisted that he have
his own separate headstone because, and she'd had to say it just once,
he had been a husband and a father as well as a son.

Two years earlier, when Margaret and Bill had updated their wills
at Patrick's office, Bill had announced that whatever happened, if it
became necessary, she was to go below him or above him. He said

he'd checked it out and they sometimes allowed this in special circumstances. He said he wanted her as close as Sylvia because why shouldn't she be?

Margaret was not at all convinced about the likelihood of this arrangement. Recently, Bill seemed to have no compunction about claiming something was true when it clearly wasn't, when he simply wanted it to be true. But she'd let it pass. To tell the truth, she didn't much care any more where they put her.

She turned in her seat now to look at Stephen and John and thought, These are Sylvia's handsome grandsons. "There used to be a bank of trees on either side of this road," she said. "They were as massive then as these few are now." She pointed out the five old remaining maples. "All the men who could would take a turn carrying the coffin," she said, "relieving each other as they got tired." She shrugged her shoulders. "It was just the way people thought it should be done." Facing the front again, she told them, "You did a good job today. Your grandfather and I are proud of both of you."

She was thinking finally about Paul when he was a very young man. About his attentiveness to Andy, their easy affection for each other, their complete and amazing lack of shame. About his climbing up on a kitchen chair to unscrew the light fixture when Sylvia was dying, simply because he had been asked to, because she couldn't think of any way to be useful except to clean and cook and wash and tidy. About his Grandmother Ferguson taking him aside and scolding him quietly in the dining room, for his tears. And about her own cowardice. She was a grown woman. She could have gone to him after his grandmother had left to go home. She could have told him tears were exactly the right thing.

1995

MARGARET assumed Bill called her Sylvia only because he could
clearly see how it aggravated her. In all these years it had never once
troubled her that he might sometimes remember Sylvia and their life
together in the privacy of his thoughts, because how could he not,
but when he said, "Thank you, Sylvia, that was very nice," or, "Why
don't you drive down and get us some corn for supper, Sylvia," she
would flinch in spite of herself, never expecting it, never quite getting
used to that one thing. She had indeed adjusted to the rest of it, as
you would adjust to anything that happened with such regularity.

She had read things, pamphlets from the young nurse up at the
clinic, magazine articles slipped to her by her old friend Norma
Fawcett, who had more time for such things now that her own
husband had succumbed to Parkinson's. These were serious articles
written by apparently qualified people. So she did have the queer
comfort of knowing she was just one among many.

And she'd watched the talk-show carnival on television, wondering as she watched what she might think to say if she found herself
up there on the platform with Bill beside her, wondering how they
could possibly capture the idiotic attention of the audience, how
they could make their own peculiar lives sound satisfactorily sad or
terrible or ridiculous in the short time allowed between commer-
cials for Rogaine and adult diapers and Walk Fit machines.

She had learned from her reading and watching that there were
specific words to put to her situation, passive aggression, codepen-
dency, patterns of negative behaviour, dementia, victim, but she was
not at all sure of their meanings. Lots of words seemed to her to have
taken on new meaning, or they were used differently now, to mean
new things. She much preferred an old word, one she remembered
from her first years here with Bill when the kids were studying

Shakespeare at the dining-room table, asking each other the hardest questions out loud, looking up and defining words like melancholy and gentlewoman and equivocation, repeating the definitions over and over, back and forth, memorizing them. The word was *tragedy*. It was a plain word and it told you plainly that there was no solution in sight.

When she could manage, to lighten her day a little or to pull herself right up out of her day, she thought of his attacks on her simply as a suddenly compelling new hobby, like black-and-white photography or car mechanics taken up late in life.

THEY'D been married now for thirty-nine years and Bill had had all that time to discover ways to get under her skin, as had she, under his. But where he thoughtfully used to avoid doing so, for the last few years, and with more and more relish, he had been spending his time sitting in his chair in the living room going haphazardly back in time to collect scattered bits of ammunition.

He conjured incidents that no one else could quite remember, or home in on, and when he told things, he told them with a twist. His little stories were such a tangled mess, such a chaos, that no one could even begin to sort them out. He revised scenes and comments and behaviour to make everyone but himself look not very good. And he would not be corrected. If he sensed correction coming, he'd just say, "Now, I'm sure about this," or "I remember that a little differently." His sentences were brief and shaped, had been carefully shaped before he spoke them, always with a bite on the best words and a cocky challenge to anyone who would dare contradict a man who had lived so long and seen so much.

Although most of the other surviving vets still donned their navy blazers and their proud grief on grey November 11 mornings, and although he was as physically capable as any of them, Bill refused the observance of the walk to the cenotaph now, and when a small, informal delegation, the men who still could be heard to say that they had come of age together, the men who missed his presence in their thinning ranks, came over to the house to try to boost his spirits, he refused the gift of their faded camaraderie. He did talk as he had never talked before about the specifics of the war, about the

North Atlantic, the soaking cold and the black distance, which he said was utterly unimaginable to the rest of them, the rest of you, he called them. He unearthed his stiff wool uniform, which had been buried on its half-a-century-old wooden hanger at the back of the upstairs hall closet, displayed it for admiration on the swinging dining-room door, where it stayed for a week, tainting all the rooms with the bitter smell of the mothballs that had been dropped, each of fifty springs, into its pockets. He pulled Sylvia's old atlas down from its shelf and traced his war through the wide blue ocean with a red magic marker, circled quarter-sized areas of water off Iceland and at the entrance to the English Channel. He talked about his ship, its size and its smell, explained to them how steel could hold the cold forever. He could not remember the ship's name. Didn't matter, he said. He could and did name several of the men who had been over there with him, an Alex, a George, a Frank, and he named without fail the men who had not gone overseas at all, many of whom were still alive. He called these men the untouched.

He had concrete evidence that the people closest to him were idiots. He slammed his fists on the upholstered arms of his chair, they were flattened with his slamming. He said wisdom would never be given its due, not in his lifetime, said the truth was evidently not valued, that he was a fool to think it would be. He said he was ready to vote Reform, just give him the chance, and he cursed Margaret when she told him she was equally ready to cancel his vote.

Sometimes he was sly, sneaky, oblique. When he complained to visitors about Margaret's stupidity, how she couldn't seem to stop blowing fuses, how she would use nothing but cushy expensive toilet paper, how she wasted his gas making small trips back and forth all over town, he couched it all in a late-twentieth-century concern for waste. He looked right at Margaret and called her *she*.

Standing at her sink or sweeping the back porch or sitting waiting for Doctor Mang to save two more of her teeth, Margaret was very thankful for the healthy function of her own brain, which she could still count on to click into gear more or less as it was meant to. She would rather be dead a thousand times over than live on the way he did. But of course that's what he would have said too, before. When she thought these words she heard his young man's voice, content again with an ordinary young man's strength, speaking them, "I'd rather be dead a thousand times over."

As it was, he didn't mean to die at all. He talked about death's avoidance matter-of-factly, as if the ending of a life was a virus that smart people could protect themselves from, given enough common sense. He gathered what he called the relevant information. He went to the doctor almost weekly, had himself thoroughly checked over even if it was only heartburn that had got him his appointment. He boldly printed the number 911 on a piece of cardboard he'd stapled to the cupboard above the phone in the kitchen, in case he was struck, he said, when she'd left him on his own. He told her that her main job was to protect him from stress, from other people's nonsense. He said it could kill him.

After Paul was gone they had faded off in their nighttime attentions to each other, settling instead for the occasional comfort of sleeping warmly bum to bum. When he'd started up again, started to grab at her like some randy kid, snorting when she tried to settle him down, apparently propelled by her resistance, she left their bed to sleep in Daphne's room. And then she had decided it might help. She returned to him, tried to teach him his own forgotten style, the ways and means. He would have none of it. When she tried to cuddle into him, as he used to urge her to do, he took her by the shoulders and pinned her to her pillow, his strength recalled abruptly, as if he'd had it just yesterday. He prodded her and moved her limbs around to suit himself, turned her over and over again, slapped her rear not playfully but hard.

Margaret had lived a very long time without a rough hand on her body and now here it was. She moved permanently into Daphne's room, bought herself a new, firm mattress and a thick duvet, filled the empty closet and the dresser with her clothes and her mementoes, with the few pieces of nice jewellery she hardly ever wore now, most of them gifts from the kids. She slipped away during a shopping trip to Sarnia with Andy to buy a dead-bolt lock, which she kept in its box under the bed until one day she got the nerve to take the drill and the screwdriver upstairs. Bill followed her up, sat on her bed and watched her struggle with the instructions until the thing was secured on the door. She kept the key on a long string around her neck, wore it wet in the bathtub.

He had struck her only once, otherwise. She'd told him she was taking the car down to the garage to get the oil changed, that she was going to leave the car and they would bring her back right away. When he called from his chair to say that it was his car, he would decide when the oil needed changing, she picked up the keys from the basket on the counter and said he mustn't worry about it, she had arranged that they would keep the car for only an hour or so, and then she heard him leave his chair. He came into the kitchen and charged her. When he grabbed the keys, she'd told him, only firmly, she thought, kindly, "I'll take those keys, thank you." And then the slap.

It was the sound that would stay with her, loud for a simple smack, that and the heat of his open hand on her cheek. The pain wasn't much. She'd banged her hip bone harder on the counter going out the door too fast, many times. But she could feel her skin burning with the rush of blood and she expected him, seeing it, to feel her shock, perhaps to cry. When he didn't she pried the keys loose from his clenched fist, digging her nails into his flesh to give him something else to think about. At the door she turned back, said, "You go and sit down." And he did.

Uptown she stopped at the grocery store to buy him a half gallon of Butter Brickle ice cream. When the Vanderlinde boy dropped her off home she quickly presented it to him, soft in the bowl the way he preferred it, and he reached for it eagerly. "How nice, Sylvia," he said. "Just the thing for a day like today."

For the first while, old friends still came to see him with some regularity. A few men, a few women. He was during that time unaccountably affectionate, generous, and false. He began to kiss women on the cheek when he shook their hands, women he had just seen the week before, women who had never been particularly important to him but who had the time now to visit around town. No one knew where he'd seen this gesture or why he took it as his own.

After the kiss he would graciously offer a chair and then sit down himself and begin to talk, looking, as he talked, up at the ceiling as if it was all recorded there to prompt him. If visitors interrupted him with a possible change in direction for the conversation, mentioning perhaps their own grandchildren, or a recent, unusual trip, or a slight variation on something he'd said, he would resume, undaunted. "Anyway," he'd say. If he was interrupted once too often, he would stop talking altogether and listen intently, hating every word spoken, and at the end of it, before the door was fully closed, he would call out to Margaret in the kitchen, "Lock up if you see that particular battle-axe coming my way again."

Once the McKellars from down the street brought over their only great-granddaughter, who was a nurse in training in Kitchener. She had driven two hours to see them because the McKellars always helped her with a small cheque at Christmas. This pretty young nurse in training sat down beside Bill on the couch to look at the Florida pictures and, perhaps thinking that what she offered was compassion, perhaps thinking that here was the chance for a practical application of what she'd learned, she took his hand. When she called him "honey," Margaret wanted to lean over and slug her. Because there was absolutely nothing else she could do to stop it.

The first two times the young woman said the word, Bill stopped talking, stopped turning the pages altogether, which was meant to be a clue, and after the third time he threw her hand off his own, looked directly at Stan McKellar, and said, "Honey, my ass."

Oh, Margaret thought, you bet, Bill. This one you can have. Then she made an offer of more tea, which the McKellars gratefully took as their chance to go home.

PATRICK and Murray and Daphne and Sarah believed it was Paul's death. They had said this to Margaret alone and in pairs and all together. They said psychological shock was a phenomenon that was little understood and they seemed happy to take their comfort from this. But she knew it was not Paul's death. It was Bill's brain cells, so minuscule they couldn't even be imagined, his brain cells collapsing inside his skull, dying off, exploding as silently as the stars she had seen dying on television. It was his death, enjoying itself coming slowly.

At eighty-one Margaret understood death's ways and means with a clarity she would never have anticipated and she half surrendered herself to this understanding, as if the surrendering could go some way toward appeasement. Death could come hard and fast, as it had come to Paul, ensuring that nothing could get done, nothing could get said before and not much after that was any use to anyone. Or it could come over a few decent months, as it had come all those years before to Sylvia, giving everyone time but not too much of it, not so much you couldn't get through it. It could come with the thunderous, bloody repetition of slaughter on the other side of an ocean, having itself a heyday in the muddy fields of France. Or it could come in slow time, taking show-off, brazen, slow-march strides. It could let you watch, knowing with cocky confidence that you wouldn't look away.

Margaret missed Sarah. Sarah's absence was almost the hardest thing on her plate. After their first few years out West, unable to discipline herself to silence, she had asked about the possibility of a transfer back for Rob, his company was national and had sent him out there in the first place, but Sarah had said no, it didn't look like they could come back. They were going to make their life in Vancouver.

They did return every two or three years to visit and Sarah came immediately for Paul of course. And Margaret still had her open invitation. But she had never gone, never flown out, never flown anywhere in her life. They'd got to Florida all those years ago on their own, driving, and they had taken the car to Expo, too, just the two of them, she and Bill fighting through the Montreal traffic, staying at the private home of an older French couple who had opened very pleasant rooms to paying visitors. Although they had liked what they saw, especially liked trying all the food, some of which they had never even heard of, when they got back home, very tired and disorientated, they decided they weren't really travellers. The crowds especially had got to Margaret. So those two were the only trips they'd taken, except for a half-dozen times over to Detroit to see a ball game and of course once in a blue moon in to Toronto.

Sarah was disappointed that Margaret wouldn't get on a plane and fly out to Vancouver but she knew enough to stop coaxing. She said what they didn't spend on airfare they should spend on pictures and phone calls, so there were albums filled up and regular Sunday telephone visits. Margaret made notes for herself before the phone calls so she could be sure to give Sarah just the most significant news. Sometimes, if she'd called after eleven when the rates dropped, she would relax maybe a bit too much and talk about people Sarah didn't remember at all and Sarah would bluff her way through it, saying, Yes, she remembered Norma Fawcett and yes, she remembered the damage from that November storm, and then she'd kick in with her own news and complaints and modest boasting: the extended deck, seven-year-old Natalie honoured at school for her confidence, her brother Jake, so old for nine, playing the guitar, imitating some kind of music from Seattle, the bonehead neighbours with their yappy dog.

Margaret had early on asked Sarah to draw her a floor plan of their never-painted wood house in Vancouver so she would know what she was looking at when she saw the pictures, know where Sarah stood with the phone in her hand. And for Christmas, two years earlier, they'd sent a VCR, which meant that Margaret now had tapes to watch in the afternoons: Sarah's kitchen with not a thing out of place, not one stray crumb, their living room, all glass and leather and chrome like something in an expensive magazine, Rob cutting the grass, diagonally, making a nice pattern; Sarah on her treadmill, her hair a helped-along blonde, her middle thick like Margaret's own but her legs still as finely shaped as Betty Grable's; Natalie lying in a chaise in her bathing suit, reading a paperback book, showing little enthusiasm for the camera; Sarah and Rob dressed up to go out for the evening with the neighbours with the yappy dog; Rob bare-chested in tartan boxers, scraping moss off the deck, getting ready to treat it with something or other.

Watching with her, Bill said, every time, "He won't win against that moss. Any halfwit could see they have no business living there. It's not a fit place for housing. It's always been a forest and that's what it means to be."

Sarah could read between the lines as well as anyone and she'd had several long phone calls from Patrick, just so she would know what was happening, he told her when he called. She did understand that her father was going through something extremely difficult but it was all entirely in the abstract for her because there was nothing she could do except listen to whatever got said and babble on about life as she knew it. Life as she knew it a continent away in a magnificent city tucked between the mountains and the ocean, with friends and neighbours and colleagues more likely to be called Wong than Chambers.

Although Daphne was settled into the McFarlane house, she didn't come over any more, ever. She was almost worn out, driving back and forth from the hospital in Sarnia, still working shift. She did welcome Margaret into her own kitchen and she did send the girls to visit Bill, Maggie occasionally when she was home from university for the weekend, Jill more often with jars of rhubarb jam or marmalade or loaves of lemon bread.

Daphne had celebrated her fifty-fifth birthday in March and the girls had given her a party. They'd sent invitations far and wide and opened the doors of the McFarlane house to over a hundred people. By all reports it was a blow-out affair. Murray and Kate drove up from Toronto, stopping in London for Patrick and Stephanie and Meg, from the home, and Andy came, and most of the kids. Friends came from Daphne's old apartment in the city, people who had known the girls when they were small, and from all three of the hospitals where Daphne had worked and from her years in training.

Some of Maggie's and Jill's own friends turned up a few days early to help get the house ready and several of Daphne's oldest friends, from town, from her own time as a girl, the people she had been getting to know again since moving back, helped the girls with the planning and the preparation of the food. The younger women stood around the dining-room table listening as the menu and its attendant complications were discussed, waiting for instruction, and soon, chopping a bag of onions or taking a cloth and a bottle of furniture polish to one more deep, dusty windowsill, they began to imitate these older, relaxed women, their confidence in the face of a big party, their casual talk of recipes for fifty, doubled. In particular, the younger women began to take as their own the much-repeated phrase, "Just leave that to me," laughing as they said it, assuming they'd screw up and hoping it wouldn't be noticed.

Halfway through the evening, when the McFarlane house was

pulsing for the first time in fifty years with music and wine and with the raucous noise of conversation, with stories and anecdotes and praise and questions and lies, when the air was filled with the steamy temptation of good food well prepared, chicken pot pie and beans and ribs and curried shrimp and stir-fried vegetables and paella and leek and potato and squash pie, which was the new recipe, because there was always a new recipe waiting to be tried on a crowd, someone lifting freshly laundered sheers to look out a window noticed a March blizzard gaining strength under the street-lights, so many of the guests who had come from out of town stayed for hours after the party was supposed to end, stayed the night, filled the beds and couches and slept on the floors in sleeping bags like middle-aged kids, pulling each other upright in the morning and stretching and complaining about their lower backs as Jill carried a large tray of orange juice through the rooms, loving it.

Margaret and Bill had been invited to the party but Margaret had declined for them, as she was expected to. Instead she sent a wild-rice casserole and a big silver tray of miniature lemon tarts and, at the last minute, two dozen glads from the new flower shop uptown, the card saying what she always said on cards, "With all our love, Your Dad and Margaret."

When Bill finally got a partial description of the evening out of Maggie and Jill, the gory details, he called them, he said to the girls, "I expect they were all drunk as lords. What else do they know how to do?"

The next night he turned off a debate about a Gay Pride Parade and phoned Daphne to give her hell. "If they were too drunk to get home, why didn't you send them over here to sleep?" He listened to her scrambling for a response and, fed up, overspoke her. "If you're fifty-five, you're old enough to know that not even drunks like sleeping on the floor."

Maggie and Jill sometimes brought one boyfriend or another to meet Margaret and Bill, young good-looking men who had been well warned on the way over, prepped to listen and nod and lie according to their best judgement, which was, on the whole, surprisingly reliable.

Margaret had sat Daphne down just once to ask her to forgive her father, simply because she knew she was the only one to do it and she would hate herself later if she didn't make some effort. She did not believe for a minute that Daphne would be able to offer this imagined forgiveness. Like any daughter, Daphne had never seen her father up close and defenceless, not the way a wife does, so she didn't have that to fall back on. And his words had been obscenely cruel and said in front of the girls, just after Daphne had moved them back to town.

Right out of the blue he'd asked her, "So where's the father?" As if this information could make any difference now. "In all this time," he said, "you've never shared that with us."

When Daphne stood to leave he got up from his chair and followed her through the kitchen to the door. "Just took what he wanted," he said. "And you too stupid and ugly to deny him."

They had all spent a good part of their lives, Bill as much as the others, more than the others, much more, trying to help Daphne believe that she was not ugly, not "dee-formed," as she used to like to put it. Her load was plain when she was still a teenager, you didn't have to be a brain surgeon. Margaret thought now that Daphne was like a small boulder pushed almost to the top of a hill by a dozen willing hands, and then comes a sneaky well-placed kick. Premeditated, guaranteed. The bastard, she thought. And that's what she'd said to him at the time, playing rough, breaking for once the firm promise she had made to herself. "You bastard. You God damned bastard." Knowing it would do no good, except that Daphne and the girls would have those words too, as a modest entitlement from her.

She marked his words to Daphne as the first outside attack. Until then no one would have believed what he could say. But Daphne had taken it to heart. She apparently thought it was real.

Andy came over regularly, as she always had. Once in a while she would have Neil or Carol in tow, or their kids, or Krissy, who was married now and the mother of three boys, the little hellers, Bill called them, taking them back to explore the creek, his control of their loud, confusing play firm but not unkind. He didn't scare them. For nearly a year, Carol and Krissy had been sharing a dark green Jag XJS. They'd bought a Dream of a Lifetime ticket together, partly because Carol's mother had won a thousand dollars in the previous draw but mostly to support the hospital, and then they'd won the car. Everyone expected them to sell it and split the money but they didn't. They'd taken the train into Toronto to pick it up and they traded it off month by month, loading their kids into the back seat, which was not intended for kids, and taking Bill for a short spin around town whenever he asked, which was often.

When Meg was brought home from London for a visit, she and Andy would come in and stay for part of the afternoon. Meg had needed a hysterectomy soon after Paul was killed and the surgery had frightened her, subdued her more than any of her drugs. She hadn't been herself since.

Bill still tried to make a big fuss over Meg, although one afternoon when they were at the kitchen table playing their version of crib, he laid down his hand and backed away from her and scowled and barked at some little thing she'd said. Not understanding at all what she had done wrong, Meg stood up and started to bawl, loudly, and then she banged the table with her fists, which made the cards and their glasses of Coke jump.

"Just like old times," Andy said, coming in fast from the living room.

Margaret steered Bill out of the kitchen quickly so Andy could tell Meg that her grandfather must be very tired, that sometimes old people just got very tired, and then it was over, forgotten. In ten minutes the two of them were sitting on the couch together, one on each side of Andy, looking at the pictures from Florida.

Andy didn't farm any more, she leased to a neighbour, putting most of that money aside, but she was still managing the mill, wisely, still getting her living from it. Neil, who was thirty-four now and, like his father, tall and fast and sometimes funny, worked for her, and between the two of them they knew almost everyone around, who could be trusted, who shouldn't be. Over the past five or six years she had been going to Europe for a few weeks every spring. The first time, she took Krissy and Carol to England,

another year Daphne and Maggie and Jill flew over to join her for a
week in Italy and then a few days in Spain. And one year Mary went
with her, although this was long after Mary had divorced Patrick, so
it went without saying that the pictures of the two of them, standing on the Pont Neuf looking down at the Seine or sitting at a sidewalk café having breakfast or drinking wine, would not be shoved
under anyone's nose. The last time she was over, so much more
confident than she'd been when she started, she had gone to Italy
again, with Meg, just for a week. After Meg recovered from her jet
lag, which had made her cry with confused exhaustion, they'd got
along fine. Meg had liked Rome best, the hot slices of pizza bought
right on the sidewalk from dark men who flirted with her, the
narrow winding streets she walked holding her mother's hand, the
women who could run across these streets on very high heels. She
had liked the churches especially, their thick stone walls, the high,
dark emptiness inside, the echo if you shouted.

Andy didn't seem to be bothered by anything Bill said or did.
Nothing fazed her, not even Bill's insinuations that she and Neil
were spending far too much money, that they were running Paul's
mill into the ground. One morning, after a visit when Bill had been
tired and thoughtful, when he had talked for a long hour, for which
she was thankful, about Paul, jumping around in time but still so
obviously and painfully filled with love for his dead son, she went
to Daphne under the full steam of nervy anger to tell her that she
thought anything was better than having your father die so young
your kids had no actual memory of him. "Do you even remember
my father?" she asked. "Does anyone?"

Daphne told Andy yes, she did remember her father. She remembered dancing with him at the wedding and out at the Casino in the
summers, many times. She said he was the one who first took her
out onto the floor to teach her to dance. This wasn't true, he had
been only one of the first, but Daphne thought, It's true enough.

Murray came. He had always come up to visit a few times a year.
During Charlotte's reign he came alone, the reasons for her absence
usually having a nice ring of truth to them, but Charlotte was almost
forgotten now. For the last twelve years he had been bringing Kate.

He often looked tired. Well dressed, impeccable in his habits and manners, but tired. His hair had thinned and finally disappeared from the top of his head, although from the ears down it was as thick as when he'd been a boy. Standing behind him, rubbing his hand over Murray's pate, Bill said, every time, "Your father's hair. Nothing to be ashamed of."

Murray never went near the mill, although Bill had been pushing him lately. "Let's go on over," he'd say five minutes after Murray was in the door. "Let's go see how they're pissin' away my son's money now." He especially despised the newly purchased computer, which he'd never seen.

Bill enjoyed asking Murray about his trips and about the paper he'd quit and the one he worked for now, the corporate world, he called it, and about the stories he said Murray supposedly wrote. He wanted to know what was really going on in Ottawa and at NATO and in the Middle East, said he was after the inside dope, the truth of it, the story the average man would never get to hear. He hated every move Ottawa made and had messy files of clippings to back up his many suspicions, which he would set out on the dining-room table if he knew Murray was coming. He told Murray every time he sat him down that the real story, the unwritten story, was the occupation. The whole country, right down to every God damned song in every God damned elevator, taken over by American this, American that, and why the hell wasn't anyone writing about it? Exposing it? So maybe people would sit up and take notice? And the stand-off at Oka had convinced him that it was high time the government settled properly and fairly and finally with the Indians and stopped all this bloody screwing around, because in the blink of an eye bloody screwing around could lead to war, and who in his right mind didn't know that? You didn't need to have fought a war to know that, he said. Anyone who'd cracked a history book knew it. He said if he was lucky enough to be writing for some big paper, he would be inclined to tell the truth, which was that Ottawa was at war with its own people, that NATO had become a scam, and that the factions in the Middle East had been at some kind of war one with the other from the beginning of time, so what's newsworthy there?

Murray's wife Kate charmed Bill, because she was new and had the energy and the inclination. She asked each time to look again at the pictures from the family's big trip to Florida. She brought him glossy magazines dedicated to sports and hunting and fishing, although she would have known if she'd asked that when Bill was young he'd never had time to play much of anything and had gone hunting up north only once or twice before the war, when he still had his trigger finger. And she brought him thin butterscotch medallions in a fancy foil bag which he held on his lap while they talked, taking one candy after the other into his mouth, not waiting or savouring but biting down hard with his good left molars.

She asked about his garden, allowed him to lead her through it and name for her the plants and the insects and the small anticipated blights. One evening they took the lawn chairs down to sit at the edge of the creek and when he began to complain that something was getting at his sweaty ankles she went back up to the house and returned with the Off! and two empty bread bags, which she slipped over his shoes and tightened on his calves with elastic bands. As she knelt to do this, he reached down to touch her hair. He told her she was the prettiest of the bunch, and the kindest. He said she should have been with them in Florida instead of what's-her-name, that other cold little fish. He warmed to his metaphor, laughed quietly, intimately, said Murray had been smart to throw the first one back, set his hook again.

After she had the bags secured, Kate straightened and took his hand into her own as a nun might or a mother. He pulled his hand back as if he'd got a small electric shock, and then he leaned down and snapped the elastic bands, kicked the bread bags from his feet, and staggered off. He walked along the creek bank through three of the neighbours' yards and then stopped, confused, to yell for her to come and get him.

Some of this Kate shared with Murray in the car on the way back to Toronto. She was a fine little storyteller, although she usually kept the coarsest things to herself. The first time, after telling Murray that Bill had squeezed what he called her fanny as she turned to get into the car, when she'd suggested, "Why not laugh?" Murray had taken his eyes off the road for a few deliberate, unsafe seconds. "What a concept," he'd said. "I'll get you a bumper sticker."

After she'd apologized, and she was sorry, she hadn't meant to do anything except perhaps make getting through these visits something less than grievous, he told her it was obviously harder if you'd known him for a long time, if you'd known him when he was young and clear, that was all it was.

Once, after Murray and Kate had pulled out of the driveway to return to Toronto, Bill said to Margaret, "I never took Murray for an ass man but, then again, you can learn something new every day if you keep your eyes open."

IN his busiest years, Patrick had come only intermittently, sending Mary and the kids in his place, but he visited fairly often now. Although he had watched the disintegration from the beginning, it was all just small changes to him, first this, then that, too much of something, too little of something else. He decided it could be managed and he didn't want to spend much time giving it a name. His experience with clients divorcing and squabbling over money and children had long ago convinced him that if people could just handle the small things as they came, complete breakdown could often be prevented. He used words on Margaret like *adapt*, thinking only to help her. She didn't bother to try to spell things out for him.

Stephanie, Patrick's second wife, almost always accompanied him on his visits and once in a while they'd bring Teresa, Stephanie's poised and beautifully made-up daughter from an earlier marriage, who called herself Tess and who was of all things a fashion model. Sometimes Margaret turned on the VCR and they watched Sarah's tapes from the coast. The movies, Bill called them.

And Stephanie, too, was asked to sit down to look through the old pictures from Florida, even though she was not the tanned and voluptuously pregnant wife who stood beside Patrick on a balcony in the sunset, brilliant in a white linen dress that exposed her bare and bony Jackie Kennedy shoulders. Not much effort had been made to eradicate this first, much-admired wife and Stephanie understood how this could happen with a woman who was the mother of grandchildren. She understood, too, that Mary had experienced some bad luck with her health and she was careful to take no offence when her name came up, naturally and casually, as if she were just someone they used to know.

Looking through the pictures with Bill, she said what a good idea it had been, going away together for a big holiday, and as he turned the pages she put a name to everyone, pointing to this person or that as if the others didn't know who they were. "There's Sarah," she said. "What a pretty teenager she was." And, "Daphne always tans so well, I envy her." And, "I can't believe Murray would be caught dead in those ridiculous sandals." She said she could see an easy resemblance between Bill and Paul, whom she had never met, she said anyone would see it. No one corrected her. Paul had never looked like any of them, least of all Bill, although his long tall son Neil was clearly his own.

If Mary had still been involved, still the one coming to visit an elderly father-in-law, she would have put up a resounding struggle. She would have talked to her own doctor and to a specialist or two, she would have read every recent article on dementia and stroke she could get her hands on, and not in the *Ladies' Home Journal*. She would have called Bill's doctor up at the clinic, made an appointment for herself, talked to him frankly about the evident debilitating strain on Margaret and about the possibility of a drug regimen to take the edge off. But, although one or two or all three of Patrick and Mary's grown kids still arrived once in a long while, Margaret and Bill no longer received visits from Mary, understandably.

Mary had come up to see them the last time on her own. It was in 1987, the summer after Paul died, just when Margaret, at least, was beginning to adjust herself to his terrible absence, to accept his absence as an ever-present, always visible scar across all their lives. She had known there were people who had to live that way, people who grieved daily. And now she and Bill were among them.

Although neither of them had formed even half a sentence to indicate their concern one to the other, for some time Margaret and Bill had both noticed, had separately believed, something was very wrong in Patrick's marriage, something worse than the usual kind of thing that people had to live through.

In the ten minutes before Mary stood up from her favourite lawn chair to leave them herself for the last time, she'd said what she'd driven an hour to say.

"Six months ago," she said, "I found an earring in Patrick's car. A big cheap earring. So I cornered him, I nailed him and made him tell me who she was. She is twenty-two. He met her when she came into the office for a job interview. A job for which she was not even slightly qualified."

"Oh, Mary," Margaret said, thinking, This is going to be an awful story.

"I tracked her down last month," Mary said. "I interviewed her myself. She was appallingly confident for someone so unqualified, sitting in her tawdry little apartment with the sentimental posters taped all over the walls, the pink walls that matched the pink coverlet on the bed that matched her rosy cheeks. She was very soft-spoken, very polite as she advised me that I do not really know my husband, that if I'm not careful, I am going to be his wife in name only, and perhaps not even that. She isn't even pretty. She is a plain, sentimental, stupid little mouse of a girl. I don't know why I didn't slap her down. I don't know how I stood it. But apparently he can cry in her capable arms. He rides up her elevator to cry in her arms and she gets to pretend that she is a wise young woman. Theirs is not a very complex affair."

"Perhaps the loss of a brother ...?" Bill said, dropping his head back heavily, staring straight up at the empty sky.

Sitting between them in her lawn chair, Margaret concentrated on the willows moving in the breeze above the creek. For days she had been watching a pair of cardinals settle in, although there was no sign of them now.

"Miss Rosy Cheeks was keen to share with me something Patrick should have told me himself," Mary said. "I think in fact it might be the one thing, the only thing, he's never told me. She said it should be obvious to me that he has worked so hard and so long because he wanted so badly to live up to his mother's wish that he use his time and energy, his life, to help people. She told me that in her experience, *her experience*, men like Patrick almost never get the credit they deserve. And she was kind enough to reassure me that I don't really have anything to worry about because he is going to continue on, he doesn't even want out. He is just very tired. She said he needs a place for himself. A safe, separate place where he is not needed."

"She said that to you?" Margaret asked, lifting the pitcher to refill Bill's glass and then her own.

Mary appeared to be winding down a little and very soon Margaret would be expected to have something to say to her about this business, something useful perhaps or, at the very least, not hurtful. But sitting there so close to Mary, waiting for the cardinals to appear, and where did they go when they stayed from their nest so long, out to the fields for grain, for the simple pleasure of the flight? she could think of nothing honourable to say.

At the time, after the war but before Sylvia's death, before she'd imagined the possibility of Bill, when for almost three years she herself had so gladly comforted and taken comfort from a man who had a perfectly good wife, a wife he never spoke of because she would not allow it, she had believed that what she'd given and received truly was, in its essence, a kind of love. She had believed that even in its secret, sneaky, rushed articulation, there was a legitimacy to what she'd done. That those heavy, middle-of-the-night footsteps on the stairs that she'd listened for with such patient, sympathetic hope had been legitimate steps. That there had been a necessity.

Although she had been more than old enough to fear the possibility of consequences, there had been no consequences. Certainly she'd felt heartache when it ended but she'd understood from the start that it would have to end, and the heartache was only for a time, and it was as nothing against his presence in her narrow bed. She could not have known then that the only cost to her would be the requirement for a difficult, respectful silence on an afternoon such as this, an afternoon that could not have been anticipated.

"I've invited him to cry at home," Mary said, "where the rest of us cry. Apparently it's not going to happen." She shook her head to

Margaret's offer of more lemonade. "But really," she said, "she is nothing. She is only the thing I can describe."

Oh, Margaret thought, she is not nothing. Such women are rarely as little as that. You could ask Daphne, for instance.

"I am asking him to leave," Mary said, "not because he's been soft and weak and stupidly self-serving. I'm almost sure I could have lived with that. But because of the thing that must have driven him, the thing that prompted the recklessness of his needing such a vacuous, stupid young woman, which is *not* nothing, not at all. Of course he remembers whatever it was his mother said to him, of course he has been a helpful man, an extremely strong, cold-blooded, steadying influence on his miserable clients, hundreds of them, year after year after year, but he *has taken* his pay-off. He *has taken* the right to stand tall on his own self-satisfied moral high ground. And he's very much enjoyed overlooking everyone, judging everyone. I am sure you've noticed that Patrick and I have both been playing around at righteousness, for years. And now he's got himself locked in. Even with his own kids. Often with his own kids, who should not be expected to bear it."

She stood up from her chair. "I think it's a simple addiction," she said, "like any other. And now that I've said the word, I would guess you have noticed he's drinking more than he should." She leaned down to kiss Bill's forehead. "But perhaps it doesn't matter. Perhaps the drinking is only a predictable, secondary repercussion."

The cardinals had returned to the willows, had soared in, the male arriving a few long minutes behind the female, and with their return, with the evidence of their deep red devotion so plain, Margaret was able to understand things differently. She understood that if all of this had happened before Paul's death, before the ground had shuddered and then gone out from under them, she and Bill might have tried to help Mary change her mind, or counselled her to at least give it some time. They did like her so much and they certainly did not have to be convinced that Patrick was not perfect. If Paul had been still alive, still among them with his laughter and his long legs and his quick movement from a chair to a door, from a truck to a back porch, they might have invited Mary to settle into her lawn chair for the afternoon and just let it pour out, hoping as mothers and fathers almost always do that the difficulties could be examined, could be broken apart and fixed one by one by one. If everything had been different, without a moment's hesitation she would have turned traitor to her own past self, would have argued for the rightness of Mary's cause just as fiercely as she'd fought for the rightness of her own when she herself was a proud, young bit-on-the-side. And she would not have wallowed, as some might, or paused to deplore the slippery nature of her fidelity. She would not have slowed down to acknowledge the fraud.

But neither of them had the strength for it, not that year. Soon after Mary's kiss, Bill left them to go into the house alone, to go up to bed, and Margaret, hearing Mary's rage fade from humiliation down to a mute, humbled grief, felt only regret for her own exhaustion. She was ashamed of her exhaustion.

Walking out to Mary's car she'd thought, It's true what they say about timing. So much in this life depends on timing. And then, believing that, whatever had transpired in their marriage, which surely was, like any marriage, beyond the comprehension of those outside it, Patrick had a very large responsibility to this woman, and believing too that perhaps this was the one way she could help, she asked Mary a normally never-asked question. "Will you be all right for money?" she asked. "Will you keep your wonderful house?"

But Mary assured her that money would probably be the least of her worries. She said she was going to dust off her M.A., and if it turned out to be as useless as she suspected, she would go back for another, more relevant degree. She said Patrick had agreed to help until she had established herself.

"I think the kids are old enough to live through this," she said, opening the car door, assuming that Stephen and John and Rebecca would be on Margaret's mind, would be claiming their proper place there. "You and Bill will still see them," she said, "as often as always. I promise you that."

When she turned away to get in behind the wheel, Margaret pulled her around and hugged her tight, aware as she patted the thick Jackie Kennedy hair that she took the embrace not for Mary but for herself, both for the young, loving, deliriously happy adulteress she'd briefly been and for the lifelong wife she had so unexpectedly, so thoroughly become. When she said goodbye, for the first time in her life she used the word *dear*, thinking, I'm an old woman now and I'll never be anything else. Except dead.

"I came because I thought you and Bill were entitled to an explanation," Mary said. She was not even close to tears. "I've worked as hard as he's worked. I have a right to be happier than I am."

"Yes," Margaret had said, helping Mary close the door and then standing back from the car. "I agree."

And so, eight years later, they had in their midst Stephanie, a lovely, grown-up woman who was all you could ask for in a second wife. Neither Bill nor Margaret had ever spoken of Mary's visit that last afternoon, not to each other or to Patrick or to anyone else, and the soft-spoken girl who had been nothing, who had no name, had disappeared without a trace, had sunk like a stone, had become by now, possibly, some young man's affectionate, trusting young wife.

Stephanie appeared to be more even-tempered, more relaxed than Mary, but maybe this was because they didn't know her so well. They would never have the time now to know her so well. She seemed to assume, not quite correctly, that everything that could be done for Bill had been done. Patrick told Margaret that she had watched a favourite aunt go in some similar way.

PATRICK had been the force behind the garden, which they'd just put in that spring. Years before, when all but one of the big hickories had come down, soon after Sylvia's death, a garden plot had been marked off and worked and Margaret had laid out her rows of potatoes and corn and broccoli and tomatoes and lettuce and cukes. Then everyone but Sarah was gone and the three of them simply didn't need all that food. And it was hard work, Margaret told Bill she found it lonely work. Over time, because no shape will hold forever, because lawn grass like any grass will want to spread, the hard garden rectangle had been reduced to a barren, rounded pond of earth. No one had put any effort into taking it back, it had never been rolled and properly reseeded, although Bill did go at the weeds once or twice a summer with 2-4-D.

And Margaret had found a use for the old plot. Soon after the town council had invoked the new bylaw against any kind of private burning, tired of raking the leaves all the way down to the burn patch at the creek, she had begun to gather them onto the plot and put her match to them there, usually taking the trouble to sink a few chestnuts, listening like a kid for the hot pops in the smouldering piles. And almost every fall a small pack of neighbourhood kids who had smelled the smoke in the air would arrive with their rakes to help her, to watch her break the law, and when it was finished she would hand out quarters or, more recently, loonies, from her apron pocket.

It was her habit too in very late winter to watch from the kitchen window for the pond of brown earth that always appeared a week or so before the sun took the snow from the grass, and a little later, in the true spring, she watched as the plot became a mucky, muddy mess, a good measure of the rain they'd had, and, more enjoyably, a soft brown platter that drew the birds to worms.

Patrick had arrived on a May Friday afternoon with a second hand wagon hitched to his newest Lincoln. In the wagon he had a Rototiller and a wheelbarrow, two bags of sheep manure and three of peat, and a bunch of long-handled garden tools, which were not made of ordinary steel but some kind of hard green plastic.

Margaret and Bill went out to the gravel driveway to meet him, and when he began to explain that they had discussed this the last time he was up, putting in a good garden, sharing both the work and the results, Bill insisted that he had no memory of any talk about a garden. "You talked maybe," he said.

Unloading the tools while Patrick and Margaret set up a make-do ramp to get the Rototiller off, holding up the business ends of the shovel and the hoe and the fork for inspection, he proclaimed them too damn weird for words.

"No rust," Patrick said.

When he asked just how much was all this going to cost him, Patrick told him, "Zilch, Dad. Father's Day."

Patrick was fifty-eight. His very short hair had lost all traces of colour, it was no longer mottled but pure steely grey, and the creases on his face, deep rays of them back from his eyes and two sturdy grooves from his nose down to his jaw, were set, he could no longer erase them with a change of expression. He claimed he had earned the lines. "Those lines and a few hundred thousand more than you're worth," Bill was fond of telling him.

This was one of Bill's steadiest rages, the amount of money Patrick made. "I cannot comprehend," he announced one Sunday, "where all this money is coming from." When Patrick talked about proportions, the high price of housing and cars and insurance and education and hospitals, Bill said the real problem was that people were being educated beyond their intelligence. "Can you tell me who's going to do the shit work?" he asked. "Can you tell me who's going to be satisfied living on the wrong side of the tracks?" When Patrick ignored him, left the living room for the kitchen, Bill raised his voice and made sure it carried. "If there ever is another war," he called out, "no one will be willing to go. No one will be able to go, everyone's so blessed soft. Then we'll see where all this improvement got us." He loaded everything he had on the word *improvement*.

Patrick had held on to a squash player's fitness, which Bill said was a city fitness that fooled no one. He liked to remind Patrick, as he sometimes reminded other men, that his hands hadn't been dirty in thirty years.

After the unloading and a short visit in the kitchen and a beer for Patrick, Bill sat on the garden bench with his arms folded while Margaret walked the plot with Patrick to find and collect any bits of refuse. Margaret told Patrick if he came across a rare coin, it was his to keep but she'd take any diamond rings. The first thing she found was an ash-smeared length of tartan ribbon similar to the ones mothers used to tie into the hair of their pretty little girls. "I didn't chuck this out here," she said, suspecting the birds. Within a few minutes she had picked up several bits of tangled wire, a half-buried pop can, and three good-sized spikes, old and crusted with rust, that must have been left behind when the fence had come down, soon after the war. Margaret knew that Bill and Sylvia had bought the house in part because of the picket fence, she had seen pictures of the kids climbing it, but when Bill got home from overseas he'd declared it rotten and pulled it down.

Patrick had found only stones, and when he said he guessed they were finished, Bill got up from the bench to walk every inch himself, to double-check them. On his second pass he found an open diaper pin with a faded pink head. As he dropped the pin into Margaret's hand, she told him it must have been extremely hard to spot.

"I'm going to put in corn and asparagus," he said. "Nothing else."

When Margaret insisted that she would like a few potatoes and some broccoli, he grabbed the strange bright green hoe and cut a line through the earth, marking a section off. "That's yours," he said.

Patrick had found some ancient stakes in the shed and after he got the four corners established, he slit the bags of manure and peat and emptied them across the dirt with the new shovel. When he had it all spread he fired up the Rototiller. He slowly covered the ground once and then again, as if he'd read about this somewhere, at a right angle. Margaret brought him lemonade, his mother's recipe, made from a boiled concentrate and loaded with ice. She stood beside him while he drank it and said very loudly above the noise of the Rototiller, didn't the soil look rich and cared for?

Bill had decided to open the croquet set he'd bought at Canadian Tire for the great-grandkids. He pushed the loops into the ground at long intervals stretching down to the creek and then he got out a mallet and a few balls, dropping the balls randomly at his feet. When Patrick finally turned off the Rototiller, the absence of the sound of its whiny engine filled the yard with a slightly unnerving silence that was broken only by Bill's determined knocking of croquet balls toward the creek.

Watching his father swing the mallet, too hard, Patrick called out, "Are you winning, Dad?" Bill ignored him and Margaret shook her head, firmly. No jokes today. Then she helped Patrick load the Rototiller onto the wagon, and after they got it on and tied down, she led him over to the barbecue. The barbecue had been an anniversary present, from everyone, and it had not had a good cleaning since the ribbon had come off five years earlier. "I want you to show me how to thoroughly clean this thing," she said, lifting the rain cover. "I'm not that anxious to get blown to smithereens. So what exactly do I disconnect?"

Patrick opened the lid. The barbecue hadn't been used much so it wasn't really that bad for char or grease but they watched together as several dozen earwigs paused on the grill and then quickly scrambled away from the daylight. Margaret leaned closer, counting as fast as she could. "Seventeen, eighteen, nineteen." And then she said, "Maybe I'll get you to show me how to clean it another time." As she bent down she recited the instructions. "Turn on the gas. Open the burner valve. Push the starter button." Watching until she was sure of the flames, she closed the lid.

With the earwigs cooked, the three of them went inside for a supper of Margaret's recipes: whipped potatoes and jellied vegetable salad and baked beans and, Patrick's favourite, the thing he claimed to like better than anything, breaded pork tenderloin. After supper Margaret took care of the dishes while the men changed the filter on the furnace and then they all sat down to watch "Jeopardy" together, Patrick and Margaret leaning back comfortably into their corners of the sofa and competing without shame, calling out the questions to the answers with either dead, but often conflicting, certainty or with wild, educated guesses.

"Oh, you two are smart," Bill said. "You don't need to convince me."

Halfway through the program he stood up and headed through the kitchen in a huff, calling back through the bang of the screen door that if they couldn't rouse themselves to get at the planting, he could do it himself. He said if they'd decided that this was his part of the work, that was fine, but he was going to get at it now while there was still some daylight left.

Patrick went out after him to tell him they had no seed, they were going to buy seed tomorrow. Hearing this bit of reality, Bill stopped at the garden bench and sat down hard. "There are days when I believe my brain is haywire," he said. Then he dismissed Patrick with a sharp head-jerk toward the house, so Patrick left him there. He stayed until dusk, until Margaret took him his sweater. And then he got up and followed her in and climbed the stairs to bed without a word.

After a while, just as Margaret and Patrick were settling down in the living room for one of their tired, interesting talks, Bill came halfway back down the stairs and called out to them. When they came into the hall he stood over them and asked, "After you're gone, how am I expected to manage? I am without my best fingers, you know." He held up his hands. "The tools seem not very heavy, but how lightweight can they be when you're the one doing the work?" Patrick told him not to worry himself over it, the tools were not heavy and would not get heavy, that's why he'd bought them. He said it would be fine. He said, "Go back to bed, Dad." Bill turned on the stairs and started up, but they heard him, as he meant them to. "Get it all talked through, now. Talk it all through."

Patrick and Margaret had been enjoying their little talks for some time. Some of the others seemed to be puzzled by this, as if Margaret was secretly teaching Patrick how to knit, or can peaches. It had begun soon after the morning they'd gone to the hospital together to see Mary, not long after Patrick had married Stephanie. Patrick's son Stephen had phoned him at his office to tell him about his mother's breast cancer, not before, but two days after Mary's surgery, which had been fast and major, a double mastectomy, and, without thinking, Patrick had immediately called Margaret, to let her know.

"Well, then we're going to go and see her," she'd told him. "You and I. Today." When Patrick hesitated, because he was not prepared, not quite ready with a legitimate defence, she didn't sit quietly on the other end of the phone as was her considerate habit. She spoke quickly and with not a hint of patience. "Not loving each other any more is no excuse."

He had waited for Margaret at a window table in the cafeteria, drinking a tolerable cup of coffee and looking out at the ugly rooftops of the office buildings that surrounded the hospital, at the bright winter sky and the streaks of clouds, which were still so white above the filth of the city air. He knew many of the office buildings he was looking at but more usually from the street-level perspective of their elaborate, arched entrances, their heavy plate-glass doors, their hushed, serious lobbies. Although it should not have been, it was a bit of a surprise, and an offence, this complete absence of architectural finish to the rooftops. Looking at the flat gravelled surfaces and the blown garbage and the old chimneys and the air shafts and the filthy pigeons flying from one building to another, concentrating on the pigeons, counting the pigeons, fighting it off but not nearly hard enough, not hard enough to stop it, he remembered the warmth of Mary's breasts and her undiminished modesty about her breasts, which had been so unexpected and so beautiful and, a long time ago, twenty years ago, so heavy with the tracing of veins, with the blue-white nourishment that he himself had taken, more than once, carefully, listening in the midnight quiet of the house to the sound of her soft, patient laughter, like a mother's laughter, drifting above him, through his hair. He imagined the breasts now, disembodied. Carried away with other breasts. Burned?

To kill the image, and his one true hope for Mary was that it would never come to her, he pulled back hard to the cup of lukewarm, tolerable coffee in his hands and allowed himself to become doubly worried, about Mary and what this diagnosis might mean for her and for the kids, and about Margaret, who had turned seventy-five in the fall and was now driving alone on the snow-covered highway.

When Margaret sat down at the cafeteria table and began to pull off her gloves finger by finger the way she always had, he asked her to promise him that she wouldn't drive the highway any more. She did promise him and she'd stuck to it, as far as he knew that trip behind the wheel had been her last beyond the town limits.

Riding down to Mary's room on the elevator with a nurse who was attending to a hairless but still cheerful child on a stretcher, a boy who held his X-rays in his arms, Margaret told Patrick, "She won't want anything from you but your support. And you should be able to give her that with no disrespect to Stephanie." And just before she pushed Mary's door open, with an obviously willed authority, as if this fight was now her own as well as Mary's, as if, three years after Paul's death, she had finally rediscovered some small part of her strength and was happy to see a chance to put it to use, she'd told him, "It's not always the death sentence it used to be. Mary can live through this." And so she had, fighting like hell all the way, seizing her luck.

Now Patrick often found himself talking to Margaret. This too could be done with no disrespect to Stephanie, whom he enjoyed and loved with almost no reservation, partly for her solid and unheralded accomplishments as a lawyer, partly because she was full of lusty wit and shameless in the dark, and partly, and perhaps this was the largest part, because she had far too much respect for her own difficult history to launch an assault on his.

And when he did talk with Margaret, usually quietly over a cup of tea or a drink of Scotch, she never hesitated to make an honest comment if one came to her.

MARGARET had made a big pot of tea. She had asked Patrick for an update on his son Stephen and he was telling her that Stephen had finally got on with the symphony, that he was at thirty the youngest French horn player the orchestra had ever hired and how proud they all were. "Whatever divorce does," he said, "it does not diminish pride."

Then he confessed that he felt quite bad for the times he had wished Stephen would set the horn aside and go out for a baseball team or sign up to be a camp counsellor or something. He said he hadn't mentioned this to anyone, only thanked God he hadn't pushed the kid any harder than he had. He said he had no idea what stopped him.

Taking this in, Margaret told Patrick that he wasn't about to hear her say he was a model parent. "You've got lucky," she said. "Good parenting is just watching for your luck, trusting it to make an appearance once in a while, and sitting up straight when it does." She poured him his cup of tea. "Bad parenting is mostly bad luck," she said. "I believe that."

Listening to Patrick go on about his thoughts, his secret achievements, his small feared badness, had turned out to be one of Margaret's old-woman pleasures. It wasn't like hearing guilt or hesitant pride or regret from a woman. It was, in her experience, much more rare. She watched him talk the way you might watch an animal grooming himself in the dark of night. She kept still, maintained a certain distance.

As he talked this time, Margaret was getting ready to make her own confession. She had decided after Patrick's last visit that she was going to own up to the lie she'd fed him when he was a boy, just after Sarah was born, the lie about his mother and the ball games. She was not inclined to tamper with their other lie, his pretence that he had never faltered, never spent his evenings crying in the arms of a mousy, loving young woman. Which had been the only place for it he could find. Obviously. Although she was willing to expose herself as a self-serving liar, a woman who would lie to a belligerent, grieving boy, she was by no means finished with restraint, with the shelter provided by restraint.

"When I first came here I didn't know your mind," she started. "I just knew that you'd lost your mother and had this new woman in your house. Me. You were so very quiet, not sulky exactly, but too quiet for my taste. So I lied to you about something."

Patrick put his cup down and briefly closed his eyes. "Sulky would be the word," he said. "I know I wasn't helpful to you. Like Paul, for instance. Paul always turned up when he was needed."

"He must have been born with his easygoing heart," she said. "I never once saw it fail him."

They were quiet for a minute. This was the thing given to Paul, a quiet space around his name.

"Anyway," she said. "About the ball games. Truth be told, your mother and I hardly knew each other when we were young. She was one of the girls who finished high school, which was supposed to guarantee you the chance for a different kind of life. I didn't, of course. My family was on the outside of things. Rougher. Not much money. No one educated. So your mother and I did not play on the same ball team. But I do remember her when she was young. When the men were away. And I remember you kids on the park bleachers, already bathed and ready for bed, you running loose, Paul and Daphne wrapped in blankets in your grandparents' arms." She waited a little while before she continued, as if she had made a picture they could look at together.

"They'd just put in the lights for night games, sometimes there were two a night, and I remember warming up behind the bleachers, glancing over once in a while to see how the other game was going, seeing your mother on first base, slamming a fist into her glove, yelling ball talk with the other women, jumping funny little jumps on the bag to keep herself revved up. I remember this so clearly."

"She wasn't very big for first base," Patrick said.

"No, she wasn't," Margaret said.

"She was a showy player," he said.

"Showy and funny and very determined to win," Margaret said. "That's what people would have thought."

"And the purpose of the lie?" he asked.

"Only to give you something," she said. "Or maybe to win you over. Maybe I was just covering my bases, or my ass."

"Well, it worked," Patrick said, smiling because he liked it when she swore, which was not very often any more. "Perhaps I can tell you a lie some day."

"That would be nice, dear," she said.

He sat up straight to finish his tea and then he asked, "You never thought of getting married before you came to us?"

"Thought about it all the time," she said. "I was lonely. Take my word, it's not good to be alone."

"I'd know that," Patrick said. He got up and walked into the dining room and opened the buffet door to find the Scotch, his own bottle, his own brand, kept there and replaced as needed. He sat down again and lifted Margaret's cup from the saucer to drink the last of her tea. Then he poured them both a healthy shot.

"Your dad saved me," she said. "Asking me." She lifted the teacup and the saucer together to take a sip. "A life wants work."

"There must have been others," he said. "Before."

"Almost all the men were married," she said, "all the good ones. And that didn't appeal to me much. Sneaking around." These were the necessary words, the lies that betrayed nothing. "It could have got known."

"But before," he said. "Before everyone was married."

"I was very tall," she said. "About as tall as I am today. Most men then didn't even like to stand beside a tall woman. Let alone lay her down."

Patrick laughed, leaned his head way back. In the middle of his pleasure he noticed for the first time in his life the array of fine spiderweb cracks in the plaster ceiling. He thought maybe he should acknowledge the cracks out loud and offer to fix them or to have them fixed, but then he thought he would probably let them go. It had to stop somewhere.

"Men your age have had to learn to hide their egos," Margaret said. "I've noticed this. And it's a good thing. But they didn't hide them then. A woman had to have a certain look about her. Not weak exactly, but if you looked like you could make it on your own, mostly they let you make it on your own. The last thing wanted was a partner."

"That's pretty harsh," Patrick said, watching her face.

"And pretty true," she said. "In my judgement."

"Too harsh," he said, shaking his head, refusing to believe.

"Your dad needed a partner," she said. "Because he'd been stopped. Because he had something under way here that had to be carried on with."

"Us," he said.

"And himself," she said. "He was a settled man. He needed to stay settled."

"I heard once," he said, "just after you came to us, that you had someone who went overseas. Someone who didn't get back."

Came to us, she thought. Like a revelation? Is that how he thinks about it now? "Heard that, did you?" she said. "I didn't think busy boys had time for gossip."

He most certainly would have described her joining them differently when he was a boy. But at the time, although she'd been casually affectionate with him, and careful and smart and patient, she had not really concerned herself with how Patrick judged her decision because at eighteen he'd been just too young to comprehend much about how a life got built. And she would have to say that she didn't really care now, either.

"Was it true?" he asked.

He wasn't going to stop. He was going to keep at her and that was fine. "It's still true," she said.

"And ...?" he said. "And ...?"

"I'm an old woman, Patrick," she said.

"You are old," he said. "An old tall woman."

She thought she heard something and looked toward the stairs, stretched back to look around the archway into the hall to make sure it was empty. She coughed, once and hard.

"He was," she started, just loud enough to be heard across the coffee table, "tall. Not noticeable, not handsome or extraordinarily smart. But he would have been able to make a good living somehow. He would have been as steady as a rock, not unlike your father. And he had the best possible body."

"Whoa," Patrick said. "Do I really want to hear this?"

"His body almost matched mine," she said. "We used to take our bodies out to the inland lakes, over to the east side where there weren't any cottages." This is quite nice, she thought, this memory of an innocent young woman, before the war. And she did remember a purity, the pure grace of good sex just discovered, and she felt so lucky to have had that when she was starting out, when she surely could not have survived without it. "I loved him," she said, finishing her Scotch, "and he most certainly loved me."

Patrick topped up their drinks. "And then there was a war," he said. "And because he was young and fit he got sent overseas. And then he was killed."

"And then he got blown to bits in a field in France. And he wasn't alone. There were sixteen from just here, so multiply that. And lots of the ones who did get back were lost in some other way. Some of your father's bits got left behind, remember. Bits he could have used."

"Were you engaged?" Patrick asked.

"Not officially," she said. "They came to tell his mother. I didn't find out how and where and when for hours." She drained her cup again. "His mother would not have liked me much, although I didn't ever hear that for sure."

"Because you were rough," he said.

"But I wasn't," she said. "I've never been rough. Only my family, my background."

She sat up straight to begin to gather things on the tray. "I kept myself busy," she said, "remembering him, all the things about him. It can pass a lot of time. I wouldn't have noticed another man's interest if it had parked itself outside my door." Oh, such easy words, she thought. And said with such a convincing firmness, as if she had been always ready, always on guard, for questions like this.

Patrick picked up the bottle to fill his own cup again and reached across to hers but she stretched out a hand to block the flow.

"Sometimes I used to take Sandra Elliot out to the east side of the inland lakes," he said. "For years I never travelled without a blanket."

"You and Paul both," she said. "I was the one who pulled your blankets from the trunk every fall and washed them. Did you never notice that they didn't smell as bad as they might have?"

"Maybe we found the same dunes," he said. "Do you remember where you went exactly?" He lifted his eyebrows, mimicked an exaggerated, prurient interest. "Perhaps we spread our blankets on the same warm, moonlit sand."

Margaret laughed, abruptly, loudly, covered her mouth to stifle the sound.

"You're blushing," Patrick said. "This I've heard about but never seen." He reached for her arm. "Take your hand away."

She brushed him off, stood up and turned her back on him, bent to gather the cups, her laughter muted from sound to the familiar shaking movement of her broad shoulders.

She lifted the tray and started toward the kitchen, through the hall. She stopped in mid-stride. Bill was sitting on the stairs, on the steps that fanned to make the turn, curled up in his pyjamas, his arms wrapped around himself for warmth, his eyes shut tight against God knows what.

"You're there," Margaret said.

Bill stood up, pushed himself up, staggering a bit against the wall. "Sylvia," he said. "Come to bed. Both of you."

Patrick recovered quickly. "Yes," he said, loudly, cleanly. "It's about that time." He pulled off his work socks and held them tight in his hands, did not drop them to the floor and leave them for

Margaret as he had when he was a young man. "Our room?" he asked, meaning his and Paul's. He knew it was up there waiting for him, the sheets on his old bed newly washed and ironed so they would feel cool on his skin, the faded quilts stacked three thick the way he liked them, the air in the room freshened with the late afternoon breeze. Earlier, standing sweating in the garden, he had looked up at the sound of their window being thrown open. He had seen his father's arms spread wide to grip the heavy sash.

He understood that he was expected to get up and follow his father. This day, the work he'd done this day, had exhausted him, as he had wanted it to. His body needed and for once had earned the deepest sleep. But he stayed put. Hearing the stumbling footfalls on the stairs, he thought about the man who was still supposed to be his father sitting out there listening, knowing, if he still knew anything, that he would soon be discovered, and then climbing the stairs to his bed to lie there alone and rage about what he'd heard or thought he'd heard. A man who had possessed for most of his life no talent for rage at all, now lost, now helpless, without it.

He lowered his head. He could not, for anything, have lifted his head. He thought about Paul, how good a man he had been, how terrifying it must have been to die so fast, without warning, to be killed instantly, although surely not absolutely instantly, surely not without a brief, black comprehension, and then he thought about sweet Meg, who had not for one moment of her life been sweet and who would never again now be her beloved, difficult, ragged self but always something else, some doped, defeated thing, and he thought about his mother, a mother he could remember not only sick and dying but just as clearly alive at the kitchen table and in the car and in the yard, dying the furthest thing from her mind, her quick, light voice calling out to all of them with praise or correction or surprise, and he thought about Daphne, the steady nerve of her mothering and how wildly, recklessly courageous she was before she fell, pumping the makeshift trapeze as hard as she could above the watching crowd, above the mattresses, smiling her showmanship smile for Murray. At the end of it he thought about a finely wrought first marriage broken by a stupid, sanctimonious man, himself.

He thought if Margaret had not been standing in the hall, he might have ... might have what? What? Broken down? Wept? Lost control? Lost himself? No. Except for the one time, the one long moment of losing Paul, the sharp, blunt shock of losing Paul ... None of that had ever made itself available to him, not even when he was a boy. His options, if that's what they were, had always been much more limited.

Margaret hadn't moved. "Are you sitting there thinking about all of it?" she asked. She didn't approach him, didn't put the tray down. "Perhaps you shouldn't," she said. "I don't."

He looked up at her. "Who knew?" he said.

"Who could have known?" Margaret answered. "None of us." She steadied the tray against the long moon curve of her stomach. "It's all right, Patrick," she said. "You are a kind man. I am a kind woman. There are lots of us around."

He covered his face with his beautiful tired hands as if to hold something back, as if something behind his face was asking to be held back. "Do you ever pray?" he asked.

"I don't waste my time asking for anything," she said. "Although once in a while, perhaps two or three times a year when some small thing happens or maybe doesn't happen, I catch myself feeling thankful."

"Thankful," he said.

"Or maybe lucky," she said, leaving him there, calling back to him from the kitchen. "Your towels are on the dresser. Have your shower now or in the morning, it doesn't matter to us one way or the other."

Patrick got up to put the Scotch away and then he climbed the stairs. Margaret rinsed the cups and saucers in the sink and followed him. There was no further talk. They slept quickly and soundly, all three of them, their separate exhaustions quietly absorbed by the house, by its safety, its comfort, its simple, blessed walls.

AFTER a breakfast of bacon and French toast with whipped butter and a pitcher of this spring's maple syrup, the kind of luxury breakfast Margaret allowed only once or twice a year now, Patrick and

Bill unhitched the trailer from the Lincoln and drove out to the nursery on the highway for seed. Bill had the list in his hands, held it up close to his face.

"Geraniums," he said. "I don't remember that we decided on geraniums." He reached toward the radio and Patrick, anticipating his wish, turned it down for him. "Tell me if this is right," he said. "Corn. Geraniums. Peppers. Potatoes. Broccoli. Asparagus. Peas."

"Sounds about right to me," Patrick said.

Bill reached out again. "Who is this guy?" he said. "What the hell is he talking about?"

When Patrick told him it was the CBC, it was Arthur Black, and that he talked very quickly, that was his style, Bill said, "I don't like broccoli." He was studying the radio, trailing his good left fingers over the buttons. When he finally found the right one, he punched it off. "They don't necessarily pick up on it, what you don't like."

"So tell her," Patrick said, glancing over. "It shouldn't have to be any big deal."

Bill shifted in his seat to look directly at this son of his. "Whatever difficulty Margaret and I might have," he said, "would never under any circumstances become a concern of yours." He turned away, muttered, "You worry about your own God damned life." When they pulled into the parking lot, to close it off for good, he said, "I don't intend to be eating very much broccoli."

The nursery was having a busy morning. They had recently expanded, there was a bigger, better sign over the doors and a bigger, paved parking lot. Bill claimed to know a dozen cars. "Everybody's here this morning," he said, throwing off his seat belt, checking his tie, opening his door wide before the Lincoln had come to a full stop.

They were nearly two hours finding what they'd come for. Bill said he wanted to see where things were now, what was new. He said they had no reason to rush. Patrick let him lead them around the old greenhouse and then outside and into another and then into another. In the courtyard behind the main building, looking over several neat rows of small "accent" trees, most of them stunted, grafted at a modest height for small properties, the grafts gnarled like a big man's hard fist, Bill laughed out loud and slapped Patrick on the back as if they were compatriots, as if such obvious stupidity must have been staged for their enjoyment. "Whatever these are," he said, "they sure as Christ aren't trees. Imagine," he said, "passing these things off as trees. And people falling for it."

As they wandered around and around again, he made several of the other gardeners stop and shake hands with Patrick. Some of them remembered Patrick, of course, some of them did not. Bill told everyone that he had decided to replant Margaret's garden and that he'd asked Patrick to come up and give him a hand. He told them they would have to come over to see his new space-age garden tools, said they were beyond belief. He walked up and down the same soggy aisles a dozen times, reached out to touch the barely blooming plants on either side as if he loved them. He had words for everyone he passed, smiled grandly, bent to kiss all the women who would be kissed.

On the way home with the seeds and the geraniums, Bill checked the time and then told Patrick to turn at Albert Street, to swing by Turnball's barn down at the creek. He said the Old Babes' Committee was dedicating the new park today and why didn't they stop off for a few minutes to watch the proceedings.

"Who are they dedicating it to?" Patrick asked.

"Oh, themselves, I expect," Bill said.

Turnball's barn was gone but there were a dozen cars parked where it had once stood and about thirty people standing around down near the creek. The park wasn't big. It was only a cleaned-up section of Stonebrook Creek with a wide footbridge over the water to an open expanse of cleaned-up land on the other side. Whoever was behind the park had got enough money together for an elaborate wooden swing set and a slide and a complicated climbing gym on the far side of the water and the grass had been roped off and reseeded, although it was still pretty patchy. Several small red maples and a clump-birch had been staked for strength against the hazard of wind and there were three large picnic tables placed in the shade of the willows at the water.

And it was obvious even sitting in the car that they had tampered with the creek bed, that rocks and stones had been either hauled in or substantially, carefully rearranged. Someone with a forklift or a front-end loader had tried to make themselves a little work of art, tried to complicate the course, the appearance and sound, of the current. As if the random placement, the natural state of things, was not worth watching. And all of this effort, this expense, all of it for the benefit of someone who might want to stand for a while on a footbridge.

Bill didn't get out of the car this time. "Too blazing hot," he said. "It's going to be one of those days when walking is more like swimming. Our first this year." He was leaning forward studying the controls on the dash. "We'll just sit here with the air on if you don't mind."

Patrick adjusted the air-conditioning. "What a fine park," he said.

"Maybe," Bill said. "We'll hope so." Sitting there, he began to play at the stubs of his missing fingers, a habit he had begun only recently. Soon after the war, the scarred skin had healed and faded back to an almost fleshy pink but now it had been rubbed raw, it was once again a wound. "They came knocking," he said. "I gave them fifty bucks and Margaret gave them her own fifty. You should give some thought to doing the same."

Patrick did not respond to the admonition. After Mr. McFarlane's note was paid off, years before, he had found his own private way to move that generosity on down the line. Now, with student loans, no kid was as trapped as he would have been, and he believed this was a good thing, removing the chance for success from the realm of sheer, dumb luck. And it certainly had been sheer, dumb luck, Mr. McFarlane being there to decide that he was worthy of risk. Anyway, if he remembered correctly, such things were not to be bandied about.

Bill was searching around for the control that would make his seat go back. "Your mother would have been pleased as punch to be part of this," he said, nodding toward the crowd. "It's just her kind of thing. Improving the filthy creek." He'd found the right knob to push and he stretched out his legs and crossed his arms. "And she has always supported Margaret. Don't ever doubt that. All these years not a word against Margaret." He pointed his left index finger, directing Patrick's attention to the activity at the creek.

Patrick looked from face to face and finally recognized Charles Taylor, who was dressed as he'd always been dressed in pressed pants and a shirt and tie, maybe the same tie. Except for the snow-white hair, Charles hadn't changed much. From this distance, at least, he still had the body of the young man who'd spent one of his summers watching a bunch of kids get ready for a circus performance. Patrick tried to calculate just how elderly the rarely seen Mrs. Taylor might be by now and then he recognized the woman standing beside Charles. It was Margaret's friend Angela Johnston, who was old and small and bent over a stainless-steel walker that reflected the sunlight. Perhaps Angela was the mother now.

A middle-aged man who was probably the mayor spoke briefly and then a woman Patrick was sure he had never known stepped forward to bend down and pull a bright red cloth off a plaque. The plaque was affixed to a rough chunk of black granite that sat low to the ground like a modest grave marker and as soon as the words of dedication were exposed everyone standing down at the creek began to applaud. When some of them lifted their clapping hands high in the air to signify a particular pleasure, Bill joined them with his own hands, shouting, "Hurray for the Old Babes."

MARGARET had taken a plate of cold baked beans out to the garden bench and she continued to wait with the back door open and her ear half-cocked to the phone. She could catch the phone in four rings, she had counted many times before. She knew their delay could be either very bad or very good, she realized there might be consequences for which she was unprepared, but she was enjoying herself nonetheless.

Looking over the newly enriched, perfected soil, she decided it was a shame to bother with the vegetables. Why shouldn't the earth just stay as it was? Undisturbed. Dark and rich and tender. The May sun was directly overhead. She could feel its heat on her thinning hair and on her scalp and on the back of her large freckled hands, the skin there like all of her skin now, no longer tight to her body but loose and thin. The slats of the bench, exposed since sunrise, warmed her backside, a backside which Bill, having just read a borrowed, beat-up copy of *Lady Chatterley's Lover*, had once affectionately called a great sloping arse, and which was more and more often now, unaccountably, chilled.

She stood up slowly from the bench and stretched her long muscles, arched her long back. She dropped her head alternately to each shoulder, then let it fall heavily back so that her face was flat to the warming sun, to the drifting clouds, eased it slowly forward until her chin touched her chest. She bent at the waist to try to touch her toes, extended her long arms skyward as she straightened, splayed her fingers. She did this three times. Then she swung her arms, made five windmill circles with each arm in turn. She inhaled deeply, pulling new air down into her body, knowing it would do her good.

Although she had never been a particularly fit person, neither had she been slovenly or slow to rise to an occasion, and she credited her relatively good health, her usual feeling of well-being, to her day-to-day living, and to the quiet, lifelong, persistent energy that day-to-day living demanded of a person. If her eighty-one-year-old body already carried within it the seeds of its own demise, a murky possibility she allowed herself to entertain only on the worst of days, Well, she thought, tell me something I don't know.

Warmed up, she stepped into the plot. With wide-open, calculating eyes she imposed a mental grid, marked off the earth square foot by square foot in her mind. She had to be careful to plant her steps firmly because the earth could easily be soft where it looked hard and hard where it looked soft but she believed there was a very good chance that Patrick had unearthed something more with the deep cuts of the Rototiller. She believed, too, that such a search might require a promise. I will never tell, she thought. Whatever I find, I will never tell. I will hide it on my person, take it back into the earth with me when I go.

She was looking, she supposed, for an artifact unique to another century, something rarely seen any more, some small thing meant to be solid against rot. She assumed the treasure would be shiny, expected the sun to throw the necessary light.

1997

MAGGIE dreamed the night before her wedding day that Kevin Costner, or someone like him, who was with her at a run-down rainy cottage on some river, had a very short, perky penis that he proudly called a smart penis and that someone else, some dark Robert Mitchum film-noir type, standing half dressed and hunched in a shadowy alley doorway smoking a cigarette, had one that was a foot long and thin as a pencil and apparently exhausted, worn right down to almost nothing. As she came to consciousness, these disparate images, these quite separate men crowded together in one lusty dream frame, tried hard to cling to the rafters of her brain. But they were fading fast, they were being booted out the back door, asked to leave with the sleep that made them. Well, she thought, not quite ready to open her eyes, that wasn't very bridelike.

When she did open her eyes to the light from the window, the men were gone, completely and immediately gone. It was almost as if they had not been real at all. Throwing off the duvet, getting up to walk to the bathroom, she thought, I am only anticipating fidelity, I am only putting foolish things behind me. And then, levelling a steady gaze at her face in the dappled mirror above the cracked pedestal sink, she thought, Hollywood. Nothing happens without Hollywood. Not even the dreams of a bride. She turned on the tap and laid some Colgate along the bristles of her toothbrush.

When Maggie and Jill were teenagers Daphne had often asked about their dreams, perhaps as a kind of quick, maternal, psychic check-up. As with nearly everything else in those days, sometimes they played it straight and sometimes they did not. Only once in a while, when they were at some loss or in some muddle, when they really needed her to be tuned into them, did they actually tell Daphne a version of the truth. Otherwise they thought and said that

[257]

she was being invasive, that she was just trying to shove herself into their lives.

The water was pouring out steaming hot so she knew no one else had showered yet. She wanted it to be as hot as her skin could stand, tested it on her open palm, told herself that even the water pressure this morning might be taken as a good omen. She stepped into the tub and pulled the curtain closed.

One summer she and Jill claimed to be having the same dreams, the details varying only slightly, the promise or the menace easily reflected from one dream to its sister dream. Daphne stopped asking after that summer. She told them that, try as she might, she could no longer make any sense whatever of the insides of their heads, that they were now and possibly forevermore beyond her comprehension.

Jill had proposed a theory then that dreams were really alien life forms, floating around at large in the night air, wafting through clouds and shingles and ceilings and blankets in search of an empty, welcoming brain where they could relax and thrive. She said she figured by the time the dreams discovered that they could not make it in a human brain, could not thrive, it was too late to get out. They were already dying. "Pffftt," she'd said, snapping her fingers. "Dead and gone."

Daphne's ordinary conversation with Maggie and Jill had always been loaded up with words like *wafting* and *welcoming* and *thrive* and *gone*. The only children's stories they'd had from her were those filled with what she named the best words, the weird, strange, yummy words. She said what actually happened wasn't nearly as important, and besides, if they were paying close attention, it was always pretty much the same old story anyway: "Be careful, children. You are all alone. Be very good or else."

By the time Jill was old enough to hear this, Maggie was in grade four and quite used to asking the hard questions. Of course she had challenged her mother, of course she had wanted to know, "Or else what?" and Jill had chimed in after her, imitating almost everything Maggie did then, everything she could manage.

Cuddled together with the two of them, her own body solid and calm in the middle of the bed, their two small clean bodies wiggling and wrapping themselves tight around her, their lovely little fingers pulling on the ribbons that were threaded through the bodice of her nightgown, Daphne told them, "Well, something will come and get you. Eat you up. There won't be a trace of you left. You know that." She gave them this nonsense to make them snort and giggle, to make them flail their arms and legs in theatrical fear, to allow them their beloved dramatics. She could offer such nonsense because she believed and they believed that they were both already smart enough to seriously doubt many of the things the world offered.

Their storybooks had been packed and brought with them when they moved from London into the old McFarlane house. They had their own shelf on one side of the small fireplace in the den, where they sat unread but dusted, waiting patiently for grandchildren, Daphne said. All the other shelves were filled with the small boxes Daphne had started to collect when she graduated from nursing. Many of the boxes were finely crafted wood, some of them were glass, some were clay. One of them, Maggie's favourite, brought back from Italy by Aunt Andy, was pressed tin.

So Maggie knew what any kids she might have with Josh would get to hear at their grandmother's knee. And she had wondered how Josh might counter Daphne if and when they did have kids. He would counter her. Josh liked to believe that he himself relied exclusively on logic and consideration, and because of this, or in spite of this, he had no patience with Daphne, with what he called her never-ending attempt to influence. The first time Maggie had brought him home from graduate school to meet everyone, to show him how her life had been, he hadn't been able to restrain himself. Sneaking across the hall, into her bed, holding her in his beefy arms, he'd started to mumble something he obviously considered benign about the implications of feminism, about women making very odd choices and how those choices could have a severe impact on other, innocent people.

She'd thrown him out of her bed, before she knew she was going to do it she'd pushed him to the floor, the thud when he landed a loud giveaway in the nighttime quiet of the house. He had been very surprised. The following night, back in Toronto, she'd noticed a bruise on his hip in the shape of a pear.

Standing under the hard stream of hot water, thinking about Josh's resistance to her mother, which by September would be moot because they'd be three thousand miles away and up to their ears in books and papers and seminars, and then thinking about the tone of his voice when he'd said that word *choice*, the cool, academic detachment, Maggie thought, not for the first time, Isn't it peculiar that the people who love me best know so little about the way life, my life, works.

Above the noise of the water bursting out to cleanse her long bride body she could hear Jill at the bathroom door, pounding. Jill was more excited about this wedding than she was, had been for weeks. "Miss," Jill yelled. "I've got some breakfast for you."

Maggie opened the door wrapped in one of the nearly threadbare beach towels Margaret had picked up for them in Port Huron ten years before, when they'd first started swimming every chance they got. This one was hers because it had the clipper ship. Jill's had a giraffe.

Jill was clowning, standing erect like a French maid holding a tray of coffee and orange juice and two banana muffins. She had just turned nineteen. Recently and often, Bill had told Margaret it was like having Sylvia back and it was almost true, Jill was very much like Sylvia in the face, maybe especially in the gestures. Maggie had always looked more like Daphne, although just lately shades of Murray's tall and quietly elegant mother were seeping through, the way she sometimes lifted her chin when she was listening, her long feet, her confident, muscular hands.

Jill set the breakfast tray down on the sink. "One last day a virgin," she said, picking up a banana muffin, looking it over. "You lucky girl."

"Really?" Maggie said. "Well, I'm certainly relieved to hear that."

Jill took a bite of the muffin. "What are we going to do with ourselves all morning?" she asked. "Josh is coming when?"

"I'm pretty sure it was left that Patrick would meet the plane in London," Maggie said. "Patrick has their tuxes, so I expect Josh and Mark will arrive when Patrick and Stephanie arrive."

"Then we have at least some time," Jill said.

"I think," Maggie said. "I think we should put on our bikinis and lie around the backyard until someone comes out and tells us we have to go get dressed. We could take a dip or two in the pool."

Just after they'd moved into the McFarlane house, when the girls were nine and sixteen, the Stewarts beside them had installed a backyard swimming pool. Making his approach, the backhoe driver had been forced to cut across Daphne's property and when all was said and done he'd chewed up the grass pretty completely and nipped several chunks out of the hedge. Daphne had watched him from the dining-room window but made no complaint and since that day the girls had been offered generous access to the Stewarts' pool. Some afternoons Jeannie Stewart, who was still trim enough to look good in a bathing suit, brought out a pitcher of lemonade and joined them for a quick dip before she stretched out on her chaise with her novel. They were fish in that pool.

They swam and sunbathed until twelve-thirty, when the guys Daphne had hired came around the corner of the house to start setting up the chairs and the sound system and then they went up to shower again, to wash the chlorine out of their hair before they put on their gowns.

Daphne was already dressed, waiting in the kitchen for Maggie to call her. She had written down what she wanted to say, the small, folded sheet of notepaper was tucked in her pocket, but when Maggie did call her she walked up the stairs and into the bedroom totally unprepared for what was waiting for her there. Seeing these young women put together so beautifully, in their light-as-air make-up, their thick, naturally wavy, summer-streaked hair falling, just falling, on their shoulders, she thought, I've done this. I've done this with Murray.

Jill, in pale yellow silk with very high clunky heels to match, was bent down fussing with Maggie's satin hem. Hearing her mother behind her, she carefully lifted the heavy skirt of the bridal gown to reveal Sylvia's white lace garter high on Maggie's thigh. "It is kind of pretty," she said. "Tacky but pretty. Did you already tell us what she's supposed to do with it?"

"She's supposed to take it off at the dance and toss it over her shoulder at the men," Daphne said. "To see who will be the next groom."

"The next groom," Jill said, laughing. "That's mint."

Daphne almost asked Jill to leave them for a few minutes and then she thought, No, if I say it to both of them at once, they will have exactly the same words in their heads later, when they might want to talk about this. She sat down on the bed. "Love," she said, taking one of Margaret's deep breaths. "I am happier for you today than I can say. I'm happy that you are so very accomplished and still able to give yourself over to someone."

She waited for one of them to speak but they were occupied, they were very busy bracing themselves. They both knew there would be more than this, knew just looking at her face.

"We got along all right," Daphne said. "I'm very sorry if the way I decided to do things has hurt either of you in any way, but as far as I can tell we got along all right."

Maggie was lifting her heavy hair in her hand, fluffing it the way she'd once fluffed Margaret's breast. "Everything's fine, Mom," she said. "It is."

"Yeah," Jill said. "Let's not do this today, shall we?"

Jill was smoothing Maggie's skirt again, adjusting the modest satin train. She was thinking about the several thousand times the word *father* had come up in her life when she was a kid, taking her by surprise every time, like a string of firecrackers thrown at her feet. She was thinking about all the other times she could have used, would have been grateful for, an explanation, or a justification, or the truth. When she would have kicked down a door to hear some version of the truth. But of course, of course, the thing would get told not when a daughter needed to hear it but at some other, decided time, when a mother needed to tell it. As if a daughter's place inside a secret was nothing. As if the waiting was nothing.

A little later in their lives, when they did talk about their father and to their father, when they and everyone who mattered to them knew and knowing was all right, Maggie and Jill both confessed that listening to their mother the day of the wedding they had been terrified that she was going to stand up from the bed and pronounce a name, that she was going to just hand it over on a tray, like the head of John the Baptist. Jill confessed that what had frightened her most was the possibility of two different fathers, the possibility that they were not full sisters which, looking back, she could see was just enormously, wondrously stupid, because how could that have made any difference?

Daphne had not written down anything more and she had made a promise to herself that whatever happened in that room, she would not start rambling. She picked up Maggie's headpiece from the bed and handed it to Jill.

"Have you cut my rose yet?" Maggie asked.

When they were in the planning stages for this day, Maggie had refused an elaborate bridal bouquet, asking why couldn't she just carry a rose from the garden instead. Soon after they'd moved in Daphne had started to bring Mrs. McFarlane's garden back to life, had taught herself how to keep the roses going, replacing worn-out bushes one at a time as necessary. And she'd got the house itself almost back to the casual elegance of its Mrs. McFarlane days. It hadn't taken much, a softer green for the kitchen cupboards, a new kitchen floor laid over the old grey linoleum, fresh paint for every wall, the woodwork properly cleaned and buffed to a shine, the floors stripped of their yellowed varnish. And all the French doors brought down from the third-floor attic and hung again between the living room and dining room and at the vestibule and at the entrances to the sunroom and the den. It was Mary who found the stack of French doors under a tarp in the attic and she'd found an ancient, stunningly ugly but carefully boxed chandelier up there too, which Mrs. McFarlane must have decided against years before. Even after she'd announced she was going to leave Patrick, Mary had still come to help Daphne and the girls get settled in, her own affection for the house evident in the way she touched the heavy front doors, the banister, the thick plaster walls.

Standing up from the bed now to leave her magnificent daughters, Daphne asked, "What colour rose do you think?"

"Oh, I don't know," Maggie said. "Pink? Red? White?"

"Red," Jill said. "Dark red would be extremely, utterly sophisti-cated."

Maggie had asked no one but Jill to stand up with her. She had never had only one best friend because she had seven or eight really good friends, a couple from summer jobs, two from university, three still from high school. And having only Jill simplified things because Josh had just one good friend, Mark. Anyway, she had never dreamed of a big production.

Daphne was going to give her away, although Daphne said, when she was told by the United Church minister that this was still the custom, "Just so we understand each other, I'm not actually giving her away. Not on your life."

And Patrick. After the minister's visit, Daphne had told Maggie if she wanted a man there too, she had a couple to choose from, although perhaps Grandpa shouldn't be asked. "Then it has to be Uncle Patrick or Murray," Maggie said. "And I suppose it should be Uncle Patrick, because he's blood."

"Blood," Daphne said. "Is that what he is?"

WHEN she came in from the garden with Maggie's dark red rose, Josh and Mark were sitting in the living room, looking a bit stiff but nonetheless exquisite in their tuxedos. They were having an early and likely necessary drink with Patrick and Stephanie. Murray and Kate's Toyota had just pulled into the driveway, and Sarah, in a wide-brimmed straw hat and a wonderfully short peach dress, with Jake and Natalie, the cousins nobody knew, following close behind her like goslings, was walking over to the Toyota with her arms flung open. She was laughing, calling out something Daphne couldn't hear. Although he'd had his plane ticket, Rob had not come back with them for the wedding. His job had disappeared out from under him, the result of some multinational cost-saving merger, so he was in Seattle, at an interview set up by an old friend from home, from England. He was scrambling, this was how Sarah had put it to Margaret. When Margaret told Daphne, clearly worried and angry and rattled because there was nothing she could do to help them, she'd been as close to tears as Daphne had ever seen her. "God, there's a lot of costs being saved," she'd said. "Every new day, wherever you turn, costs being saved."

Margaret and Bill were sitting out on the wraparound porch in the wobbly, many-times-repainted Muskoka chairs. Through the big living-room window, Daphne watched her father reach over to take Margaret's hand, looking for comfort against the onslaught of his family. They had just yesterday had word that his brother Gerry, Uncle Gerry, had died after a long stay in hospital in Windsor, and that Aunt Eileen was not in good shape at all, so there was that, too, to think about today, and the funeral to attend on Monday. And another funeral on Tuesday, at least for Margaret and Bill.

Charles Taylor, who had become an old man, had also died, some time in the last week. He'd been missing for a few days and finally some kids had found him under the railroad bridge two miles past the golf course, beyond Livingston's gully, drowned in Stonebrook Creek. It had never been a particularly hard crossing under that bridge but it was thought that Charles had lost his footing on some mossy rocks and gone down hard. On hearing this sad bit of news, Bill had told Margaret he only hoped Charles had knocked himself out cold before he had to suffer the insult of drowning. Margaret did not tell Bill or anyone else that she believed the tarnished silver whistle she'd found in the turned garden soil that May afternoon must surely have belonged to Charles at some time, or that its presence in their garden was a mystery she sometimes pondered.

Until very recently, Margaret had been determined to resist what she considered to be the too-easy solution of drugs to control Bill's moods, but she'd told Daphne she would give him a little something extra with his lunch today, to keep him steady. She'd said it was going to be a long day for Bill and he wouldn't want to do anything to spoil it for Maggie.

At five after three, after all the wedding guests had been seated on fold-up chairs in the backyard and just before it was time for Patrick to join Daphne and Maggie, to offer Maggie his arm and escort her down the aisle to the recently built arbour, to the minister, to Jill and Mark, to Josh, he walked over to Murray, who was sitting near the front with Kate and Stephanie, and pulled him up out of his chair.

Murray hesitated, understandably, and looked a bit worried but this did not prompt Patrick to explain himself. "Just come," he said.

Then he looked down through the rows for Andy, who had been late arriving because she'd had to drive into London for Meg and when she'd got to the home Meg wasn't dressed because she thought maybe she didn't want to come. Andy had been watching Patrick, had watched Murray stand up from his chair and head for the back. She was waiting, ready to understand what Patrick wanted to happen, ready to catch his eye if it came her way. When he found her, she nodded and got up quickly, grabbing Sarah on her way to the back.

Maggie had been watching Patrick too, anxious for him to come to stand beside her. Someone had given the signal. The processional music had already started. Jill had gone down the aisle, she was already up there, and Stephen, with his Lab, Sailor, sitting at strict attention beside him, had started his video camera. People would be wondering what the hell was going on.

And then she got it. When Patrick moved in beside her offering his arm, and Murray and Andy and Sarah gathered in close behind them, she looked straight ahead down the aisle and muttered, "It *would* have to be a cast of thousands. Silly me." She patted Patrick's back. "Anyone else would likely be surprised," she said. She took his arm because what else was there to do?

Daphne did not turn around. She was thinking, This is good enough, this is more than good enough. But Patrick wasn't finished. In the instant before they would have started to move forward down the aisle, he frowned and pulled his arm away and stepped back behind Murray, whispering loudly that he had to fix his damned cummerbund again, Jesus, he hated cummerbunds. Murray quickly moved to help him, to lift his jacket and check the hooks, but Patrick shoved him off, pushed him forward. "Go," he said.

When Murray moved in close to offer Maggie his own bent, available arm, Daphne did turn around. If she could make Patrick meet her eyes, she would not even have to speak, she would not have to ask him if he couldn't please just cease and desist, please, for once in his manipulating life, couldn't he just stop the manoeuvres. But he would not meet her eyes. Of course he wouldn't.

[266]

She started them off. Patrick and Andy and Sarah followed, Andy comprehending, finally, and nearly blind with tears.

When they got to the arbour, no one but the minister and Josh could see Maggie because she was so surrounded and those were the words she whispered to Josh before their vows began. "God, look at me. I'm surrounded."

But they left her to him soon enough. They split off, took their separate places in Daphne's backyard to listen attentively as Maggie and Josh made their many promises.

The Presbyterian women had been signed on to do the buffet, which they'd decided to serve on long tables in the side yard, and as soon as the ceremony was over they started to pour out the kitchen door with covered platters of food. The wedding party was going to use this time for photographs and while they waited the guests were expected to more or less take care of each other, to find someone to engage in conversation and to help themselves to canapés and punch, both kinds. The little kids, some of whom were Patrick's grandchildren, some of whom were Andy's, moved together through the crowd in spinning, dressed-up clusters, the girls holding hands and swinging their hands together in quick friendship, the boys following along, kicking at the grass, sometimes jumping in front of the girls to entertain them with clumsy taunts.

Bill shouldered his way up to the head of the line for punch and as soon as someone poured him two cups of it, he got away from Margaret and moved determinedly past the people he should have talked to until he found Patrick. He handed Patrick his punch and told him that he wanted everyone to go up to the Town Hall steps for a picture. Because it would be gone soon.

"You know the bastards are tearing the Town Hall down," he told Patrick, pulling on his sleeve, fidgeting. "When the boys in Toronto are finished there aren't going to be any more towns, just one big stretched-out mess. Those assholes think we'll all be happy as clams to live in one big stretched-out mess." He paused to give Patrick a chance to join him in his rage. "A city," he said. "That's what they think they're going to call us."

Patrick knew that the province in its wisdom had recently

decided that amalgamation was the way to go. To save money, five separate towns much like this one would soon be joined at the hip so that all the administration, which the government proudly and loudly described as suspiciously expensive, could be handled in one central place, which was not here.

Of course it cost something to keep a building like the Town Hall running, heat in the winter, maintenance, insurance. And not surprisingly it needed substantial structural repair. Margaret had told Patrick that some of the guts, the dance floor upstairs and a few of the ceiling beams, had rotted almost right through. But now that it was going to be more or less useless there seemed no point in sinking good money into it. She told him those in favour said either nothing lasts forever or progress sometimes hurts and those opposed were mute, made impotent, because it was their money the government was wanting to save and how could any sane person argue with that? In one of their last motions, the town council had apparently decided that after the building was levelled and gone the lot could be used for a skateboard park, with maybe a ramp or two, to keep the high-flying baggy pants kids off the streets.

"Get everyone organized," Bill said, spilling some of his punch on Patrick's just recently purchased one-size-larger tux, then pulling a crumpled handkerchief from his back pocket to blot it up. "We can be up there and get this thing done in no time."

Patrick left Bill with Stephanie and Kate to go and look for Daphne. He found her on the front porch steps, heading for one of the cars. She wouldn't look at him and she didn't stop walking. "When this is over," she said, "you and I are going to have ourselves a little talk."

"Fine," he said.

"It wasn't your decision to make," she said. "It was mine."

"Fine," he said.

"What the hell did you think you were doing?" she asked. "Did you think it would go unnoticed?"

"Most of the people watching thought it was a simple screw-up," he said. "And that's what I was counting on." He stopped following her. "I do know people."

He knew too that he should have gone straight to Maggie with Bill's request but he asked anyway. Hearing the request, Daphne was able to remember where she was, she was able to let the other go, temporarily. She turned to tell Patrick that she found herself in a difficult spot, that she wasn't sure the photographer would have time. She said he was a friend of Josh's parents, they had arranged for the pictures, and unbeknownst to her the plan appeared to be to use the time between the ceremony and the reception to go over to Stonebrook Park. The photographer had come early enough to spend a half hour driving around town trying to find some place suitable and he had decided they should go over to the park to take advantage of the footbridge and the water and, of course, the rocks. "They want picturesque," she said, shrugging her shoulders. "It's their call."

When Patrick reported back, Bill poured the last of his punch on the grass at his feet. "I would have paid for the pictures." He was beside himself. "Why didn't someone ask me to pay for the God damned pictures?"

THE dance was at the arena, because it was close and because Daphne had said there was no good reason to ask people to drive back into the city. Maggie's friends, who were staying out at the golf course motel, had spent the earliest part of the hot afternoon decorating the hall, drinking Long Island Iced Tea and filling each other in on their lives as they draped steamers from one side of the room to the other and covered the walls with clusters of white balloons and oversized satin bows. Krissy and Carol had helped the florist, who was the granddaughter of the late Archie Stutt, bring in all the centrepieces, the sweetheart roses and the mums and daisies, and Margaret had set up her old bridge table just inside the door and covered it with one of Sylvia's mother's embroidered cloths to hold a display of pictures: Maggie at about six months settled securely in Bill's arms, looking up confidently into his face, Maggie and Jill swinging hard on park swings somewhere, Maggie off to her first day of school when they still lived in the city, and another picture of her as an older student, looking embarrassed and annoyed to be holding a plaque for second prize in public speaking. Maggie almost as she was now, posed on the diving board of the Stewarts' pool like a pin-up girl, rudely shaving her legs.

A deejay friend of Jill's boyfriend Ryan, Crank, they called him, took care of the music and it wasn't half bad. He was young but he was very good at gauging exactly this kind of crowd and he had something in his repertoire of CDs for nearly everyone who wanted to dance. Jill had told Daphne that given enough to drink, Crank would do a really funny Elvis impersonation, an ironic imperson-ation, and Daphne had told Jill that she would leave it in her hands then, making damned sure Crank did not get enough to drink.

Maggie and Josh had started things off. They were obviously uncomfortable with everyone staring at them, watching to see them do the thing newlyweds were supposed to do, whatever that might be. As soon as she decently could, Maggie whispered something in Josh's ear and stepped away from him. She found Patrick and Josh got his mother and soon the newly formed couples broke off again, and again, collecting more dancers, filling the floor.

When Bill heard the first bars of what he considered to be a legit-imate waltz, he bowed low to Margaret and guided her in among the others. He was astonishingly smooth for a man in his eighties, smooth as butter.

Daphne moved from table to table alone to talk to the guests and to thank them. Maggie and Josh had opened many of the gifts and people had been thoughtful in the choices, and generous. After she'd finished her rounds, as she was making her way back to her table, she noticed Patrick walking across the floor toward her. He was going to ask her to dance, and what could be more normal, more civilized? Of course he would be counting on her not to make a scene in front of all these people, "a public spectacle of yourself," as Grandma Ferguson used to call it, which, when Daphne was a girl, had never failed to make her extremely curious about private spectacles. She had imagined these going on behind closed doors all over town, muted and bound by walls and unwit-nessed, but still, as the word itself suggested, spectacular, still some-thing to be part of.

Those nearly forgotten Saturday nights out at the Casino dances had not been for naught. Unlike Josh, unlike John, neither of whom was old enough or experienced enough to understand that it was necessary to take control of a woman on the dance floor, Patrick guided her with confidence and grace, and listening to the old Motown song, she was almost charmed. But she was waiting for him to acknowledge his responsibility, his mistake. It did not have to be complicated, he did not have to dredge up a fake humility. He could say, for instance, All right, I'm sorry, I likely overstepped. I am sorry. When he tried instead for the pretence of oblivion, nodding at people and smiling, lifting his arm from her back to wave to someone sitting at a table, she let go his hand and pinched the flesh above his thumb, hard. "I want you to leave us alone," she said.

Anyone watching them dance and talk might have thought Patrick was having one of the best nights of his life. His reportedly brilliant niece was successfully launched into the world with her equally brilliant young husband, and Daphne looked so obviously, deservedly content. Many people assumed it had been Patrick's money that had made things a little easier for Daphne.

"Don't you ever ask yourself," he asked, nodding again at someone behind her, "if this might be too much for the girls to carry? If *you* might be too much for them to carry?"

"No," she said. "That is *not* something I ask myself. You think you know them but you haven't got even a partial understanding of how strong they are." She pinched him again.

"Jesus," he said, dropping his hand to his side. "Are they in the habit of inflicting pain on innocent bystanders like their brat mother?"

"We can only hope," she said.

The song ended and Patrick took her back to her table, and before she could sit down Murray was beside her, leading her onto the floor again.

After he got her surrounded, buried in the crowd of dancers, he asked, "Did you get a chance to share a few thoughts with Patrick?"

"One or two," she said.

He pulled her a bit closer but only to steady her. "There is a small possibility that he's right," he said. "He sometimes does have a wonky kind of instinct. You have to give him that."

"Are you ready to give him that?" she asked. "Is Kate ready?" Saying Kate's name, she realized that it was not very fair to Kate, using her for this.

"I'm just wondering if it could be time," he said. "We didn't ever decide that it would never happen. Did we? Was that our intention?"

"What if it doesn't make them happy?" she asked, shaking a bit now, her hands and her arms and her bare shoulders. "What then?"

"Why wouldn't it?" he asked, pulling back to look down at her face, which meant he expected an answer. He didn't get his answer but in the expectation, in the blunt calm of his expectation, the conceit that had long since settled in a dark, guarded corner of her heart, the conviction that it was enough to mean no harm, that this could keep her safe, and innocent, shifted. Shifted and broke apart and came scraping out into the open chambers of her heart like jagged shards of shrapnel. For better or worse, Murray had decided that this was the day to let her know what the lie had cost him, and that he might want recompense. That he might be prepared, finally, to desert her.

When he turned her to move off the floor, he put his hand, absently, on the firm rise of her rear end. She could feel in the dead weight of the gesture how little it meant to him now and she remembered that hand, or an entirely different hand attached to an entirely different man, resting comfortably on her body, at home on her body, anywhere.

Just before they joined the others at the table, he bent down to her. "This is something we could do," he said, already leaving her, reaching out for Sarah, who apparently had made him promise her a jive, if jives there were.

She watched Murray and Sarah go at it. They were not the only ones on the floor, as Murray had no doubt feared, because Jill and Ryan and Rebecca and her boyfriend soon joined them. Watching Murray spin Sarah, watching him pull her in close and fling her out again, she wondered where on earth he'd learned to do that. And then she thought, Things are going to change.

She excused herself to go to the clammy cement-block washroom, telling herself as she skirted the dancers, as she nodded and laughed at her dancing guests, this whole damned wedding was a mistake. My mistake. The kids didn't care if they had a big day, it was me, greedy for a good time. For all of us to be together, to mark their happiness with a bit of our own. She was almost at the washroom door when Patrick's John grabbed her hand and suggested with some quick footwork and a quirky grin and a hopeful tilt of his head that they could join the jivers. "Can't," she said, pointing to the washroom. "Sorry." John just shrugged and gave her a quick bear hug before he let her go, holding her a few seconds longer than he might have because Stephen was coming at them with his video camera, ducking through the dancers in his beautiful waistcoat, a fine blue silk shot with gold thread.

She was making her way to the washroom to cry and John's bear hug had nearly brought it on before she got herself free. And what might John have done if this middle-aged woman, this aunt whom he probably assumed to be entirely grown up and without any serious doubts in her heart, and certainly without shrapnel, had started to bawl in his strong, innocent arms? Laugh and hug her harder, that was her best guess. People like John, young people, seemed to put a lot of faith in a big, spontaneous display of physical affection and, from what she'd seen, most of them were absolutely sincere with their hugs, as if the raunchy pleasure of sex, so highly prized and so hard won by their parents, was finally not quite enough.

The washroom was stuffed full of high-spirited young women touching up their lipstick and blush and mascara and trading earrings and hiking their carefully understated but elegant dresses high to adjust their pantyhose. Friends, all of them. Brash, beautiful, and dangerous to know, that's what they'd called themselves when they were teenagers stretched out on Daphne's sofa and across her chairs and sprawled on the rug with pillows, their legs intertwined as they talked far into their teenaged nights, deciding together exactly what kind of women they were getting ready to become.

She could not retreat back out to the dance floor because in this riotous company she herself quickly became what these young women believed her to be, which was nothing more or less than their friend's middle-aged mother, the lovely, proud, and evidently beloved mother of the bride. Pleased for her and with themselves, because in fact almost all of them had grown up to be what both she and most of their own mothers had promised they might, they passed her around the small crowded washroom, from embrace to embrace, and after she finally got herself safely locked in a cubicle she couldn't even pee, let alone cry.

Sitting there waiting for a reasoned calm to overtake her, willing it, because it was something very much like calm she was going to need, she listened to the excited voices on the other side of the partition as they interrupted and contradicted and verified each other, each one of them fighting to hold her own in the chaos. It is chaos, she thought. That's what they provide for each other. There was a softening of the voices and then the more distinct sound of only two or three of them still standing at the mirrors and then the certain silence of an emptied room. Calm in an empty washroom, she thought. Well, fine.

She opened the cubicle door to a wavy, squared-off reflection of her small, proud, evidently beloved self in a deep raspberry linen two-piece dress, the colour Jill's decision and just exactly right for this day, for this night of dancing. Turning on the tap at the sink, at the mirror, which was not wavy at all if you stood close enough, she saw in the damp, godawful light that her bare shoulders looked cold but that her hair, a thick, robust, and envied silver grey, was holding fine, and that the skin on her neck beneath her jaw was smooth and taut, and that her face was broken, illuminated by a clean, white, unanticipated smile. A smile from nowhere.

At the house, before they'd come over to the dance, she had gathered her hair and tied it at the nape of her neck with a soft, wide silver ribbon and she understood now, in this clammy quiet, that she had gathered and secured her hair deliberately, to expose the widow's peak, to remind at least a few of the dancers, to remind herself, that there had once been among them a very pretty woman named Sylvia. Who would have danced her heart out on a night like this. So, she thought, placing a hand over each bare shoulder, watching the smile die off like one of Jill's alien dreams, this is the kind of thing I might do with my life. I could amuse myself with the arrangement of hair, and memories. I could make myself smile.

The music had stopped. When she came out of the washroom, she saw that Maggie and Jill had gone to the middle of the cleared dance floor. Everyone made a large circle around them as Maggie lifted the satin hem of her gown and Jill pulled Sylvia's white lace garter down and slipped it over Maggie's arched foot. A small herd of young men stood ready, not one of them even pretending to look anxious to be anyone's groom, and when Maggie turned to throw the garter over her shoulder toward them, it was caught by Andy's six-year-old grandson Tom, a soccer player in his first suit, who dove hard to the floor to make his catch. It looked as if Jill had decided that she might want to wear the garter too, some day, because she kicked off her buttercup yellow heels and chased the squealing Tom through the crowd to make him give it up.

Patrick and Murray, after they'd had their turns with Maggie and Margaret and Daphne and Jill and Andy and Sarah and Meg, danced with their wives, sometimes switching off, although Stephanie and Kate tried to assure them they didn't have to be babysat. These two women did have much in common and when they were not up dancing they were content to huddle together at one of the front tables, a white woman in a black dress and a black woman in a white dress, watching the dancers and drinking wine and chatting easily, guessing correctly that the people who moved past the table who couldn't recall their names would call them simply the second wives. But they didn't care. This was what they were, almost happy sixty-year-old second wives.

After several glasses of wine, certainly more than she might have had under normal circumstances, Kate leaned close to Stephanie's ear. "So tell me," she said. "Has everyone just always known?"

Stephanie shook her head. "No," she said. "No. Not at all. I've always assumed it was some married doctor. Or two married doctors."

Kate lifted her wineglass at Patrick's son John, who was dancing past with a child lifted up into his arms, his own sweet daughter done up in a layered froth of pale organza. As they danced, the child rested her fat cheek on his shoulder and watched the strangers' faces floating around her own, fighting with all her small might to resist the pull of sleep.

"I wonder if I did realize," Kate said, "at some subterranean level. And it would be interesting to know now how much I actually care."

"I'm sorry for you in this," Stephanie said, thinking, God help me, what a paltry combination of words.

"Maybe it's all right," Kate said. She was grinning at Margaret, who looked almost jubilant in the sturdy young arms of the best man, what was his name? Mark. "There is a possibility that I can live with this," she said. "It would take a very large effort to foul things for Maggie and Jill. And what kind of person would do that?" She turned to look at Stephanie's face. "Am I such a person?"

Stephanie, too, was smiling at Margaret and Mark, who were approaching the table now. "This Mark," she said, just under her breath, "is an astonishingly handsome young man. Oh, if I were young again," she said, "I'd have me some of that." Studying the small movements of Margaret's face as she came near, a face that was at that moment a miraculous combination of absolute control and a beautifully aged contentment, Stephanie decided that this thing they had ahead of them, the death of Daphne's private, puzzling lie and the subsequent exposure of the bald and simple truth, could easily, with just a bit of carelessness, turn into something beyond even Margaret's orchestration. "I can't say if you are such a person," she said to Kate, quietly. "I shouldn't say. But I think not."

Kate had pulled her chair up closer to the table to allow Margaret to pass behind her. "I suppose I think not too," she said, and just as she was saying these words, Margaret leaned down to kiss the top of her head. A coincidence, she thought, surely. Margaret was the last person who would believe she could be bought with a kiss on the top of the head.

After the short visit from Margaret and Mark, Sarah drifted by the table and throughout the evening Andy sat down with them several times and started to talk, but she never stayed long. Someone always turned up to coax her to her feet and she went every time, eager and laughing and by the end of the night sweating, which she said had embarrassed her once upon a time but didn't now. All night people made a point of telling Andy how wonderful she looked. For some reason, maybe Krissy had given her a nudge in that direction, she had started to colour her hair blonde again and she could still dress because she hadn't gained an ounce in forty years, not since she was a teenager. She'd tell you this.

It was an open bar. Murray had asked Patrick to cut a cheque for the liquor. There was still some money left in the girls' account, the bulk of it held there to cover Jill's tuition. Most of the guests had danced this floor many times before, most of them had no memory at all of a time when they couldn't dance and they thoroughly enjoyed a night of nothing else but. When things were well under way, some of the outsiders who had been claiming that no, they couldn't really dance, were being pulled reluctantly to the floor to confess that well, maybe they could, and when some of them started to sing as they danced, Crank tried to play songs they might know.

Late in the evening, Patrick and Murray excused themselves from Stephanie and Kate, freshened their drinks at the bar, and left the dance to walk out through the lobby and then through the big double doors that led to the rink. They found it all in empty darkness, hot with summer heat and full of the threat of echo, and after their eyes adjusted to the absence of light they stood together at the boards and saw that where there used to be a summertime grid of water pipes laid on a bed of sand, there was now only an expanse of dull cement.

They turned and found the balcony stairs and climbed up in the dark, sat down together front and centre. "Best seats in the house," Murray said.

Patrick leaned forward. "I have to say that it is small," he said. "Even if that's what people usually say coming back to something, it's nevertheless true."

"It was, my friend," Murray said, "always small."

Patrick was looking out over the ice and up to the scoreboard, which even in the darkness he could see was new and much larger, much more elaborate than it had been in his day. "You would have seen that," he said, "sitting up here watching. We didn't. We thought we were the cat's ass and then some."

"That I remember," Murray said.

"It felt so damned big. Although that sheet of ice was a good deal smaller for guys like Paul." He stopped for a minute, looked down at his drink. "Every coach likes a long stride. Guys like Paul could get the puck from anywhere."

"It's been eleven years this summer," Murray said. "And I have not yet found a way to think about him being gone."

Patrick drained his Scotch. "Andy our travelling lady seems to be doing all right," he said. "It's much better for her with Meg in London. There was never any other way to go with that."

"She should remarry," Murray said. "She shouldn't be on her own now. There's no reason that I can see."

"Well," Patrick said. "People marry and people don't marry. You've likely noticed." He stood up quickly to start down the dark stairs. "Although looking at Andy tonight makes me suspect she's not entirely on her own. Daphne mentioned something to Stephanie about a guy from Toronto, some stud in his forties, no less."

"I hope he hasn't got his eye on her money," Murray said.

"I hope not too," Patrick said. "Because he won't be seeing much of it. Andy is extremely close with her money. Instinctive and careful and firm. In that respect, she's quite a bit like your mother."

Murray laughed quietly at the memory of his mother's financial acumen, and as he got up to follow Patrick back to the dance he finished his own drink and crushed the plastic cup in his hand, tossing it behind him into the darkness. He was perhaps a little drunk, something he had not intended. Just before he took the first step he put a question to Patrick's descending shoulders. "How's the cummerbund now?"

Patrick didn't stop or hesitate. "It seems to have got itself straightened around," he said. "Although I'll be glad to take the damned thing off. I always am." He continued down the steps. "In case you're wondering, this afternoon was understood to be just a simple screw-up," he said. "That's what people think. And more to the point, it's what Maggie and Jill believe."

"Is it?" Murray said, beginning his own descent. "Then maybe you would be kind enough to tell me what Daphne believes." He had to raise his voice because Patrick was almost at the bottom of the balcony steps. He could hardly see him down there and what he saw wasn't so much a man as the probable shape of a man. "And what Kate believes."

AT Daphne's the next day, after the rest of the gifts had been unwrapped and lunch was being served by the Presbyterian women, this time on card tables set up on the wraparound porch, Bill arrived. He was unexpected because he had told everyone he wasn't going to be there. He'd walked over, had got himself dressed in his suit pants and a fresh white shirt, which he'd buttoned wrong down near his belt. He had even remembered his tie, although he hadn't knotted it. He wore the tie draped over his small hunched shoulders the way you would wear a harmless carnival snake. The old camera he'd dug out of Margaret's kitchen junk drawer swung down heavy from his neck and as he approached the porch it bounced against his sunken chest.

It was not his intention to go inside Daphne's house, so he stopped to talk to the Presbyterian women for a minute and one of them soon fixed him a plate of food he said he didn't want, bits of strange cheese, slices of lukewarm spiced-up chicken, cold chopped broccoli that was supposed to be some kind of salad. He stood waiting, holding his paper plate and eating what he could manage to get down. The women were right there hovering over him, he could hardly refuse to eat. And Patrick's Stephen had that godforsaken video thing pointed in his direction again.

He was waiting until word got to Maggie that he was on the porch. He knew she'd come out to him. He was here to insist on his picture. Maggie and her new husband and himself and whoever else wanted to be in it. He was not going to listen to any talk today about who arranged for things, who paid for what. He'd paid for enough things in his life to get a picture out of it. If no one would drive them uptown, they could walk. It wasn't that bad a day.

When Maggie came out through the wide open doors, he was annoyed to see that she wasn't in her beautiful white gown and when she got close enough he said so. "Where's your dress?" he asked, squirming in her strong arms.

"Oh, Grandpa," she said, giving him her biggest bride smile. "Silly Grandpa." Maggie had not seen much of Margaret and Bill since she had started her doctoral work and soon, after she and Josh got packed up for the big move to California, she wouldn't be seeing them at all, although she would be closer to Aunt Sarah in Vancouver. She did realize that there was every chance that one or both of them would die while she was gone. Unlike her mother, and unlike Jill who argued loudly with her grandfather, and because she was not required to exercise it very often, Maggie had been able to adjust herself to Bill's condition with a firm, one-time-only decision. If he said something offensive, she simply didn't hear it. It did not compute. Today she was just happy to have a flesh-and-blood grandfather to tease. Some of her friends didn't. "That was for yesterday," she told him. "The bride dress was only for yesterday."

By this time Daphne and Margaret had come out to the porch to see what was going on. They were standing outside the open doors at the head of a bunched-up pile of the rest of them, Josh, Jill, Patrick, Murray, Andy, Sarah, Meg, all of them together in a cosy little group holding their plates of food, their forks hanging in mid-air as they listened. Margaret noticed the unknotted tie immediately. "Oh, sweet man," she said quietly, meaning it to be only to herself. "So this is what you've forgotten today."

"Go get your dress back on," Bill told Maggie. He set his plate of food down, balanced it gingerly on the porch rail. "We're going up to the Town Hall for my picture." He lifted the camera in his hand to show everyone that he meant business.

No one stepped forward to try to tell Maggie what she should do. They stood just where they were, waiting to see what might happen, quiet and wary and ready, one way or the other, for things to proceed.

Standing at the edge of the steps, Stephen lifted the video camera and began to record again. He focused first on the weird old camera trembling in Bill's hand and then he panned to Maggie and Josh, who was beside her now with his arm around her bare back, and then he swept across the tables of food and some of the Presbyterian women and back again to a medium shot of Daphne, who seemed to be close to laughter, and then over to Margaret and Sarah, who was still in her peach dress, and to Stephanie and Kate, who were leaning side by side against the railing, their arms touching as they talked quietly between themselves.

And then he zoomed in on wild and crazy Jill who, after she'd grinned and pulled him up to dance last night, had responded to his first, hesitant, hopeful telling of his news, which was not news of course to the people in his real life, the young men who would never be grooms, whose lives would never provide an excuse for family celebration, with an immediate and brutally confident equanimity, as if she'd been waiting and ready to be told, as if he had flattered her with his trust. As if she believed it would be helpful, would be best just to throw him over her shoulder and carry him through whatever was to come. He could imagine this, his own body gone slack, Jill pushing forward undaunted by the extra weight and singing at the top of her lungs, yelling fierce obscenities to intimidate the enemy. And wasn't that the risk with rescue? If you allowed it, you could find yourself in someone else's hands? Although Jill's hands, of all these beautiful hands, were perhaps the most beautiful.

Hearing the girl behind him, hearing them come, he turned the camera toward the street to get two guys flying past on Rollerblades, pulling between them a long-legged girl who was squealing in either terror or joy, and when they were gone he got all the cars parked at the curb, the Jag and Patrick's new Lexus in particular, and from the cars he lifted the camera up to the dappled light in the just-quivering leaves of the front-yard maples and to the bright blue Ontario sky exposed between the leaves. Finished with the sky, he came back to the wraparound porch, to the far corner of the porch where the kids were climbing over and under and around the overturned Muskoka chairs, to Patrick and Murray, grey-haired men in cut-offs and stupid hats who had moved to stand one on either side of Bill, and then to Andy and awkward, hesitant Meg, who was the only one looking directly at the camera, the only one on the porch who seemed to realize she was being captured. And then he began to move down the steps, thinking if he stood far enough away, maybe as far away as the sidewalk, he might be able to get a full, wide-angled shot of everyone, the whole mess of them, together.

"Come on, people," he said, moving carefully backwards. "Strut your stuff."

A FEW days later, after three carloads had driven down to Sarnia for Uncle Gerry's funeral and then most of them had gone their way, those left behind would sit around Margaret and Bill's living room to watch Stephen's wedding videos, to see themselves in action. They would watch Jill as she came down the aisle ahead of her sister, grinning at Josh and Mark, and wasn't she an incorrigible flirt, and they would once again admire Maggie's beautiful gown as she walked slowly forward, followed by her unanticipated crowd of escorts. They would see themselves standing up from their chairs after it was done, after all the promises had been made. They would laugh watching the bridal party fool around down at Stonebrook Creek while the still photographer worked so hard to pose them, first on the wide footbridge for several shots and then down at the water. They would see Josh reach back to help Maggie, their hands lifted and extended to each other like dancers from another century as she tried to get a foothold beside him on a large, flat rock that had been placed deliberately and probably with some difficulty at the edge of the current.

Then, as Stephen's camera work was softly praised, they would move with him away from the bridal party, away from the bridge. They would follow for a few minutes along the bank of the creek, the water moving fast and churned to mud in the middle of the current but much cleaner, almost crystal clear, in the pools along the edge, the surface of the water there held calm by clusters of rocks and stones and bright with reflected sun, with the slow, reflected swaying of trees. They would watch Sailor run ahead along the water and then turn back at Stephen's call. And from a perfectly focused, extreme close-up of a Scotch thistle, so sharply, delicately barbed, its small, spiny flowers so perfectly mauve in the sunlight, they would be quickly lifted back to a long view of Stonebrook Creek turning through town on its way to the lake, its movement like a muscle twisting and their perspectives briefly jolted, just as Stephen intended.

Near the end of the second video, which was partly the dance and partly all of them at the house the next day, they would watch the scene on the wraparound porch and Stephen's brief, unintended narration, his overheard command that they strut their stuff, would prompt a round of easy laughter. Pleasure would pass among them not because they knew Stephen well, they didn't get to see him very much any more, but because what little they knew of him they quite liked, because even when it hardly mattered he had taken the trouble to choose his words.

Bill's pictures, snapped by Cheryl and Tara, young curly-haired twin sisters who just happened to be walking past the Town Hall with their arms full of groceries, would be ready a week later. Although it was tight, there had been enough steps to hold all thirty-seven of them, Maggie and Josh and Margaret and Bill front and centre, Maggie in her beautiful gown with Sailor stretched out at her feet, panting, and all of them, except for Bill, looking perhaps a little too serious, Daphne and Jill perched on the step above, and the others standing not in their natural groupings but scattered, a husband separated from his wife, a sister nowhere near her brother, little kids content in the wrong arms.

Studying the pictures with a cup of tea at the kitchen table, Margaret would almost regret her insistence on knotting Bill's tie for him. He likely would have been all right as he was. And she would decide that before too much time passed, someone with a fine hand should write all their names on the back of the pictures, in full, the placement of the names replicating the placement of the bodies, like a key, or maybe it was more properly called a legend.

Yes.

Acknowledgements

For the precision of their own memories, gratitude is extended to Mona Huctwith, Catharine Wynne, Jean Hishon and Lana Reeder, and most especially to Mel Huctwith.

Printed in the USA
CPSIA information can be obtained
at www.ICGtesting.com
JSHW031911070823
46136JS00005B/24